CW00321363

WALTER H. HUNT

A SONG IN STONE

A Song In Stone

Printed in the U.S.A.

Book designed by Matt Adelsperger

First Printing: November 2008

Library of Congress Cataloging-in-Publication Data

Hunt, Walter H.
A song in stone / Walter H. Hunt.
p. cm.
ISBN 978-0-7869-5067-6
1. Television personalities--Fiction. 2. Time travel--Fiction. 3. Middle Ages--Fiction. I. Title.
PS3608.U59S66 2008
813'.6--dc22

2008004432

---

9 8 7 6 5 4 3 2 1

ISBN: 978-0-7869-5067-6
600-23927720-001-EN

U.S., CANADA,
ASIA, PACIFIC, & LATIN AMERICA
Wizards of the Coast, Inc.
P.O. Box 707
Renton, WA 98057-0707
+1-800-324-6496

EUROPEAN HEADQUARTERS
Hasbro UK Ltd
Caswell Way
Newport, Gwent NP9 0YH
GREAT BRITAIN
Save this address for your records.

Visit our web site at www.wizards.com

DEDICATION

To the love of my life, my wife Lisa, who has always believed in me and stood with me. The music I hear is that which we have made together.

ACKNOWLEDGEMENTS

This book came about as a result of a visit to Rosslyn Chapel in August 2005. I received a first class tour of the Chapel courtesy of a Masonic brother, James Munro; his descriptions of Rosslyn and the high points of his tour are part of the narrative of the book. He appears in this book as Rob Madson, and I hope the rendition does him justice.

During the development of the story, our Scottish friend Dinah Tennant was of inestimable help, not only with plot points, but with Scots authenticity. She will be able to tell all of her friends that she has become *La Vierge sous-Tierre* – the Black Virgin of Chartres, and Ian's Gran MacPherson.

Thanks to Tom Easton and Jack McDevitt for their timely advice, to Paul Bourke (whom I've never met, but who has an outstanding web page on Chladni plate interference), to the Bowdoin College Library (especially Ms. Virginia Hopcroft, for her assistance during my research efforts there), to Cecily Christensen, the Reference Librarian at Bellingham Public Library for her great help, to Bruce Coates, my Edinburgh Masonic friend, and of course to my dear wife Lisa, who read parts of this book many times and helped me get it right. Thanks also to my editor Cortney Marabetta and my agent Don Maass, who have helped me move forward on the path of light as a writer with this new venture.

The esoteric pilgrimage described in this book is based on the one detailed in *Rosslyn: Guardian of the Secrets of the Holy Grail*, by Tim Wallace-Murphy and Marilyn Hopkins, to whose work the author is indebted. While neither the most detailed nor the most definitive work on the subject, it served as an inspiration at many points and opened up avenues of inquiry and research that helped articulate the plot and background.

For more information on my books, please visit http://www.walterhunt.com on the World Wide Web.

PART I

CLIMBING THE HILL

And the light shineth in darkness,
and the darkness comprehended it not.
—Gospel of St. John I:5

"The Divine Logos . . . is the Light that
shineth in darkness, by which all things
are made, and that enlighteneth every
man that cometh into this world."
—Denis the Areopagite

CHAPTER 1

It was half ten in the morning; I was sitting in my flat in Leith half-watching the television, the morning *Scotsman* spread out on my breakfast table.

For the last seven years it had been nothing like this: I'd been up at dawn, tuned in to News 24 or the Beeb blaring so I could catch the headlines, down a quick cup of tea, take two or three calls on my mobile, then out the door. It was never quiet—never like this.

This was a new experience, though it was beginning to wear: get up, turn on the TV, look at the paper and wait for the phone to ring.

Surprising, really, when it did. I fairly jumped.

"Graham," I said, with my polite Channel 4 voice.

"Ian! How's the lad?" If he had work for me, my agent, Rodney Weiss, always sounded as if I was the long-awaited Messiah.

"Unemployed."

This was a month or so after *Ian and Lily* became *Alex and Lily*, six months after Jan left the show. Remember *Ian and Jan*? That was me, Ian Graham. We'd been the toast of Scotland; people turned us on at tea time as we sat at our coffee table or traveled abroad, shaking hands with celebs, telling them what everyone was wearing, or showing off the latest recipes.

I'd been hired on there seven years ago, one of Gerard Lamont's bright young men at Channel 4. Gerard lost to cancer—good old Gerard, watching out for me—and I'd thought I didn't need anyone to do that anymore.

"Not for much longer," Rodney said. "Are you listening?"

"Lost in my own thoughts. Go on."

"Well," he said after a moment. "I've got a simply *marvelous* offer. ITV called—they asked for you personally."

"ITV?" My thoughts ran to soaps, quiz shows, sport. Mostly soaps and more soaps. "What do they want?"

"They're looking to do a documentary, Ian. A sort of edgy hour-long thing, investigative reporting. Uncovering the mysteries."

"Geraldo." *Ian and Jan* had taken us overseas a few times, and I'd seen a lot of American telly; their broadcast and cable networks were filthy with that sort of thing. "You mean, sex crime and conspiracy." *At least it's not a quiz show,* I thought.

"Well, they'd like to be a bit more tippie than that, Ian," Rodney said, sounding like he was pouring on the patience. I cringed when he used the Edinburgh slang, especially in his annoying Midlands accent. "That's why they wanted *you*: to be the heid-bummer, add a wee bit of class to the programme and bring over a better sort of audience."

"And they asked for *me.*"

"Yes."

"Personally," I added.

"Yes," Rodney insisted. "Yes, personally. They thought you'd be just the chiel."

Rodney had been working with Scots for better than twenty years. He prided himself on his ability to mix the lingo into the conversation—he probably kept a £3 Scots dialect dictionary on his desk. A night stroll in certain neighborhoods in Glasgow or Edinburgh would cure him of that someday; one *chiel* out of his mouth and he'd get the crap beaten out of him.

Still, he was a good agent for all that. "What does it pay, Roddy?"

He hated the nickname, but every Rodney in Scotland is called Roddy. He sighed and named a figure; it wasn't insulting. Turned out they were willing to put half a dozen programmes in the can and try me out at half seven in the evening.

It wasn't my usual brief, but it would get me back on the air at least. Show the face to the viewing audience. Six hours of this sort of stuff couldn't be that bad.

No, not desperate, I added to myself. *Not Ian Graham. Not me.*

"Tell them yes."

"Splendid, splendid," he answered. "I knew you'd be pleased."

Beggars can't be bleeding choosers, I thought but instead said, "Where do we start?"

"Rosslyn."

—•—

It was a step down from *Ian and Jan*, but after a month of waking up alone in the flat, nothing to do but read the papers, drink coffee, chain-smoke, and listen to voices from the telly that weren't mine, it was *something.* It beat lying about the flat all day waiting for the phone call.

It wasn't the money: I'd put aside enough to be comfortable. But to be honest—and after I rang off and began to dress, I knew it was past time to be honest with myself—the lunches and drinks with producers and telly execs had resulted in no more than vague promises that turned into nothing. In no time I'd become old news. I wanted the audience, the spotlight, the feeling of being that *chiel* that everyone knew and tuned in to watch.

I only knew a little bit about Rosslyn Chapel; I'd lived in Edinburgh all my life and never visited. It had been much in the news lately; they'd been shooting some sort of movie there, as I recalled.

Look the part, I thought as I finished my shaving. They'd get the top shelf Ian Graham with no desperation in his eyes: it would be as if I walked straight off the set of *Ian and Jan* and into ITV's documentary. I needed a look around to get my bearings and feel comfortable with the setting. Damn it, this—whatever it was, whatever sensational thing that ITV wanted—wasn't why I'd climbed the hill in the industry: to be *ordinary*.

But a question kept crossing my mind. *How the hell did you let it come to this, old lad?*

As I left my flat and walked down the street to where I parked my motor, then started it up and pulled it out into traffic that late-July morning, I realised that I didn't have an answer.

—•—

Any heavy-drinking chain-smoking television pro will tell you that once you're in the business you're always in the business, and you don't lose the skills you've picked up—still, it had been damned hard to think about really *working* for a living instead of smiling into the camera and telling the afternoon crowd what book they should take to the beach with them.

It had been seven years since Gerard Lamont had hired young and handsome Ian Graham from the Kilts and Heather Club of the Scottish BBC to pair up with sweet, sophisticated Jan Pierce to do lightweight interviews, talk about summer reads and host cooking demos for the late-afternoon telly watchers on Channel 4; six years since my loving wife Liz had gone from thrilled at my success to jealous of my success to becoming my ex in a matter of months. Jan's husband, by comparison, hadn't been jealous even when he should have been. Jan and I were good together, better than my marriage ever seemed to be. I took the parting in stride: divorce was a part of the backdrop in the business. *That's show business,* we'd say. *Can I buy you another drink?*

It was six months since Jan had decided to move on—she'd been offered an opportunity in London with the National Trust of all things. 4's upper management wanted the programme to continue and had replaced Jan with Lily Burton: young enough to be Jan's daughter, and what she lacked in native talent she made up for in pure spite. Lily must have had some spitfire quality they liked—she was everything that Jan was not—but the viewers took to her straight away.

Then a month ago, *Ian and Lily* had become *Alex and Lily,* with Alex maybe two years out of university. "Younger crowd watching, you know," they told me. "Nothing personal," they added as they pushed me out the door. At thirty-four I was old news and not fit for the afternoon crowd. Word came through the grapevine that Liz and her friends were laughing their socks off about my "fall from grace." I felt old—angry and betrayed as well, but mostly just old.

—•—

It's only a few miles to Rosslyn from the centre of Edinburgh. I took the BMW down South Bridge and twisted and turned my way out of the twenty-first century; the road changed its name three or four times as it took me out into the countryside. Past the retail centre, round the roundabouts, and down a lane into the village of Roslin.

Edinburgh's busy and loud late in the summer, what with the Festival and the Fringe and all—I'd been stunned when Channel 4 made me redundant, so I'd noticed it much more than usual—so my first impression of Roslin was how little it was. Used to be just the faithful and the conspiracy nutters who came there—now it's people who read best-selling novels . . . some of whom are the faithful and the conspiracy nutters. Somehow I expected something more grand.

I knew blessed little about it. Out of old habit I envisioned tracking shots all the way to the end of the lane as I drove down and pulled into a little car park opposite the entrance: the wind in the elms—remarkable, really: hadn't seen many of them since Dutch Elm disease took hold—leaden clouds behind. All very photogenic.

I joined the tour, with one of the handheld audio guides, turning down the volume so that I could gather my own impressions. I had a polite smile and nod from the clerks but I didn't have the feeling they recognised me. Old news indeed.

When a half-dozen of us were assembled, a guide led us through the gift shop and down a little hall, then through a door and into the courtyard—and there it was.

From the outside Rosslyn Chapel's not much to look at these days. The outer shell is surrounded by scaffolding, put in place to keep it from crumbling. It was a fanciful thing at first glance.

"Welcome to Rosslyn Chapel," the guide began: a tall, balding man with a bit of an overbite. "I'm William MacLeod, one of the Friends of Rosslyn, and I'll be showing you around the building and grounds this afternoon."

He squinted at the low clouds. It was one of those summer days when the grey and threatening sky bends down almost to touch the earth. It was a bit cool for July, and the air felt as if a storm was waiting to come on stage.

"This structure was founded in the year 1446 by Sir William St Clair, the third and last St Clair Prince of Orkney. It was—or was intended to be—the Collegiate Chapel of St Matthew, one of more than three dozen such chapels erected between the reigns of James I and James IV of Scotland, a period covering roughly the entire fifteenth century."

He delivered it with crisp efficiency—more information than I really needed. MacLeod stopped and smiled: a tourist had a video camera inexpertly aimed right at his face—and even from the rear of the group I could see the light was all wrong. He glanced away and looked up—and gave me a wink. I assume he recognised me.

"For more than forty years there was construction at this site. Indeed, this building was intended to be only a part of a larger cruciform structure—excavations a few centuries ago revealed foundations that extend more than ninety feet—almost thirty metres—beyond the west end of the Chapel, and underneath the baptistry—a later addition to the building intended to support the organ. But when Sir William died in 1484 it was still incomplete."

MacLeod gestured to the building, turning away slightly; he

was clearly used to the patter. *If I can get him to cut it to fifteen seconds we may be able to use this,* I thought.

After getting us from the fifteenth to the eighteenth centuries in a few more minutes, he beckoned us inside through the north door, where the monks entered. Gargoyles, soldiers on horseback, foxes and geese, and green men and musical instruments attended us.

We walked along the north aisle to stand in the northeast corner of the Chapel. What was left of the afternoon light strained to pass through a beautiful stained-glass window of St Matthew, the patron of the Chapel that had been. I stifled a yawn; it was an amazing confection, reminding me of the sort of thing my Gran had kept in miniature in her china-closet—but it was still just a church.

"There are many remarkable aspects to this structure," MacLeod continued. "A brief visit can scarcely do it justice, but I would like to point a few of them out to you.

"There are hundreds of individual carvings on the walls and ceilings of this place. If you look up along the Lady Chapel"—he pointed to his left, facing us; we obligingly followed his hand and saw the intricately carved ceiling, filled with carved animals, people, musical instruments, and square boxes formed into curved arches that met at a middle round projection that looked a little like a light fixture—"you'll see the work of the artisans. For decades they labored to build this place, this wonder—this exquisitely beautiful mystery."

"Are you saying—" The man with the video camera stepped forward, with the damn thing still running. "Are you saying that there's no meaning to all this—this stuff?"

It was an American accent. MacLeod looked at me again; I was trying to be unobtrusive, "drinking it in"—but by now he'd *surely* recognised me and was showing how he could play the audience like a pro.

He shrugged the tiniest bit. "No, sir, that's not at all what I meant."

"But you said—"

"What I *said,*" he interrupted, his voice patient, "was not that the stonework has no meaning—but rather that it has some meaning that we do not at present understand." The tourist looked ready to jump in again, but he raised his hand slightly. The dim light glinted for just a moment off a ring he wore, but I couldn't see the device. "This place was chosen, laid out and founded, and the artisans worked for more than four decades to build it. Though Scotland was torn by religious strife for more than two centuries afterward, and though great harm was done to the outer shell of the building and to the fragile work within, the carvings and artwork you see in its stones have survived virtually *intact* since the late part of the fifteenth century."

It was really getting a bit thick, I thought; it would have to be cut down to thirty or forty seconds at most—perhaps I might be able to do a quick gloss.

"Sir William of St Clair wrote a message in these stones, we believe," MacLeod continued. "It is our greatest regret . . . that we can not decipher it."

I pricked up my ears at that. *This* was the sort of thing that would play well on television. *A Geraldo moment,* I thought, only half-facetious: mysterious stone carvings that had survived intact, with a meaning lost to history.

Mr Video Camera, meanwhile, didn't know how to respond. Without speaking further MacLeod led us along the Chapel, beneath the three stone light-fixtures, to the opposite corner.

As we passed through the centre of the Chapel, I heard a sort of low humming. It was almost like someone had left a wireless at full volume, tuned to some frequency that had no broadcast. It was annoying; I stopped and shook my head to clear it, even stepping back a few steps and then forward again. It was only really there when I was directly in line with the west doors.

As I looked that way I glanced up at the ceiling and saw the beautiful decorations—stars and flowers, mostly, hundreds of them—marching their way toward the baptistry entrance. The rest of the group moved past me. It wasn't until I moved along to where they'd gathered that the sound seemed to dissipate.

"Are you feeling all right?" the guide asked, coming back to me.

"Yes. Fine," I said. "Nasty hum."

"I beg your pardon?"

"The hum. The noise."

He shrugged and smiled slightly. No one else had appeared to notice—not MacLeod, not Mr Video Camera.

"Don't you hear it?" I asked. I stood directly in line with the west doors, open to admit weak early afternoon sunlight.

"Perhaps you should sit down for a bit," he said, gesturing toward a bench, and began to turn away. He was being polite. I decided that there was no point in pursuing it as MacLeod returned to the rest of the group. I followed, getting a curious glance from the Yank with the camera.

"This is the Apprentice Pillar," MacLeod said, indicating the rightmost of three great stone columns that separated the Lady Chapel from the rest of the church. It was different from the others. Instead of being straight vertical, it was like a braided cord, its incredibly intricate designs swirling around from bottom to top. "I would wager that this pillar is the one thing that anyone who has heard of our Chapel would recognise."

It'll certainly get a few seconds on camera, I thought. *Closeup from the base, pan slowly upward and then zoom out for Ian Graham's face, caught in a thoughtful moment, contemplating . . .*

"Why is it called the Apprentice Pillar?" one of the other tourists asked—an older English lady.

"Aye, there's a story that goes with that," MacLeod said. "It's said that many different craftsmen worked on this building, and that one of the masters was given the assignment to create a work of exquisite design. Before undertaking it, he decided to leave for Rome to examine the original.

"While he was gone, a talented apprentice dreamed that he had finished it and set about to complete it." He reached his hand out and touched the pillar gently, affectionately. "When the master returned and found that the apprentice had created this, he was so enraged that he took a mallet and struck the apprentice on the right temple so"—he made his right hand into a fist and gently tapped his own head—"and slew him. But justice caught up with the master, and he was executed for his crime."

"How awful," the lady said.

"What a load of bull," the American with the camera interjected. "Sounds like a story for tourists."

And telly watchers, I thought. *Maybe there is an interesting story here after all.*

"That is as may be," MacLeod responded evenly. "But you'll find among our carvings the head of the apprentice showing the mortal wound, the head of the jealous master, and even that of the apprentice's grieving mother. Believe it or not as you wish, but it *is* recorded in the stones of the Chapel."

MacLeod's tour ran on a dozen more minutes. He pointed to the ceiling, the stained glass, and a number of other photogenic places in the church. Each time I crossed the centre line of the Chapel, I heard the same low humming. It was clear to me that no one else noticed.

You need to get out more, me lad, I thought. *Hearing noises no one else hears?*

He ended the tour in the sacristy, a sort of crypt area reached through a flight of stairs in the southeast corner of the Chapel. It was a bare place, with a flat stone floor and artificial light. On one side there was an opening with darkness beyond, and a polite National Trust sign indicating that the area was off limits to tourists.

The wall beside the opening had a number of drawings and traceries: triangles and circles and such. Before it was a stone plinth with an upright stone, like a grave marker, set into it. At either end was a carved statue of a man; one had his index- and ring-fingers pointing to his mouth, and the other stood with his hands pressed palms inward to his chest, one above the other.

It wasn't likely to be good footage, but it was certainly intriguing: a collection of little mysteries to go with the bigger one above.

When MacLeod's standard speech was over, he asked for questions. The English lady asked, "What are these sea shells?"

There was a little collection of them set on end in an alcove at the east end of the sacristy. At a glance, they could've come from anywhere—a child's collection from a beach holiday.

MacLeod was about to answer, but a professorial-looking chap piped up with, "Those are from Santiago, aren't they?"

"That's right," MacLeod answered. "Pilgrims who had visited the shrine of Saint James in Spain would often come here as well and deposit their shell badges."

All of the tourists nodded appreciatively.

The question and answer went on for a bit longer. I found myself drifting back to the wall with all of the tracings. It was hard to imagine that they were hundreds of years old, but there was some pattern there—something elusive, that I couldn't quite pick up. I was sure that I could have ITV get someone to research it for me.

And then, from the passageway beyond, I heard voices in the dark.

"It worked. I'm sure of it. It's all here."

"Yes—but where is 'here'? It could be anywhere—Orléans, Chartres—"

"The Saturn Oracle," the first voice said. "Where we expected to be."

The second voice was one I'd never heard—but the first one I knew very well: my agent.

"Rodney?" I said, stepping into the opening. "Roddy, what are you doing there?"

"Sir," MacLeod said, stepping through the other tourists toward me. "Sir, that area is off-limits to visitors." He was polite, but firm.

"I heard something. I heard . . ."

I stopped, not sure how to finish the sentence. The chamber beyond was dark, except for the intrusion of electric light; everyone else had stopped speaking. I stood for a moment longer, but all was quiet except for the incessant whirr of that damn video camera.

"I'm sorry," I said. "I thought I heard something."

"I'd be surprised," the guide answered, smiling. "Those are the crypts. Tradition says that the St Clairs were buried fully armoured, ready to spring to the defence of the chapel—but that's never happened."

I smiled as well. It was the easiest course. I was no celebrity—just another tourist.

With the guided portion of the tour done, I made my excuse of a headache and took my leave of Rosslyn Chapel, after buying a guidebook in the gift shop. I don't think I could get out of there fast enough. Humming that no one else heard; voices in the dark—*disquieting,* I thought, *that's a good word for it. Not "spooky"—that's Geraldo for sure.*

As I put my car into motion up the lane away from the place, the storm broke, sluicing the area with rain.

—•—

I came home tired and depressed. Not that it mattered, but the guide probably hadn't recognised me after all. I'd just been a tourist—an ordinary tourist.

I tried to do my reading that night while the rain pounded down and lightning crashed, threatening to take out the power in my flat. It was hard to concentrate, and at last I gave it up as a bad job; there'd be a script, I'd give my lines, and ITV would be happy to have such a fine talent as Ian Graham describing the mystery of Rosslyn Chapel for the conspiracy folk.

How the hell did you let it come to this? I asked myself again as I got ready for bed. I sat up and watched News 24 for a while, but kept finding myself being maudlin and autobiographical.

Ian Graham. Local lad. Born and brought up in Edinburgh, attended chapel at St Giles when I was a wee boy, Bible class and all—"he'll go far, that Ian," they always said. For a while they were right.

Edinburgh College of Art. Married to Liz. Radio with the Beeb—reading the headlines for Newshour, then moving on to hosting—then on to Channel 4, dropping in practically at the very top, when Gerard Lamont hired me for Ian and Jan. No one disagreed with that—everyone was scared of Gerard, but he was a good judge of talent.

Locations all over Britain, on the Continent, overseas. Celebrities coming to sit at our little coffee table on air, talking about their latest film, their newest venture. Politicians, philanthropists, rock stars—they all dropped by.

And now Ian Graham would be reading the lines from a Tele-Prompter while they got the light just right on a fifteenth-century puzzle box filled with stone carvings that no one understood.

How the hell was this going to be a vehicle to get Ian bloody Graham back into the spotlight?

It's not, I told myself. *Not a chance. Especially if he keeps talking about himself in the third person.*

I snapped the light out, turned off the telly, and went to bed.

—•—

It was some kind of interview, in an ITV boardroom. Seven executives were sitting around a polished wood table, but there was no seat for me. They were dressed like something from a costume drama—*The Lion in Winter* came to mind—robes with hoods thrown back, beards for the men, head cloths for the women.

They didn't look happy, and they weren't even looking at me.

Somewhere in the distance I could hear music. It sounded like the sort of thing my Gran used to favour: Satie or perhaps Poulenc coming from a phonograph.

"It's obvious that you've chosen wrong," the one in the middle said. "Look at him: he's obsessed with his own image."

"Hey," I began. "That's a bit over the top—"

"You're right, of course." The man to whom the comment was addressed didn't even seem to hear me. "But he'll need to rely on his own strength."

The first man snorted. "It can't work. It astounds me that you think it can."

"What won't work?" I said.

"I know it will. It already has."

"Only the past is immutable."

"But this has happened in the past," the second man protested.

"Not *his* past," a woman interrupted. She sat near the end of the table. She was young—twenty-five, perhaps younger, and very attractive.

"I don't understand," I said, but it was obvious that I wasn't even there to them.

"I don't take your meaning," the second man said.

"For him, what we believe to be the result has not yet occurred. It is possible that it may never occur."

"But we know—"

"We know very little," she said. "We know what we see, but we do not know if this moment is part of what has happened to lead to where we now sit. It is in *his* hands: all of it. We cannot be sure."

"What do you propose, then?" the second man asked. "How can we bring this about?"

"He may turn away; he may give up. He may not even complete the task once he starts it. We can only have faith—and hope."

"He can be told—"

"No," the first man said finally. "He *cannot* be told. He must not—it would jeopardise all." He placed his index and middle fingers to his mouth.

The others followed suit.

The music swelled louder all of a sudden.

"Amoun," he said, and for the first time looked directly at me—

—•—

At a crash of thunder I woke up in my bed, sweating. The clock at my bedside glowed, showing the time: 0210.

For a moment I considered speed-dialing Rodney, asking him what he was thinking putting me—*me!*—on this ridiculous programme and what the hell he was doing in the crypts at Rosslyn that afternoon.

“Get a grip,” I said to myself. “Too much caffeine. Too much stress.”

I laughed, and that sounded as hollow as my self-assured comments. Most of my dreams weren’t so memorable.

I felt for the remote and flicked on News 24 again. Tragedies, repetitive weather reports, and meaningless sport flickered across the screen—and at some point I fell into a dreamless sleep.

CHAPTER 2

THE STORM HAD MOSTLY PASSED THE NEXT MORNING BUT THERE were still hints of it when I awoke, the telly still blaring on. The dream was nothing but a faint bit of undigested anxiety by the time I got out of bed and had my morning coffee, nicotine, and something for my headache.

There was nothing for it but to go forward; I wasn't going to duck out on the job. Whatever it amounted to, they'd get the best that Ian Graham had to offer.

—•—

A few days passed. ITV sent out a sample script which seemed fine. Rodney took care of the contract details. In the meanwhile, there were no more dreams.

On the day shooting was to start I drove out to the country again, down the lane to the Chapel, and into the car park in a grassy field. As I stepped out I saw someone wave to me.

"Hello," I said, walking across to the entrance-door. "I'm—"

"Ian Graham," the man completed my sentence. He shook my hand. "Of course. I'm Rob Madson. Some of your crew is already here, but I've been asked to look after you especially."

"Thank you very much, I'm sure," I answered. "You don't need to trouble yourself."

The voice seemed slightly familiar, but I couldn't place it—not surprising, considering the number of people I met in my line of work.

Former line of work, I added mentally but shrugged that thought away.

"No trouble at all," he said, smiling. Rob Madson was a middle-aged man, gone white on the top; glasses framed deep eyes. The smile was something else again—the look of someone who knew a secret he wasn't sharing. "Rosslyn's something best experienced with a guide."

"You know it well, then," I said. He led me through the gift shop and down a short corridor, handing me a visitor badge with the ITV logo.

"I'm one of the Friends of Rosslyn," he explained. "I work part-time for the Trust."

"I was out here a few days past and had a wee tour then," I said. "The presenter—MacLeod, I think his name was—was quite good; I think we might be able to use him."

"MacLeod, you said."

"Yes, that's right. William, Warren, something like that. Tall fellow."

Madson looked thoughtful for a moment but didn't comment further. He didn't follow up as we passed through the gift shop. We stepped through the doorway and onto the path, and there stood the Abbey before us once again.

"Remarkable, isn't it?" Madson said.

I'd seen it before, but the light seemed different—the day was overcast, but there wasn't fog toward Mountmarle and the castle; I concentrated on what it would look like on screen. I'd stand *there,* and we'd need the light over *here* . . . "Yes," I finally said.

"Shall I give you the usual tour, or did you get enough of that?"

"No, that's all right. I've done some reading also." I'd gotten enough of the "usual tour" the previous time out.

Madson shrugged, with a small additional smile. "Let's go in, then."

—•—

Through the north door again.

Inside was all abuzz. The ITV crew was there already. They hadn't set up equipment, but a production man was pacing it off, measuring with his light-metre; a younger tech was standing near the front, bent over a laptop that he'd set up on a stone altar. I noticed Rob Madson catching sight of this and frowning.

"Graham!" I heard from across the nave. "About damn time you got here." Madson seemed to flinch a little bit; it bothered me at the time too, for reasons I couldn't explain.

David MacDougal, ITV's Production VP for Scotland, was making a beeline across toward where my guide and I stood. He seemed heedless of anyone else there. Most of the ITV folks were trying to keep out of the way of the tourists and visitors, but MacDougal wasn't having any of that. I'd met him years ago—a fairly typical media exec, a climber. Still, he had a good track record; it was one of the things that Roddy had used to convince me this was a good idea after all.

"I was told ten o'clock," I began to say, but MacDougal wasn't interested in that either. He rolled his eyes.

"We only have a few days to shoot," he said, sounding exasperated. "Studio One sat on this for long enough and now I'm behind schedule. There are already enough problems without prima donnas. All right, you're here now. Had a look at the script?"

"Yes, it seemed fine—"

"You've met Madson, I see," he interrupted.

"Just now."

He grabbed my elbow and steered me a few metres away and said in a stage whisper, "Don't let him get started, for God's sake. Mystical claptrap. My script man has done a little revising for you—take a look at it. We'll take a break in a couple of hours and go over the idea. Think you can manage it?"

Think you can be more insulting? I thought, but shook my head. "No problem, Mac." Only his friends called him Mac, but I didn't care.

He gave me a look meant to peel paint, then shrugged. "All right. Get a look at the script edits and we'll meet—let's say twelve noon in the trailer. Suit you?"

"Brilliant."

He nodded, gave a last look at Madson, and moved off toward the baptistry, shouting for some other victim.

Madson came over to stand by me. "He's been here since early morning. He thinks this is a sound stage with carvings, but it's the Collegiate Chapel of St Matthew, or was meant to be."

"Has he shown you the script, Mr Madson?"

"Rob's fine."

"Rob."

"I only got a brief look. I don't think there will be anything in it that will surprise you, Mr Graham."

"Ian."

He smiled again; a stray bit of sunlight found its way out from the lowering clouds and passed through the stained-glass of St Matthew in the northeast corner.

"Mr MacDougal has prepared a fairly standard hour of television programming, as far as I can tell. Best-sellers have put Rosslyn in the public consciousness, but it's been a significant place for hundreds of years."

"The Templar treasure," I said.

"Oh, yes, that," he replied, adjusting his spectacles. "All the tales about the Templars that got away from the Inquisition, coming up here and helping Robert the Bruce win at Bannockburn . . . the Grail's supposed to be buried here, you know. The Grail, the head of John the Baptist, the Ark of the Covenant—here."

We had begun to walk toward the east end of the nave on the north aisle, and he stopped me with a gesture a pace from the Mason Pillar—the straight one, not the Apprentice Pillar on the other side. I'd gotten a good look at that yesterday, and in any case it was presently under scrutiny by two dozen tourists.

"Stamp your foot here," he said. "Gently." He pointed to a place where the carpet had been rolled back a bit to accommodate one of the ITV techs.

I did as he asked; there was a reassuring, solid sound.

"Good," he said. He pointed to a spot only a metre or so beyond, in the north aisle to the left of the Pillar. "Now try it *here.*"

I stamped and immediately understood: the sound was hollow and quite different.

"Crypts?"

"Oh, yes," he answered. "At the very least. A number of St Clairs—the lairds of Rosslyn, the ones who built this place"—he gestured—"are buried down there. But there's more."

This must be what Mac was trying to warn me away from. It wasn't likely to make it to the screen, but I was intrigued—there might be a hook there to help make the presentation more interesting.

"What else?"

"Good question, Ian. Good question indeed. The Earl of Rosslyn isn't inclined to let us scan, and we're not going to go digging it up. But there's a transverse hollow corridor running from just near the sacristy"—he pointed to where the steps led down—"to just beyond the north wall. Could be more graves, could be treasure—hard to say."

"That's where the 'Keep Out' sign is placed?"

"Well, yes. Can't have people tramping about in there. I don't expect you'll have any need, and I don't believe the Earl would grant permission."

"Still, someone's working in there."

"Oh, aye?" he said, looking at me curiously.

"I was here a few days ago. While I was down in the sacristy I heard voices."

Rob Madson gave me a searching look then said, "It was probably an acoustic trick—someone outside on the grounds. The Earl doesn't permit anyone down there."

"I know I heard something."

Rob smiled slightly, just as the tour guide had done at my first visit. No one heard humming; no one heard voices from the crypt—no one but Ian bloody Graham.

"Rosslyn has an effect on people," Rob said quietly. "It's an unusual place."

I wasn't going to get a definite answer—it was something to file away. The reporter part of me wanted to get to the bottom of it. The rest of me just decided to move on.

"I have a question for you," I said after a moment. "I understand that this building was intended to be only a part of a larger one and it was never completed. But . . . why build it here? It's a good distance from the castle, not terribly convenient for a collegiate chapel at all."

"William St Clair chose this spot for a reason," he said. "Like so many holy places, Rosslyn Chapel is built upon another, earlier place. If the Templars did come here, they chose *this* place for a reason as well."

"There was a pagan temple here?"

"Almost certainly. And in the Celtic tradition, even more so than in the Roman one, there's a remarkable amount of syncretism. You see it all over the Isles, including my native Tiree. There are countless sanctified places that were holy long before Columba reached Iona."

He placed his hand on the Master's Pillar, touching it almost reverently. "You see, Ian, the new religion doesn't replace the old—it molds it to a new shape. As you walk around this place look at the walls, the pillars, the ceilings. Green men, nature symbolism, pagan emblems. Even the dimensions of the place have meaning."

We had been looking up at the St Matthew stained glass—a beautiful piece of work, but a recent one, I knew. All of the original work had been swept away by the Reformation in its usual dour and efficient manner. Now Rob Madson turned around to look south, along the Lady Chapel—the portion of the church separated from the main area by the three great pillars.

"Look up there," he said, pointing to the ceilings. I could see the stone light fixtures—*pendant bosses*: I'd learned the term from my reading—hanging down from the place where four arched supports met. Each arch was decorated with hundreds of boxlike projections and an assortment of carvings and decorations—animal and human figures, angels and devils, nature emblems and Green men.

"Extraordinary," I managed.

"Unlike anything else," he said. "There are countless numbers of places of worship, holy places, all across Europe and the world. But this is different, Ian. This is not merely a work of art: it's a text written in stone. More than that—it's a *song.*"

"I don't understand. A song?"

"Look round the arches. There are seven slightly different shapes for those boxes. There are seven notes in the scale. In fact, if you've a good ear, you could strike each of them and hear a slightly different sound.

"Now imagine if all of them—there are more than fourteen hundred—were arranged as music. It intrigued the young man over there"—he gestured to the tech with the laptop—"enough that he's set some sort of computer programme to sort them out. I wish him good luck—that's been sought after for generations."

"What's been sought after? The pattern of the song? What is it, 'Jerusalem'? 'And did those feet in ancient times . . .' "

I was trying to be lighthearted; years on daytime telly will do that for you. This was an important subject for Rob Madson—he might well have tried to talk to MacDougal about it. God knows what Mac had told him; probably to shut up and do his job.

Rob smiled politely but I could see that I'd touched a nerve. It was the sort of moment we edited out.

"I'm sorry," I said after a moment.

"Don't trouble yourself," Madson said, still smiling.

"Why is the song important, Rob?"

"It's the healing music of Rosslyn," Madson said softly, looking away from me as if he were trying to remember something.

"I don't think that was in my briefing."

"No, it wouldn't be," he said. "But if it could be found . . ."

"What happens then?"

"It heals the world."

"What does that mean?"

Madson didn't answer. Our attention was drawn away by the tech working at his laptop, who said something under his breath that didn't bear speaking aloud in a church.

We walked toward him. As I approached the centre line, I again felt the beginnings of that same hum I'd heard yesterday. I hesitated; my guide seemed not to notice.

The tech looked up at me angrily—then his face softened.

"I'm sorry, I thought you were Mr MacDougal. You're Ian Graham, aren't you?"

"I certainly used to be." I had a brief warm feeling—it was good to be recognised.

"I'm Sean Ross. I got out here a bit after eight, but there's nothing for me to do until they've blocked everything out. I was admiring the Lady Chapel, and Mr Madson was kind enough to provide me with some information."

"About the . . ." I lowered my voice. " 'healing music'?" I didn't want Mac to think that I'd let Rob Madson "get started."

"It's an interesting mathematical problem," Ross answered. "There are a number of different ways the song could be arranged: a simple sequence of notes, or more likely something much more complicated. I thought perhaps it would work as a motet or a rondeau."

I smiled. That wasn't in the briefing either.

"Mr Ross studied music," Madson explained. "He seemed to be keen on this little puzzle. Royal Scottish Academy, wasn't it? And St Mary's too."

Ross smiled. "Except I can't get the damn thing to run," he said. "My laptop keeps crashing. I can't explain it—it's brand new." He shrugged, a helpless slave of technology.

"Perhaps it's where you've placed it," Madson offered.

Ross frowned. He adjusted its position slightly on the altar. I could see that the machine was picking up a wireless signal from somewhere but not very efficiently.

"I mean . . ." Madson gestured toward the far end of the chapel, toward the Victorian baptistry attached to the west end of the building.

"Oh. I see. Faraday cage," Ross said cryptically. He closed the laptop and picked it up, carrying it with him as he walked down the centre aisle.

Madson watched him go, then carefully adjusted the altar cloth where the machine had been placed. Then he looked at me and stamped softly with his foot—a hollow sound.

"You think . . ."

"What I think is not as important as what I believe, Ian. Come, look at this." He walked over to the south aisle; for just a moment I caught David MacDougal's eye—he looked impatient and annoyed at his current victim. The humming grew in intensity and then diminished. I wanted to stop my guide and ask him about it, but I also wanted to see everything he had to show me before Mac decided to throw his weight about—there might not be time for it later.

We turned to face the sacristy steps. Madson gestured to a horizontal stone beam—an *architrave*, the guide book had said; I mentally patted myself on the back—with faint script writing on a scroll ribbon, interspersed with elm- and oak-leaf carvings.

"What does it say?"

" 'Forte est vinu. Fortior est rex. Fortiores sunt mulieres: sup om vincit veritas.' "

"Strong wine," I ventured. "Uh. . ." Latin was a long way in the rear-view. "The king is strong . . . and something about truth winning."

"Not quite full marks, but well done," Rob said. "The actual translation is 'Wine is strong. The king is stronger. Women are stronger still: but truth conquers all.' It's from Esdras: one of the books of the New Testament that the Council of Nicaea voted out. It describes Darius' challenge of wisdom. The words are attributed to Zerubbabel, the Jewish prince who led the people of Israel out from Babylonian exile to the Holy Land to rebuild the Temple.

"Truth," Rob Madson said, looking directly at me. "Rosslyn is a destination. Not just for tourists and television producers, but pilgrims. And others."

"They bring seashells from Spain."

"Yes," Rob said. "That's where the pilgrimage begins." He looked at me thoughtfully, almost as if he was looking at me for the first time.

I was distracted by a snatch of music: a soft piping and a gentle brush of a hand on harp strings.

"What's that?" I asked.

"What's what?"

"That music." I heard it again: a regular theme, with embellishments working their way into and out of it—rather like the carvings around the scroll. It was probably one of Ross's motets or rondeaux or something.

"I don't hear any music," Madson said. "Where—"

"From the baptistry, I think," I said, and began to walk down the south aisle. I could see Sean Ross sitting on a stone projection with the computer in his lap, completely absorbed by something. Madson walked alongside me, and people seemed to flow out of our way as we traveled the length of the church to the west entrance.

The baptistry, I knew, was not part of the original building or the original plan; it had been added in the 1880s, in part to accommodate the organ. As we stepped across the threshold the music seemed to swell: it was playing continuously now . . . and even though I was directly in line with the centre aisle of the church, I wasn't hearing the hum.

I seemed to be the only person who could hear any of it.

"Take a look at this," Ross said, turning the laptop to face me. Whatever programme he was running—some sort of mathematical modeling software, from the look of it—was building up a regular arrangement of cubes in three dimensions in a variety of different colours.

"I—I don't—" I began to say, but the music filled my ears. Neither Ross nor Madson nor any of the threescore other people in the Chapel seemed to notice anything.

Beyond the west door the sky was dark. I felt, rather than heard, a rumble of thunder.

The model continued to build, block upon block, as the melody became more complex. In the baptistry there were two stained-glass windows, one on either hand: one of an airman, some St Clair killed in the Second World War, as I recalled; and the second of St Francis, dedicated in honour of another member of the family. As I glanced at them, details jumped out at me and seemed to move of their own accord: the wings on the airman's helmet, the woodland animals to either side of Francis.

"Truth," I heard—perhaps aloud, perhaps in my head. "Truth conquers all."

The last thing I saw was Rob Madson, looking curiously at me as I fell into nothing.

CHAPTER 3

I COULD STILL HEAR MUSIC WHEN I BEGAN TO WAKE UP. IT WASN'T quite the same, and it was being interrupted by a steady drum of rain outside.

Storm must've broken, I thought, then added, *Passing out on the first day of work—that'll help my prospects.*

"Ian."

I didn't open my eyes. My head was pounding—maybe I'd hit it on the stone floor when I fell.

I could feel something digging into my back, and there was a smell nearby—something like an open septic tank. Maybe there was some sort of works project being done.

"Ian," the voice said again—Rob Madson, my guide. "Come on, we're going to be late."

"MacDougal can wait. Can someone get me a coffee? And maybe some—" I couldn't come up with the word: I wanted to say *aspirin* or *ibuprofen.* "I've got some in the car. What happened? Did I . . ." I put one hand to my head and stretched the other one out.

Five seconds later I was sitting bolt upright, eyes open. Something—a smelly, wet dog, actually—had done a pretty solid job of slobbering all over my hand.

"Did we lose power or something? And where am I?"

Rob Madson came into view. He was dressed for play acting from the look of it: a knee-length robe and sandals, and he'd got a few weeks' growth of beard, maybe from some overzealous makeup artist. He wasn't wearing his glasses either.

"Are you feeling all right, Ian?"

"I'm . . . I could use a coffee. Even a bottle of Irn-Bru would do—to pick me up. I feel like I've been asleep for a week. Did I hit my head on something?"

"That'd explain it." He knelt down next to me and began pressing on my forehead. The beard growth came with several days' stink from his body; I felt like I hadn't recently had a wash either.

"Get off," I said, pushing him away and hauling myself to my feet. Five seconds after that I was flat on my arse with an even more pounding headache; the ceiling couldn't have been quite much more than five feet high. My dog friend was making free with my hand again; I pulled it away and he shuffled away to find someone else.

"Watch your head," Rob said, smiling. He reached for a robe like his own and tossed it to me.

"You think this is funny? Wait until I talk to MacDougal about this," I snapped, pulling myself up. "I'm still the star of this programme." I reached down for my mobile—and found that I wasn't wearing anything but a pair of loose shorts.

I swung my legs onto the floor and looked at him. "Where's my gear? My—" I wanted to say *mobile* or *PDA,* but again couldn't come up with the words. "My wallet?"

Rob looked baffled. "Your pack's over there, lad." He gestured toward a dim corner of the room. "Now put on your robe and let's go. I don't want to miss Matins. Not today."

I picked up the robe; it looked as if it hadn't been washed since Maggie Thatcher's time. As I sat there for a moment and came to myself, I took a look at my surroundings.

I'd been asleep on some sort of straw mat in the middle of an airless, foul-smelling barn three-quarters filled with mats, the remaining quarter filled with dogs and piles of possessions—packs and such. What light there was came from a few dim, flickering torches. It was as if I'd been kidnapped by Walkabout Scotland.

"What happened? Did we lose power?" I repeated. There still had been no answers.

He looked at me curiously. "I don't know head or tail of what you're talking about. Now will you get dressed?" He turned and squatted down, rummaging in a pack—the one he'd said was mine.

"I don't know what this is about," I said, getting myself to my feet and keeping my head low as I went over to stand beside him. "Where are we?"

Rob didn't answer. He turned and produced a rope belt to go with the robe and thrust it into my hands, then pointed to a pair of sandals on the floor nearby. The pack and the clothing didn't look like anything I owned.

There was no sign of MacDougal or the tech crew; I was in strange underwear in near-darkness in a smelly barn. The only thing I recognised was the man next to me—my guide at Rosslyn Chapel—who was next thing to a complete stranger.

"I'm not going to put this bloody thing on," I said, holding it out at arm's length.

"Well, they won't let you in without it," he said, not turning.

"But my clothes—"

"This will do, lad. No one will be looking at you in any case."

At least the robe looked like it would cover me. I began to pull it over my head. As I did, I felt beard growth on my own face.

I had no idea why I was here. This was some sort of weird dream or some very nasty practical joke—and at some point I wouldn't feel like playing along. At that moment, I needed coffee and something for my head and wasn't getting either.

"Why don't you want to be late today?"

"This is St James' Day, you lackwit," I heard Rob say. "Don't you remember? That's why we're *here.*"

—•—

We came out of the building onto a wide field. The moon was just above the horizon, cloaked by clouds, and I could see that our building was one of a number of hostels, or maybe barracks was a better term, lining an avenue that climbed from a river to a fortified wall. There was a crowd of dozens—perhaps hundreds—of people dressed as we were, climbing the hill through the mud and the rain to a wide gate in the wall, open to admit us.

I was still a bit groggy. It felt like a dream as Rob and I moved with the crowd toward the gate to the deep sound of a bell.

I could hear the music more clearly now: two or three distinct themes wound their way in and out of each other, but it was all voices: no instruments at all. The underlying theme hinted at the music I'd heard at Rosslyn.

The healing music, Rob had called it. I wanted to stop and ask him about that, but had all I could do to put my feet straight and not slip.

"Have they decided to make this some sort of costume drama?" I finally managed as we passed through the gate and into what looked like a medieval city.

There were a couple of bonfires lit in a great plaza, illuminating a few very large buildings, one to the left and one in front of us. It was to that one that the crowd was moving. In the flicker of the firelight, I could see a strange expression on Rob's face.

This is a pretty strange dream so far, I thought. *What the hell did I say now?*

I was still half-asleep. Thinking back later, I wondered that I hadn't pressed further. It might have done me no good, and I suppose that I might have been taken for a witch—or worse. Shrugging, I touched my head, pretending that I hadn't said whatever it was. Rob looked away.

"They'll have started Matins already—we'll go through the west door along with everyone else. A few Poor Knight initiates weren't going to get much of a view anyway."

Poor Knight, I thought, and looked down at the half-sodden wool robe I was wearing: a plain brown thing secured by a rope belt.

"I don't understand."

He pulled me a few feet out of the press. Two men just behind cursed as they were forced to step around me; the rain continued to pelt down. "Templars who haven't taken their vows have very little leverage here, lad, no matter what you've been told. This is *Santiago,* and this is St James' Day. Now let's get in there before Terce, all right?"

Templars.

He turned and walked away: I continued to stand there, trying to understand what he'd just said. He was ten feet away when he realised I wasn't walking next to him.

"Ian?"

"Rob, did you say we're in *Santiago?*" The shells sitting in the alcove of Rosslyn's sacristy came to mind.

"Yes. And we're standing in the rain. I'm getting wetter by the minute, and I'd rather be in a nice dry sanctuary. Come on."

"Santiago? As in *Spain?*"

"Spain." He repeated the word as if he'd never said it before. "This is Galicia. About as far west as you can go before stepping into the western ocean."

"I didn't sign on for this. I don't know what's going on—I'm—"

"You're what?" he said, holding his hand above his face to shield it from the rain. "What is it?"

"How did I get here?"

Rob wiped his hands on the front of his robe. "Don't you know?"

"I—I can't remember." I listened to my voice, then tried to concentrate on Rob's voice.

He stepped close. "You and that Asturian, La Rosa, walked in here yesterday afternoon from Cintra. I thought you weren't going to make it, but you got here just before the weather broke."

"The last thing I remember is standing next to you in the baptistry in Rosslyn, watching that—" I wanted to say *computer programme*. Again no words.

"Never heard of the place."

He grabbed my elbow and began to march me across the plaza toward the church, its summit lost in the smoke from the bonfires. "I think the heat's got to you, lad. You're a long way from your home in Edinburgh. Of course, *I'm* a long way from Tiree, but unlike myself, you haven't done any tours of Outremer to get you used to the heat. Whatever happened yesterday in there"—he gestured toward the church—"we're going to sort it out inside."

He didn't seem to be in the mood to argue; I was in no shape to protest, so I kept silent. If this wasn't another strange dream, then someone had gone to great lengths to set this up: the costumes, the players, the *stink:* and they were going to get top shelf Ian Graham. Professionalism would let me do no less—that and the hope of steady work in the spotlight.

I shrugged and let him lead me along. But something about the conversation still bothered me—and as we entered the church I realised what it was.

Not a word of our conversation had been in English.

I couldn't place the language—it sounded like French, but it was nothing like the French I'd learned in school. If this *was* a practical joke, someone had gone to a lot of trouble. If David MacDougal had decided to go the costume drama route without telling him, I had Rodney on my mobile's speed dial—assuming I could lay my hands on it—and between the two of us we'd rip Mac's head from his shoulders, regardless of the consequence.

On the other hand, if this was just a vivid dream, I'd suddenly developed the sort of imagination that leads to blockbuster movies and novels that come in threes.

There hadn't been any Templars, no *real* Templars, in seven hundred years. They were driven into hiding or burned at the stake. Something happened with the King of France. I reached for my PDA to look it up on the Net—but the robe didn't have any pockets: no cash, no PDA, no mobile either.

This is crazy, I thought.

"Galicia," I said, as others hurried in ahead of us and pressing in behind. "On St James' Day."

"That's right," Rob said. "St James' Day, in this year of Grace thirteen hundred and seven. Any other questions?"

You could've knocked me over with a feather. I'm sure that if he hadn't been holding on to me I would have fallen down. As it was, there was quite a press for the middle of the night.

"Uh," I said. "1307."

It was a third explanation I hadn't even considered. I was actually in the *fourteenth century. No,* I thought. *They don't really believe that and neither do I.* But we were speaking French, or something like.

What in hell was happening?

"Yes. Now be quiet. I want to hear." He craned his neck and stood up straight, looking over the crowd in front of us down the main aisle of the church.

'Haud your wheesht, child,' my Gran used to say when she was fairly worked up. It sounded no more strange than the French, or whatever it was, we were speaking.

Without anything else to say, I hauded my wheesht and listened.

Two lines of monks were entering the great church by the north door, singing solemnly as they went. The air was rank with sweat, with a vague overscent of sweet incense; it didn't smell like St Giles or any other Presbyterian kirk I'd ever been in. But the voices . . . unaccompanied by instruments, they sounded angelic.

Annua gaudia
Jacobe debita
Sunt tibi danda.
Organa dulcia
Conveniencia
Sunt resonanda.

At least at the moment, I seemed to have a good command of Latin to go with the French—or whatever it was—I was speaking with Rob, so I could make out the meaning: "James," the monks sang, "each year we rejoice in praise of you. Sweet instruments will play in harmony." The language was Galician, I knew—though I had no idea how I could possibly know that. I could hear a few of the pilgrims singing along quietly as the procession made its way into the nave.

Maybe something got slipped into my coffee, I thought. What was going on around me was very believable.

Very real.

"Sorry I'm late," someone said nearby. Another pilgrim, dressed as we were, elbowed his way toward our place—and I recognised him as well: it was Sean Ross, but with a scraggly beard and long greasy hair tied in a queue.

"Did you—" I began, startled. "What about the—" I tried again, but couldn't come up with the words. I had no idea what to say to him, but at least he was something else familiar.

Rob looked back at him and scowled. "I'm surprised you made it at all," he said quietly, crossing his arms.

"Oh, wouldn't miss it," Sean said. "They're going to do all of the *Cantigas* between now and Vespers."

"*Cantigas?*" I asked. "Sean, what's—"

A hand cuffed me on the head and I turned angrily, but noticed the hand was attached to a pilgrim who stood close on seven feet tall and must have weighed twenty stone. He made the international gesture for quiet, followed by a few other equally understandable international gestures about what would happen to me if I didn't hold my tongue, then serenely turned his attention back to the singing.

—•—

It went on, song after song in that lyrical language, until watery grey light began to filter through the high windows at the east end of the sanctuary. Every so many songs—it was hard to tell, since they seemed to meld one into another—there seemed to be one song particularly in praise of the Virgin Mary. That too was a long way from my good kirk upbringing, and I was at a loss to know how I recognised them.

Finally at some unseen signal we all began to filter out into the pre-dawn. Smells of cooking wafted across the plaza, mixing with all of the other odours, and I suddenly felt very hungry. If I had any cash, it was back at the hostel. I had no idea whether I did or not.

Fortunately Rob provided for all three of us. We walked out into the morning light, and he steered us to the right and into a wider plaza where the great cathedral stretched along one long side. It was filled with vendors of all kinds, along with entertainers, beggars, and folk going to and fro on errands. It was rather like the Canongate during the Fringe, but with animals and without electronics.

Rob strolled along the food-sellers until he found one that satisfied him, and held up three fingers. After a few words in Galician and an exchange of coin, he handed a sort of fried pie to each of us and took one for himself. We found a spot off to the side of the plaza to sit and eat our breakfast.

"Empanadas," he said, biting into it. "Fish."

They smelled wonderful. "What sort of fish is in them?" I asked.

Rob stopped eating and looked up at me, paused for a moment, and said, "They have two kinds. 'Meat' and 'fish'. These are the 'fish' ones. I think that's about all I need to know. Would you rather have the 'meat' ones?"

"What sort of 'meat'?"

Rob scowled. "I don't know. *Meat.*"

Sean and I looked at each other. "Fish," we said at the same time.

Whatever sort of fish it was, it hit the spot, as did the skin of wine—*ribiero,* I was told—we passed between us. I'd tried my hand at wineskins when Liz and I had traveled to Spain, so I was able to manage. The empanadas were delicious—better than anything that I had in my fridge back in Leith.

We ate and drank, wiping our mouths on our sleeves. The rain had mostly drifted off, leaving a high, overcast sky. For a few minutes I think I even forgot about the absurd idea that I'd been transported back to the fourteenth century.

"How are you feeling, lad?" Rob asked finally, when we had done justice to the empanadas and the wine.

"Better. But I still don't understand why I'm here or how I got here from Rosslyn."

"You'd best leave thoughts of her behind," Rob said.

"Who?"

"Rosalynn," he said. The two men smiled and continued to eat.

"It's not a girl. It's a place."

Rob looked at me, cocking his head and frowning. "The two of you hiked in yesterday afternoon—you said you'd come up from Cintra in Portugal. You went in to the church to pray, passed out from the heat—or by hitting your head too hard on Maestro Mateo's statue in the Pórtico, I don't know—and we had to carry you back to our doss. You didn't wake up until I had to drag you out of bed for Matins."

The cover story, I thought. *But that's not where I remember having been.*

"You said . . . you'd been expecting me."

"Yes." He crossed his arms in front of him. "I was told to expect you," he continued, and then at what must have been a blank expression from me, added, "You don't remember a blessed thing, do you?"

I wanted to say: *I remember you telling me about what might be buried under Rosslyn Chapel.* But that was yesterday—and, who knew, seven hundred years in the future. Instead of answering, I squinted at the watery sunlight.

Maybe I was in the fourteenth century after all. It was impossible, some kind of science fiction thing. But the rock felt real, the fried pie tasted real. The sunlight and my itchy wool robe and the smells of the market were all real as well.

I was bewildered, light-headed, and sore. But at least I wasn't hungry.

"What has Sean told you?" I asked, gesturing toward our

third companion, who was just finishing his meal and appeared to be looking for more.

"You mean *Juan?*" he said, looking at the other man. "Brother Juan la Rosa."

"Sorry. Juan." *What the hell,* I thought. *Juan.*

Ross—la Rosa—nodded, still eating, and said something incomprehensible. He swallowed, took a drink of the wine, and said, *"Misil me Dominus."*

"That's as may be," Rob said, offering no explanation for the Latin remark. "But he's told me more than I want to know about motets and rondeaux and the *Cantigas de Santa Maria.* Which is all fine but won't let me pass any more easily through the eye of the needle, if you follow my meaning."

"Philistine!" Sean—Juan—managed around the last bite of his empanada, then swallowed and wiped his face on his sleeve. "This would not be the first time I've had this argument, Brother." He looked at me. "You enjoyed the music last night, didn't you?"

"It was remarkable."

"It tells the whole story of this place. More than four centuries ago, the Lord God led the hermit Pelayo to discover the grave of the blessed Saint James, Jesus' companion, in the very spot where it now lies." He pointed toward the church in the distance. "The great king Alfonso *el Sabio* of Castile wrote beautiful, beautiful music about Santiago, all in the native language."

"All right, all right," I said, holding my hands up. "More information than I needed."

"Every tenth song is a *loor:* a hymn to the Blessed Virgin," he added, as if he had to sneak that last comment in. Rob rolled his eyes. Juan stopped and crossed himself, and each of us followed suit. It was one more thing we didn't do in kirk.

Quickly, I thought, *okay—spectacles, testicles, wallet, watch:* every Low Church worshipper's memory aid for the thing High Churchers learned when they were just lads. I must have done it right, since Juan hurried along. My Gran would be spinning in her grave, and I felt uncomfortable with such a Popish gesture—but years in front of a camera helped me keep that feeling to myself. And as for Gran, she had a weakness for liturgical music she never admitted to anyone—but played it for me sometimes when I visited her for tea . . . so maybe she'd understand after all.

"It's wonderful." He spread his arms wide. "Not just chant, but multiple voices—and there are diagrams for the singing so everyone can see how it goes together."

"Sheet music," I offered, and got another blank look from both of them. "Musical notation. Every Good Boy Deserves Favour."

That struck both of my companions dumb for another few seconds. Presumably they were starting to get used to the idea that I would say things they didn't understand.

Juan hurried on. "It's all written down in this beautiful book. You can see it if you ask the monks."

"You've seen the Codex?" Rob perked up, leaning forward.

Juan reached into his scrip. "I have a letter of introduction." He pulled out a small wrapped parcel, a piece of weathered canvas. "My abbot, Father Corvão—"

"*Crow?*" Rob asked. "You should show proper respect."

"Well, his Christian name is Tomaso, but everyone calls him Corvão—Raven—on account of—" He made a gesture at his own nose. Rob snorted.

"He sent this letter to the Father Abbot here," Juan continued, "asking them to let me see the book." Juan's eyes were full of light, as if he'd had a spiritual experience—which, upon reflection, he probably had.

"And the Father Abbot here let you see it," Rob said, sounding a bit skeptical.

"Yes he did."

"I'd very much like to see it myself," Rob said. Juan smiled—he gave the impression of being the third in our little pecking order, and this was something that gave him importance to Rob.

"I think I can get us all in," he said. "Maybe after Compline."

—•—

Afterward Rob and I strolled through Paraiso, the large plaza north of the cathedral; Juan disappeared somewhere on his own errands. It was like a flea market—there were food vendors, cloth sellers, every kind of gem and jewel imaginable. Then there were the chemists: healers, they'd say, selling cures for anything that might ail you from an itch to a cramp. And even in my reduced condition I was smart enough to avoid the stalls with thorns from Jesus' crown, fragments of the True Cross, strands from Veronica's veil and who knew what else.

I took it all in with a good reporter's eye, still considering the possibility that this was some elaborate test. In the meanwhile, I tried to play the role that I'd somehow been assigned.

"Thieves and whoresons," Rob hissed at me when I turned to look at a display of herbal remedies. "Look at what they charge—ten *sueldos* for something worth no more than a few *nummos*. The prices are supposed to be regulated, but most pilgrims don't know that."

"Hmm." I looked around. The vendors were all trying to get my attention now that I'd stopped. There didn't seem to be any price controls in force here.

"Just looking," Rob said, steering me away. He gestured toward a nearby cloth-merchant, measuring out lengths of fine blue-dyed linen for a wealthy-looking woman. "That one uses his crippled arm to measure ells of cloth, so he never gives good value. If you must, go to *that* one—" He pointed down the row at a bearded man in a dark robe and an odd, peaked hat, whom some customers were going out of their way to avoid. "He may be a Jew, but he's honest."

"Why—" I began to ask why it mattered if he was Jewish, but I realised that I shouldn't ask the question. The bias was part of this society, something muted in my time but not completely silent.

Every fourth or fifth stall was selling the scallop-shells, called *vierias*, that marked one as a pilgrim. Most of the people in the crowd had one pinned to their clothing; I noticed one clipped on my own hat. Evidently I'd already picked one up, perhaps in this market, sometime yesterday; but the yesterday I remembered was back where my car was parked, at Rosslyn Abbey presumably seven hundred years from now.

—•—

Finally Rob said, "We should go back to our doss and rest. Have to conserve our strength."

"*Now* you're interested in conserving strength?" I answered, as we disentangled ourselves from a very persistent craftsman who had tried for fifteen minutes to sell us a set of knucklebones carved from jet. "Juan doesn't seem to need to do that."

"Young men have all the luck. Youth is wasted on them. Though he wants to spend every moment in the church, which is worthy of praise." Rob added, running a hand through his hair and then smoothing his beard. "Come on."

We wound up back at our hostel outside the gates. I was fair knackered and ready for a rest, but wasn't about to sleep just yet.

"I need some answers," I said, as we took seats on a two-tiered stoop outside the hostel. The late-morning sun was far preferable to the smelly dimness within.

"Certes."

"I'm not sure I belong here, Rob," I began, not sure how to begin.

"But you're here on pilgrimage. No one comes to a place like this save those who want to be here."

I didn't know how to respond to that, so I continued, "You say we never met before yesterday." *True enough,* I thought: as far as I could tell, only a single night had passed since we were both at Rosslyn.

"That's right. I was told you would be here by St James' Day. The Lord knows I've got enough sins to expiate that I'd earned one more pilgrimage; I was sent off from Paris at Eastertide—and here I am."

"Who sent you?"

"Why, the Grand Master himself," Rob answered, as if it was obvious. He bobbed his head slightly. "He's taken a very special interest in you, lad. You should be honoured."

"The Grand Master . . ."

"Of the Poor Knights of Christ. That's right, the Grand Master of our Order."

"I'm even more confused. I'm—not sure I'm supposed to be here."

"You said that. Why shouldn't you be in Santiago?"

"I don't think I should be here . . . in 1307," I said, not sure what kind of reaction that would bring. *If this is a test,* I thought, *I'm admitting failure. And if it's not . . .*

Rob looked at me curiously for a moment—and then let loose a laugh fit to shake the thatch from the hostel roof. "By all the saints, lad, what year would you like it to be? I don't think we have much choice in that. You're—what? Thirty summers?"

"Thirty-four."

"And still have all your teeth. Thirty-four—you're halfway to the grave, Ian. The Lord only grants us threescore and ten. This is the day the Lord hath made: you might as well rejoice in it. It's the year of Grace 1307, the second year of the reign of His Holiness Clement the bloody Fifth, no friend to our Order." He glanced around, mock-furtively. "But you didn't hear that from *me.* It's 1307, lad, and you might as well get used to it."

I stood up and took a slow walk. Rob didn't seem to be suffering from any sort of dislocation—both he and Sean—Juan—were at ease in this place at this time. Every reference I'd made to the present day seemed to draw a curious look or a laugh. It was as if they weren't the men I'd met at Rosslyn, but their twin brothers—or great-many-times grandfathers.

Or they were very good actors, and this was on camera somehow.

I'd been in the television business for most of my adult life; I knew that there were any number of ways to conceal cameras—trees, rocks, and steadycams carried by costumed extras. Television was getting very talented at it. I took a look around: low one- and two-story buildings, a few market stalls, a city wall—they could be anywhere, I suppose, but I couldn't see anything. Mid-morning, most people were up in the city or sleeping off the night before.

It didn't seem as if anyone could really be filming this—this vivid dream I was having.

"Why did the Templar Grand Master expect me to be here at Santiago?"

"Ian." He patted the stone bench next to him; I went and sat down. "Ian, you are here because you are ready to follow the road. Here and all of the other sites along that road you'll learn to see with new eyes."

"But I'm not—" *Catholic,* I wanted to say. Of course, I really wasn't much of a Presbyterian either, not by this time. Truth be told, I didn't know what the hell I believed at that moment. But the idea of seeing with new eyes—whatever he meant by the expression—might go even beyond that.

I didn't know what would happen if this was actually happening and I tried to tell him what I was . . . where I was. I needed some sort of rope to grab onto, and Rob Madson—Rob, the man sitting next to me—was all I had.

"I'm not ready," I said finally.

"Ready enough," he said. "Time's wasting. Thirty-four summers. How much longer do you think you can wait?"

—•—

Time was governed by the offices being sung at the cathedral and the dozen other churches up in Santiago. We rested through the worst heat of the day and headed back into the city just before Nones. Juan met us near the gate—he'd had a few hours to pray and listen to the music, and his face was full of light.

"What do we do now?" I couldn't help but ask as we got into another queue, one that snaked around the cathedral to the west-facing side, near the archbishop's palace.

"We're going to go through the Pórtico de Gloria," Juan said. "The Gate of Glory. It is a true wonder, Ian."

Rob nodded sagely, and several others around us in the queue agreed. I tried to keep my face impassive—another church façade, I supposed; Lord knows I'd seen enough of them when we did locations with *Ian and Jan*.

"What's so special about it?"

"Well, of course it's beautiful," Rob said, giving me the curious look I'd already become used to. "A masterwork. Especially the Tree of Jesse."

I quickly searched my memory for a Jesse that might appear on a cathedral façade in a tree. None presented itself. "I see," I said, not seeing.

"King David's father, Solomon's grandfather—and the ancestor of our Saviour." He gave a small smile. "David. The one with the slingshot."

"I know who David was," I answered.

"Of course you do, lad," Rob said. "At the Pórtico there's this great pillar called the Tree of Jesse. It's the centrepiece of the whole gate."

"Oh, yes," someone said nearby: an older man, bent with age, who walked with an improvised crutch. "I've been here five times and will touch it again." He erupted in a phlegmy cough that took a few moments to sort out—I expected him to pitch over dead in front of me; the others nearby gave him a little room in case he was planning to do just that. "This might be my last visit," he said, looking up at me and giving me a toothless smile. "The Lord gave me strength to get here one more time."

"Amen," several people echoed. I said it myself—he seemed to have just made it.

"I'll walk away from here too, mark my word," the old man said. "My hand in the Lord's hand." He turned away, shuffling forward. There was a lull in the conversations in the queue.

To Rob, I quietly said, "What did he mean, 'I'll touch it again'?"

"That's what we do at the Pórtico, Ian," Juan said. I guess I hadn't said it quietly enough. "You place your hand where God placed His hand."

Though there were enough people around us to make a good queue for a Stones concert, the crowd seemed to part in front of me as we turned a corner, passing under an arch, and I got my first view of the Pórtico de Gloria—the Gate of Glory, the sculptured west door.

The sun was well down in the sky; it lit up the Pórtico like it was on fire, etching it in brilliant relief like nothing I'd ever seen.

"My God," I managed to say, more quietly this time; but all around me pilgrims were crossing themselves and mouthing prayers. I absently made the gesture myself, offering silent apologies once again to my long-dead Gran.

Ian and Jan had done remotes from various parts of the world—we'd been to St Petersburg and Rome, to Greece and Jerusalem and Rio and any number of other places and seen impressive monuments. I think I was expecting something like those things—well-used or gilded, decorated and set up for perfect viewing—picture postcards 40p, three quid for the guidebook. The Pórtico, on the other hand, was the real Mackay.

The gate consisted of three portals, carved in stunning detail. There must have been a few hundred people perched on capitals, crowded onto the transoms, arranged in curved arcs over the doorway. In the middle of the centre portal was the man himself, Saint James, a cane in one hand and his shopping list or something in the other, perched on the top of the Tree of Jesse. The pilgrims were moving forward, watched by several burly monks, and touching the pillar at shoulder level.

"The hand of Christ touched the pillar," Juan whispered reverently. "He turned the church a bit north of east, and the pillar bears His mark."

Why would He do that? I wondered, looking at the younger man. And then I thought—*Juan really believes that. This is an age where God goes right ahead and puts His hand on anything He feels needs it and leaves His mark behind.*

And what, I added silently, *will this thing look like in seven hundred years?*

—•—

The old fellow we'd met had his turn; he shuffled forward and placed his hand gently on a spot where there were five hollows for fingers and thumb. He closed his eyes and murmured, then took the hand away and moved clockwise around the Tree to the rear, letting the next *peregrino* take his turn.

Rob nodded toward the statue of Saint James as Juan waited, balancing on one foot and then another like a nervous greyhound. "Look at the scroll, Ian."

I squinted in the afternoon light and made out the legend: *Misil me Dominus.* It was what Juan had said this morning.

" 'The Lord sent me,' " Rob obligingly translated.

"The Lord sent him here?"

"Aye, that's right," Rob answered. "He brought the word of the Lord to this land—the unconquerable Truth."

Truth conquers all, I thought. I must have looked surprised, but Rob had looked away. "Right," he said, "Juan's done. Your turn, lad."

Juan crossed himself and walked around the centre column to the rear, where he knelt at a smaller statue, touching foreheads with it.

"Seeking wisdom," Rob said as I took a single step forward. "That's supposed to be Master Mateo himself. Make sure you do it yourself—maybe knock some sense into you, too."

Rob gestured me toward the pillar. I looked back at him; he smiled, just as he'd done at Rosslyn.

All right, I thought. *For form's sake I'd best do this.*

I took my turn, reaching my hand up to touch the Tree of Jesse, placing each finger in a well-worn hollow—

—•—

And the scene changed.

It was night, with a pale light limning the beech trees in front of me. A low stone wall was a few paces away, between where I stood and the nearest tree; a black bird—a raven, I think—perched on a wide, gnarled branch, blinking, its eyes catching the same light. There was no moon; I couldn't tell where the light was coming from.

As I began to turn I heard Rob's voice say, "No, lad, don't turn around."

Waking up into a costume-drama dream was one thing, but this was quite another. I tried to continue turning and found that I couldn't.

Instead of being disoriented or angry, I felt afraid—out of control and afraid.

"What's happening now?"

"I need to tell you something."

"I'm listening," I said. I took a deep breath to calm myself. *You're on camera, me lad,* I told myself. *Relax and smile.*

"Are you?" I heard him step closer; I resisted the urge to try and turn around. "Are you really listening, Ian? Have you ever listened?"

"I've spent my professional career listening. Anyone who had anything to say, I listened."

"You need to listen to the music."

"The hymns to the Virgin? I listened all bloody night. It was spiritually uplifting. Bravo."

Rob sighed. "Not just the *Cantigas,* Ian. They're a part of it, but there is more. You heard the music at Rosslyn."

"I certainly did. Just before—this—started. And I'm listening now."

"You could hear the song: that's why you were chosen."

"For what?"

"Do you know about the year 1307, Ian? When you took your Highers, did they teach you about what happened to the Knights Templar in that year?"

I had an uneasy feeling in the pit of my stomach. I'd done my reading prep for Rosslyn and that date stuck out in my mind, more so than anything in my Highers half a lifetime ago. "Is that when they were outlawed?"

"That's right. On Friday, the thirteenth of October of 1307,

Philip le Bel, the King of France, and Clement the Fifth, the Avignon Pope, outlawed the Templar Order."

"Thus fulfilling the fears of paraskevidekatriaphobics everywhere." *Ian and Jan* had done a programme on it three or four years ago, and I'd been taken with the word enough to memorize it. More evidence of my ability to pick up on odd facts—great for interviews.

"Make light of it if you wish, Ian, but just remember that it really is 1307 and you're a Templar."

"I'm not a Templar," I answered. "I'm not even *Catholic.* This—thing, this adventure, whatever in hell it is, is a colossal mistake or someone's idea of a joke. I'm just a bloody reporter. A talking head. If this was a test, I'll take the failing grade and go look for other work. You should send me back and get someone who's truly interested in . . ." I began to turn, intending to give the rest to his face.

"Don't," Rob said rather forcefully, and I found myself unable to do more than move one shoulder. From the corner of my eye, though, I could see brightness: it was where the light was coming from, and it had grown in intensity.

"I'm a Templar, and it's 1307. Go on," I snapped.

I heard him sigh again behind me; the illumination returned to the level of moonlight. "You're making this difficult. I only have a few minutes to talk to you."

"Ah. Are all abductees so recalcitrant? I'm terribly sorry, Rob. I've scarcely known you a day and I'm already a disappointment."

"You actually don't know *me* at all. The Robert du Maison who is with you at Santiago right now doesn't know what I just told you. He only knows that he's to help you along the path of light, beginning at Santiago."

"I thought Santiago was a pilgrimage destination."

"It is, Ian. But it is not the end of the path: it's the beginning. Most of those who travel the pilgrim road go to Compostela—you will begin there and visit each site in turn until you reach your final destination."

"Oh, no. I'm not traveling anywhere. This isn't real—someone put something in my drink, or something happened when I hit my head. I'm going to wake up in a hospital—"

"Perhaps so," Rob said.

"—with a nurse to tend my fevered brow," I finished. "My agent is going to sue everyone at ITV for this."

There was no answer from the figure behind me.

"Did you hear me?"

"Every word, Ian. If that's what you must do, so be it. But you can't do it here, and you can't do it now."

"Because this is 1307 and I'm a Templar."

"I realise that it's difficult for you to accept this, but it's absolutely necessary if you ever want to get home."

"Rather than just waking up—or walking off the set."

"You must travel the pilgrim road. That's the only way."

"Until I reach the final destination. Which is?"

"Rosslyn."

"Wait. That's not possible—Rosslyn wasn't built until the 1440s. If Rosslyn is the destination, how am I supposed to get to it in 1307?"

Rob didn't answer that. "Santiago is the beginning, Ian. Look up."

I looked up at a sky full of stars. The wide swath of the Milky Way was directly overhead: if I was more knowledgeable, I might have been able to determine where in the world I must be—Spain or somewhere else.

"The Milky Way—the *camino de las estrellas*. One end is anchored at Santiago, the other at Rosslyn. This is how you get home—to follow the *camino*. And to do so you must first learn humility—and then listen."

"I'm listening."

"Listen *carefully*," he added. I felt and heard him step up behind me, laying a hand on my right shoulder. The pale light caught a bronze ring on his hand set with a small ruby.

He leaned close to my right ear. "This is the first initiation, Ian. The Moon governs this sphere. *Amoun*. Be discreet."

Amoun, I heard, and had the image of a row of people sitting at a conference-table, their fingers touching their lips. The dream of a few nights ago—

"And what happens now?" I asked.

He didn't answer. I tried to look back, but my gaze was drawn forward toward the raven on the branch before me. Its wings were ruffled by a faint breeze, but its right eye seemed to grow and grow until it filled my entire field of vision: I was falling into it, deeper and deeper—

—•—

"Now," Rob said, his hand on my shoulder, "you cross yourself like a good Christian, and you knock your broo against Master Mateo there."

I turned around suddenly enough for Rob to drop his hand. He and the two or three pilgrims just behind all stepped back, wondering what I might do next.

I looked around. I was standing before the Pórtico de Gloria, with Jesus, his disciples, and a few hundred other stone figures watching. My hand was a few inches from the five depressions on the Tree of Jesse where I'd just laid it.

"It's all right," Rob said softly. He nodded his head toward Juan la Rosa, who stood near Master Mateo. "Let's go in."

CHAPTER 4

THE NIGHT AFTER I HAD MY VISION AT SANTIAGO, WHAT *THAT* Rob had called the "first initiation," I collapsed on my pallet and slept soundly. I'm not sure if there was anything that could've got me up in the middle of the night. When I awoke again it was bright and clear—and it was still 1307. It was all too elaborate for a practical joke and too persistent to be a dream. As for the initiation—whatever that meant—I didn't have any idea what to make of what I'd been told. Why an initiation? What did he mean that it was the first one?

It was the only way home, I'd been told. The only way off the stage. I wasn't letting myself consider that too closely.

—•—

That morning I queued up with dozens of other *peregrinos* outside the Pórtico de Gloria to have another go at the Tree of Jesse. The crowd had thinned the day after Saint James' feast-day, but it still took time for me to reach the front of the queue.

When it was my turn I stepped confidently up to the Tree as if I were walking onstage for *Ian and Jan.* I stopped before the Tree of Jesse, bowed slightly, crossed myself—and placed my fingers and thumb into the depressions—my hand in God's hand. I may have offered a prayer—I don't remember.

But I do remember that nothing at all happened: no visions, no pretentious voices, no revelations of mysterious quests with mystical properties.

I was hurried on into the church, leaving the Pórtico and the Tree behind.

The next morning we were up early; Rob was ready to leave Santiago. I didn't know what was to happen next and when I found out, I wasn't at all happy.

"You're not serious."

"Serious?" Rob shook the water from his face and beard and rubbed them dry with a cloth from his pack. "Of course I'm serious, lad," he continued. "How did you expect to travel? Take wings and fly?"

Juan laughed and began to peel an orange; he was sitting on the edge of the fountain where Rob had just finished his morning toilet.

"I don't even know where we're going," I said, splashing my own face with water.

"Toulouse."

"You want to walk to *Toulouse?* Are you insane?"

Rob seemed to be considering an answer to the question. He sat down on the stone rim himself and began to arrange things in his pack. I waited a few moments and said, "Why do we want to walk to Toulouse?"

"It's the next stop."

"Next stop?"

"On the pilgrimage," Juan said around a mouthful of orange. He offered me two sections.

I remembered what Rob-in-the-vision had said: Santiago was the beginning of the journey—Rosslyn was the end. Rosslyn Chapel—whose builder, William of St Clair, wasn't due to be born for a century.

"Toulouse," Rob said, ticking it off a finger. "Then Orléans, Chartres, Paris, and Amiens. That's where we're going, lad. And the only way to do it is to walk."

I tried to imagine how long it would take to get to Toulouse on foot, and then to all of the other places—and I tried to fit that in my mind with what I'd been told was coming in October.

Amoun, I heard in my mind. *Be discreet.*

"All right," I said at last. "When do we start?"

—•—

We left Santiago to travel eastward on Shank's pony. During the first few days my legs and lungs reminded me that in my own place and time I wasn't much of a hiker—but then I began to let my Templar initiate's body take charge of the business of walking. He—I—was apparently used to it. I had a memory of some quote of Sir Walter Raleigh's I'd learned in school about the pilgrim's path—but fortunately I couldn't bring it to mind. He'd written it down on his way to meet the headsman, as I recall.

Still, the idea of a quiet road, a few possessions, and some knowledge of destination and purpose was appealing enough to keep me walking on that road, crossing the Galician Plain in the summer of 1307.

—•—

We were an interesting threesome. Rob was the oldest, perhaps ten years younger than the one I'd met at Rosslyn Chapel. He was tall and greying, but clearly in top condition. He'd done this route before, escorting one or more Templar initiates making the pilgrimage. Six stops and none of them Rosslyn, of course. He knew all of the by-ways and places to stop, every hostel and roadside shrine—who to bargain with and who to avoid.

Juan was the youngest, lean and agile, almost acrobatic. He loved to sing—and to eat. He also loved to run: when we had a straight section of road with no one around he would poke me in the rib or give me a gentle slap in the back of the head, then sprint off, tossing his pack to the side—and I'd oblige him by chasing him until I could return the favour. Our guide would remain where our packs had been left, his arms crossed, mock-serious and patient for us to return.

I was the odd one out. Juan was more full of life, Rob more firm in his faith. In the daytime I listened to Rob's stories and Juan's songs, trying to see everything as we walked. At night, when the sky was clear, I looked up at the *camino* in the sky and wondered why I was here—and received no answer.

—•—

Ten days after leaving Santiago, we reached the city of León. The days had begun to look the same—and it caught me a bit by surprise when Rob said that we'd be stopping.

"What's in León?" I asked as we passed through the western gate into the city. "Another church?"

"Among other things," Rob said. We unslung our packs and found a spot to relax in the shade, on a low stone wall at the edge of a wide, busy square. It was late afternoon, past the restful middle of the day, and the vendors and pedlars of the Saturday market were doing their best before the sun set.

"Brilliant," I said, drawing a waterskin from my pack.

"Ian, they revere Saint James here too," Juan said. "Or had you forgotten?"

My first answer was *I never knew,* but instead of saying it I shrugged.

"We'll visit Santa Maria," Rob said. "The new cathedral. I was here when it was consecrated four years ago; I was escorting three initiates on this route."

"How many times have you done this?"

"Eleven times," Rob said. "This is my twelfth trip. The pilgrims usually come up from Cintra as you did, and we travel the same route. It's a shame that King Sancho never had a chance to see the fruits of his labours—it's a beautiful church. The windows let in more light than any building I know—except perhaps Chartres."

"Enough light to be able to see with new eyes," I said. I took a drink from my waterskin, but glanced sidelong at Rob to see what kind of reaction that might get. He seemed to let it go by.

"This is just a stopover." Rob leaned forward, elbows on knees, resting his chin on his hand like a piece of Rodin sculpture. "They worship the blessed Saint James a different way in León than in Santiago. There he is the patron of the *peregrinos*—the companion of our Lord, the apostle of this land. But here, lad, they also call him *Matamoros*—the slayer of the Moors."

—•—

I must have drowsed, because for the next few seconds my mind held the image of a battlefield. I was running across it, a sword in my hand, my vision partially obscured by a helm held tight to my head by a chin-strap. My long-legged shadow ran ahead of me. All around was blood and noise and death—and over the shouting and cries I could hear a snatch of music—familiar music that haunted me at the edge of my hearing—and that word *matamoros.*

Santiago Matamoros. Saint James, Moor-slayer.

—•—

"Ian?"

I shook my head. Bright sunlight cast my shadow on the dusty cobbles beyond where I sat, waterskin lowered and held loosely in my hand.

I'm getting pretty damn sick of this, I thought.

"Of course," I said, putting on my best stage face. "Well, we'd better go up and pay our respects."

Santa Maria de Regla was a gorgeous cathedral, and truly was only a few years old; building had apparently begun only about fifty years earlier and it had been consecrated in 1303. And as Rob had said, it was full of beautiful windows; the most striking of those was the huge rose window on the west façade between the cathedral's two towers. It was divided into petalled panels; the afternoon sunlight cast the rose pattern into the central nave.

Rob, Juan and I stood at the back of the sanctuary; it was crowded with pilgrims paying their respects to the martial aspects of my new favorite saint.

"Rob."

"Hm." He was admiring the architecture.

"Rob, why are they walking like that?"

I gestured toward the high altar. The pilgrims in the church were not approaching the altar directly; they seemed to be walking in some sort of pattern—advancing along slow curves and short straight lines. They didn't all take the same route but moved in groups, twos and threes, changing directions as if they were dancing in a slow pavane.

He looked up above where we stood, a few paces from the western wall of the church. The rose window cast a beam filled with motes of dust, making it visible like a shaft of light from the heavens.

"They're following the path of light," Rob said, smiling. And it was true: the path the pilgrims walked toward the east end of the church was along the shadows cast by the rose window divisions.

"Why?"

"It's the way you get to the east, lad," he said, smiling.

—•—

There were no visions in Santa Maria de Regla. No voices spoke to me, no warnings were issued. We heard offices—Nones, Sexte, and Compline: we spent most of the day and a good part of the evening at the church before retiring to our beds at a pilgrim hostel in the city. The music was beautiful, but it wasn't the music of Rosslyn. I'm not sure if I was more relieved or disappointed.

—•—

It was ten more days from León to Roncesvalles. Some of our days had rain, but our weather was mostly favourable; hot, humid days and warm summer nights with star-filled skies—the *camino de las estrellas* was bright and clear, helping to point our way. No ravens, no troubling dreams for me—only the disturbing feeling that this wasn't my first time in this country. I'd been in a battle where men shouted the name of Saint James as they fought and died, and I'd walked this road before.

Roncesvalles was a place full of echoes. In school I'd had to learn some bits of the *Song of Roland* for a play, and I'd got Bishop Turpin to do—

That Emperour sets Rollant on one side
And Oliver, and the Archbishop Turpine;
Their bodies bids open before his eyes.

I'd never forgotten those lines for some reason. Roncesvalles, where everybody died. Of course Roland, Turpin, and Charlemagne himself were all real people, and possibly Oliver as well, all made more real by the presence of Roland's Cross and the other landmarks of the place, though hardly the people depicted in the *chanson:* I knew in school and recalled as we walked through the marketplace of the town that the song and story was dressed up in feudal costume, even though the battle and the participants were from centuries earlier—just like we Brits had done with King Arthur. But in this time—1307—the *Chanson de Roland* was an amazingly popular story, sort of a *Coronation Street* for the inn-and-tavern crowd. It was all over the place: the story of the heroes of Roncesvalles, and the music that went with it.

—•—

"Look at them," Juan said, half of an empanada in his mouth. "They'll dance for anything."

We were watching a line of people, arm in arm, dancing across the square. Rob had gone out in search of a place for us to doss down; Roncesvalles was crowded, even a few weeks after the saint's day—lots of folks still making their way westward to the Tree of Jesse.

"It's like music," I said. "You feel it in your bones."

"Mmhm." He swallowed what he was eating. "That's true, I suppose—music is like life to me, you know. But this. . ." he did a little jig-step, one arm akimbo, making me laugh out loud.

"You've got the talent, I think."

"And you'd make a good court fool, you great big—"

He let the sentence drop. Instead, he cocked his head to listen to the music. I thought about continuing, but decided to listen as well, and watch.

The dance was full of life and energy, but despite that it was precise and almost geometric. I couldn't see the pattern from where we were standing; I nudged Juan and we walked up a set of stairs to get a better view.

From a few dozen feet further away and several feet further up in the air, I got a clearer view. It took me a little time to make any sense of it.

"Juan," I said. "That's—"

"Shh," he interrupted me.

"That's the same thing we saw at Santa Maria in León. We watched them walk along the shadows cast by the window—the dance is the same pattern."

He looked at me, then back at the people down in the square. "You think—you mean that the *aragonesa,* the dance they're doing, is some kind of . . . worship?"

"I don't know. I don't know what it is, Juan, but it's . . . there's a pattern. The same as at León. So yes, that's what I think it is."

Juan looked thoughtful but didn't answer.

We listened and watched for a few more minutes; finally they took a break from the dance, to applause and praise from the audience. Juan and I began to walk slowly along a crowded avenue.

"Will you answer a question for me?"

"Sure. I'm still hungry. Are you?" Juan said. "Let's find something to eat."

"I don't need anything else." I stopped walking, and he stopped as well. "Tell me something. When you touched the Tree of Jesse in Santiago, did something happen?"

"What do you mean, 'Did something happen'?" Still, I could tell from the way he said it that the question had caught him by surprise.

"Just what I said."

"Rob said that I shouldn't discuss it."

"I know." I rubbed my forehead. The sun was hot; the crowd was loud. There were snatches of music making their way to the front of my hearing: not more than a note or two, but a hint of something more. "I got the same message. *Amoun*, wasn't it?"

He frowned. "Don't say that. Don't say the word."

"I don't understand what's going on, Juan. I don't remember—I don't know. I—"

"You hit your head," he said. "But you're here, aren't you? You're on the road east, walking to Toulouse. You're a part of this now." The words hurried out of him. "No matter what brought you to this point, Ian, you're here now."

He looked away from me, down the street where afternoon sunlight painted the buildings and cast long shadows. There was some emotion trapped in his eyes, something he was trying to conceal from me.

"Juan, what's—"

"Amoun," he said, and touched his index and middle fingers of each hand to his lips. "Come on, let's find Rob—and dinner."

—•—

Since Roncesvalles was a major landmark on the *camino* where the road came down from Somport in the Pyrenees into Aragon, the town was filled with hawkers and thieves—it more reminded me of one of those dress-up Renaissance festivals than one of the sombre tropes you usually see of the Dark Ages—dour monks marching along singing some dirge. A regular tourist trap, Roncesvalles.

By the time we caught up with Rob and found where we'd be sleeping, it was early evening. Roncesvalles was crowded with pilgrims going both ways: some still headed for Santiago de Compostela to say their prayers before St James even though they'd missed the saint's day, the *día santo;* some few leaving, as we were, scallop-shells pinned to their scrip or their cloak or their hat—whatever style was in fashion. All, other than we three and possibly a few others like us, were likely at the end of their journeys, with Santiago just a few weeks away. For us, the journey was just beginning.

Juan never mentioned what had happened to him at Santiago, and our conversation at Roncesvalles never came up again. The next morning we were on the pilgrim's path once more, headed north and east toward the Pyrenees and France.

—•—

The night before we began our ascent toward Somport—the 'highest pass' in the Pyrenees between Aragon and Gascogne—we were in a small roadhouse, crowded in with pilgrims going in each direction. Juan was eating while Rob and I relaxed on a wooden bench, our backs against the wall of the building, listening to the music. A group of performers had done some of the *Chanson*—the cheerier bits, staying clear of the treachery and blood-soaked death while we were eating and drinking, thank you very much.

I'd begun to drift off, drowsy from the fatigue of the day's walk, when of a sudden I was brought bolt upright by something familiar: bagpipe music. Scotsmen are supposed to love the bagpipes, just like they love to eat haggis and drink themselves blind. Haggis, properly prepared, I could enjoy well enough, and I'd done my share of drinking—but left it behind when I moved on from radio to television where image is everything. As for piping, I avoided it as much as possible.

The offenders were set up on a small platform halfway across the room from us. Rob pulled his knees up and leaned his chin on them, smiling; Juan finished gnawing on a bone and set it aside, clapping with the rest as the two pipers—accompanied by two drummers and a tambourine player—whaled away at a tune that sounded hauntingly familiar, squeezed and distorted through the instruments being used to rend it apart.

"You look like you've never seen a *gaita* before," Rob said to me as the music went on—and on.

"I didn't know—" I began, then found myself needing to shout a bit. "I didn't know there were bagpipes in Spain."

"They're a bit different from the ones you hear in Scotland, lad," he said. "But the principle's the same: blow in that bag there and finger the tubes."

"Brilliant," I couldn't help but say. I rolled my eyes, and my two companions laughed. Setting my dislike of pipes aside as best I could, I tried to listen to the tune—there was something about it that struck me.

We'd heard bits of it on the road already. One thing I noticed was how similar all the music had seemed to be, as if everyone was singing from the same book both in and out of church. Juan knew every note and seemed to have perfect pitch: it was his first and greatest love (eating whatever came by seemed to be a close second)—he seemed to live and breathe through music.

But there was something else: a theme, or maybe even a phrase, that repeated and twigged a memory. My first thought, sitting in that roadhouse listening to those bloody pipes, was of a TV advert theme song—the kind that invades your head and won't get out.

Then it hit me all of a sudden, so abruptly that I was on my feet and trying to push toward the ensemble through the assembled crowd.

It was the music from Rosslyn again.

Rob's strong hands caught me by the shoulders before I'd made it more than five feet; he and Juan muttered apologies as they hustled me outside into the hot August night.

"What's got into you?" he managed after a moment, spinning me to face him. The moon was nearly full and halfway up in the sky. Juan stood off a few feet, not interested in getting involved.

"I heard something."

"What? What did you hear?"

"Music. I heard—"

The *gaita* players had shifted off to something else. The moment was gone; the music was gone. I was standing outside in the sweaty darkness with two men who were dead nearly seven hundred years: I was alone.

I looked up at the stars. The Milky Way was visible, brighter and clearer than I'd ever seen it—except during that dream or vision or whatever it had been at Santiago.

Amoun, I thought. What was I going to tell him? That I had heard something that might lead me back to the future?

"I'm sorry," I said, touching my forehead. "Nothing. My fault." He let me go, and I turned away, making my way toward the privies. Neither of my companions followed.

—•—

Brilliant, I thought again the next day as we climbed up through Somport. *I hear the healing music that got me thrown into this mess, and it has to be on the bagpipes.*

Rob and Juan had very little to say as we tramped along. The road was less crowded now: many of the pilgrims used the valley road through Navarre and avoided the challenge of the mountains. Apparently no challenge was too great for Robert de la Maison—and Ian Graham, Templar initiate. It didn't really seem all that bad to me now that I was becoming accustomed to the walking, letting my soldier's body do the work.

We stopped after midday in a shaded spot beyond the summit, pulling bread, cheese, fruit and a wrapped package of sardines from our packs along with a skin of *Cariñena* wine, local Aragonese stuff the color of dark blood that was strong enough to grow hair where it was never meant to be grown.

"Lad," Rob said to me when we'd eaten and drunk our fill, "I'm beginning to think that you're going daft. You could've got us into a brawl down in Roncesvalles just because you don't like the sound of the pipes."

"It wasn't that."

"Then what was it?"

"Nothing."

"No, by God's blood, it wasn't *nothing,*" he answered, frowning. "You said you heard something. What did you hear? Did someone say something about your mother?"

"I heard a strain of music I'd heard before," I said, and it sounded as weak and lame when I said it. "It was important, and I needed to know what it was."

"That sounds like Juan's area," Rob said, looking at the other man. "Maybe you can help," he continued.

"Certes," Juan said. "What is it?"

"The first tune they played on the *gaita,*" I offered. "What was it? Do you remember it?"

Juan la Rosa closed his eyes, as if remembering. Then he began to sing: the same strain of music, but slower and more melodious, free of the piping harmonies and the clapping and shouting of the crowd in the roadhouse:

> *"J'ai encore I tel pasté*
> *Qui n'est mi-e de lasté*
> *Que nous mengerons—marote*
> *Bec a bec et moi et vous*
> *Chi—me ratendés maro-te*
> *Chi venrai par—ler a vous*
> *Marote veus tu plus de mi."*

When he was finished he opened his eyes again and all was quiet, but for the chirping of birds and insects and the soft sound of the breeze in the chestnut and beech trees that covered the mountainside.

It was a fragment of the same music I'd heard just before the twenty-first century disappeared around me. Juan had rendered it note for note—his voice was beautiful and his ear was perfect. I couldn't help the few tears that rushed into my eyes before I looked aside and brushed them away.

"It wasn't *that* good," Juan said.

"It was beautiful. What is it?" I said after a moment. Rob was watching this very carefully but keeping silent.

"It's from *Li Gieus de Robin et de Marion*. It's a play with singing—you've never heard it?"

"No," I said. Fourteenth century drama wasn't part of my brief as part of the preparation for Rosslyn. Rob shrugged as well.

Juan looked between us as if to suggest that we were unlettered peasants, then sighed. "The greatest of the *trouvères* wrote it. Adam de la Halle. Adam le Bossu—Adam the Hunchback, as they called him."

"That doesn't sound very complimentary. Is it accurate?" I'd never heard of him.

"He picked that up when he was in Naples," Juan said. "He wasn't really a crookback at all, but some of his enemies called him that because he bowed so much to the King. He was a genius."

"He wrote"—*the healing music of Rosslyn,* I thought, but didn't say it—"that piece? It sounds like a love song, though I can't make out all the words—it sounds almost like Occitan."

"It's in Picard," Juan said. "I learned it by sound." He smiled. "But I know what it means. Robin and Marion are lovers, and Robin promises Marion that he'll share a . . . treat with her."

"The *pasté.*"

"That's right. He will have it with her *bec a bec.*" He made a rude kissing noise. Rob reached out to cuff him, but he ducked under it with the practised skill of a younger brother. "And he tells her that she's the woman that he can't live without."

"Gluttony," Rob said. "And lust. Does he pack the other five deadlies in there? Those thoughts will cost you a few *Aves* when we next stop, Brother. And you *too,*" he said, pointing at me. "That's not a fit subject for any of us. Even if it comes from the throat of an angel."

Juan beamed at the praise, giving Rob a chance to cuff him properly. His eyes flashed momentarily in anger, but he shrugged it off and went digging for something more to eat.

Rosslyn's music is . . . what? I thought. *A suggestive love song written by a dead troubadour?*

I was more confused than ever.

—•—

The road through the mountains was straight and well-maintained. We left Aragon and Navarre behind us and descended into the valleys of western Gascogne—Rob pointed out the sights as we went. After a night at St Vincent monastery, where Rob made sure we gave our Hail Marys in apology—and he offered a few himself for his oaths—we headed off across St Jean-Pied-de-Port and eastward toward the great city of Toulouse.

I had only the most general map in my head, and it was hundreds of years out of date. Liz and I had taken a holiday down here toward the end of our marriage; we'd crossed through the Pyrenees at Port Bou coming from Nice, and at Hendaya on our way back to Paris, sipping cocktails and looking out the windows of a high-speed train. My impressions of that trip were scattered and random—later I only remembered scenes and names and sometimes can't relate the two even now. But every day brought us closer to Toulouse.

—•—

Long before we could make out the red brick buildings or clearly see the forest of spires or the rambling western walls of Toulouse, we were struck by an offensive, unpleasant reek—not just the usual offal and animal smell, which I'd become fairly used to, but something much more grim. It hung in the air like a greasy, acid cloud that reached us long before we reached the villa of Saint-Cyprien on the west side of the river.

"Mary, Mother of God," Juan said, after a drink from a waterskin. "What a stink. We're a German mile away from the city and it's in the air. What is it?"

"Coquagnes," Rob answered. Of course he knew. "Filthy stuff. There's a plant they grind up and mash together until it becomes like blue mud. The *pastilleurs* make it down on the dockside"—he waved in the general direction of the river—"and when it dries out they roll it into little balls of dye. Makes the most beautiful blue cloth you've ever seen. The waste makes the river blue too. Thank all the blessed Saints the factories are downriver from the Temple."

"What plant makes blue?" Juan asked.

"The same one our heathen grandfathers used to paint their faces," Rob said, gesturing to himself and to me. "Up in God's country we call it *woad."* He smiled, apparently thinking about the heathen grandfathers; all I could think of was the actor who made William Wallace out to be some sort of Pict in a top-rated movie a few years back—and the idea of my granddad, a postman, painting his face with woad. Not a pretty picture.

"And that causes that stink?"

"That, and the fur skinning. And the tanning and the leather-working and the runoff from the wineries in the Daurade. If we could bottle the stuff, we could hurl it at the infidels in Granada and the *reconquista* would be over in a week."

Mustard gas, I thought. But fortunately that particular atrocity was six hundred years in France's future.

—•—

Today we don't think of Toulouse as the city I saw crouching along the Garonne that sweaty summer afternoon, standing on the hill between Isle-Jourdain and Saint-Cyprien. The twenty-first century city is a picture-postcard place, full of art and architecture and—at least recently—high technology. When the City of Space was dedicated a few years ago *Ian and Jan* was there to see the full-size model of the Ariane and the huge planetarium.

It was all gone. Or, more accurately, it wasn't there yet.

Rob, Juan and I stopped by the roadside to rest late in the afternoon, the smell hanging around in the thick summer air. The heat was oppressive: it was a few hundred percent humidity, what Gerard Lamont used to call "weather you can wear." A wool robe didn't do much to help the situation but that wasn't my choice.

There was a little falling-down shrine in honour of the Blessed Virgin there, where a track led off into an overgrown meadow; I had the drill down pretty well by then—we each took turns with a silent, kneeling prayer, and then came out and sat on a stone block worn smooth by the hind ends of many earlier travelers.

After sitting there for a short while—none of us was in any hurry to move along in the heat—I began to sense, rather than see, something nearby: a sort of line passing through the place we stood, leading off toward the mountains in the distance, dappled by the late-afternoon sun.

It evidently attracted Rob and Juan's attention. I suspect that they'd begun to relax, since I hadn't done anything wild and crazy for a few days, but they showed no inclination toward dumping me in a sack or dunking me in a river—they just stood there quietly until I looked at them.

"You can feel it, can't you?" Rob said, looking from me to the city and back.

I nodded. "There's a path or something." I wasn't sure what else to say.

"Places grow up where these paths cross. There's been a Christian settlement there for a thousand years or more, and once there was a Druid temple there. And here," he added, gesturing toward where we stood. "A sacred grove of oak trees. All long since hewn down, of course, by good iron-bladed axes, but that's progress for you."

"What am I feeling?"

"There's a path that runs roughly east and west, at least as far as Arles to the east."

"And to the west?"

"Santiago."

"What sort of . . . path?"

Rob shrugged. "An earth-path. There's a water-path that runs through Toulouse there, all the way to the sea at Bordeaux."

Juan nodded, agreeing with what Rob was saying. He seemed to be less surprised by this discussion than I was. It didn't seem doctrinally sound, but I wasn't completely versed—perhaps it was some part of Templar rites that I should've known but didn't.

"A river, you mean," I said.

"*Yes,* a river," Rob agreed, sounding a bit annoyed. "The river mostly follows the path. They cross in Toulouse. We're going to follow the earth-path straight to the doors of Notre-Dame la Dalbade. It's where the two paths cross."

"There's water under the church?"

"There was," Rob answered. "The Petite Garonne—it's a bit farther to the west now. But the path is still there."

"And . . ."

"We'll pay our respects at Saint-Sernin, and then we'll go to the Dalbade and see what there is to see," he said, picking up his pack and shouldering it. I didn't have anything by way of an answer, so I did the same.

Things had seemed strange before, but they were just getting stranger. The music of Rosslyn seemed to creep in everywhere, I had had one long vision and the briefest glimpse of another one, and now there were magic paths running under my feet. I remember hoping at the time that there might be just enough strangeness to actually get me home when this was all over.

—•—

We crossed the Garonne at St Pierre-de-Bazacle, the bridge farthest down river; the toll-keeper saw our scallop shells and Templar emblems and waved us on without taking our pennies—and in exchange we got a snifter full of the stink from the dye factories that lined the east bank of the river almost as far down as the largest bridge that spanned it. Juan pointed out a whitewashed church that stood out plainly from the red-brick buildings all around it: Notre-Dame la Dalbade. As I glanced from the church to Juan, a familiar reverent look came across the young Templar initiate's face.

We arrived at the Cathedral of Saint-Sernin at dusk. It stood at the crown of a hill in the Bourg, a vast wall-enclosed northern suburb. After washing our hands and feet in a fountain at the Place de la Trinité we got our first view of the great cathedral from the south. We had a good look at the portal called the Porte Miègeville, with Rob providing the details on what we saw. Saint James stood on the left—he had the scallop shell on his hat; Saint Peter held the keys to God's BMW, or something, on the right. James stood between two cypresses, the Gospel in his hand, surveying the scene, watching the three pilgrims who had walked all the way from his shrine at Santiago to visit this cathedral. Even Juan seemed subdued as we passed through the portal and into the church.

We were between Vespers and Compline; though there were a good number of pilgrims still in the church, its vast spaces seemed to swallow sound making us feel as if we were alone in the huge sanctuary.

I knew at once that this wasn't the Saint-Sernin that I had visited when Jan and I came to Toulouse to do our programme: sometime between the now I was experiencing and the century of my birth, something had happened to the cathedral—something that was still in the future. It's the sort of thing that dissuades you from letting yourself be hurled back into the past . . . but, after all, it hadn't been my idea.

I must have stood there gawping like a tourist; it took Rob grabbing my arm and giving it a good pull to bring me back to my senses.

"Something's happening out in the street," he said, gesturing toward Juan. "Let's just stay here and be a part of the crowd, I think."

The atmosphere had changed—everyone seemed tense of a sudden.

"What's going on?" Juan said.

"Someone's here," Rob said. With a gesture we made our way to the front steps of the church, where a procession was passing through the plaza before Saint-Sernin. Rob was the tallest of the three of us, and was looking over a cluster of people who had reached the door before we did and now stood on lower steps. In the procession, several liveried servants held torches aloft, with a small group of well-dressed persons walking in between.

In the centre of the group was a man of medium height, fashionably dressed; a golden pendant on his breast was embossed with a fleur-de-lys, the symbol of the King of France. He had a slightly bent nose and sunken features, with deep, dark eyes. He seemed ideally suited to the scene, lit in flickering shadow and torchlight—if I were staging a costume drama I wouldn't have changed a thing.

He walked with measured step, looking slowly from side to side as he progressed across the square; wherever he looked, people looked away. Even Rob—hardy, brave Rob—seemed to shrink down, as if he didn't want the man's gaze to fall on him.

We were well back when the man was met by two well-dressed priests who bowed and scraped. I caught a name as they addressed him: Monsieur de Nogaret. It didn't mean anything to me, but I heard Rob suck in a breath when he heard the name.

"What's *he* doing here?" Juan whispered.

"He's from here," Rob answered. "His father was a citizen of Toulouse—and a Cathar," he added in a very low voice.

It was loud enough, though, that someone in front of us heard it and said without turning, "Don't say that too loud or Monsieur will personally put your balls in a vise, Templar."

Like most people in earshot who had balls, I cringed at the thought of having them in a vise. I wasn't sure whether that was the prize you won for being a Cathar and wasn't eager to find out. For his part Rob meekly nodded agreement, which really wasn't like him: in the month or so I'd traveled with him he hadn't seemed willing to take that sort of comment from anyone, particularly someone eight inches shorter who didn't look as if hefting a weapon was part of his daily regimen.

Nogaret and his party moved off toward a building on the side of the square, after one last look around. The two portly priests went right along with him—I overheard that they were going to escort him to the abbot, and something about manuscripts.

After several seconds it seemed as if there was a collective sigh, and people went back to doing what they had been doing. Rob seemed eager to get away from the church as quickly as possible; he wasn't alone and neither Juan nor I were interested in arguing.

—•—

Notre-Dame la Dalbade was near the river in the main part of the city. The streets were already dark as we made our way there—south along the Carraria Major from the Portaria until it played itself out in a warren of narrow streets.

"It feels like we're being watched," I said to Rob. Juan held a single torch, all the light we had to hold back the darkness.

"This part of the city is deserted, lad," Rob said as we ventured past a particularly imposing building, a squat stone structure that appeared to be boarded up.

"How do you know?"

"It's the Jewish Quarter," Rob said. "That's their temple right there. But none of them come to worship."

"A synagogue?"

In the light of the torch he glanced at me. "Know much about Jews, lad? Aye, it's a synagogue as they call it. But the French king sent them out of the country last year."

"Why?"

Rob snorted. "The usual reason. He owed them money. But they'll be back—when he needs more."

—•—

Our destination was just down an avenue from the imposing synagogue: Notre-Dame la Dalbade, its white walls almost luminous, ready to receive the full light of the moon when it rose in an hour or so.

Within the church the pervasive smell of incense drove away most of the reek from without. But as soon as I stepped across the threshold of the church, I could feel something else—and I knew that this was our reason for coming to Toulouse.

I walked slowly down the centre aisle, the clerestory vaults to either side, toward the high altar. It was as if there was an invisible but very tangible line on the stone floor that I could follow. What was more, I had a distinct feeling that I was being escorted: two rows of figures, just out of sight, walking alongside me in the main aisle of the church. I'd never been much on the business of having a sixth sense, but this certainly felt like it. Like visions and mystical paths, it seemed to be a part of my all-inclusive fourteenth-century tour package.

The scene became slowly more indistinct. I could see the altar and somewhere I heard the sound of slowly coursing water, the sort of noise that comes from a decorative waterfall in a Japanese garden: loud enough to notice, soft enough to be unobtrusive. With each step I took, it became harder for me to contemplate the next one—as if I were growing more and more heavy.

Earth and water meet, I thought suddenly. The two paths. I wanted to ask Rob more about what he'd meant, but I couldn't see him and I couldn't turn my head—all I was able to do was walk forward, one difficult step after another . . . but when I placed my foot on a square of red marble just before the altar the terrible lassitude was released so suddenly that I nearly fell on my face.

And just as suddenly, the church—which was dim, lit only by candles—was full of light, and I was completely alone.

But not for long. Behind me I could hear someone singing a snatch of the music from *Robin et Marion* and the soft tread of sandals; unlike the vision I'd had at Santiago, I was able to turn around to see the figure of Juan la Rosa walking toward me.

"What's happening, Juan?" I asked, looking around. The huge church was completely empty other than myself and the Asturian.

"There are several ways to answer that question, Ian," he said, coming closer. "Do you mean, 'what is happening right now,' or 'what is happening in the world,' or 'what is happening to you,' or is it some sort of general greeting—'hello, Juan, how are you today?' "

"Answered like a true—" I wanted to say *geek*, thinking of the tech at Rosslyn, the laptop in the baptistry. But *langue d'oc* had no more a word for that than it had been capable of providing the term *computer programme* a few weeks earlier. "Like a true jurist," I finally decided, since Lord knew advocates split hairs like that; perhaps that's why they wore wigs.

"You wound me," he said, placing both arms across his chest, the right above the left, his palms flat against his chest. It struck me as familiar at the time, but I couldn't place it. "My forte is not the words but rather the tune."

"Would you like to answer the question? Or all of the questions?"

"Very well." He let his arms drop to his sides, and leaned back against the nearest clerestory pillar, smiling. "I'll take them in turn. What is happening *right now* is that you are standing at the centre of Notre-Dame la Dalbade in Toulouse—not the one you know from a future century, but an earlier one soon to be consumed by fire—and when we are finished with our visit, you will still be there. In the meanwhile, I am here to provide you with information that will move you along the path of light.

"As for what is happening in the world, I know that you are aware of why this time is so important. In a matter of weeks, the King of France and the Pope whom he has installed at Avignon will betray the Knights Templar—of which order you, and I, and Frére Robert are all members. Bad luck for us. Of the three of us only you know the truth. Just to add spice to the soup, as we say in Asturias, you are in possession of some very important knowledge—and there is someone who is seeking to discover it, and you with it.

"Now. As to what is happening to you." He looked off into the middle distance, as if the answer was written on one of the arches of the clerestory. "You have learned to listen; now you are learning to see."

"And the music I hear is part of—what? A bawdy song?"

"Not the words, Ian. The *music.* You can hear it. Now *see.*"

He gestured, and I found my glance suddenly jumping from place to place around the church, as if I had a hand-held zoom camera taking in the high spots for a TV documentary: statues of patron saints and apostles, gargoyles and outlandish creatures, Christ enthroned with the keys of Heaven in his hands—and everywhere I looked, *croix-pattés,* symbols of the Knights Templar. I felt as if I were whirling around—I was dizzy, almost drunk with sensation; I was unable to remain on my feet, and found myself sitting on the floor of the nave in a fairly undignified position, trying to overcome vertigo.

"But you'll need to understand this a little better," Juan said, walking slowly forward and extending his right hand. I took hold, but he let the hand slip to my elbow, then grasped it with his other as his own elbow touched my palm; it had some symbolic significance that escaped me at the time. "This is . . ." He helped me to my feet and let go, stepping back a pace or two, then beckoned me down along the southern clerestory aisle. I followed him past three pillars until he stopped and pointed up at a portion of the wall, where I saw a figure with wings on his feet, a caduceus in his hand. "This is the Divine Messenger, Ian. The Greeks called him Hermes; the Romans Mercury; and to the Druids who built the sanctum here more than a thousand years ago he was Abaris, one of the teachers of Pythagoras."

"You're saying that he was a real person?"

"What does that mean, Ian? Are you a real person? Am I? Is this place—" He spread his hands wide, then returned them to his chest in the same gesture he'd made earlier. "Is this place real?"

"I don't know."

"No," he agreed. "No, you don't. But you can't really afford to assume otherwise—not if you want to return whence you came. The key to *that* is the music you hear, that you have heard, that you will continue to hear."

"Rosslyn's healing song."

"Call it what you wish. It was composed before Rosslyn was built, but its secret is there, written in stone. It will be forever lost without you."

"Does that explain why I'm here? In this place, in this time? Who sent me here—who did this?"

"That isn't a question I can answer now. I can only help you along the path of light." He stepped close to me, placing his hand gently against my chest, then touching his own. "Nothing escapes the notice of the all-seeing eye. 'For the eye is the lamp of the body. If your eye is sound, your whole body will be full of light.'

"As above, so below. Hermes presides over this place, and Mercury governs this sphere. This is the second initiation, Ian."

—•—

The light all around was suddenly extinguished when he said the last word and I was back in the dark at Dalbade. Juan was standing in the south aisle looking up at something obscured by dimness, but I knew what it was: the bas-relief of Hermes-or-Mercury.

Rob stood next to me, his face concerned. Somewhere in the distance I heard a note or two of the music.

"I'm all right," I said. "I just . . ."

Rob held up his hands. "I think it's time for us to present ourselves at the Temple."

—•—

A stern gatekeeper gave us entrance after a few hushed words with Rob. He'd passed this way before—and I suspect that the Templar who served as night-porter had heard these same excuses from him on previous visits, explaining why he'd come so late to the Temple. His gaze followed us along the torch-lit tunnel until we were out of sight and up the stairs, the iron-barred door clanging shut behind us.

The Templar priory in Toulouse was near the southern gate of the city, overlooking the Petit Garonne and the Île de Tounis; as Rob had said, it was well upstream from the noxious dye factories that lined the river to the north. We were assigned to beds in a part-empty barracks, and soon had cold supper and mugs of wine from the refectory; we sat at a rough wooden table in a small room that adjoined our cells and ate and drank before retiring. It gave us enough privacy to talk.

"Why is everybody afraid of this guy, this Nog—" I began. A stern look from Rob kept me from saying the rest of his name.

After a moment, la Rosa began to speak.

"Four years ago," he said, "under orders from his master, he went with a group of ruffians to the Holy Father's home in Anagni. A Florentine spy and some well-placed *soldi*"—he rubbed his fingers together—"and they seized His Holiness' body, making him a prisoner. Only the blessing of God stayed his hand from killing the Pope, and only the outrage of the townsmen freed him—but it was too much for the Holy Father, and he died before he could take any action."

"But the next Pope *did,*" Rob said. "Benedict XI forgave the King, but not his minister. His father may have been a heretic and burned for it," he added softly, "but the son is the devil himself. Monsieur and his accomplices—members of a prominent Italian family whose name I will not speak here—were excluded when the new Pope absolved his Highness the King of France and all others involved in the humiliation at Anagni. They were all summoned to appear before him on the next St Peter's Day—"

"Which they did not," Juan added.

"Which they did not," Rob agreed. "But before the new Pope could take any action he died as well."

"Poisoned," Juan hissed. "And then he was replaced by a creature of the French king who hasn't yet even gone to Rome. But *he* pardoned Monseiur for his acts as soon as he was enthroned." He spat on the floor near him, as if he were ridding himself of a foul taste.

Rob looked into his wine mug and didn't like what he saw there. He stood up, gathering our empty—or near-empty—mugs as well, and walked around the corner to a pantry where the wine-jugs were kept.

"Why be afraid of him?" I asked Juan quietly. "The world is full of other lands and other kings."

"The Grand Master fears no one," he said. "Not—" He lowered his voice to a whisper. "Not *el diablo* Nogaret, not the King, no one. But for the likes of us . . ." he crossed himself. "I still don't understand why Monsieur Nogaret is here in Toulouse."

I suddenly thought of my vision in the church, and remembered what that Juan had told me: *You are in possession of some very important knowledge—and there is someone who is seeking to discover it, and you with it.* I wondered whether Nogaret, the King's confidant and bully boy, was here to find me.

"Rob said that he's from here."

"Oh, certes, sure enough, Ian. His father was a heretic Cathar and burned here at the stake for his blasphemy. I would have thought that was enough to keep him away—but perhaps he simply goes where he pleases, regardless of any of that."

I didn't know much about the Cathars, though obviously Juan did; I'd have to get that information at another time—it was bad enough that they had to explain this Nogaret fellow to me.

"What do *you* think?" I asked.

"He's looking for something, or someone."

"What? Or who?"

Rob returned at that moment, placing three stoneware mugs on the table in front of us. "I may have an answer to that," he said quietly, sitting again.

"Say on," Juan said.

"I have heard," Rob answered quietly, "that a few days ago—at the suggestion, nay, insistence of our Grand Master—the Holy Father signed a writ commanding that our Order be investigated. For heretical practice."

"Heretical—but that's absurd," Juan replied, taking a long drink from his mug. "Who has been calling for renewed crusade against the infidel? Who has—"

"I don't need to be convinced," Rob said. "His Holiness's inquisitors do. And I wouldn't be looking them up and confronting them. Leave it to your betters."

"What does that mean to us?" I asked. The revelation of the vision returned to me: very important knowledge and someone looking for it—and me.

I wondered what Juan had seen this time. Maybe I'd been nattering to him in *his* vision, telling him cryptic things about telly and the internet.

"I don't know, lad," he said. He leaned back in his seat and scratched his beard. "It means we must tread very carefully. I think we're done here—I had hoped to stay a few more days, but we'd best move on. There's bound to be a boat that will take us downriver as far as Médoc, and then we can make our way northward toward Orléans from there. We'll go to Mass and be off with first light."

I nodded. Based on our experience at Santiago, I'd done what I came to Toulouse to do—and there now seemed to be greater urgency.

"Drink up," Rob said. "A long road ahead of us still. And evidently the Devil himself is walking on it." He crossed himself against evil and took a long drink.

I drank and considered the problem in my head. It was the twenty-sixth day of August, meaning that the fateful October thirteenth was a bit under seven weeks away.

I was traveling the path of light: both Rob—in the first vision—and Juan in the second had used that term. I didn't know how many more stops this train had to make, but I did know that the last one: the end of the *camino de las estrellas,* the path of stars—was at a place that wouldn't be built for another hundred years.

Each of the first two visions told me that a "heavenly body" governed it: first the Moon, then Mercury. I was reasonably sure that the last heavenly body known to the ancients was Saturn—Uranus and the other two farther out weren't discovered until much later—and that they considered the Earth, not the Sun, to be the centre of the universe. I counted Venus, Mars, Jupiter, Saturn, and the Sun: five more. If each body got its own stop on the Enlightenment Express, then we'd done two of seven, and there were four more to go, plus Rosslyn, however the hell we got back there.

Five more stops, and seven weeks to do it. Even with the urgency that this writ put on our journey, I still couldn't see the end of the path—or why the King's henchman was crossing it.

CHAPTER 5

THE FIRST DAY ON THE BOAT WAS UNEVENTFUL. THE *BATEAU*—A flat-bottomed vessel used on the Garonne—was crowded with passengers and cargo headed for Bordeaux; it was nothing like the luxurious river cruise Jan and I had taken five or six years ago—a bucolic, comfortable tourist experience that provided wonderful footage for the programme. After filming we'd sit on the deck and watch the sun go down, drinking wine from crystal glasses. The fourteenth-century trip provided us a sheltered spot on the deck between wooden cartons and straw bundles that kept us out of the sun.

The Garonne wound back and forth through Aquitaine, headed for the sea. For a mile or so downriver from Toulouse the river was tinted greyish-blue by the runoff from the *coquagnes*—it was like rafting across a chemical waste dump. A few hundred years in the future, that sort of thing wouldn't be allowed; and by then there would be the Midi Canal to straighten out the kinks and allow deeper draught vessels to use the river. For now the flat-bottomed barges ruled it, guided by pilots who knew most of the eddies and sandbars (though the passengers had to set to work with long poles more than a few times to push us back into the flow, accompanied by more colorful *langue d'oc* curses than I'd imagined could exist.)

By the time the sun set we were fair knackered, but the boat captain took good care of his passengers and provided hearty fare for us.

"Rob," I asked as we sat on the deck later, our knees tucked under our chins as it drifted on through the night, "what's going to happen in Orléans?"

"What's that?"

"Orléans."

"Ask me in the morning," he said, the light of the waning moon etching his features in the semi-darkness.

"Morning," Juan mumbled to himself. He had the ability to go to sleep anywhere, anytime—a good habit for a monk. An even better habit for a soldier, which I was supposed to be, but I couldn't sleep. Apparently Rob couldn't either.

"I want to know tonight. What is the third initiation?"

"What did you say?"

"The third initiation. What will it be?"

Rob let his long legs stretch out. He took his hands and placed his fingers to his lips—a gesture I'd seen before, but still couldn't place where I'd seen it. I knew what it meant, though: *Amoun* again—*be discreet.*

"No, I've had my fill of that," I said. "You know what's been happening to me. At Santiago it was the first initiation and the Moon. At Toulouse it was the second initiation and Mercury. The third initiation must be—what? Venus? And who walks out of the wings this time? Who gets to be Mister bloody Mysterious this time?"

He let his hands fall to his sides.

"This is my last one, Ian," he said, not responding to my question. "I've been doing this route for years: someone comes up from Cintra, ready to pass through the first initiation, and I guide them to it. We walk along through Aragon and Navarre, across the mountains to Toulouse, then down the river and up the road to Orléans, and so on.

"But this is the last one. I've had enough of it. There won't be another trip for me next summer."

You have no idea, I thought. *Or do you? Do you know what's going to happen?*

I'd been told what lay a few weeks in the future: the betrayal by the King of France, the outlawing of the Templar Order. I'd also been told that Rob—the one sitting next to me—didn't know any of that.

Truth? Or more mystery—more gestures, more steps on the path of light . . . I'd had four weeks, more or less, in the fourteenth century and I felt just as adrift as when I arrived.

This is the last one, I told myself. *Juan and I are the last ones. And I mustn't tell him what I already know.*

Be discreet.

"The third initiation will be the most challenging," he said at last. "Since Sainte-Croix collapsed it's been more difficult for initiates to make their way through it."

"Collapsed? What do you mean?"

"The roof caved in. Some of the cathedral roof collapsed recently and the sanctuary is partially obstructed."

"How recently?"

"About thirty years ago."

"Thirty—" I must have done a comic turn. "Well, why haven't they rebuilt it yet?"

"It's only been *thirty years,* lad. You can't rush these things. But don't worry: we'll see you through it."

"And what will I see there?" *It's only been thirty years, he says,* I thought. *Here. Step into this heap of stone and we'll send you the next mysterious stranger.*

"I told you that I don't know. When true pilgrims become initiates and begin walking this road, most of the time they see . . . something, but it's different for each person."

"As opposed to what *you* may have seen."

"Aye, that's right. I don't know what you saw or heard except in the most general way. And I don't need to know, lad, and you don't need to know *my* experience as an initiate," he added. "It's between you and the Lord God.

"But yes, the sphere of the third initiation is governed by

Venus. It represents the Warrior, the one who can fight for good against evil—and the free will to do it."

"I've not had much in the way of free will, Rob. I feel that I've been led along like an ox with a ring in its snout."

"You have been 'led along paths that you know not,' " Rob answered. "That's the way of the initiate, Ian. You had to pass through the first two spheres to reach the point where you can decide what you want to do. Will you follow the path of light or turn aside?"

"*Do* people turn aside?"

"Of course they do. Sometimes they stand at the door and knock and the door is opened unto them—and sometimes they never reach the door at all."

"Is that how it happens?" I leaned my forehead on my knees and closed my eyes, just taking a few moments to listen and think. "Is this where these warriors come from? Knocking around until they happen to ask the right questions, then puzzle out what people like you say to them? How are we expected to fight for good against evil if we have no earthly way of knowing what to do?"

"Faith, Ian," Rob said. "Faith—and hope."

I wish I had it, I thought. *I wish I could dismiss my doubts and fears that easily.*

And while I sat there listening to the filthy water of the Garonne lap against the sides of the boat, I could also hear Juan la Rosa, full of faith and hope himself, snore softly on.

—•—

It took four days in all to reach Médoc, where the Garonne joined the Dordogne before rolling on to the sea. Our conveyance wasn't an express: it seemed to stop every hour or so to load or unload, with the periods in between ranging from peaceful drifts to sprints along rapidly-moving stretches of dangerous water to fights with treacherous snags and underwater obstacles that had evidently appeared since our captain's last trip through. Still, it was a pleasant change from walking—we would catch the foul odour of a tannery or a stable and then it would be gone as we moved around a bend in the river. . . but we lost sight of beautiful vistas just as quickly.

The banks and nearby hills were full of fortifications: England and France had fought over this area, and would continue to do so even when the Black Death brought them to a standstill half a century from now. All of that was history that hadn't happened yet.

Rob and Juan weren't the Rob and Sean I met at Rosslyn. They looked like them and sounded like them: but Robert de la Maison and Juan la Rosa seemed to be thoroughly at home in this time and place. Their resemblance to the men I'd met in twenty-first century Rosslyn was part of the pattern of events that had brought me here in the first place. Each of *them* was a Templar, and the Ian Graham that I was in this time was a Templar as well. What that meant for the Ian Graham I remembered myself to be: God only knew.

And as of this date, the end of August 1307, we were all in mortal danger . . . and only I knew how it was likely to turn out.

—•—

The last time I'd seen the Midi I had been on on a high-speed train between Barcelona and Paris; Liz and I enjoyed a nice glass of claret and watched the vineyards fly by— hills and valleys were covered with them. We'd had a holiday on the Costa Brava to get away from *Ian and Jan*; Jan had gone off to the Baltic with a cousin—we'd spent the whole fortnight exchanging late-night text messages at Channel Four's expense.

By the time the train passed through the Midi Liz and I were barely speaking. It was our last holiday together.

—•—

We left the Garonne and the Midi behind in Médoc, taking the high road north toward Poitiers and eventually Orléans. It was great stock footage: most of the land was boggy, desolate moorland interrupted by marshy meadows and clumps of dark forest. I was too busy making sure I didn't step off into a bog with water over my head to pay much attention.

The Templar priory in Toulouse had provided us with stout quarterstaffs to replace our makeshift palmer's staffs that had served us as we crossed through Spain and the Pyrenees. Evidently the armourer and the prior felt—and I couldn't help but agree—that we might meet with some hostility on the road.

Both Rob and Juan carried their staffs with the confidence of two blokes who knew what to do with them. My staff felt vaguely familiar to me, but I couldn't place from where, and offered a silent prayer that I wouldn't have to use it.

—•—

My lack of faith served up a nice portion of dramatic irony two days after we parted from our riverboat.

It had rained much of the previous night, which we'd spent huddled up inside the remains of a small abandoned cabin. The day had come in cool and damp, giving us a light ground fog and reducing our sight and hearing to almost nothing. Up ahead we saw a shape on the road; as we approached, it became obvious that we were looking at a human figure—a body, sprawled face-down on the road.

"Heya," Rob said, stopping and looking around. He gripped his quarterstaff tightly; Juan and I did the same. Rob gestured to Juan to go forward and check the body.

"Stay close, lad," he said to me as the Asturian approached the figure. Juan poked the body gently with his staff, then a trifle harder when it didn't respond.

I began to answer, but Rob held up one hand, returning it to his staff. He cocked his head as if he was listening closely.

Juan placed his staff beneath the body and flipped it over. From the smell and the level of decomposition it had been there a while. While we stood there, Rob suddenly gave me a shove, sending me sprawling into the mud: before I could yelp a complaint it became obvious why he'd done so: two *some-things* zipped through the air approximately where I'd been standing. A third one narrowly missed Rob as I watched, flat on my arse.

"Come on," he said, grabbing my elbow and lifting me to my feet. We began to run directly at a stand of tall pine trees ten or fifteen paces away in the direction from which the shafts had come. Rob had his staff in front of him like the handlebar of a bicycle, gripping it toward the middle with both hands. Juan was up and with us in an instant.

"We've got one try at this," Rob shouted as we ran. "They don't have time to shoot again!"

"What—" I said. "What if they do?"

"Then we're buggered!" Rob said.

They didn't have time to shoot.

The next few minutes seemed like hours. We were on our assailants almost at once: there were three of them—strapping fellows with lanky hair and unkempt beards. Two were still cranking their crossbows for another shot; the third one, evidently the leader, had seen us coming and had dropped his weapon and drawn a nasty-looking short sword.

Rob took on the leader, whirling his staff forward and down at his opponent's head—then turning it around and delivering a sharp blow at the fellow's knees. The swordsman blocked the head shot but I heard a sharp *crack!* as the second blow landed solidly.

Juan's technique was a bit different—lighter and more agile, the little Asturian used his staff end-first, catching one of the others straight in the chest, knocking him back against a tree—and then lifting it up to catch him just under the chin. Then they were wrestling, rolling over and over on the ground; Rob and the leader exchanged blows until he finally connected with the lead bandit's skull.

I literally fought for my life. I swung the staff like a cricket-bat, the only wooden stick I'd had much practice with. I aimed for the knees as I'd seen Rob do—but my man was ready. He batted the staff out of the way with the crossbow he still held in his hands and used his shoulder against my chest, turning my momentum against me. My man was clearly enjoying the combat; he grinned, showing his few remaining teeth, and somewhere along the line got a long pointed dagger in his hand. He kept daring me to come at him with the staff, grabbing for it as I attacked or dancing out of reach. Finally we wound up in a clinch—I was strong enough to hold on to the staff and push him back, and was trying to knock him off his feet, when suddenly I felt a sharp pain in my midsection.

I shouted in pain and jumped back—then did the one thing that should have convinced my companions that I was no fighting man. I dropped the damn staff and touched my chest. My hand came away covered in blood.

"Oh," I said. It was the only thing I could manage.

The next few minutes went by in slow motion. The nasty bloke who had just used his Ginsu knife on me was getting ready for another blow as I went down on my backside; as I watched, the end of a staff came into the frame and struck his head with a sickening crack and he fell away sprawling, the dagger flying out and landing a foot from my left hand. I reached out and picked it up.

Blood was pooling on the ground in front of me, but I was fascinated by the blade itself: crudely made, a bit rusty up near the hilt . . . *but it does the job, now doesn't it?* I thought.

This is really more than I bargained for, I mentally added to myself. The dagger still in my hand, I felt myself fall onto my back and watched a leaf, blown by a breeze and weighed down by the rain, drift slowly and lazily down toward me, blotting out my vision . . .

—•—

. . . I remember what he had said to us on St Magdalen's Day as we stood in our *schiltrons:* "I half brocht ye to the ring—hop gif ye can!" William Wallace, Protector of the Realm, the hero worshipped by many of us—myself included, though I was twenty-five and should have known better—we held against the mailed cavalry but no heroism, no confidence would be enough against the longbow. We stood and fought, except the Comyn, who did not find the battle to their liking and followed their chief from the field.

Some few of us escaped the horrible slaughter. That very day we rode with Wallace himself for Callender—and thereafter became raiders, nipping at the heels of the English overlords and vanishing into the dark wood before they could catch us. For Longshanks, King Edward of England who styled himself "Hammer of the Scots," Wallace became his greatest enemy.

We could hop, just likc thc spearmen of the *schiltrons.* We fought with bow and sword, staff and spear—but after six years I found that I no longer had any taste for that kind of war: hit hard and run away. A soldier waits for the arrow that will find him, whether it comes from an opponent's bow or King Death Himself . . . I knew what fate would probably await me if I remained in my homeland, so I took myself away.

I was as capable of killing infidels for Castile, or Aragon, or Portugal as I had been in defending the land of my birth. The variety of weapons and styles made me more capable of surviving and more valuable as a mercenary. I left enemies dead on the battlefield; I left gold behind in taverns and brothels, and probably left behind a squad of fair-haired half-Scots bastards spread across the *reconquista.*

In the end, I was numb to the violence of a soldier's life. The greatest fighting men died, I knew, and if left to rot, vermin would crawl across them . . .

—•—

. . . and suddenly I was wide awake and watching maggots crawl across my own wounded chest.

I was propped up against a pine. Juan was walking toward me, his hands cupped before him: more of the filthy things were trying to make their escape as he came forward.

"Aaah!" I shouted. I wanted to scrape them off with my hands, but found my arms pinned. I looked frantically down and saw a ring with a ruby stone: Rob was holding my arms to my sides from behind the tree.

"What in bloody hell is going on?"

"It's to clean the wound, lad," Rob said quietly. "They'll keep it from being infected."

"Maggots? Are you—" I reached out to kick Juan, the only weapon available to me. He grinned and dodged out of the way. "Get the hell away from me, you madman. And let me go!"

"I'll not do," Rob said, holding yet more tightly. "They've got a bit more work to do. Then we'll bandage you up."

My stomach was ready to revolt at the thought, so I looked away and tried to calm myself. . .

They'd done it. I'd seen it on battlefields all across Aragon and Castile: the little bastards cleaned out the wound, kept it from going septic. And *Ian and Jan* had looked at doing a programme on biosurgery a few years back, but it didn't get out of the planning stage—

I looked away from my chest; Juan was squatting on his heels, safely out of range of my boots.

"How much time . . ." I began.

"A few hours," Rob said behind me. "We'll have to get ourselves somewhere to have you looked at. But you fought well, lad, you truly did. We'll make a Templar of you yet."

"What—" I began, then looked back at Rob, then away at the trees, giving up their leaves one at a time to drift lazily toward the muddy ground.

"Are you a real person? Am I? Is this place real?"

Juan asked me that at the second initiation. Now I had two sets of memories: one of being a mercenary, a soldier with William Wallace and of the *reconquista*—and the real one of me, the telly talking head.

What was real? I didn't know. I couldn't answer that question. As the leaves drifted down from the trees, I passed out again.

—•—

I woke to the sound of music: a human voice singing softly. It should have come as no surprise that the tune was the one I'd been hearing all along—in Rosslyn, at Santiago, in Navarre and now wherever I was. There had been no dreams this time, of William Wallace or of anyone else.

Wherever I was, it was comfortable—on my back under a soft blanket, a pillow beneath my head. I kept my eyes closed, my breathing steady, and waited for the sound of the voice to come near. When I felt someone nearby I reached out and grabbed, getting hold of a wrist. I opened my eyes and pulled myself up—then collapsed onto my back, pain stabbing my midsection.

"You're awake." The singer was an older monk with a carefully trimmed beard and almost no hair on his head. "I was beginning to worry, Brother."

"I'm sorry to worry you."

"I was only beginning to worry," the monk said, smiling. "Your companions are much more concerned. They had no reason. God willing, my patients all awaken."

"You are a doctor?" It came out *magister:* my Occitan vernacular dipped into Latin, causing the monk to raise one eyebrow. Evidently I didn't look the sort to have any Latin other than the Mass at my disposal.

"I haven't been to Salerno, if that's what you mean," he answered, walking off to a sideboard. "Just a modest servant of the Lord and St Luke. A *medicus,* if you please." He poured a bit of water into an ewer, washed his hands and wiped them on a cloth, and came back. "Brother Andre at your service. I can assure you that Frère Robert has rarely had cause to complain."

"You know him well?" He nodded. I let my hand touch the tender spot near my belly, but stopped when I saw him frown.

"Nay, leave it be," he said. "I'll clean it out myself. They're like as not all dead at this point anyhow."

"There are still—"

"Ah," Andre said, stepping to my side and taking my near hand, palm up, as if examining the lines on it. "Now *you* have become a healer, Brother? Yes, there are still maggots in your wound. The flesh in the wound should be . . . *débridée?* Dissolved. They've done their job."

I thought I felt them still moving around down there—it was probably just my imagination. It would have turned my stomach again, but I realised there was nothing in it.

"What day is it, Brother?"

"Why, it's Saint Giles' Day," he answered. "But you'll recover just fine, son. A penny or two to the patron saint of cripples wouldn't go amiss, but you should have a full recovery."

"Saint Giles' Day? What day is that?"

"Why, the Kalends of September," he answered, looking at me curiously. I didn't say anything to that—*kalends* wasn't exactly part of the vernacular. "The first," he said at last. "The first of September."

"I've been asleep for two days?" I started to sit up again and thought better of it almost immediately, collapsing back as the wound reminded me what a bad idea it had been.

"Almost three." Brother Andre pulled down the sheet and began methodically to unwrap my bandages. I concentrated on the September sunshine streaming through a window on the opposite side of the room.

"Where am I?"

"The infirmary at Saint-Eutrope," he answered. "Saintes. Your brothers brought you here with this"—he took the opportunity to give it a good poke, and I winced—"and you slept while they attended to their souls."

"I've a few days' catching up to do."

"Oh, yes you do," he said. "All you talked about was the girl."

"What girl?"

"Rosalind. Roselin. Something like that. All you've talked about in your sleep—all that I could understand, any rate. The rest was in whatever Scots dialect you favour." He poked the wound once more, then began to lay clean bandages on it.

"What did I say?"

"Oh, I'm not sure—something about wanting to get back to her." He raised an eyebrow; his eyes twinkled. "My brother, you'll really have to let this go. You must serve God by leaving such things behind."

"I'll keep that in mind."

"You do that," Andre said. He finished his work and pulled the blanket up again. After a while I began to drift and soon was back to sleep.

—•—

I awoke again near sunset and ignored the discomfort in my chest to attend to bodily needs. After I'd taken care of business I returned to the infirmary, where Rob and Juan were waiting for me.

"I must have been appointed as your groom," Rob said, smiling and tossing me a clean robe. I stripped off my sweat-soaked one and dropped it on the bed—a few weeks in their company had taken away any sort of modesty for me—then pulled on the fresh one, which smelled of soap and summer air.

"Thank you." I sat on the bed and bent over to pull on my sandals, which turned out to be an adventure, but I didn't feel as if I wanted to ask for help.

The great bell was ringing by the time I was done; I followed Rob and Juan to walk through the cloister to the church nave, where the monks were in procession to Vespers. While we waited for them to pass, I stopped Rob, placing a hand on his arm.

"I've slept for three days," I said.

"You needed it, lad. Your wound—"

"We don't have time," I said. "We couldn't afford to—"

"To what?" Rob smiled. "To wait for you to heal? All in good time, Ian. We'll go on toward Poitiers in the morning. Brother Andre doesn't think your wound is too serious—now that you've had your wee nap."

"But it's already the first of September," I said. "We have to—"

"We have to pray," Rob said. "There is a caravan leaving tomorrow; we'll go with them as far as Tours, then make our own way to Orléans."

I wondered again to myself whether I should reveal what I knew of the terrible thirteenth of October—and if Juan and Rob would put me in the nearest asylum if I did.

And *Amoun* still plagued me, along with what else I'd been told. To go home meant continuing with the pilgrim's path, and to have done with it before that date.

"But—"

"Pray," Rob said, removing my hand from his arm. "We'll pray, lad. That's why we're here."

Juan nodded, smiling. "We'll get to Orléans soon enough, Ian," he added. "I'll teach you how to properly handle that staff along the way."

I had no argument. If I had been a soldier with William Wallace and in Spain and Portugal, I knew how to handle a staff—but I'd need help to rediscover the skill.

"Let's hear the word of the Lord," Rob said, and we did.

Saint-Eutrope was new by medieval standards, completed less than a century earlier. It was dominated by huge piers of stone supporting the central nave; the capitals were decorated with angels playing instruments—harps, tambours, flutes and a number of other things I couldn't readily identify.

As the office was sung I could hear strains of that elusive music that had followed me through my journey.

—•—

In the half-light of morning Brother Andre changed the bandages again.

"You must have spent your pennies wisely, Brother," he said, looking at the wound and sniffing. "I told Robert that it was really too soon for you to be on your way, but St Giles—or someone—has blessed you."

"I'm fit to travel then." I certainly felt well enough—it still hurt like hell, but Andre had done a wonderful job.

"Quite fit, quite fit. I understand you'll be able to ride for a few miles with a merchant caravan that leaves at first light. But have a care," he said, reaching out a hand to grasp mine and help me to my feet. As he helped me up, he let the hand slip to my elbow, then grasped it with his other as his own elbow touched my palm.

I froze, looking directly at him. I'd had that done to me once before—by Juan during the initiation at Toulouse.

Andre held my gaze a moment longer, then reached inside a fold of his sleeve and drew out a copper medal, pressing it to my right hand. "Keep this," he said. "Saint Giles. May he protect and guide you."

“I—” I began, not sure what I wanted to say. “Thank you,” I managed.

Andre looked away, as if he had a hundred other things to do before the sun came up. As I walked away I looked back over my shoulder, and his gaze followed me every step.

CHAPTER 6

I THINK I KNOW NOW THE TRUTH OF THE MATTER—WHICH OF my lives was true: the Ian Graham who went out to Rosslyn and fell into history and lives to tell the tale, and the Ian Graham who fought with Wallace and for glory and profit against the Moor . . . dust and forgotten seven hundred years by everyone but me. Still, as we traveled with the caravan from Saintes to Tours those rainy September days, I didn't know what to think.

—•—

The caravan was a dozen wagons full of goods, fifteen tradespeople that all seemed to be related to each other, and a half-dozen hired guards other than the three of us. I remember thinking that for the distance involved, it was a surprise that so many armed men were involved in the business—but the experience on the way to Saintes had thumped me on the head as well as stabbed me in the gut.

Meanwhile, I was getting thumped in a lot of other ways.

—•—

"No, no, no!"

Juan squatted down on his haunches and waited for me to get back to my feet. He never let go of his staff and never let his gaze leave me as I got myself up.

"What did I do wrong now?" I asked.

The caravan had camped in an open field near St Cyprian's Abbey, across the river from the walls of the city. As he had done for the past few days, my Asturian friend took the opportunity to do some staff work with me.

He stood up and walked over, his weapon held loosely in his right hand. As usual, we'd attracted a bit of an audience—kids, the other guards, and Rob. They seemed to be enjoying my discomfort.

"What you did wrong," he said softly, "is to forget that a staff isn't a sword." He tapped it gently on his head. "It's for cracking skulls, and knees, and"—he placed it lewdly next to his crotch—"other places."

It drew a laugh from the audience. Juan smiled appreciatively and offered them a little bow.

"I know what a sword can do," I said, bringing my staff to a defensive position. Juan crouched as well and we began to circle. My bandaged wound twinged a bit as I moved, but I ignored it.

"You should know"—he said, thrusting and then quickly moving out of my range—"what a staff can do as well, Scotsman. You'll get it if I have to beat it through your thick woolly head."

He blocked my sweeping attack, dancing out of the way, grinning in a way that always seemed to get my back up.

"Thick, is it?" I said. *Witty response, Graham,* I thought. *Billy Connolly would be proud.*

The little ones always think they're funny, I added. *Remember the sneak-thief in Barcelona, the night we were all drunk*—

"Pay attention, you great lummox!" Juan beat on my staff and then cracked me sharply on the shoulder; I didn't quite let go of my weapon, but staggered out of the way and barely blocked his next move that intended to slash my legs out from under me. I shook my head, trying to determine where that memory had come from—and did my best to avoid the next few attacks.

I've done this before, I said to myself. A brief glint of sun through clouds reminded me of a practice-yard somewhere, and another sweaty, humid day where I'd beaten back attacks from a big brute of a man with most of one ear missing. It had happened somewhere in his past—my past.

"I *am* paying attention," I shot back. *I* am *paying attention,* I added to myself. *All right, you've done this before—let's see what you've got.*

I don't quite know how I managed to do it, but I pushed my modern self away: all of it—wanting to be back in my flat in Leith, wanting to have my TV and my mobile and my PDA . . . wanting to drive my BMW again.

I put it all aside.

Attack.

Juan noticed it right away, when I flourished the staff in my hands. It felt light, as if it belonged there—as if it had always been there and I'd just put it down for a moment. I could see the other man's weaknesses just by looking: he favored his left a bit, and would place his feet in a particular way before he moved to attack from that side. I had the longer reach and the greater strength, he the greater quickness. His ability to knock me on my arse was based on making me watch the feint and miss the blow that followed.

I let him come. I followed the feint and made sure to just barely parry the next attack, but evidently I gave too much away: he could see that I was ready. I easily stepped out of the path of a thrust to my midsection, shifting my weight from left to right, smiling as I went through the manual of arms that One-Eared Diego had taught me when we served *el Justo*, Count Jaume de Barcelona, three years ago. I tapped away his attacks as if I was swatting a fly.

"You learned something from the last crack to the head," Juan said, but I could see that his heart wasn't in the taunt. He could smell the wind; he could believe his eyes.

"You're not getting tired, are you?"

"Not at all," he came right back. But he did seem to be tiring. His parries weren't as crisp—his feet weren't as sure.

It was time to give the insolent Asturian the clincher. I knew—*knew*—that I could finish him at any time, but it was far better to let him come at me.

He knew he was running out of time. He feinted once, then twice, then came: but I was ready. I stepped aside, pushed his staff out of line, and then swung around and cracked him across the back. He sprawled face-first headlong into the mud, his staff skittering across the cleared area to land a few paces from where Rob sat on a stone, his arms crossed, a smile on his face.

The folk in the audience stamped their feet and shouted. I walked to where Juan had fallen; he'd rolled over, reaching wildly for his staff.

"Ian?" he said, as if he wasn't sure it was really me. He looked up, crouching as if I might kick him in the midsection to finish him off.

In a few minutes I reflected on how easy it had been to call up skills and abilities I didn't know I had—and push myself, my twenty-first century self, aside. I admit that it frightened me how quickly that happened when I took the time to think about it.

But at that moment I didn't want to think about that.

"I told you," I said, leaning down to help him up. "I know what to do with a staff."

—•—

Our route to Orléans led through Tours, which was as far as the caravan went. Rob and Juan were intent on visiting the "new" church and shrine of St Martin before we moved on to Orléans—new, as in thirteenth-century new. I had never been there in the modern day and I had no memory of doing so in the fourteenth century.

Rob found a place to pray in the nave. Juan was most interested in the acoustics of the place; without someone to show me around or a colour guide, I found myself wandering through the ambulatory—the array of shrines around the central aisle of the church. I followed the north aisle and then wandered down the north transept to stand before the brand-new rose window beneath the *Tour Charlemagne.*

After a few minutes, I realised I was not alone. The beautiful window was evidently interesting enough that I didn't hear him approach.

"Peace be with you," someone said behind me. I turned at the sudden interruption of quiet to see a man of medium height and build, standing quietly and calmly behind me. He had a carefully-trimmed beard but no tonsure. There was nothing really remarkable about him except that he seemed somehow familiar. He was carrying something woven of dark-blue cloth draped over his arm.

"And also with you," I answered by reflex. "I'm sorry, I didn't hear you approach."

"I didn't want to interrupt your contemplations, Brother," he said. "You seemed . . . rapt."

"Distracted," I said. "There's a lot to see."

"It's what's left of an old sanctuary in our new church . . . you're right, of course. It's easy to be distracted. I believe you dropped this," he said, handing the cloth to me.

"I don't think so—"

"No, I'm sure."

I took the bundle from him and inclined my head. "As you say." I wasn't about to shrug it off.

"I'm sure you will find it useful."

"I suppose." I turned my head to look at the window. "Tell me," I continued, "do you know the names of the two men shown on the far right? I can't make out the inscriptions."

There was no answer. I looked back at my benefactor—

But he was gone again, as suddenly and as quietly as he had appeared. The cloth was still there, though: a heavy wool cloak, edged on three sides and ragged along the fourth where a seam should be. At the top there was the hook end of a clasp, but the eye was missing. After looking at it for a moment I shrugged and swung it around my shoulders—or, rather, one shoulder, for the garment was scarcely big enough to cover half of my back.

—•—

"What did you say he looked like?" Rob asked.

"He was medium height—about my height. Modest clothes, a close-trimmed beard. Not tonsured like a monk."

"Describes almost every man in this church that isn't one," Rob said, sweeping his hands toward the nave and across the wide open area of the ambulatory. "And you say he gave you *this.*" He fingered my damaged garment.

"He said it would be useful."

"It's a cloak, from the look of it." Rob unwrapped the bundle as I did and snapped it open. He fingered the clasp, looking for the other piece—but by the time he realised it was missing, a look of complete astonishment had come over his face.

"What did he say to you?"

"He told me that it was easy to be distracted in this church because there was so much to see—and then he gave me this. Said he was sure I'd dropped it."

Rob carefully smoothed the cloth. "Is that all he said?"

"He said 'peace be with you', too, but I don't—"

"Lad, this isn't a cloak," Rob interrupted me. "Don't you know what this means?"

"No."

"It's half a cloak. Ian, I think you were visited by Saint Martin himself. That's part of his legend: he parted his cloak to share it with a poor man." He gently ran his finger along the ragged edge—it would have been along a vertical line from the top to the bottom.

"Saint Martin?" I looked up at the vaulted ceiling of the ambulatory. "You mean, as in 'Saint Martin of Tours', Saint Martin?"

"Yes." He took me by the elbow and steered me along the north aisle to a particular alcove, which showed an elderly, saintly figure bending down and offering a cloth to a ragged, kneeling one. "Saint Martin. You've—this is a *relic,* Ian. This is from the hand of a saint." He handed it back to me and genuflected, bowing toward the statue.

"I guess that makes me a beggar."

"You could do much worse, lad."

"He didn't look like *that,*" I said.

"Artists." Rob frowned and rolled his eyes. "He lived centuries ago. Who knows what the man actually looked like."

"Then how do you know it wasn't someone playing a practical joke on me?"

"Why would anyone do that?"

A memory came to me: a little Irishman, drunk half the time, who enjoyed doing just that sort of thing in the encampment on the southern shore of Loch Ness. Gave a hotfoot to every man in camp—except the Wallace, of course: he was afraid what sort of revenge the great man might take—

"Ian, are you all right?"

I shook my head. "I—yes. I need some air."

"Let's get a drink of water," he suggested. I nodded, carefully folding the half-cloak as we walked out into the square.

Juan was already sitting on the edge of the fountain. We'd had quite a bit of rain, but there was welcome sunshine brightening the day. Rob and I took seats next to him, reaching into our packs for cups to dip in the water of the fountain. As I reached down to fill my cup, I stopped short.

Looking up at me from the water, features etched clear and plain by the bright sunlight, was the face of the man that had handed me the cloth.

—•—

Juan and Rob spent the evening looking at me sidelong, not sure whether I was touched by a saint or cursed for a fool. I didn't know myself. Truth to tell, I didn't actually *know* myself: I had met a person who looked just like me and I hadn't recognised him. Me. This is the point in the movie when the hero becomes overloaded with information and freaks out; fortunately, there was no word in fourteenth-century French for "freak."

—•—

"Lad," Rob said to me after we'd heard the Vespers office at our hostel, "I think you need to pray."

We'd obtained overnight places in the Benedictine pilgrims' hostel attached to St Martin's. The place was largely empty; pilgrimage season was nearly over, and the great city of Tours was customarily near the beginning of the route rather than somewhere in the middle as it was for us.

Juan was in his cell already, but Rob was sitting with me at the rear of the quiet sanctuary; two monks were tending the candles beyond the rood screen, but otherwise there was no one present.

I wanted to answer, *As if it would do any good*—but I wasn't sure I even meant it anymore. I wasn't a good Catholic, despite my newfound skill at crossing myself. I wasn't a good Presbyterian boy from St Giles' either. Things were changing too fast; I could scarcely understand it myself.

"I want to know what I'm supposed to do," I said. The half-cloak was spread out in my lap; the patterns were unfinished somehow, as if whatever was depicted was spread across the missing seam to be completed on the other side. "I'm the beggar. I'm the fellow kneeling at St Martin's feet waiting for some random act of generosity."

Rob scratched his beard thoughtfully and looked off into the darkness of the church, his face only dimly lit by distant candlelight.

"You don't trust much in the Lord, do you, lad?"

I knew what my answer must be, but didn't want to give voice to it. Of course I didn't: those that didn't have great faith in my time usually had no faith at all. The Sunday-school boy from St Giles had been in the first category, while the co-host of *Ian and Jan* had moved steadily into the second.

"I don't know what He wants me to do."

"I think He's already told you." Rob turned to face me. "The problem is that it's not clear to you what He said."

"My prayers don't usually wind up being answered."

"*All* prayers are answered, Ian. Since we know you're listening, you must learn to believe what you hear." He gestured toward the dimly-lit sanctuary. "Do you want me to stay with you?"

"I don't think so."

He nodded. "That's the answer I expected. Very well, lad. Don't be too late—we've got to be off early." We stood, and he grasped my shoulders. "Remember that He never demands more of you than you can actually perform. Trust in the Lord, Ian."

With those words he gave my back a pat and walked away along the west corridor toward the cloisters, past which the hostel was located.

I waited until the slap of his sandals was almost inaudible, then took a deep breath and walked down the south-central aisle to a place near the transept where there were small benches set out for kneeling. I genuflected and took up a place to the left of the aisle where I could lean on a low railing; the monks gave me the briefest glance and went back to their work. I placed the half-cloak on the stone floor in front of me.

Several minutes passed. I offered some of the standard prayers: the Lord's Prayer, the good old Twenty-Third Psalm . . . but I was distracted: too many foreign smells, small noises from near the high altar, echoes of night-time activities in the church. At some point my devotions—if you could call them that—drifted off into the theme song from 'Coronation Street.' It was as if I didn't know where to begin.

It was maddening. For the first time in God knew how many years I genuinely wanted to pray and I couldn't concentrate. For the thousandth time since I was thrust back into the fourteenth century, I genuinely yearned for a strong cup of coffee and four aspirins.

I heard the slap of sandals coming up the aisle and turned, expecting to see Rob coming back to offer some more cryptic advice. If that was all it turned out to be, I would've been only impatient—but instead I saw someone else: an older man, tonsured and dressed in a brown robe, walking slowly up to where I knelt. He was unremarkable except for the most prominent hooked nose I'd ever seen.

At first I didn't know him, but then some dim memory made me realise who he was: Father Corvão—the Raven, the Abbot of Cintra. I stood as he approached but he waved me down and took up a position next to me.

I had no idea why he might be there, but I had stopped being surprised at anything that seemed to happen these days.

"Father Abbot," I said, trying not to sound annoyed. A moment later I realised that it had come out in Portuguese.

Another vision, I thought. This was becoming tiresome.

"Brother Iano," he said, smiling. "It's good to see you again. You have come far."

"I wouldn't say that, Father."

"You need not. I have said it for you. Are you keeping a vigil?"

"No, not really . . . well, I suppose I am in a way: I'm trying to find some answers. But I don't know what questions to ask."

"Do you have too many questions or too few?"

"Too many." I gestured at the folded square of cloth in front of me. "I was given that this afternoon. I don't know what it means."

Abbot Tomaso looked at the half-cloak. "Nice material," he said, with another smile.

"It's only half a cloak. It's a puzzle with half the pieces missing. Very appropriate for this place," I said, waving at the sanctuary around me. "But what am I supposed to do with it?"

"Perhaps you should try to find its mate."

"That makes sense, I suppose—but why was I given it in the first place? And why was I given it by myself? And why in Heaven's name didn't I know it was me at the time?"

"Three questions. That doesn't seem to be too many." He knotted his hands in front of him, leaning on the rail. He gazed at them for several moments before continuing. "If you receive a gift as you walk the path of light, my son, it is because it will be useful: not now, perhaps, but sometime. Even if it is only half a cloak, it might be a whole something else.

"Why did you receive it from yourself? That's a bit more difficult. Perhaps the 'you' that gave it is more wise than the 'you' that received it. Just as I am from your past, perhaps your benefactor is from your future.

"And why did you not recognise yourself? Tell me, my son—how well do you know yourself? When you came to Cintra you confessed to me that you did not know yourself anymore—has that situation improved?"

"Can you tell me more of how I came to you?"

The abbot cocked his head, giving me a thorough going over. He bit his lip—a nervous habit that I seemed to remember quite well. "You don't remember?"

"Not yet."

"That's an interesting turn of phrase."

"I *don't* remember," I said. "Please, Father. This may be of great importance."

"Very well. You arrived in the late spring of this year. Your mercenary company had been disbanded after the death of your commander—Lamontaigne, I believe his name was. Rather than sign on elsewhere, you had come south and west and had found yourself at Cintra.

"At first you wished employment as a guard. But each night at Vespers I found you in the sanctuary, listening to the night office—often with your eyes closed. Sometimes you seemed angry, sometimes you wept—but you told me that you had lost yourself and didn't know how to find the broken pieces."

"An interesting turn of phrase," I said, which made the Raven smile to hear his own words spoken back to him.

"I thought so at the time, my son. But it was very apt—not just for you, but for many men who devote their lives to battle and death. Surviving the battle means that you die a little. You think that the blood washes from your hands but it never does—even in the holy cause of crusade.

"I could be burned for saying this, my son, but I do not believe in my innermost heart that any confession, any repentance, or indeed any pilgrimage serves as absolution for the taking of a life. The longer you practice at war, the more it becomes part of your being."

"And it had become part of my being."

"It had sunk roots deep into your soul. It troubled you so much that it turned your feet toward my abbey. And now—here you are."

"But why? Why am I here?"

"Here in Tours?"

"Here." I turned to face him, placing one foot on the stone floor, kneeling on the pad with the other. I felt a twinge at my gut where the wound was still healing but it could be ignored. "Here in France in 1307. Why am I here, Father? I don't belong here."

"Don't you?"

"No." I stood up; the abbot remained kneeling, looking up at me with the kindly face that seemed so familiar and was yet completely unknown to me. "No. I don't. After all of it—Santiago, Toulouse, the fight in the Midi—I don't know why this is happening to me. All I wanted to do was a—" I wanted to say, 'programme about Rosslyn Chapel', but of course couldn't find the words in Portuguese any more than in French. I let the sentence trail off. He looked puzzled, but was still listening as I struggled to find words to continue.

"Please, Father Abbot. I beg of you. *Why am I here?*"

"The music," he said quietly. "You could hear the music."

From far off in the darkness I heard it again: soft voices singing two and then three and then four distinct themes, intertwining and separating and then joining again. It seemed to be coming from the cloisters.

Without hesitating I turned and ran down the central aisle, the dim light casting weird shadows behind me. The music began to come more rapidly, changing to accomodate the rhythms of my feet and the beating of my heart. At the end of the nave were two great pillars, rising from the floor toward the arched ceiling: I came closer and closer—

And suddenly my agility failed me. One of my sandals caught in a loose stone and I went sprawling headlong. I threw my hands out in front of me as if I were sliding for a wicket in a cricket match, but I fell instead, far into the darkness, with no floor below . . .

—•—

"Ian." Someone was shaking my shoulder: Juan la Rosa. I sat upright so suddenly that he took a step back in the near darkness.

A waxing moon sent a sliver of light through the window of my cell. It was dark; I could hear a bell calling the monks to prayer.

"What—"

"It's Prime, Ian. Rob's getting ready to leave."

"At Prime?"

"Someone is here. Someone asking questions. He thought it best that we get ourselves on the road to Orléans."

I swung my legs on to the floor. I was evidently in my own cell: my pack was set on the floor beneath the window. "I was in the sanctuary . . ."

"Yes, yes. You must have fallen asleep. Probably hit your head again," he added, stepping back as if I might give him a swift kick. "They helped you back to your cell a few hours ago. By the rood, Ian, it'll be a wonder if you have any skull left by the time we reach Paris."

I grabbed his arm as he turned away. "Juan, was I alone?"

"In the sanctuary?"

"Yes. In the sanctuary. Was anyone else with me? Did the monks see me talking to anyone?"

"I don't think so. Why?"

I was talking to Father Corvão, I began to say. But I wasn't sure whether Juan would believe me. Probably not.

Another dream. I put my hand to my forehead. I'd fallen and hit my head and that's what had brought it about.

"Nothing." I let go his sleeve and reached for my sandals, trying to find some inner calm to combat the turmoil that swirled in my brain; as I found one, my hand brushed against the half-cloak, neatly folded beside my pallet.

"I'm going to stop in the refectory—they'll have some fresh bread. Want to come along?"

"I'll catch up."

Juan shrugged. "Central courtyard." He held up one hand. "Five minutes. The bell should have finished tolling by then."

I nodded. "I'll be there."

Some things are not just dreams, I thought as he walked away down the hall. The cloak was real—as real as anything that was happening to me, but it was another piece in a puzzle that was becoming increasingly more complex.

With a sigh, I stood up and began arranging my pack for the next step on my journey toward the destination that wasn't built yet.

CHAPTER 7

IN SANTIAGO, I'D BEEN TOLD, THE HAND OF GOD HAD REACHED down and turned the cathedral a little bit north of east—for some purpose that He never explained, nor needed to. The marks of His fingers on the Tree of Jesse were evidence of His deed—though they were more likely the result of the pressing of uncounted fingers of *peregrinos* over the years. Still, the more the story is told, the easier that sort of thing is able to move from legend into the realm of truth.

Orléans had its own similar story, one that was told to us when we paid our first visit to the Cathedral Saint-Croix. Apparently when the church was being consecrated the bishop fell ill and there was no one available to do the blessing. Instead, God's glowing finger came down and touched each part of the building, which was enough to do the trick—there was no other evidence of the consecration ceremony left to mark it. The God of the Middle Ages was, dare I say it, a very hands-on God.

It was another, more sinister hand that was moving, however, as we prepared for the next step of our journey along the path of light. God's hand in the consecration of Saint-Croix hadn't kept the roof from collapsing because the arches and vaults were too ambitious for the available materials, and God's hand in my pilgrimage—if He was paying any attention at all—couldn't keep me concealed forever from the enemy who wanted to know what I was supposed to know, or at least wanted to hear what I clearly heard. I learned that lesson in Orléans and it changed the nature of my quest.

—•—

"That can't help but be trouble," Rob said, looking across the courtyard of Saint-Croix at Juan la Rosa. The younger man was having an animated conversation with a young woman. Even from twenty paces where we stood, it was apparent that she was very pretty: a few wisps of auburn hair escaped her wimple and caught the afternoon light from the courtyard, and the modest clothing that befit a house of God couldn't completely conceal a graceful shape.

"Why do you think she's trouble?"

"All women are trouble, lad." Rob turned away, frowning, and squatted down to examine a statue propped against a wall. It was a somewhat damaged saint, one that had evidently fallen from some part of the still-unfinished roof of Saint-Croix when it had collapsed.

I watched Juan continue to talk with the young woman; he seemed full of energy, the way I'd seen him when listening to music.

"You'll get no argument from me."

"Oh? Had much trouble with women, then? I would think a soldier's life leaves that sort of thing aside."

I wasn't sure what he meant by 'that sort of thing,' but he made me think of Liz. A memory teased at me: something about the tilt of the young woman's head as she replied to Juan's most recent comment. She smiled when she spoke, which was unlike Liz: her smile had gone to the curbside, out with the rubbish, long before we'd split.

"Enough that I'm unable to forget," I finally managed.

"Well, you're past that now," Rob said, straightening up. "The path of light doesn't lead that way."

"Path of light," I repeated.

"That's right." Rob scowled. "Our purpose here doesn't include . . ." he waved toward Juan. "That young man can't tell the difference between light and fire."

"That's a bit harsh."

"Is it really." It was more of a statement than a question.

Juan began to walk across the courtyard toward us. He whistled as he came, his face caught up in a smile; he kept looking over his shoulder at the woman, who returned to work sweeping dust from the flagstones. By the time he reached us he'd picked up on Rob's scowl and stopped smiling.

"Have a care," Rob rumbled at him.

"I'm sorry?"

"You are here for a reason, Brother," Rob said, his brows knotted together. "And *that* is not the reason."

"It's not what you think."

"What do you suppose I think? That you're being led astray by a Jezebel? If so, then you're right."

"That's hardly fair."

Rob put his hands on his hips. "This is the path of light," he said softly. "It is not a matter of fairness."

The two men stared at each other for several moments. I began to say something, thought better of it, and began to say something else and thought better of that.

The Order had a vow of chastity; it was recommended, but not required, of initiates who had taken the Cross but hadn't been formally received as full Brothers. I hadn't realised that it included not speaking with half of the human race—but Rob was adamant and angry.

Finally Juan looked down, appearing to give in. Rob's face relaxed. Years on television had made me a good student of faces: he thought he'd won. He was wrong, of course.

—•—

Toward the end of the thirteenth century, church builders and architects had begun to build vaulted roofs with tall, pointed arches. All across France they'd rivaled each other's efforts to reach farther and farther into the heavens—but shortcomings in materials and basic misunderstandings about force and stress had made a number of those roofs collapse. Orléans was one of those. God had consecrated the church with His own hand, but He was also responsible for gravity—which wouldn't get a name for another four centuries, but worked just as effectively in this one.

On the afternoon of our arrival, we paid our respects at Saint-Croix. The main sanctuary was covered over by wooden scaffolding draped with canvas: the interior was drafty and the temporary shelter leaked. Regardless of weather, indifferent to the dignity of the holy offices being conducted beneath, construction went on; at Nones we heard the Lord's word with a works project going on in the background. Still, it was apparent that this would be magnificent when the current builders' grandsons finally finished it.

I wondered how an initiation could take place in such a place but didn't want to speak of it in the church. I waited until we'd gone back to our hostel: a place called *La Maison de la Coquille.* It was down by the river—a peaceful place with a little garden guarded by an enormous old willow tree.

After the service Juan and I spent an hour in *Coquille's* stableyard doing quarterstaff work; he didn't underestimate me now, and I kept discovering things I had apparently already learned. When we were done Juan went in to rest, a bit uncharacteristic for him. I went into the garden, where I found Rob sitting quietly, his eyes closed, hands folded in his lap.

I found a bench and thought about nothing of consequence, waiting until he looked up at me.

"We have picked up a shadow," he said.

"What does that mean?"

"Someone has followed us here. Or, perhaps, someone was waiting for us to come."

"Someone working for—"

He held up a hand. "Yes. Do not speak the name." He gestured to a seat near him; I came over and took it. "You saw something in Tours. Juan said that you asked him if you were alone, if he saw someone."

"That's right. I spoke with . . . Father Corvão."

"From Cintra?"

"Yes. I realise it's hard to believe—"

"You might be surprised what I'd be prepared to believe, lad. What did he tell you?"

"He told me why I'm on this pilgrimage. He said it's because I can hear the music."

"Music?"

"The healing music of Rosslyn."

Rob frowned, as if that wasn't the answer he was looking for. But he didn't laugh it off or dismiss it. "When did you last hear this music?"

"At Saint-Eutrope, when I was recovering from my wound. But I've heard bits and pieces since—" I took a deep breath. "Since the beginning."

"Since Cintra."

"If you like." I wanted to tell him, *No, since you showed me around the Lady Chapel at Rosslyn;* I was ready to spill the whole story, how much I really didn't belong there. But there was the ghost of William Wallace to deal with, and the soldier running across the battlefield casting his shadow before him, and the one-eared giant who had taught me to fight with a quarterstaff . . .

"He believes that you have something he wants, or possibly know something he wants to know. He knows where we're going and why—and may mean to stop us."

"You mean the pilgrimage. The path of light."

"Yes. Amiens, Chartres, and the other places. His servants will be at each place. He may have even set the bandits on us on the road north of Médoc."

"What does he want?"

"I thought you might be able to tell me that, lad. A warrior can't fight in the dark."

"I'm no warrior."

He cocked his head and looked at me. "No, I suppose you're not, not until tonight."

"What do you mean?"

"When we were on the Garonne you asked me about the third initiation. I had a quiet word—we're to do that tonight; you and Juan will be elevated to Warriors." I heard the capitalization.

"What does that mean?"

"We don't customarily discuss it. You should experience the initiation without prejudice or foreknowledge."

"A warrior can't fight in the dark, Rob."

For a time he considered his own words thrown back at him. It was quiet but for the sound of the river flowing past, the soft sigh of the wind in the willow tree, sending a few leaves to drop to the rough cobbles of the hostel garden courtyard.

"I can't tell you what will happen."

"Can you tell me what it's about? What I'm here to do?"

"Here?" He smiled. "Here in Orléans? Or . . . here in this year of Grace 1307?"

"I'll take any information you're ready to offer."

"A thousand years ago," he said, "the Romans built a temple to Venus on the site where the Cathedral Saint-Croix stands. The stones they used were previously used for a Druidic structure that marked the earth-path."

"As in Toulouse."

"As in every site on the path of light, lad. All of them honoured Abaris, who marked them out before our Saviour walked the earth."

During my initiation in Toulouse, Juan had mentioned that name. *Abaris, the teacher of Pythagoras*, he'd said.

"The great druid."

"That's right. He became Hermes and then Mercury. Every civilization found a way to represent him: and every pilgrim on the path of light follows his footsteps."

"Surely—" I began to say *Nogaret,* but stopped. "Surely our opponent knows that. Why would this pilgrimage be any different than the, what, eleven others you've led? Or Lord knows how many other ones you haven't?"

"I should think that would be obvious."

"Me."

"That's right. You. Missing memories, strange words and ideas. You don't fit here, Ian. I can't quite understand why."

"You can't imagine."

"All right," he said, nodding, as if he was trying to do so. "All prayers are answered—but I don't quite understand what I've been told so far, except that I must help you through this."

"So Juan and I are to visit Saint-Croix tonight and become Warriors."

"Yes. The third initiation is the beginning of self-awareness." He leaned forward, elbows on knees, chin resting on folded hands. "You may understand more of your own personal quest after tonight—perhaps you will be able to explain it to me."

—•—

The sun had set behind lowering clouds when Rob and I returned to Saint-Croix. Juan wasn't with us: he wasn't in the hostel when we went looking for him. *Probably off looking for dinner,* Rob had said, shrugging; he gave a message to the innkeeper to pass to the Asturian, to join us at the church at Vespers.

But he wasn't there either. It was unlike him; Rob was worried, and so was I. Three or four times I began to ask him, but stopped: he was walking around with his fists clenched, and didn't seem to want to talk about it.

The sanctuary was dark after the evening office. The wind caught the canvas and flapped it against the stones and made the candles flicker and the scaffolding creak. We made our way through the nave, offering a brief prayer before the high altar before descending into the crypt. Our companion was nowhere to be found, but there was another man waiting for us: a tall, middle-aged man dressed as a monk, tonsure and all. Monk or not, he held himself like a warrior. His cingulum was knotted in an intricate pattern, and he wore a ring on his right hand that depicted some sort of flower.

"Brother Ian, this is Brother William. A MacLeod, if I'm not mistaken—from the Isles as I am." The other smiled and nodded. "I leave you in his hands."

I must have looked startled at the name and the appearance of the man who'd first shown me around Rosslyn Chapel. For several moments none of us spoke: Rob looked as if he wasn't sure what I'd do next, while Brother William didn't know how to react. They waited patiently for me to say something, but I just composed myself as best I could and waited.

"There were to be two," William said at last.

"I know." Rob answered, tight-lipped. "I have a bad feeling."

"Shall I wait?"

Rob looked at each of us in turn and then said to William, "No. I speak for this initiate, Brother," he said. "I ask that you receive him as a Warrior." He bowed, and then turned and walked back the way he came.

William waited for the sound of his footsteps to disappear, and then said, "Don't be afraid, Brother. The Lord is with you. Though to be honest," he added, smiling, "I think that this would be easier if we gave the initiate a wee dram before taking him in."

I couldn't help but smile as well. "The sun's past the yardarm."

"A sailing man," William replied. "Robert said you were a city boy. Ah, well. No dram is forthcoming. Are you ready?"

"If I said yes, would you believe me?"

"No."

He nodded and took me by the elbow. We walked several paces down an aisle marked by burial stones on either side until we came to a stone baptismal font. With some effort we removed the cover and set it aside; the font was dry and empty.

William reached into the centre, where the bottom of the font was raised in a little knob that reminded me of the pendant bosses of Rosslyn's Lady Chapel. He pressed his ring into a depression in the centre and twisted his wrist, and I heard the sound of stone sliding against stone.

We turned to face an opening two paces away in the wall where nothing had been before. Without another word, he gestured me toward it. I took a deep breath and walked forward into darkness, the stone polished and smooth beneath my sandals.

"All right," I said. "What do I do now?"

There was no answer except the sound of stone against stone again. I whirled around to see the door closing again, the last bit of stray candlelight disappearing. By the time I came back to where it had been I couldn't find an opening or handle.

I was in the dark and alone.

—•—

It was worse than waking up in the fourteenth century. It was worse than being stabbed in the gut. Being trapped in the dark and feeling the rough stone wall that had closed behind me was possibly the most frightening thing I'd experienced on my quest—possibly the most frightening event of my entire life.

"Let me the hell out of here!"

I banged on the door—or where the door had been. There was no answer to my shouts or my pounding on the walls.

My pulse was racing; I was breathing rapidly and shallowly.

"Great," I said to no one in particular. "Let's hyperventilate. I'm sure that'll help me get through this initiation." I sat down, leaning my back against the missing door. "It'll be like . . . passing out on the first day of work."

That made me laugh. I'd said that to myself when I was waking up in Santiago—when Rob first introduced me to the fourteenth century, before I knew I'd been sent back. And now here I was, scarcely able to breathe and my blood pressure going through the roof.

We'd done a location with *Ian and Jan* once several years ago—Jerusalem at Christmas. Part of the programme had included descending into the crypts and corridors under Temple Mount, where Christian sects tried to outpray and outsing each other. It took only a few minutes for me to find it difficult to talk, and then difficult to breathe—I had to get out of there.

I *could* say that it took every bit of my professional self-control to get through the segment. In truth, however, it took every bit of my professional self-control to avoid soiling and ruining a thousand-pound Armani suit. Getting out of the filming was no more than walking off the set and retreating to my trailer like the good self-absorbed telly star I was. Jan had to finish it off herself, with some additional work done in the studio to let me add my usual wit and sizzle. She got her revenge the following spring when I had to do the altitude shots at Christ the Redeemer in Rio—poor girl was terrified of heights.

"No celebrity trailer here," I said to myself, and laughed again. I got through that somehow. God knew how, but I was going to get through getting locked in the dark under a fourteenth-century cathedral too.

I thought I could make out the chants of Armenian monks from under Temple Mount as I squatted there in the dark. It was probably just the monks of Saint-Croix performing one of the night offices—or maybe it was just my imagination. Whatever the case, I couldn't find any escape back the way I'd come.

"I can't have come all this way to die in some damn crypt," I said to myself. My voice sounded small and frightened.

Small, I thought, after I'd said it.

When I'd been under Temple Mount my voice hadn't carried far: it was all tunnels and hewn corridors, duck your head here and mind your elbows there. But this was different: wherever I was, it was big.

I turned from the wall, standing straight, and stretched out my arms. "Hello," I tried. It didn't quite echo, but it seemed to carry for quite a distance.

There was no answer, but somewhere in the darkness I thought I could pick out a faint point of light. It seemed far away, a wavering little ball of fire—a will-o'-wisp, a distant torch.

"Hello," I repeated.

"Give the pass," I heard. The voice was familiar but I couldn't place it.

Pass? I thought. *What pass?*

I tried to remember where I'd heard the voice. I closed my eyes—it made it no more or less dark—and tried to concentrate on it. Where had I heard it before?

It has to be something memorable.

I remembered. It was a cold day in January or February—the wind was whipping through the camp. I was with a dozen others recently come to the company: four or five other Scots, a couple of Italians, a German, and some lads from Muscovy or Kiev or somewhere similar.

It has to be something memorable, the voice said. *Something most of them can pronounce, but not so simple anyone can figure it out. What about* . . . and there had been a long pause. *What about 'veritas'. Yes, that's it: make the password 'veritas'.*

Truth.

Truth conquers all, I thought.

"Veritas," I said, opening my eyes.

"That's right," the voice said. The point of light—clearly a torch—had come very close. "I was beginning to think you didn't remember."

Looming into view almost abruptly, a face came out of the dark, illuminated by flickering flame. The rest of the figure was dimly visible: he was dressed in fighting leathers, a sword belted at his side.

"Hello, Ian."

Lamont, said one part of my mind.

Lamontaigne, said the other.

"I thought you were dead," I managed after a moment. It applied to both men: one, my first producer at Channel 4, had been taken a few years back by cancer; the other, my mercenary commander when I'd fought in Spain, had had his gut carved open by a Saracen blade several months before I came to Santiago.

"You thought right," he answered, winking. "I am."

"Does that mean . . ."

"That you've crossed over to the great beyond?" He smiled. "Shuffled off the mortal coil? Started to feed the worms, to push up a few daisies—"

"I get the idea."

"No, you're quite alive." He pinched my arm—his fingers felt long and bony, but seemed to still be sheathed in flesh. "What would be the point of all this bit if you were dead?"

"I was wondering that myself."

"No point at all. None at all. Come along," he said, and began to walk away. I wasn't about to argue—or get far from his torch. I fell into step. "You seem surprised to see me, Ian."

"Well," I said, "You're dead. Both of you, I mean."

"Yes. And you're not. Old ground, Ian. We'd already figured that out. My God, it's a good thing you could fight—you sure as all hell are no tactician."

"Wait." I stopped walking. So did he. "So you're not just Captain Lamontaigne."

"I am, in part."

"And the other part . . ."

"Gerard Lamont, old boy." He held his torch up high—and I saw he was now dressed in the tweedy suit that Gerard had always favored. "I was the one who originally recognised your talents. Can't stay long though: must do what I came here to do, then . . ." he made walking motions with the fingers of his free hand. "Then back where I came."

"Back where you—"

"But enough about me." He lowered the torch a bit and looked off to his right, into the darkness. I looked there and saw nothing; when I turned my attention back to Lamont he was Lamontaigne again, the mercenary captain.

"So there are two of you."

"Not quite. There are two *echoes* of me. One here, and one in the time you came from. But both echoes are gone, except as they are remembered. Most people are echoes, no more . . . the background music of other people's lives."

I wasn't sure what to make of that comment. "Are there two of me as well?"

"That would be telling."

"Yes, damn it, it would be telling. Which one is the real me? The mercenary who fought with Wallace—who fought with you—or the TV talking head?"

Lamontaigne began to walk again; I walked with him.

"What do you think, Ian? The answer is, both are real. What

happened here, in this time, is what made it possible for you to be in both places, both times."

"And what happened is . . ."

There was a sound of distant music: a series of notes like a waterfall, a cascade descending from one phrase into another, then climbing to the top of my range of hearing so it could do it again. Then as I listened it was joined by another theme—slightly different, but completely compatible with the first.

It was a part, but only a part, of the music of Rosslyn. Standing in the darkness under Saint Croix Cathedral with a dead man, I felt tears come to my eyes.

"Polyphony," Gérard Lamontaigne said. "And the genius of one man, who captured something essential, something capable of creating echoes." He placed one hand on his chest, palm facing in—half the gesture I had seen in the second initiation. "He created it, and he wrote it down."

"De la Halle."

"That's the one." Lamontaigne stopped walking for a moment and turned to face me. "You must find his music, Ian, and bring it to the other part of yourself. It will be difficult, but it must be done—and only you can do it."

"How . . . how does this knowledge make me a Warrior?" I capitalized it as I spoke the word. "I thought I'd be given a sword or something. I assumed I'd be given some knowledge so I could go to war."

"Part of you has already learned that and gone past it. You learned it with Wallace and learned it with me. When I was killed you turned away from that life. What was it you said to Father Corvão? You'd lost yourself and didn't know how to find the broken pieces.

"The Warrior learns to tame the dragon: to achieve the inner wisdom, access to the Higher Self. This passage of arms is not for everyone. Many turn away, most do not understand."

"I haven't turned away. But I don't understand."

"But you will."

We began to walk again in silence. Finally we came to a blank wall; Gérard held his torch nearby. On it I could see symbols of some sort: they looked like Egyptian hieroglyphics.

Gérard Lamontaigne took a step forward and embraced me, placing one foot next to my feet, touching my knee to his, and placing one hand on my back while letting the other fall to his side. "This is the third initiation, Ian," he said quietly in my ear. "Venus governs this sphere. Serve mankind."

The torch went out suddenly, and Lamontaigne disappeared. I heard the sound of stone grating on stone, and a shaft of light appeared near where I stood, widening to the point at which I could step through.

At my feet was a small bundle of cloth. I knew what it was even before I knelt and picked it up: it was half a cloak, a twin to the one I already had except that the clasp-piece was on the other side.

The light was coming from the crypt room, where Brother William and Rob were standing by the stone font.

"Glad to see you, lad," was all Rob had to say as I emerged from the darkness into the light.

CHAPTER 8

THAT NIGHT I DREAMED OF THE *RECONQUISTA*.

Since arriving in the fourteenth century most of my memories of the mercenary soldier Ian Graham had come to me in flashes of vision or in dreams. After being wounded, and after my experience in Tours, I began to wonder whether he was real and my modern life was some sort of extraordinary work of imagination. After the third initiation I began to understand that *both* were real—for reasons I couldn't yet grasp.

The night after my underground encounter with Gérard Lamontaigne, I dreamed of my life as a soldier—full of blood and death—and awoke to a morning in which my memories and experience had begun to return to me. Awake again, I could see the two men far more clearly: they seemed to be two parts of the same man. There was more than that to the relationship, but I couldn't quite put my finger on it.

—•—

When we returned from Saint-Croix the previous night there had been no sign or word from Juan. In the morning Rob and I went to mass and came back to *Coquille* and still heard nothing. I could see that Rob was worried but was avoiding the subject.

Rob sat in the garden carving an apple into segments with the determination and effort of someone who wanted to keep his hands busy—as if he wanted to put them around Juan's neck but regrettably didn't have it available to wring. I did some exercises with my quarterstaff, but without a sparring partner gave it up and came to sit by Rob.

"I had wanted to leave for Chartres this morning, lad," he said. "I had half a mind to do it anyway."

"I'm glad you didn't. I want to know what's happened as well."

Rob set his knife aside and spread the segments of apple in his hand, offering them to me. I took a couple of them and tasted sweet summer left behind in the fruit: perfect, fresh, no preservatives or artificial colors.

"I've got a bad feeling in the pit of my stomach," he said. "I can't tell whether he's in trouble, or just making a terrible mistake."

"You mean the girl."

"He knew her, I think. That wasn't a chance encounter."

"Then why are you worried about it?"

"Light and fire, lad. Light and fire." Rob leaned back on the bench, arms crossed over his chest. "He knew very well that we were to be at the cathedral. He knew what we were here to do."

"You were going to lock him in the darkness as well?"

Rob stared straight ahead. "If you're looking for an apology, look elsewhere."

"I'm not. I don't expect that any more than I expect an explanation. I saw—"

"It's between you and—"

"I *saw*," I persisted, "two men that I knew very well. Except they weren't two men—they were echoes of the same man. Gérard Lamontaigne and Gerard Lamont. Do you know what they told me? That most people are echoes, background music for other people's lives."

"Hmm," Rob said, not really saying anything. He still stared ahead, refusing to look at me.

"It was as much as saying that most people aren't real. Are you real, Rob? Is this real? What about Juan—is he real, or is he out of the story now?"

"I don't know what you mean."

"Oh, I think you know very well." I wiped my hands on my robe. "I think you know what I'm trying to ask, and where I'm going with this. How much of this pilgrimage is about me alone?" *You sent me here—why?* I thought, and added aloud, "Why am I here?"

"This is a dangerous line of inquiry, Ian." He always called me by my name when he was being particularly serious. "You are undertaking this pilgrimage to find out who you really are, and I'm here to make sure that you don't get yourself killed doing it."

"Me."

"Yes."

"Not *Juan and me*. Me. You're not here to watch out for both of us—just for me. Juan can take care of himself—get himself killed, get involved with a girl, whatever—while I—"

Rob stood suddenly and turned to face me. "Are you accusing me of something? If so, you'd best get on with it."

I looked up at him. My mercenary persona was quickly evaluating whether I could take him down, and how I might do it; my broadcaster persona was trying to determine how this would play on the air.

Maybe there was a third persona that brought the two of them together: the one that was trying to understand what Rob was feeling, what he was thinking.

"I'm not accusing you of anything," I said quietly, trying not to impart any emotion into the statement. "But I believe that Juan was along for the ride. The Grand Master sent you to Santiago to meet me, not us. Isn't that right?"

The anger, if it had ever really been there, seemed to have drained out of him.

"Yes."

"Why?"

"You can . . . you can hear the music."

"You can't?"

Rob clenched his fists, but instead of answering turned away and walked across the garden to a corner where there was a little statue of the Virgin. He knelt, crossed himself, and folded his hands before him. I waited half a minute and then went over myself.

"You can't hear the music."

"No one can," Rob said without turning. "No one can other than you."

"What does it mean for me to able to hear the music?"

"Aye, that's the big question, isn't it, lad?" he said. He stood again, crossed himself, and turned to face me. "What it means hasn't been told to the likes of me—except that it's critically, vitally important. I was ordered to make sure you did what you needed to do.

"A king sends a hundred men to take a fortress. Fifteen of them are killed by archers as they cross the field. Twenty more die as they climb the walls. Twenty more are killed in the fighting in the courtyard. Thirty more meet their Maker as they go up the stairs. The rest take the keep.

"In the end, if the king orders the hundred to take the fortress and the fortress is taken, then the king is satisfied."

"And the death of eighty-five men makes it a Pyrrhic victory."

Rob frowned. He knew what I meant, even if he didn't recognise the reference; no classical education for this edition of Rob.

"If Juan doesn't make it, lad, but you do, the Grand Master is satisfied. If I don't make it, but you do, the Grand Master is satisfied."

"Because I can hear the damn music and no one else can."

He cringed when I said it, but I refused to look away.

"Because the Grand Master has said so," Rob said finally. "And that, lad, is what matters the most to me."

—•—

Juan came back after midday. He was accompanied by a kid, twelve or so years old. It took me a few minutes to realise why the boy looked familiar: he bore a strong resemblance to the woman that we'd seen Juan conversing with the previous day.

Rob met the two at the gate of the hostel and, without another word, took Juan aside and walked across the courtyard to the little refectory. I was left to stand with the young man, who stood nervously, watching Juan's back.

Years of television had trained me to deal with all kinds of people in the green room: I'd put babies, animals, and celebrities at ease before they went before the cameras. This was no different.

"Come and sit," I said, and walked into the garden. He followed me along and we found places on one of the benches.

I'm pleased to say that the personalities of boys aren't much different in that time than in this. He looked ill at ease, ready to bolt at any time, disinterested in the affairs of adults. He eyed me warily and kept glancing at the garden gate for Juan to return.

"You're her brother," I said. He looked surprised for a moment, and I added, "I saw her talking to Brother Juan yesterday. You have her smile."

He smiled more or less by reflex—which was the purpose of the remark. I watched his shoulders relax a bit under his homespun tunic.

"Jean—" he gave Juan's name the French rendering. "Jean said that the older Brother would be angry with him."

"I imagine so. He was expected last night."

"He did not want to go."

"So he hadn't just forgotten," I said. "But he didn't send word where he was."

"If he had," the boy said, "the older Brother would have come to fetch him back."

"What was he doing?"

The boy looked away, kicking his feet in the dirt. "He was with my sister."

"For someone he just met—"

"He didn't *just meet* Ysabeau, Monsieur. Frère," he corrected himself. "He has known her many years. Well, he has known of her."

This was interesting. "But Juan—Jean—" *How many damn names will I have to learn for this guy?* I thought. "He's from Asturias."

"Yes, Frère. But he and my brother Julien served in the wars together. The wars against the infidel."

My first reaction was to consider how little I knew about Juan—but my memories had largely returned, and I realised that I did know about him: we'd spent some time in Cintra and on the road to Santiago and he'd talked about himself. Juan was a dozen years younger than me; I always thought of him as more talented as a singer than as a fighter. By the time he reached Cintra he—like me—had left the bloody business behind and for largely the same reason: someone close to him had died.

Julien.

"There was a promise," I said, guessing.

"He told my brother that he would come to Orléans and look after us. He held him as he died and promised on Julien's blood and by the Blessed Virgin. He promised, Monsieur. Frère," he corrected himself again. There was emotion in his eyes. "He *promised.*"

This put an interesting twist on things. Rob had refused to speak about Juan and the girl—even the previous night when he tried, and failed, to conceal his disappointment that the Asturian hadn't come to Saint-Croix to undergo the third initiation. But this wasn't some dalliance, some kind of surrender to temptation.

"What is your name, young man?"

"Thierry, Frère."

"That is a good name," I said. "Thierry, are you the—" I groped for a word; I wanted to say 'breadwinner', but the language didn't have anything handy. "Responsible?"

"Since our father died," he answered. "Julien had gone to fight the infidel. He was hoping to bring back enough to pay his guild-price."

And died on some damn battlefield in Spain instead, I thought. Most mercenaries never brought home riches—and many, like Thierry's brother, never came home at all.

Had Juan joined the pilgrimage just so he could come back here? Had he deceived Rob all along only to leave the path of light at Orléans?

He'd never said anything of this promise to either of us. He'd never indicated anything other than a willingness to take on the vows of a Templar, to undergo the initiations. He was a natural: music was life to him—he'd said those exact words to me in León.

A brief strain of music came from over the garden wall. Someone was passing by in the street beyond; the tune was familiar—it was from *Robin et Marion.* It was the music of Rosslyn.

"Juan la Rosa is a very honorable man," I said at last.

But Juan la Rosa can't hear the music. That was the problem—it had to be. At Santiago and then at Toulouse, he had undergone the Templar initiations . . . and he hadn't heard the music. I had. I had passed the tests, and Juan had not. Instead of taking the direct route from some battlefield in Spain to Orléans, he'd joined the pilgrimage hoping to hear the healing music.

Rob and Juan chose that moment to step into the garden together. Thierry looked up when they appeared and sprang to his feet, but didn't go to join them. He looked back at me, perhaps expecting me to say something.

I looked away from Thierry and at Juan.

"Juan will not be coming with us to Chartres," Rob said.

"I know."

"You do?" Rob said curiously, then glanced at the young man next to me.

I stood up and put a hand on Thierry's shoulder. "I do."

Juan crossed the garden and took my hand, then grasped my shoulders. "Thierry told you," he said, glancing at the young man.

"No. I guessed. We should be in each other's place," I said as quietly as I could. "This should be your pilgrimage, not mine."

"I wanted that to be so." His eyes were full of regret—possibly with a tinge of anger. But it didn't seem directed at me.

"If you could have heard," I said, "would you have passed by? Would you have traveled all the way to the end of the path?"

"Yes. But I would have come back. I would have come back at the end. But . . . there's no point in continuing, Ian. You don't need me. You can take care of yourselves, you and Rob."

I wasn't sure how to respond.

He dropped his arms to his sides, and looked at Thierry. "Come on, Thierry," he said. "Your sister is expecting us."

For the second time I saw the young man smile. He gave me a little bow, a poor imitation of the proper one, but good enough for a Poor Knight. "Thank you, Frère," he said. "If I could have your blessing—"

I must have looked alarmed. Juan took my hand and guided it to Thierry's head. *Don't worry,* he mouthed to me and nodded.

"*Pax vobiscum,*" I managed. "The Lord be with you," I added, and took my hand away.

And with that, Juan and Thierry turned away and walked out of the garden, offering the briefest of good-byes to Rob as they went.

Rob stood in place for a long time after they left, saying nothing. I walked over to join him, not sure what to say myself.

"I can't save him, you know," he said at last.

"He's saved himself."

"No, lad, he hasn't." Rob turned to face me; I expected to see anger or resentment in his face—but all that seemed to be there was regret and, perhaps, fear. "No. He may have condemned himself to death."

"Why?"

"We can't stay here. Go get your gear together, lad; we have enough daylight to make some progress on the road." He began to turn away, but I caught his arm. He went to jerk it away, but I wouldn't let go.

"What do you mean when you say 'condemned himself to death'?"

"Nogaret," Rob whispered. "If they find him, Nogaret's men will kill him. If he's with us I can protect him—but if I leave he could be a dead man. All of them may be dead. I tried to tell him so, but there was the promise. If he was more of a sinner. . ."

"Or if he could hear the music."

"Yes." Rob disengaged his arm from my grasp. "There's that too. If he could have heard the music, he'd not give up the path of light. You asked me if people leave the path of light, and I told you yes, but most of them turn aside because of things of the world, because they are unworthy, because they do not or cannot fulfill the path's demands. I thought that was this. I was so . . . angry. I was disappointed and angry. May God forgive me."

"Juan has forgiven you, I expect."

"Yes," Rob answered. "Yes, he has. That will have to do." He turned away and walked out of the garden, leaving me alone with my thoughts.

—•—

Rob gave me the impression that we would be walking out the gate of the city in twenty minutes. Instead, we made our way back to the cathedral and spent the afternoon praying and watching the masons and carpenters work on the building.

If any task demanded faith in that era, it would be cathedral-building. We watched the masons work: there were no plans and the tools they had at their disposal were amazingly primitive.

I don't know what Rob must have thought—but I had a bit of an epiphany as I looked at the men directing the work: they would likely never see this work completed, if war, plague, and a dozen other things didn't stop it in its tracks.

Of course, they—and everyone around us—was seven centuries dust. Everyone except me.

Our scallop-shells and Templar emblems gave us leave to walk about; I felt very much like a tourist—except that no one was demanding an entrance fee or trying to sell me a souvenir. Most of the workmen and monks simply steered clear of us as we walked around the place.

"You're full of surprises, lad," Rob said after we'd been there most of an hour. "Know much about architecture?"

"Not my field," I answered. I almost added, *studied it in Art History,* but my fourteenth-century persona helped me hold my tongue.

Rob paused before continuing. "Certes, I knew it wasn't." He ran a finger along some delicate filigreed decoration at the side of one of the western entrance doors. It was all unfinished work; the artist had gone off to enjoy a bite to eat. The thing was going to look like a huge wedding cake when he was done. "You know, building a cathedral's a mighty complex business."

"Takes years, I've heard."

"They don't just build it up as they wish," Rob continued, a bit annoyed at my flip answer. "There's an order to it. Look at it all—the walls, the pillars, the ceilings. All the things they've carved and painted. Even the dimensions of the place have meaning."

I'd heard those words before—and I'd heard them from Rob Madson's mouth at Rosslyn. Having him repeat them now made me wonder again.

Even the dimensions of the place have meaning.

For the last six or seven weeks I'd become convinced that this wasn't the Rob Madson I'd met at Rosslyn: this man, my guide and mentor—who had put my hand on the Tree of Jesse, who had brought me to the Dalbade in Toulouse, and who had most recently allowed me to be shut in the darkness under this very cathedral—wasn't the man I'd met at the little chapel outside of Edinburgh the last time I'd laid my eyes on the twenty-first century. This was his time: this was his place. He'd never heard of Rosslyn, never watched *Ian and Jan* . . .

"Do you need some air, lad?"

"Tell me about the dimensions," I said.

"The Lord has imposed a symmetry and order to all things," he answered. "All through history, civilised man has sought to imitate it. The greatest of God's houses—like this one, or like this one will be when it's finished—achieve that through a study of what's called *la langue verte.*"

"The 'green language'?"

"That's right. The language of sacred geometry. It existed before the time of our Saviour—and it is part of the secret knowledge of the builders of cathedrals. And, incidentally," he added, as we walked slowly back into the ambulatory, "it is part of the inner wisdom of the Poor Knights of Christ: a part of our treasure."

"Everything I've heard about the treasure of the order is, well, gold and jewels."

"The Lord knows there's enough of that. It turned the head of His Majesty when he took refuge in the Paris Asylum a hand of years ago—but the greatest of our treasures can't be carried away by his unlettered marauders."

"The treasure of the Templars is knowledge. The . . . what this pilgrimage has been about."

"That's right. The rest of it is earthly dross. You can clip coins, you can sell the jewels. But this is more than that."

Rob sighed. We were alone in the ambulatory; just the two of us and a large, impressive statue of Saint James; the old boy was dressed like a Orléanais burgher, his stylish bonnet adorned with the scallop-shell of Santiago, his eyes looking off into the far distance.

"Our greatest treasure," Rob said, bowing slightly toward James, "the one we brought back with us from the Holy Land, is something *le roi* Philip cannot have. It's *knowledge,* lad. You're receiving some of that yourself—with each initiation you gain more of it."

"Die Gedanken sind frei," I said. I could hear Pete Seeger's voice in my head—he'd sung it on *Ian and Jan* one afternoon. He'd done it very well.

"Aye, that's right," Rob agreed. "You really are full of surprises, aren't you? That sounds a bit like the German, though I couldn't quite make it out."

"So the Order knows how to build cathedrals," I said, trying to get us back to the original subject.

"More importantly, we know how to read what's written in stone. It teaches us about the dual nature of things: seen and unseen, light and dark, good and evil. Our entire Order is based on that: after all, aren't we men of war fighting in the cause of the Prince of Peace?"

"Is it why I saw two men—" I stamped lightly with my boot.

"I don't know why you saw what you saw," Rob answered. "I told you before, that's between you and God. But the Warrior, one who has passed through the third initiation, has learned to transform the toil of this world into the toil of the spirit."

" 'Serve mankind.' "

"That's right, lad. That's absolutely right. Our enemy, the one who's shadowing us, doesn't serve mankind: he serves one man. That one man. . ." He lowered his voice and ran his hand across a delicate pattern of *fleurs-de-lys* on Saint James' tunic sleeve.

"Rob," I said, "why are we still here in Orléans? If he—if his servants—are shadowing us, why haven't we left for Chartres?"

"Tonight," he said very quietly. A pair of canons had just passed under an arch into the ambulatory, on their way toward the chapter-house. They nodded to us, and crossed themselves as they passed the statue of Saint James.

"I thought they shut the gates at sunset."

"They do. But there are ways and ways. Scots are a very resourceful people. And as Juan told us, we two can take care of ourselves."

"Won't we be followed?"

"To be completely honest, lad, I hope we are. The alternative is that Monsieur's agents go after Juan and his adopted family. If they follow us, we will do what must be done. I don't think you'll be caught on your heels this time," he added, poking me in the chest. "I hope to God not—I don't think I could carry you all the way to Chartres alone."

"I'm ready."

"I know you are, lad. I know you are. And so am I."

Without another word, he turned on his heel and walked into the sanctuary of Saint-Croix. After a moment I followed.

CHAPTER 9

THEY CAME AFTER US.

The brother at Saint-Croix, William MacLeod, had resources I didn't expect—but evidently Rob did. In near darkness—the mostly-full moon had already set—we made our way through Orléans' deserted streets to a postern gate on the north wall. After an exchange of signs that it was too dark for me to see we were let through a low door. A short flight of narrow stairs brought us into a narrow tunnel. If I hadn't spent some of the previous night in Saint-Croix' crypt the closeness of the tunnel would have bothered me—instead it was no more than an uncomfortable passage: darkness into deeper darkness into a clear starlit night on a little hill overlooking the king's high road.

They say that those that travel roads by night court trouble as a matter of course. As Rob had said, we wanted the villains to follow us: better we had some bullies sent by Nogaret than they went after Juan, left to protect a young woman and her kid brother. Thierry came to mind as we stood for a moment on that hill, getting our bearings: he was the sort of young man that would play a hero and become a victim. As for the two of us, I suppose we were courting trouble—but I think Rob expected it on the pilgrimage. We just assumed that we could handle it.

—•—

Two hours' walk north of Orléans we were resting off the road in a thicket. With no moon there was only starlight—and with no light pollution from cities the sky was brimming with stars. The high grass to either side of the road rippled in the breeze, minor shadows chasing themselves over the fields. The night was still but that quiet was abruptly interrupted by the sound of horses' hooves approaching from the south. We kept down, out of sight of the road.

"You much of a tree-climber, lad?" Rob whispered to me.

I must have looked bewildered and didn't answer immediately. He shrugged.

"All right then," he said after a moment. "It'll have to be me." With a gesture for me to keep down and out of sight he crept forward to a large, low-limbed tree, hiked his robe around his knees, and began to climb from branch to branch.

I crouched in the underbrush and watched, one eye on Rob's receding form and the other on the road. The noise of horses was getting steadily louder. I couldn't see anything from the ground, but evidently Rob had a good vantage point, as he shortly stopped climbing.

Finally the riders came into view. Six well-armed men, star-dappled shadows, reined in their horses in a clearing twenty paces from where I hid. They had their swords sheathed and their bows stowed. It took the soldier part of me less than ten seconds to realise that if they were bent on killing us, we were likely dead—we were outnumbered and opposed by mounted men in armour. As a twenty-first century man, I wondered for the millionth time what the hell I was doing there.

They didn't appear to see either of us, or at least weren't letting on. While three remained on horseback three others dismounted. One of them drew out flint and tinder and in short order had lit a torch; another of the three pulled a scroll-tube from a saddlebag and opened out a chart of some sort—I guessed it was a map.

"I'm sure they must have come this way, my lord," he said to the leader.

"Could they have come this far?" the lord asked. He drew off his tall sugarloaf helmet and hung it from the saddlebow. He seemed very sure of himself: even in nothing but starlight, a good archer would have no problem dropping him. He swept his mailed, gauntleted hand in a circle, then tapped a finger on the map spread out on the saddle. "They could be anywhere. They could even be hiding nearby."

"Cowards," one of the others said, raising his helmet visor.

The lord whirled at the voice. "Mind your tongue, varlet," he said angrily. "They are *Templars*. Whatever crimes their order has committed, His Holiness—and our Master—has not condemned them yet."

"Surely a matter of time, my Lord," the mounted man answered, his voice sardonic. "But I beg your pardon if I have offended."

The lord waited another moment before turning his attention back to the man with the map. Whatever he saw there, he wasn't satisfied; he turned away again and began to pace back and forth. At one point he stopped and looked straight across at my hiding place: I held my breath until he looked away.

"Lodestone," he said, without looking back.

The other man rolled up the map and tucked it under his arm. He reached into a saddlebag and drew out a small pouch of dark cloth. He placed it into the lord's outstretched hand, then laid the map back out across the saddle.

The lord removed his mail gauntlets, handing them to one of the other mounted men. He undid the lacing on the pouch and drew out an ovoid stone the size of his thumb, suspended on a metal chain. The lodestone was night-dark: it looked like the jet I'd seen at the Paraiso marketplace at Santiago. It was so black that it seemed to swallow all light. I felt a chill run down my back but couldn't look away.

Cupping the stone in one hand and holding the chain with the other, he carefully moved his hand over the map and then let go of the stone—which began to spin free and then swing slowly back and forth.

"What—" began the mounted man who had spoken before, but the man who held down the map hissed and the speaker fell silent.

I began to be aware of a very slight humming, like the sound of a distant lawn mower. If I was chilled before, this seemed to somehow make it worse. A small part of me wanted to leap out of my hiding place and charge at the six armed men—but fortunately the majority of me decided to stay put.

The wind continued to gust. The lodestone continued to swing.

And Rob and I continued to hide. I didn't even dare look into the darkness above me to see Rob in his hiding place up in the tree—it might have drawn attention, though I'm not sure how.

Finally, after what seemed like an hour, the lord scooped the lodestone into his hand and dropped it into the pouch with a curse. At the same moment the distant humming abruptly cut off. With one more scathing look around the area, he mounted his horse and accepted the gauntlets from his companion. He tugged his coif into place and then pulled his helmet onto his head.

The other two mounted, after grounding the torch, cloaking the clearing in darkness once again. The entire procession then kicked into motion and rode quickly back toward Orléans.

I remained quietly in my place until well after the sound of horse hooves receded in the distance. A few minutes later I heard rustling nearby.

"They missed us, lad," Rob said quietly. "God knows how, but they missed us."

"What was that all about? The lodestone and all?"

"He was dowsing. Looking for a disturbance in the earth-path."

"Why didn't they just look for our footprints?"

"Without even a moon to go by, they'd have a tough time. As

for the earth-path . . . well, he should have been able to detect us by using the lodestone."

"This is all beyond me."

"Yes, it is, isn't it?" I could hear him smile in the dark. "It's not easy to explain. Guilbert—oh, that was Guilbert de Bec; he's one of Nogaret's hounds—Guilbert is aware of our destination. As we walk the path of light . . . as *you* walk the path of light . . . the path is altered. Our footsteps show there, even in nothing but starlight."

"He can find us with a lodestone and a map. In the middle of the night in the middle of France."

"Well, lad," Rob answered, grasping me gently by the forearm, "he should be able to. But it seems that he can't."

—•—

And so without our pursuers we continued on toward Chartres: fifty miles or so from Orléans, likely to be almost three days' walk—even if we went partly by night, we'd not come within the city gates until Saturday, the eighth of September.

Even without pursuit—a fact I was willing to accept but couldn't quite believe—I didn't think we had reason to celebrate. I'd gotten the distinct impression, probably quite accurate, that Monsieur's spies and agents were everywhere and that they'd find us soon enough; it was only a matter of time.

As the sun poked above the horizon the following morning we found ourselves a place to shelter in what had been at one time a hermit's cottage—it had evidently once been deep in a thick wood, but the trees that hadn't been cut down outright had been victimised by fire. The stone structure was a half-ruined thing surrounded by tree stumps and underbrush, but with no foul weather it did us well enough for a place to sleep.

Rob offered to watch while I slept but he was plainly bone tired; he had no sooner offered a brief prayer for his own soul than he was fast asleep, leaving me to sit on the sad remains of a stone bench that gave a good view of the high road. I waited for the sound of hooves, but other than a few drovers with big, slow-lumbering wagons, there was hardly any traffic at all. When the sun had climbed most of the way toward its zenith I woke Rob and settled down myself, but found it more difficult to rest.

"Get your sleep while you can, lad," Rob said, making a small meal of some dried fruit and a hunk of bread that was a day old when Brother William gave it to us the previous night. "That's the maxim—'when in doubt, eat. If there is nothing to eat, sleep.' Since you said you weren't hungry, you should be applying the second part of the rule."

"I know that," I said, yawning. "But I can't stop thinking about that Guilbert de Bec fellow and his lodestone. What could it mean that he couldn't detect us?"

"Hmm." He tore another hunk from the bread and chewed it. "That's a mighty good question. Either he's not as good as I thought he was, which seems unlikely, or else we're getting some help in concealing our tracks. Which also seems unlikely. This is . . . the part of the path where we'd be most noticeable, climbing the hill to Chartres."

"Hill?"

"Figure of speech," he said, almost too quickly for me to accept it. "The cathedral is built on a hill, so we say that we're climbing that hill when we go from the third to the fourth initiation. This is the midpoint of the journey, the highest point, you might say."

"All downhill after that?"

"Hmm." Another bit of bread met its end. I was joking, following along with his figure of speech, but he ignored it and continued. "From Chartres we go on to Paris, and then finally to Amiens. But if ever there was a test on the path of light, it would be at Chartres. Especially for you."

"Why especially for me?" I asked, yawning. It was clear to me that Rob was ready to provide me some information, but huddled up under the two cloak-halves with the sun practically at noon I was warm and sleepy.

"Because of the music, lad. Chartres is . . . like a musical instrument. It was designed that way, to amplify and focus the music of the spheres."

"As in the planets. The things that govern the spheres of the initiations."

"So you *have* been paying attention." Rob leaned back against the wall of the cottage, toying with a blade of tall grass that had grown through cracks in the foundation. "When the master architects rebuilt Chartres Cathedral after the fire a century ago, they replaced the old style with a new one—a Gothic one. The vaults reach toward heaven, but their size and shape echo the crypts below.

"The earth-path leads us there, but the paths of all four elements cross on that hill: the air-path in the arches of the ceilings; the water-path in the Well of the Strong in the crypt; and the fire-path, which touched the church decades ago. If there is a single, most critical destination for us, lad, it's Chartres: the great instrument that resonates in harmony with the Lord Himself." He crossed himself; I was too tired to follow suit.

My eyes were drifting shut; my reporter persona was shouting, *stay awake, damn it! Pay attention—he's never been so clear before.*

"This is a place for the eyes and the ears—but it is for your heart to discover," I heard from seemingly far away. "It is the opening way to the Abode of Mercy."

"Abode of Mercy," I repeated. The words had come adrift in my mind, like three pieces of wood floating lazily in a river, caught by currents and eddies and now each on its own mission.

"Time to rest, Ian," he said. "We'll make it there all right."

In the quiet that followed I drifted off to sleep, while some part of my mind struggled to keep awake and the rest bemusedly wondered why.

—•—

I was unprepared for the sights that greeted me when I reached the city. I don't know if Rob just wanted to watch my face when I got my first look, or if he didn't know what to expect himself—but my first look at the *cloître de Notre-Dame* looking up the Rue de l'Hôtel-Dieu—what I could see of it—was of a row of covered booths crowding the street, each holding a table covered with wooden and metal souvenirs. Tiny lead models of the cathedral, Our Lady of Chartres, and something that looked like a folded cloth were the most popular. The vendors were doing a very brisk business.

"Well," Rob said as we tried to make our way through the crowds that prevented us from reaching the cathedral close.

"Is it like this all the time?"

"No," he said. *"Septembresce,"* he added, as if that explained it. We came clear for a minute at a place where the narrow alley widened at a dogleg.

"Which is . . ."

"This is the centre of the world as far as veneration of Our Lady is concerned," he explained. "The city is packed at each of Her feasts—and today is *Septembresce,* the Nativity of the Virgin. I'd lost track. Today and tomorrow the cathedral will be jammed."

"How does that affect the—our business here?"

"It depends. If the city is very crowded, there'll be people sleeping everywhere—even in the crypt—during the feast. We may have to wait a few days."

"Monsieur will certainly catch up with us if we have to wait."

"Yes." Rob frowned and squinted at the clouded sky peeking between the buildings above, where the second and third floors extended out over the street as if they were reaching toward each other. "Still, he knew we would be coming here—hopefully he won't be able to prevent us from getting our 'business' accomplished."

"How would he prevent it?"

Rob didn't answer that question, instead shouldering his pack and leaving me no alternative but to follow.

—•—

The *place* directly before the cathedral was no better. We finally made our way out of the *rue* and into the open area, but it was a warren of tables and booths, selling everything from food to dry goods to more *souvenirs de Notre-Dame.* All that was missing for my twenty-first century eye was the colour accordion-fold postcards and ice cream sundries.

I had read Poe. For Rob that writer was still hundreds of years in the future—assuming that my guide wasn't the same man who had met me in Rosslyn in my previous future lifetime—but Rob still understood the concept of concealment in plain sight. Whatever the importance of my pilgrimage, or the music only I seemed to be able to hear, in Chartres at *Septembresce* we were just two more pilgrims.

"We should at least be able to get through this undisturbed," I said as we watched the crowd swirling through the square in front of us.

"I wish that were true, lad."

"We're just two more pilgrims, Rob—two more people coming to see the tunic of the Virgin."

"I'm afraid not," he said. "Our shadow is back. I'm not sure if he's made us out yet, but they're watching for us." He gestured toward the north porch, a staircase of several wide, gradual steps that led up to a three-arched entryway full of statues and bas-reliefs on the tympana. It was crowded, but only a few people were under the overhang on this unseasonably warm and humid September afternoon.

"Which one?"

"Two, actually. There—" He pointed at the central arch, where two men stood scanning the crowd below. They were dressed as pilgrims: stout staffs and simple clothes. "Look familiar?"

I recognised the face of one: he had called us cowards, out on the road from Orléans. The other was probably one of the ones who had been with him. But their master, the man with the lodestone, was nowhere to be seen.

I earned myself a few Hail Marys for my next comment, at which Rob nodded.

"Aye," he said. "They assumed they'd lost us. I'd guess that they rode here and arrived ahead of us. The only advantage we have now is that they're not sure we've gotten here ourselves."

"They're bound to find out."

"Sooner or later, that's true," Rob answered. "And my lord de Bec is probably in the city. I would guess he's having the Templar priory watched as well. It would not surprise me if all of his helping hands are here in Chartres, ready to bid us welcome."

"What is he going to do? Is de Bec going to try and interrupt the . . . the proceedings?" After mystery Rob, mystery Juan and mystery Gerard Lamont, I couldn't even imagine who would come to have a chat with me here—so I had no idea what the 'proceedings' might actually consist of.

"I can't say." Rob squinted at the two henchmen. One began descending the steps, headed for the alley from which we'd emerged; the other leaned back against some unknown saint or patriarch, keeping his eyes on those who came up the steps to the church. "But I think we're going to have to find out."

—•—

Rob waited until the second man was well clear of the square around the cathedral before beginning to make his way through the open-air market around the north portal. Chartres textiles were well-enough known that my fourteenth-century self had heard of them down in Spain where they were worn by the wealthy and high-born; here in Chartres, on the feast of the Virgin's birth, vendors competed with each other for our attention—even though we didn't look like their best potential customer.

A few fragments of the ells of cloth being measured against merchants' arms that afternoon would be preserved behind glass in my time, relics of this age, their bright color and soft texture long gone . . . like everyone and almost everything that caught my gaze that afternoon.

"No time for daydreaming, lad." Rob's voice interrupted my reverie: heedless of the situation, forgetting the danger, I'd stopped in the middle of the open-air market, caught by the scene.

I looked at my companion and past him to the top step of the porch, where de Bec's remaining henchman leaned against a round pillar, hat pulled down against the hazy afternoon sun, but watching all the same.

"I'm sorry. I . . ."

"He hasn't seen us yet, but he will," Rob said. "We have to give him the sense that we don't know who he is. Think you can play the fool for a bit?" he added, smiling.

"With you as my teacher, I think I can," I answered. He reached out to cuff me, but I caught his hand in a two-handed grasp. "What do you have in mind?"

"There's no way to avoid being seen: so we'd best make it work to our advantage. We want him to follow us, see where we go."

"And?"

"And Chartres Cathedral's a big place, lad. Easy place to go missing." He let go of my hands and twisted his left fist into his right palm.

"Won't he just go tell his master that he's seen us?"

"That's small beer. Now if he can bring de Bec—or even Monsieur—knowledge of what we're actually doing here, that'll earn him the leg o'mutton to go with it. This one wants to be the right-hand man—they all do. The more he comes back with, the better."

"What if you're wrong? You've given away that we're here."

"We have that. But as I told you afore, they'll know soon or late. So unless you've got any better notions, let's make our move."

I nodded. We began to make our way through the tables filled with bolts of cloth and between the shouting, sweating hawkers that wanted to sell them to us.

We came to the base of the steps. Our shadow marked us right away, trailing us at a distance as we made our way under the central arch, where a multitude of characters watched as we passed beneath, and into the west end of the great cathedral.

We'd been in a fair number of great churches by this time in my adventure. From Santiago to León to Roncesvalles; St

Pied-de-Port and Saint-Sernin and la Dalbade in Toulouse; Saint-Eutrope, where I recovered from my wound; Tours and then Orléans. As we traveled, particularly when Juan was still with us, we'd bowed our heads in a number of other sanctuaries. But Chartres was different.

As a good television reporter telling a cracking good story, I'd like to have walked into the enormous vaulted nave of Notre-Dame-de-Chartres and have been overwhelmed by the presence, the *numinousness* of the placc. Instead, the first impression I got of it was of something like the Grassmarket in Edinburgh—transported inside a huge cathedral.

"More of *Septembresce?*" I asked Rob. "Is this a special feature, that folk get to bring the market into the church?"

"Actually, yes," he answered. "For a small donation, the most well-behaved get to set up their stalls in the nave itself. No one selling animal carcasses, but lead models of the Blessed Virgin are just the thing."

"Better class of customer?"

"No, not just." He took a look around the nave, where the tables seemed primed for someone to come along and turn them over. "It's more basic than that. In here *Monsieur le Comte* can't levy a tax—so those pious souls that contribute have no need to share their well-earned profits with him."

"A duty-free zone," I said and got the usual curious look from Rob. After a few moments, he cast a casual look back toward the west portal—I could see that he was noting the location of our pursuer.

"Let's find a quiet place to pray," he said finally. We made our way up the north aisle. As we walked through the third bay I looked aside to see the labyrinth in the nave floor: a pattern made up of a few hundred white stones. None of the vendors had dared set up his booth atop it, so it formed a sort of oasis in the middle of the crowded church. Two people—a man and a woman—were slowly walking along it, their hands folded, eyes cast downward.

Somewhere I could hear organ music playing—it went on a

minute or so at a time and then it halted, as if the musician was practising or improvising.

At the east end of the cathedral, the choir was encircled by a huge vaulted corridor—the ambulatory—that permitted pilgrims to venerate the relics without getting in the way of the choir or the celebrants. We crossed the transept and entered the ambulatory on the north side. Rob seemed to have a destination in mind: the first chapel alcove, where three sublime stained-glass windows admitted soft afternoon light.

We bowed our heads and crossed ourselves, then knelt on two of several unadorned hassocks that appeared to be set out for *Septembresce* pilgrims.

"Saint Thomas. The doubter." Rob folded his hands on the back of the wooden *prie-dieu* and gestured toward the left-hand window. "Maybe you'll find yourself trusting in the Lord, lad." In a quiet whisper he added, "Let's see if our shadow decides to take a closer look."

I nodded and folded my hands in prayer as well.

As I knelt there in the relative quiet, the hubbub of the tradesmen sounding distant, I felt my mind wander. It reminded me a bit of my vigil at Tours, where I'd talked to—or dreamt of talking to—Father Corvão; but no visions came, no mysterious visitors: just the background sound, the faint organ music in the distance, and the palpable tension from Rob a few paces away, ready for something.

Good Templar initiate and mercenary soldier that I was, I should have been ready for action as well . . . but instead, the wear and tear and stress of the last few days' journey seemed to catch up with me.

With the late afternoon sun filtering blue and ethereal through the tale of Saint Thomas, I drifted off to sleep.

—•—

Every Thursday afternoon during my first two years as an undergraduate, I left my last class at the Edinburgh College of Art and made my way across North Bridge to Princes Street, then went down almost to Jenners and walked two blocks further to Gran's tidy, crowded apartment. It was a ritual: Grandmother MacPherson—my mum's mum—had been a part of my life from the time I was old enough to notice, and I'd been told that it was my duty to pay court to her since I was so close.

So off I'd go. No time for a pint or a game of darts; a few hours' library time would be given over in favour of tea with Gran. Along with refreshment I'd receive the obligatory lecture on my character failings and the extent to which I'd disappointed her . . . and in the background there'd be music.

—•—

"Right on time, I see." Gran opened the door and let me in. "The kettle's on; hang up your coat, young man, and help yourself to biscuits." She pecked me on the cheek and bustled out of sight into the kitchen.

I did as I was bid. The little alcove was warm and comfortable—it was beastly weather outside—and I took my usual chair. Music was playing in the sitting room: soft organ and a women's chorus in French.

"I don't think I've heard this one," I said, reaching for a packet of cigarettes and then thinking better of it—Gran didn't abide smoking in her apartment.

"What's that?" she said, coming in with the teapot, hidden under a cosy shaped like a swan, a gift from some enterprising grandchild.

"I said that I don't think I know this piece of music."

"I'm not surprised," she said, setting the teapot down on a coaster. She brushed a few crumbs of biscuit away from my place setting and into her outstretched hand, dropping them into a small wastebasket. Then she settled into her own chair. "No one listens to it anymore."

She fell silent. The recording had cracks and pops—Gran was a Luddite: no CD player for her, oh no: nothing would replace her reliable record player.

"What is it?"

"Poulenc. *Litanies de la Vierge Noire.*"

"Poulenc." I didn't know who he was—some Frenchman, probably a contemporary of Satie, someone I knew she liked. "Church music."

"Yes," she said, as if it was obvious. "He had a great tragedy in his life, Poulenc did, and he turned back to the faith of his childhood. He wrote this about a famous virgin."

"The Virgin Mary."

"Yes, of course the Virgin Mary."

I smiled. "Sounds a bit Popish, Gran." She'd spent all of my youth complaining about Catholics—she didn't even care for Bonnie Prince Charlie. I expected her to unload on me; after several months of this ritual, I knew I'd have disapproval served with tea and biscuits anyway, so at least I'd have a chance to enjoy it.

"It's beautiful music, Wee Ian. Just because they're singing about the one they believe to be the Mother of God doesn't take that away. The lyrics don't really matter: it's the music that matters."

She poured tea into each of our cups. I hated that nickname; my Dad was named Ian, and though I had thirty centimetres on him, I was 'Wee Ian' and he was 'Big Ian', and God help anyone who didn't abide by that naming.

The music came to an end; she stood, wiping her hands on the tea-towel, and disappeared into the other room to put on the next record.

"I don't know what they teach you at that school," she continued a minute later. The Poulenc piece came back on; she'd evidently decided that I needed to hear it from the beginning. "It's true that Catholics get a frightful amount of rubbish between themselves and the Lord God—all the genuflecting, transsubstantiating, the relics and pilgrimages and all that nonsense. But in the end they do glorify God, and that's what's important." She sat down at the table again, adding milk and sugar to her tea.

"I suppose."

"You don't believe it." She sipped the tea, looking over the cup at me.

"People approach God in different ways, Gran. I assume that Catholics keep all of the trappings because it helps them do just that."

"It's not how you were brought up. They don't speak of such things at St Giles'—and they don't play Poulenc there either."

"I imagine it would be scandalous. Sounds like fun."

"You don't believe in *anything,* do you?" she asked me, then stood and took me gently by the elbow, leading me into the sitting room. The music swelled: the organ, the women's voices in harmony. *La Vierge Noire*: the Black Virgin.

"I—" I began.

"All over northern France," she said quietly. "They're in churches all over. Statues of Mary, some with the Christ Child and some not: black virgins. Except they're not really Mary: they're older than that—they're the earth mother.

"They call her *virgini parituriae,* Wee Ian. The virgin about to give birth. The Catholics took her over from the Romans—and before that, the Celts. They took her over from us."

The simple harmony of the music seemed to wash over me. Gran shook my elbow. "Listen," she said. "Listen carefully."

—•—

"Ian. Wake up."

Rob was shaking my elbow. The music rushed into my consciousness: improvisation, someone adjusting and evolving a tune—except that the tune was from *Litanies de la Vierge Noire.*

It was the fourteenth bloody century again. Someone was playing Poulenc on the organ at Chartres Cathedral—six hundred and fifty years early.

"Rob, is there a statue of the Virgin here—a dark-coloured one? A black virgin?"

He looked at me curiously: not as if I'd said something out of character or out of period, but rather as if I knew something he hadn't expected me to know.

"La Vierge sous-Terre," he said. "The Virgin beneath the Earth. It's in the crypt, next to the Well of the Strong."

All over northern France, Gran had said. Including Chartres.

"I've heard that music before," I said.

"Oh?"

"Let's find that organ." I stood up. Rob got up quickly as well; I turned away from the chapel and walked back toward the nave, the music—and the distant echo of Gran MacPherson's voice—ringing in my ears.

CHAPTER 10

Before my experience as a Templar, I always thought of myself as a fairly deliberate sort. My career had been based on making reasoned decisions and rarely letting myself do anything impulsive. When I *was* impulsive, it was a whopper: I slept with Jan for six years and destroyed my marriage, but that was probably bound to happen anyway. But during my pilgrimage in 1307 there was nothing but impulse.

I'm not sure there was any other way for me to proceed—I had to trust what I saw and how I felt, and act accordingly.

—•—

Without considering the possibility that I was leading us into a trap, I walked out of the ambulatory with Rob at my heels. On the corner formed by the nave and the south transept, I could see the organ sitting on a carved wooden table. A young acolyte was working a set of bellows behind, while an older, heavy-set monk was playing the device, moving his hands across the keyboard to produce the snatches of music I'd been hearing. He tapped one of his sandalled feet to keep time; the thing didn't seem to have any pedals.

I'm not sure what I would have done if I'd seen a pair of heavily-muscled, bearded Templars bearing down on me—but the organ player seemed to remain completely calm, continuing to work the various themes of the *Litanies* as we walked across the transept crossing. We paused only briefly to bow and offer a genuflection to the high altar as we passed.

As we came up to stand beside him, he made a gesture to the sweating lad plying the bellows, who grinned and dashed off; they'd evidently been at it for a while. The monk turned on his backless stool to face us, wiping his palms on his robe. The last bit of the air passing through the organ gave off the sound of a dying goose before it fell silent.

"Brothers," he said in French, but his accent was clearly not native.

"I—was listening to you play, Brother—"

"Francis." He smiled. "Yes, it's a beautiful instrument, isn't it?" He looked around him, gazing up at the vaulted ceiling and then back at us, not sparing a glance at his organ.

"New organ," Rob said. "They used to have a portative, I think."

"That's right," Brother Francis answered. "It's the gift of a wealthy benefactor." He ran one hand slowly along the edge of the keyboard. "His Grace the Bishop asked leave of my abbot to have me come here to play for services—I was just . . . trying it out. I hope I didn't disturb you."

"Not in the least," I managed. "Where have you come from?"

"St Peter's in Derby. In England. I'm a long way from home—but I feel that I belong here."

You think you're *far from home,* I thought. "I was listening to you play. The piece sounded very familiar."

"It's just something I'm working on—for the choir. It's intended to be an homage to the Blessed Virgin—Our Lady beneath the Earth."

Rob nodded. "We've not gone below to the crypt yet, Brother—we only arrived this afternoon."

"I'd like to hear it again," I said.

"I sent my assistant off to refresh his thirst, I'm afraid—"

"I'll work the bellows," Rob interrupted, glancing at me,

clearly interested in where this might be going. "My friend here has an ear for music, and I'd like to indulge him."

"You're certainly in the right place for it," Francis said. "Chartres Cathedral is the most perfect setting for music I've ever been blessed to visit." He turned to face the keyboard as Rob walked to the back, pulled his sleeves up on his arms, and prepared to pump the massive bellows set on the table behind the organ.

Then Brother Francis began to play.

I closed my eyes and listened. There at the centre of Chartres Cathedral . . . the centre of France, the centre of the world, the middle of my quest atop the hill, I heard the music of François Poulenc played on a primitive organ with no chorus of female voices to accompany it.

I don't know how long Francis played and Rob pumped the bellows. I'm not sure whether our pursuer was in plain sight or hidden, or really much of anything that might have happened in the next few minutes. Guillaume de Nogaret, Guilbert de Bec and King Philip the Fair could have walked up to me and clapped me in irons, kicked me in the balls or presented me with the *Croix de Guerre*—all highly unlikely—and I would not have noticed.

I know I felt tears in my eyes—maybe it was thinking about Gran, or about Liz, or about being so far from home; and maybe it was just the music.

Listen, Gran MacPherson had said, her small hand on my elbow. *Listen carefully.*

—•—

See with new eyes.

Hear with new ears.

I opened my eyes, listening.

It was as if I was wearing the noise-canceling earphones we used in studio: I could see clearly enough, but there was no sound other than the music from Francis' organ. In this strange setting, it also seemed as if everyone in the cathedral had stopped whatever they were doing to look directly at me.

To accompany the music that rose from Francis' organ and was amplified, focused and made to surround me, I began to hear voices—the women's chorus, just like the one on Gran's phonograph record. I tried to make out the words: French lyrics, written by Poulenc that, like the tune they accompanied, wasn't to be written for more than six hundred years—but it wasn't French at all—it was Latin.

Creatori serviunt omnia subjecta, the chorus sang, and then a few more phrases. I strained to hear them as they repeated.

> *Creatori serviunt omnia subjecta,*
> *sub mensura, numero, pondere perfecta.*
> *Ad invisibilia, per haec intellecta,*
> *sursum trahit hominem ratio directa.*

I must have spoken the words aloud as I heard them, for suddenly the spell was broken—Francis left off his playing, and Rob let go the bellows.

Things resumed their normal course as suddenly as they had stopped.

"Your friend knows poetry as well as music," Francis said to Rob, looking from one of us to the other.

"Ian is full of surprises," Rob answered, curving an eyebrow at me. "I never know what will happen next with him. We're here as a part of the pilgrimage," he added.

"I see."

"I can't say as I know that much poetry, Brother," I said to Francis. "Did I . . ."

Francis rose from his seat before the organ and beckoned us to follow. We crossed the nave again, offering honours to the high altar as we passed, then turned right into the north entrance to the ambulatory—almost as if we were retracing our steps to the chapel where we'd prayed. Rob and I could both see de Bec's man now, watching us as he appeared to be haggling with a tradesman near the labyrinth on the floor of the nave; I wondered if he'd sent word to his confederate, or—as Rob suggested—he was continuing to gather information on his own.

Francis led us past two bays and then turned left to enter a wood-panelled passage. He stopped at the head of a narrow circular stairway leading down.

"That's the stair to *La Vierge sous-Terre*," Rob said. "The Virgin Beneath the Earth."

"That's right." Francis gestured toward a stone about waist-height at the head of the stair. "Read that."

"Creatori serviunt omnia subjecta," I read. *"Sub mensura, numero, pondere perfecta. Ad invisibilia, per haec intellecta, sursum trahit hominem ratio directa."* I looked below it and saw the inscription: Gau. Cast. MCXCIX.

"You just recited those words, lad," Rob said, glancing back along the passage. "Why are they important, Brother?"

"They were written by a poet, Gaultier de Insulis—or as we might say in French, Walter de Chatîllon. They praise the divine nature of mathematics."

"Was he a monk here?"

"No, no—he was the secretary to His Grace William, the Archbishop of Reims, more than a hundred years ago."

"Never heard of him," I said.

"Yet you know his poetry."

"I—" I began to say, *I heard it when you played Poulenc,* but didn't know how I'd begin to explain all of the questions that might have arisen from that comment, so I let it go.

"He wrote a history of Alexander, the *Alexandreis,*" Francis said. "You know, *'Incidit in Scyllam qui vult vitare Charybdim'*. 'He falls in Scylla's jaws who would escape Charybdis.' "

Rob stared at him blankly. As for me my mercenary life hadn't given me much Latin poetry, and my twenty-first century education didn't know who the hell Walter of Chatîllon was either. But the reference to Scylla and Charybdis—between a rock and a hard place—was common enough parlance for those who wanted to show off that they'd passed their Highers. It reminded me of my comment about Pyrrhic victories—Rob didn't understand this reference either.

"Why is this stone here?" Rob asked finally.

"I don't know. He may have visited here while the cathedral was being rebuilt—the stone is dated 1199, a few years after they started work. But he neither lived nor died here."

"Where did he die?" I ventured.

"Amiens."

Something suddenly made sense to Rob. He stepped past the organist to stand beside me. "I'd very much like to show Ian the crypt of the Virgin," he said. "I don't want to take you away from your duties."

"I should be getting after that lazy lad," Francis agreed. "I'd like to talk to you more about this . . ."

"Later tonight," Rob agreed.

"Certes." Francis smiled. "If you'll excuse me—"

"By all means. Thank you, Brother," Rob said, and gestured for me to go down the stairs. Francis turned and walked back toward the nave.

"Rob, what's—"

"We've got a clue. I don't know how you did it, lad, but you've happened on something important—something our shadow is going to want to find out. Quickly now, down the stairs with you."

The crypt was dimly lit. It was a small chamber, built around what appeared to be the foundations of an earlier part of the building—perhaps from before the fire; the western wall looked as if it had been there since Roman times. An arched doorway led out into another, wider passage. Other than the statue of the Virgin in its place of honour, there wasn't much to distinguish the tiny crypt of *La Vierge Sous-Terre.*

Still, there was a feeling to the place—the sort of numinousness that I'd expected to experience when we stepped into the great cathedral. Before I could pin it down I was distracted by Rob's voice.

"Over there." He was tense—he didn't even call me 'lad', as he customarily did. He took his staff in a two-handed grip; I hadn't even noticed him pick it up before we came down stairs. "Stand in plain sight." He faded into the shadows.

Great, I thought. *Play the fool—be the bait.*

I stood near the old wall and examined the decoration: it was a pastoral scene—the sun, a flowered strand, swans on a lake. After just a few moments I heard steps on the stairs: someone trying to come softly, but the jingle of chainmail made it difficult.

Our shadow appeared in the entrance to the stairway.

I turned, as if surprised to see someone there. "Peace be with you," I said as casually as I could manage.

The man didn't say anything at first. He took a few steps into the chamber and looked around, giving me a chance to size him up at arm's reach.

He was younger than me: in his twenties I thought, and one of those folks who walked as if he were more accustomed to riding. He was medium height—tall for this time, I suppose—and seemed to give attention to his appearance: carefully trimmed beard, clean tabard, gloves neatly tucked into his belt.

"Where did he go?" the man asked.

"Who?"

"You know very well, damn you," he replied, glancing quickly at Mother Mary and then back at me. "Your guardian angel. The older Templar. Left you alone, did he?"

"I can take care of myself," I said.

"Can you indeed." He smiled, crossing his arms in front of him. "That's not what I hear: needed to be taught to handle a staff. Is that the best old De Molay can scrape up these days?"

"Who are you to question the Grand Master's judgement?"

He stepped forward and grabbed hold of the front of my robe, slamming me back against the old wall so quickly that I almost didn't have time to react. My Templar body took over, however, grabbing hold of his arm—but he leaned in close and snarled, "I'll ask the questions, Templar. We can do this the hard or the easy way. *Where is it?*"

Onions, I thought. *It had to be someone who eats onions.* "Where is what?"

With his off-hand he punched me in the stomach, but I was able to squirm partially out of the way—still, it knocked some of my breath away.

Any time, Rob, I thought, struggling.

"The manuscript. You know where it is—the fat monk just told you." He looked around the chamber, taking his eyes off me for a moment. "It's down here, isn't it?"

"Manuscript," I managed. "What manuscript?"

He turned his attention back to me and slammed me against the wall again. "The music. The manuscript with the music, you devil-worshipping whoreson. You know where it is, and you're going to tell me."

"I am."

This would be a good time, Rob old pal, I thought. I don't know what my assailant thought of the look in my eyes, but I tried to look right at him and not past in case Rob was approaching.

"You are." He took his off hand and pressed his thumb on my right eyebrow. "I'm going to give you a five-count, then this eye comes out. Easy or hard, your choice."

"Hard," I said.

"Be it on your head," he answered—and *that* was when Rob decided to smack the side of his head with the staff. He went down in a heap at my feet. For good measure Rob landed a kick right in his midsection.

"Devil-worshipping whoresons, are we?" Rob said, frowning. He undid the man's belt and used it to tie his hands to his sides, then the two of us dragged the sorry sod to a corner of the room out of sight of the stairs.

"Were you waiting for a good dramatic moment?" I said when he was leaned against the wall. "He was ready to take an eye out."

"You played the fool well, lad," Rob answered. "Don't worry, it was well in hand." I shrugged; he gestured toward the stairs. "Keep a weather eye out."

I stepped back a few feet to keep the stairs in view; Rob put a hand over the man's mouth and knelt on top of his thighs to keep him in place.

"Wake up," Rob said, shaking the other's head violently. "I think we'll ask a few questions now."

He struggled a bit, but Rob leaned hard on his legs and gripped his face tightly.

"Easy or hard, your choice. You're willing to spy for de Bec; do you want to die for him?"

They reached some unspoken understanding. Rob removed his hand from the other's mouth, but didn't let him up from the floor. I glanced over to receive a look of pure hatred.

"You'd best watch where you place your feet, Templar," he said to Rob.

"I know just where I'm walking. Now tell me: what are your master's intentions?"

"As if I'd tell them to you." He spat in the corner, just missing the sleeve of Rob's robe.

"I didn't think I was leaving you a choice," Rob answered quietly. "I'd say you have a hand of minutes before I send you directly to your Maker if I don't get some information."

"You wouldn't dare touch me."

"Sure of yourself, aren't you? You don't know me too well. The Children of Soubise threw de Bec out of their ranks; the *Compagnons Passants* turned him away. The Children of Solomon wouldn't have him either. So what he knows he learned the old-fashioned way: as a sorcerer. That makes you tainted by association.

"After a few years in Outremer sending the enemies of Mother Church directly to Hell, it wouldn't trouble my soul a bit to do the same for you." He leaned his right hand on the man's chest. "I can start anytime."

"If you kill me you'll never leave Chartres alive."

Rob leaned hard on his prisoner's chest, making him huff in pain.

"I'll ask you again," Rob said, grabbing the man's chin, tilting his head up so quickly that his jaw snapped shut. "Let me make it clear to you, villain. We have every intention of leaving Chartres alive. We have important work to do: the Lord sent us, walks with us and guides us. No bandit"—he shook the man's head, rattling his teeth—"no prince, no *sorcerer* is capable of standing against us. So tell me: what does de Bec want?"

There were several tense seconds, and then the man shook his head free from Rob's grasp and said, "He wants the manuscript with the music in it. The music *he* hears," he added, nodding toward me.

"We don't have it."

"No, but you know where it is. It's somewhere in this cathedral, and my lord de Bec wants it found."

"So you thought we'd lead you to it, and the sorcerer would shower you with praise and gifts."

He didn't answer.

"What was your master going to do with the book? He can't hear the music."

"It doesn't matter. It would lead him to the place of perfect measure."

"It's not for him."

"My master will take what he likes." He spat again. "You aren't afraid of him, Templar," he said to Rob. "But you should be. The little man wasn't afraid until the end—"

That caught my attention. I took two steps toward him. "What do you mean, 'the little man'?"

"The Asturian. The one who was traveling with you."

"He's trying to goad you, lad," Rob said without turning around. He leaned hard on the man's chest again. "Don't—"

"She took pleasure in it. She moaned with pleasure," de Bec's man added.

A cold feeling came into the pit of my stomach. "What did you say?"

The man smiled. Rob took a quick glance back at me. "Shut up," he said, drawing back his hand as if to strike his prisoner.

"The little sister," the man whispered. "Ysabeau. We took her in turn. She moaned when each of us took her—after the little Asturian was out of the way."

The cold feeling turned to rage. My twenty-first century self was repelled by the idea—and to my surprise, my fourteenth-century self was also none too fond of that particular spoil of war. The idea that Juan had been attacked, likely killed, and that the beautiful young woman had been repeatedly violated—

Impulse. Like seemingly everything associated with my pilgrimage, I acted on impulse. Three steps and I dealt the pinned man a vicious backhand across the face, knocking him on his side . . . and as I watched, drops of newly shed blood fell to the stone floor of the crypt . . .

—•—

And suddenly, without warning, I was alone in the crypt of *la Vierge sous-Terre.* Rob was gone; de Bec's henchman was gone; and instead of the dim torchlight, the chamber was lit with the soft blue glow created by the afternoon sun's passage through the beautiful stained-glass windows of the cathedral above.

Somewhere above I could hear soft organ music: Poulenc again.

I let my gaze travel around the chamber to rest on the carved statue of *la Vierge* with the Christ-child in her lap, but instead of the dark-hued wood figure I saw someone familiar. As I watched she stood, placing the child on the floor; it crawled a few feet away and then sat, looking up at her.

"Hello, Wee Ian," Gran MacPherson said to me, her hands spread apart, her face relaxed into a smile. "I'm so glad to see you."

CHAPTER 11

GRAN MACPHERSON DIED WHEN I WAS STILL AT THE COLLEGE of Art. Her departure from my life was a relief in a way—no more Thursday afternoons spent hearing how I was wasting my talents—but it was a shock as well, the first hint of mortality for a young man to whom that idea has little relevance. She was there—and then she was gone, like a song heard clearly in a dream but scarcely remembered once awake.

And suddenly there she was in the crypt of the Black Virgin at Chartres, her arms spread wide, smiling as she always did before we got down to discussing my failings.

"Gran," I finally managed to get out. "What are you doing here?" It sounded fairly inane to me even as I said it.

"I am here, Wee Ian, because you called me forth. This is Chartres, and this is part of the song."

"I wish I knew what that meant." And God, I still hated that nickname.

I looked down at my hands—the hands of my Templar body, the one from this century. "I wish I *knew* who I was. Is there another Gran MacPherson for this Ian? I don't seem to remember one."

"You wouldn't." She smiled and looked down at the little baby playing on the stone floor; she reached into an inner pocket of her gown—she was dressed as the Virgin had been—and drew out some colorful Fisher-Price gewgaw to keep him occupied. She bent down and handed it to him and added, "The other Ian's grandmother died when he was just a babe. She never saw what he had become."

"Neither did you. And what you saw you never seemed to like."

"Oh, really," she replied, straightening up. "I don't give a toss about that anymore, young man. You had your success, for a time—and your marriage, for a time. But as one door closed another opened. And here you are."

"Impossible as it seems."

"Clearly not." She gathered the child into her arms. "You're here; you've climbed the hill to Chartres."

"Are you here to help me?"

"Of course I am. Poulenc heard a part of the song of healing; you heard Poulenc from me, and then from the talented monk here in Chartres. And so I have come to help you."

"How did you—I . . . well, we were interrogating—"

"Blood on the stones. A powerful thing. There was a time that blood was spilled regularly in this chamber, words of power spoken in that place where earth and water cross. Do you remember what I told you?"

"Of course I do. I dreamt it half an hour ago upstairs. It's all too perfect: I dreamt of you; I heard the music of Poulenc; I heard the words of Walter of Chatîllon. More jigsaw-puzzle pieces drop into place and the picture of Ian bloody Graham becomes more and more visible."

I'd let myself get angry at this point. *What the hell's the difference?* I thought. *Gran's ten years in her grave, and this is a dream.* I'd never speak to Gran this way, but I could feel bile rising into my throat.

"What are you trying to tell me? What is this all about? The music, the pilgrimage—is this some sort of adventure story, an extended costume drama, a fever dream, magical reality? I've spent seven weeks in the fourteenth century following from one place to another, Gran, listening to mysterious folks that look like people I know—some of them long since dead—and no one gives me straight answers. And just when they might answer one question they say, 'this is the nineteenth initiation, Ian. This or that planet governs this sphere. Stand on one leg and close your eyes, touch your nose with your index finger. Carry on, but watch out for the toffs that are trying to kill you—and zip zap I'm back where I was, wondering what in God's name is happening to me.

"I was told—and I *was* listening, Gran—that I must ultimately go back to Rosslyn. *But there's no Rosslyn here in 1307.* It doesn't exist yet—and won't until long after this Ian"—I thumped my own chest—"will be dust."

"Like me."

I took a deep breath. Chills ran across my shoulders and down my back.

"Like you. What's it like, being dead?"

"We've gotten off the subject," she said. She looked away from me; her eyes were bright—they might have had tears in them. "You're so angry you've stopped listening."

"I'm listening! I am." I rubbed my forehead. I was trying to find the right words—and failing. Seven weeks as a Templar had completely ruined my interviewing skills. "I think I hear too much, not too little. The song seems to be everywhere, and I keep having these visions that tell me just enough to make me ask the next question, take the next step. It's the Socratic method with dirt, disease and being burned at the stake added in for spice. The Dark Ages costume drama review, for your entertainment pleasure on Channel 4."

Gran looked at the child she held; he played with his little toy, gazing up at me innocently.

"This isn't a costume drama, Wee Ian. It's your life."

"Only half of it. Only half of me. The rest of me parked his car across the road from a half-built mystery chapel two months ago and was thrown into this pilgrimage without so much as a by your leave. I'm in some kind of novel, Gran, and I can't get out." I tugged at my robe. "Look at this. Not exactly Armani, is it?"

"What would you like from me? An explanation of it all—answers to all of your questions?"

"Yes. Of course. But you're not likely to give them to me, are you? No more than you're actually my old Gran."

She looked at me sharply. That didn't seem to be an insight she'd been prepared for.

"Caught you, did I?" I asked.

"What makes you think I'm not your Gran, young man?"

"Whoever or whatever is causing all of this to take place has miscalculated by sending me the image of my Gran. Rob or Juan I could imagine: they're true believers. Even Gerard Lamont could be a messenger . . . but Gran MacPherson? She may have reveled in mysteries, but only in uncovering them, not compounding them.

"Blunt and direct Scots ladies just don't deliver cryptic messages. 'Speak your mind, young man,' she used to say. 'As long as it's the truth.' "

Gran—or whoever it was—gave me a long look, saying nothing. Then as I watched, the blue light faded, leaving us in near darkness. I felt her hand on my elbow and saw her gesture with the other. The child she had been carrying disappeared.

"Ask your questions," she finally said.

I hadn't expected such a blunt offer. It took me aback for a moment, stopping me in my tracks—but I recovered quickly.

"Why am I on this pilgrimage? Why me?"

"You can hear the music that can heal the world. With your help, the key can be found and the music can be recovered."

"How was *I* chosen?"

"You weren't chosen, young man. You were discovered. And when that happened, you were sent back to be with your earlier self—here, in 1307."

"So there are two of me—like everyone else: Rob, Juan, Gerard—"

"Not quite. There is only one of *you*—split into two parts. One part was born in this time, grew to manhood, served as a soldier and then turned aside to make this pilgrimage. The other was born in the other time—but the music links them together. In a sense, something that happened in this time helped create you in that future time."

"Gothic architecture?"

"Polyphony. The use of multiple voices in the same musical piece. Until the thirteenth century it was mostly antiphonal, but then it began to flower. And then a musical genius named Adam de la Halle came here, to Chartres, and composed the music you hear—and it created you."

"I have no idea what the hell you could possibly mean."

She shrugged and continued, "And I haven't time to explain all of it to you, Ian. Even the greatest esoteric scholars could not completely understand it—though Giordano Bruno came closest. Scorn if you wish, but it's true: the music created you because it was composed and first played in the most perfect musical instrument of all—this cathedral—and because of that you can hear it."

"And he tucked a copy of the sheet music into some corner of this cathedral—so now a sorcerer and his thugs are trying to kill me for it."

"They think it's here."

"It's not?"

"No. It's in Amiens."

I thought about that for a moment.

"We're supposed to eventually go to Amiens. It's the last place on the pilgrimage dance, I believe. Where is it hidden there, or would that be telling?"

"The music was powerful, young man. De la Halle feared so much for his life after he conceived of it, that he put about rumours of his own death. Some scholars say that he died in the 1280s; others have his decease in 1306, just over a year ago. Neither might be true.

" 'He that hath an ear to hear, let him hear.' He left a clue of the music's whereabouts for anyone capable of perceiving it."

I noticed that she managed to avoid answering the question. I said, "*Creatori serviunt omnia subjecta*. That's what Rob figured out—so what de Bec and his bullies want isn't here after all."

"No. What *is* here is just as important, but it isn't the de la Halle manuscript. It's something you'll take with you when you leave."

"Something important . . . how will we get it out of Chartres?"

The dim illumination caught the edge of her smile. "You'll manage."

"What is it?" I crossed my arms over my chest. A visionary informer was actually informing: I was impatient to hear what she had to say.

"Let me show you."

We walked forward in the gloom to the end of the Roman wall. Ahead I could make out a low stone wall, which turned out to be the rounded front of a cistern or well: it was even equipped with a bucket attached to a long, thin chain.

"This is the Well of the Strong, Wee Ian. It's a fearful long way to the bottom—a hundred thirty feet—exactly the height of the tallest point of the cathedral roof."

"Quite a coincidence."

"Your sarcasm does you no credit," she snapped, sounding just like my old Gran for just a moment. "The depth of the well within the sacred hill is, among other things, the reason for the dimensions of the church above us; its presence here is why there is a church at all.

"Chartres—Carnutum—was holy long before the first Christian shrine was built here. This"—she leaned her hand on the stone rim—"was a Druidic well. Then it was dedicated to the earth-Goddess Demeter. And then, later, the sacred Mother was transformed into the *Virgini parituriae*—the virgin about to give birth." She snorted, again sounding like Gran.

I heard voices behind me and turned; I could see seven shadowy figures filing down the stairs into the crypt. Gran put her hand on my arm.

"Who are they?" I whispered. "And what are they doing?"

They didn't look our way—they didn't seem to hear us at all. The small group of men, their hooded robes obscuring their faces, seemed to be moving in a slow dance, following the outline of some sort of pattern on the floor I could only dimly see.

"These are the Children of Soubise," she answered. "The builders of Chartres' Romanesque cathedral. They're calling the quarters."

She said it matter-of-factly, as if I understood exactly what she meant. It made no sense at the time . . . except that the pattern was familiar: it reminded me of the *aragonesa*.

What I could see of the pattern in the crypt floor looked remarkably like the flagstoned labyrinth in the cathedral nave above. As I watched, I could feel the hairs on my arms and legs stand up, as if the air were charged with static electricity.

"Bishop Fulbert was a member of that fraternity. He sensed the sanctity of the hill of Beauce and the power of the *Wouivre*—what your friend Rob calls the earth-path—and built his great church here."

The scene seemed to ripple like the surface of a well disturbed by a hand. When it cleared again, I could see another group of figures: two men dressed in Templar fashion, and two priests—one older, one somewhat younger. They were carrying on a quiet conversation that I couldn't make out. Between them on the floor of the crypt was a stout trunk, bound about with leather straps and secured by a large lock.

"Hugues de Payens and a companion of his order came here to Chartres a few years after the Knights Templar were founded," Gran said. "They had been in Outremer—their charter was to protect the pilgrimage routes—but they had another purpose, given them by that man." She pointed to the older priest. "Bernard of Clairvaux, the founder of the Cistercian Order."

"Saint Bernard?"

"Full marks for the television personality," she answered. I caught a hint of another smile. "The same one. Abbé Bernard sent the knights of the Order to the Holy Land with a single purpose: to conduct a search beneath the ruins on the Mount, where King Solomon's Temple had once stood."

She turned to face me and added, "And they discovered many things, Ian. They returned to this place with ancient knowledge that had lain hidden since the destruction of the second Temple, the one built by Zerubbabel and those who returned from the Babylonian Captivity."

Zerubbabel is not exactly a household name; hearing it spoken reminded me of something, but I couldn't quite put my finger on it. I'd heard of him before.

"Please continue."

"Solomon—and later Zerubbabel—possessed the keys to the sacred geometry that had been developed in Egypt and perfected in the building of the first Temple. The Templars found these keys and returned them here. And they brought back that." She gestured toward the trunk.

"Souvenirs?"

"Within that trunk are, among other things, the rod of Aaron, the pot of mana and the tablets of the Law. For more than a thousand years they lay buried in the ruins of the Temple, and they were brought back here for safekeeping."

The rod of Aaron, I thought. *The pot of mana. The tablets—*

"The tablets—you mean the *Ten Commandments?* The ones that Moses received on the mountain, 'put thy shoes from thy feet?' The ones that were stored in the—"

I could feel my heart rate speed up. I was having an Indiana Jones moment: all that was missing were the special effects. The four figures before me continued to converse.

"Are you telling me that the Templars brought the *Ark of the Covenant* to Chartres?"

"I am indeed, Wee Ian. And it's still here—until you carry it away."

The Templars and priests faded from view. We were alone again in the crypt of the Virgin Beneath the Earth. I turned to look at Gran, profiled in the faint light.

"We'll manage. We'll get it out of Chartres, with every one of de Bec and Nogaret's henchmen watching the cathedral, the Templar priory, every gate, the road to Paris—"

"They're not watching the road to Amiens, Ian."

"But we're not going to Amiens, not until we do the mysterious stranger in Paris. The next one of you that will ask me to rub my belly and pat my head. And we might have to go back to Orléans—Juan needs our help."

"The brother and sister are unharmed," Gran offered. "They are being held to lure you back."

"She was raped. Repeatedly."

"No. She is . . . undefiled, they would say. Your enemy believes that if she were violated, she would lose all value as a hostage."

"Then why did the guard say—"

"To make you angry, Wee Ian. And it worked."

I heard the sound of Poulenc's *Litanies*—not Brother Francis playing, but a phonograph record with clicks and pops. I looked back where the last scene had been—and before me I saw the crowded alcove in Gran's apartment.

She walked away from me and into her apartment; I followed. The Templar part of me was looking around in wonder; I could hear the sound of traffic on Princes Street, smell the faint odour of lavender that I remembered so well. A bouquet of sunflowers sat neatly arranged in a vase on the tea-table.

She gestured me to my usual seat. Gingerly I lowered myself into it, leaning on the chair arms. She uncovered the teapot and poured a steaming cup for each of us.

For the first time in more than ten years I was having tea with Gran . . . and I was back home in Edinburgh. Still dressed as a Templar, half of me bewildered by the end of the twentieth century.

I stood up and in two strides was at the apartment door. As I placed my hand on the knob, Gran said, "Ian, don't."

"Why not? Couldn't I just go out, down the stairs, and go take a walk to Jenners? There must be someone who would recognise me, lend me twenty quid or taxi fare—"

"Come back and sit down, young man." She was using the voice of command. "You can't go out that door—it's closed to you. There's only one way for you to return to the Edinburgh you know; it requires you to pass through the remaining initiations."

My hand tightened on the knob.

"I don't believe you," I said without turning back. "I have no reason to. This could still be a long and complex dream. Maybe I fell so hard at Rosslyn I'm in a coma."

I knew that the other figure in this scene wasn't Gran MacPherson—and that this wasn't her apartment in Edinburgh. My life in the fourteenth century wasn't a vivid dream: I had no rational, scientific explanation for it, but it was happening.

I remembered Rob in the first initiation: when I tried to turn and look at him I'd been frozen in place, unable to see some figure of light speaking in a voice of command. By comparison, I knew that Gran was still sitting at the tea-table. Perhaps she might have pointed her finger at me to prevent me from opening that door—but I'll never know.

I came back to sit down. A police siren shrilled in the street below, which made my Templar persona jump; my twenty-first century hands shook slightly, realizing how much I missed my home.

"Let me come home, Gran."

"You know the answer. You can only continue and undergo the transformation that these initiations represent. You are the Lion, Ian: not just a Warrior, but something more noble. Any man can kill, but only one who is noble can spare a life. Your heart is the Abode of Mercy, and you will be led on paths you know not.

"This is the fourth initiation, Ian. The Sun governs this sphere. Go through the strait gate, and be merciful."

—•—

I fell forward onto my hands and knees. De Bec's man and Rob were both caught by surprise. I looked at the back of my right hand; it had blood from the henchman's mouth on it.

"Ian?" Rob said, never taking his eyes off his prisoner.

"Did you rape her?" I asked without looking up. "Did you touch Ysabeau?"

The man took several heartbeats to answer. "No."

"We have no reason to believe that, you lying sack of—" Rob began, but he caught my eye as I looked up and didn't finish the epithet.

"Yes we do. Let him go, Rob. He doesn't know anything, and I won't have a death—another death—on my hands. Not here in Chartres Cathedral."

"All right, lad," Rob said. "If you think that's best." He stood up, releasing his hold on the man. But as the other struggled to get to his feet, Rob decked him with a roundhouse blow and then gave him a kick for good measure; he fell like a sack of stones and once more lay unconscious on the crypt floor.

"He can report to his master later," Rob said, nodding toward de Bec's man. He looked me up and down. "What's happened?"

"The fourth initiation," I said. "I know why we're here and what we do next."

"Oh, certes?" He raised an eyebrow and smiled slightly at me. "Perhaps you don't need me to be your guide any longer."

"No. I'm apparently to be led along paths I know not. I can't manage that without a guide—so you've still got a job."

He seemed to accept this. Without looking down at the man sprawled on the crypt floor, we gave a small bow to *La Vierge sous-Terre,* crossed ourselves, and then headed up the stairs just as the Vespers bells were beginning to toll.

CHAPTER 12

It had only been that morning that I had come to Chartres, running from enemies that knew our next destination. Now with the sky paling and night beginning to fall, I considered the possibility that we might actually be one step ahead of them.

There was no guarantee that we had shaken pursuit. Our shadow, the one we'd left unconscious in the crypt, might not be the only one assigned to watch our movements; we knew he had at least one companion, and when he didn't report in there'd no doubt be others.

—•—

Rob had surprised me with his skill and his knowledge. His resourcefulness I took almost for granted. At the Door of the Initiates he found a scribe, paid a penny for a small bit of parchment, and wrote the number 21 on it along with something else I couldn't make out. He gave it a quick fold, wrote 'For the Giblumite' on the outside, sealed it with wax in which he embedded his own ring, and handed it to be delivered to someone whose name he whispered in the scribe's ear as he handed him another coin.

The other man's eyes widened for a moment, glancing up at the doorway beside him and then back at Rob.

"At once," Rob said aloud, nodding.

The scribe gestured to another to watch his place and scurried off into the cathedral.

I let my gaze travel up to the area where he'd looked. As with so much in Chartres, there were sculptured figures: two columns showing men transporting a wheeled wagon, its contents shrouded.

I could make out an inscription beneath: *Hic amitur archa cederis.*

You are to work through the Ark.

"Aye," Rob said quietly. "Come along, lad. We'd best make haste."

Anyone who's worked behind or in front of the camera can estimate time, even after seven weeks knocking around the fourteenth century in a monk's robe. Thus, I was fairly certain that it was scarcely fifteen minutes later that we were sitting on a stone pier, our feet dangling over the river a man's height below us. There was something fairly smelly in a building a dozen paces away, blocking the remaining light from the western sky that paled toward night.

Another few small coins had procured a bottle of mediocre wine and a good loaf of crusty bread to go with food from our packs, giving us an acceptable dinner. The plan had been to sup at the refectory at the Templar priory, but that was clearly not going to happen.

Rob didn't seem willing to offer any information, so I finally got impatient.

"Rob."

"Mmhm." He chewed a piece of bread and swallowed it. "Yes?"

"What does it mean to be a Lion?"

"Shirk from no toil," he answered. He tore off another piece of bread and examined it. "Warriors must do more than fight for a cause or kill an enemy. They must stay their hand when needed, and stay the course when needed."

"A textbook reply."

He tilted his head at me, conveying that I'd baffled him again.

"You're a Lion, I assume," I said after a moment.

"Among other things."

"So tell me: would you have killed de Bec's man back at the crypt? Would you have stayed your hand or stayed the course—what would have been the right thing to do?"

Rob took a long time to answer. He looked at his bread but didn't see what he was looking for there; then he gazed off and away down the river. "I don't know, lad," he said at last. "I can't say for sure but I think I would have done something foolish. I would have sent him to the hell that's ready and waiting for him."

"Does that disqualify you as a Lion? Or . . . or does some secret hand waving I've yet to see invalidate it all, getting you off the hook of that particular moral dilemma?"

"No. It only gets more binding. I . . . think I'd likely be at fault if I'd killed him. It's one thing to slay the infidel, or defend a bastion, but quite another for me to kill a man in cold blood."

"Even if he'd do the same given the chance."

"Aye. Even if he'd do the same. Of course, if sparing him leads to further harm—ah." He set down the bread, and went to work teasing a loose thread out of the sleeve of his robe. "I don't know what to say."

"You're worried about the law of unintended consequences."

Rob laughed. "Do you just save up these turns of phrase to torment me?" He opened the wine bottle and took a long drink. "Half the time I don't understand you, lad, and the other half you just mystify me."

For the hundredth time I considered the consequences of telling Rob exactly why I so confounded him: to tell him that I'd come from the future, that this wasn't my century. I held my tongue.

"So tell me, Rob: exactly how are we going to get out of Chartres?"

"We're going to get help."

"What sort of help?"

"Shh." He held up a hand and leaned down to place his ear near the stone pier. I tried to be as still as possible. After a moment he sat up and began to gather his possessions. "Here he comes."

"Who?"

"The Giblumite."

I tossed the remains of our dinner into my pack and pulled my staff close to me. From down the alley I heard the sound of boots: a steady, determined stride that sounded like the wearer knew exactly where he was going.

Someone knew we were here.

"Peace, lad," Rob said quietly. "He's a friend—or at least an ally."

The determined footsteps grew closer. In the light cast by the three-quarter moon, a figure emerged from the alley. We got to our feet; Rob stood a little ahead of me to greet our visitor.

"Thank you for coming so promptly," he began. "We—"

My impulsive nature kept my tongue a stride ahead of my brain. I couldn't help speaking.

"Rodney?" I said.

The man's hand went to his sword hilt as he stared at me suspiciously: a bearded, muscular figure—but the spitting image of my theatrical agent, the fellow who had gotten me the Rosslyn assignment in the first place.

"Who are you?" he asked, scowling at me. "And how do you know my name?"

"I—" I began. Inside I was cursing myself repeatedly. *Thank you very much,* I said to myself. *Nice job.*

Rob, alarmed, looked from the stranger to me and back again. He held one hand out, palm up. "Peace, Giblumite. My brother and friend is full of surprises. But . . ." he lowered his voice. "He can hear the music."

"Ah." The Giblumite—whatever that meant—didn't let his hand stray far from his weapon. "I do not know you," he said to me. "I do not give out my name—yet you know it. But if you can hear the song, then you know something of me."

"I apologize if I have offended." I used my Channel 4 voice, as best I could with my foot stuck in my mouth. "I meant no disrespect."

"We would do best to be away from here in plain sight," the Giblumite said. "Everyone is watching; everyone is listening."

He got no argument from us. Without another word he led us back along the alley, then up a narrow flight of stairs to a small courtyard. He withdrew a key-ring from under his shirt and unlocked one of several iron-bound wooden doors along the side of a particular building; there was a shell badge attached unobtrusively on one of the lintels. In the dim moonlight I could see stairs going down. There was no sign of a cresset or a lantern.

"I will lead them in paths that they have not known," the Giblumite said. "I will make darkness light before them and crooked things straight. These things will I do unto them, and not forsake them."

Rob looked at me. "Isaiah 42," he said at once. The Giblumite nodded, narrowing his eyes at me.

"Where does this lead?" I asked.

"Within the Hill of the Strong," the Giblumite answered. "To the deep darkness."

Rob's eyes widened. "Will we see . . ."

"Yes," the other said. "It is there. It has been waiting for us to take it from this place."

"Us?"

"Yes, Templar, us," the Giblumite said. "It is as foretold. I would accompany the stranger who knows my name, and convey the great treasure to its penultimate destination."

"Whatever that means."

The Giblumite looked surprised. "You don't know what it means either?"

"Who, me? I'm just here for the pilgrimage." *Which you got me into in the first place,* I added in my head. *You and your £3 Scots-English dictionary.*

"Lead on," Rob said, gesturing to the stairs.

Without hesitation, the stranger walked through the doorway and into the darkness; we followed a step behind.

—•—

We made our way down thirteen stairs—I counted—and then along a narrow corridor that sloped gently downward. It was completely dark: we'd shut the door behind us before proceeding. The Giblumite moved at a slow but steady walk; I was directly behind him, and Rob brought up the rear.

After a hundred steps I concluded that I should try to determine how far we walked based on how long we'd been at it. With no landmarks I fell back on a traditional method my Gran had used when I was small.

Awake, my soul, and with the sun
Thy daily stage of duty run;
Shake off dull sloth, and joyful rise,
To pay thy morning sacrifice

I sang the first stanza of *Awake My Soul* in my head. There were twelve in all, four lines each: all onerous, ponderous things written in Puritan days that were trotted out at St Giles a few times a year. She sang it frequently for a practical reason that always amused me—twelve stanzas of *Awake My Soul* was just enough time to soft-boil an egg, or about two and a half minutes.

I'd gotten twice through, just done with the only stanza anyone actually knows—

Praise God, from Whom all blessings flow;
Praise Him, all creatures here below;
Praise Him above, ye heavenly host;
Praise Father, Son and Holy Ghost.

I was about to start a third time when the blind leader of our blind procession said, "Halt," and stopped. I heard Rob stop behind me, but I collided with the Giblumite, who grunted as I did so. Evidently there was a door in front of us; I could hear keys rattling.

"Almost six minutes," I said. Two soft-boiled eggs were waiting on my mind's kitchen counter.

"Before we continue," the Giblumite said, "tell me how you know my name."

He'd turned around, and I heard a soft noise: a metal blade emerging from its scabbard.

"We're within the Hill," Rob said quietly, a few paces behind me. "You wouldn't shed blood here."

"These days we protect our names with blood. I know you well, Brother Robert, but I don't know your companion. The King's men are swarming like flies to a rotting carcass, and none of the Children of Solomon are safe."

"Our order is in danger also. The papal inquiry—"

"Wait," I said putting my hands up—not that anyone could see. "Since I'm the one being threatened, can I get a word in here?"

"Say on," the Giblumite said.

"I should not have spoken your name, Rodney," I said to the man in front of me who was apparently threatening me. "You caught me by surprise. But ever since I—" I almost said, *ever since I came to the fourteenth century,* but instead decided on "began this pilgrimage, I've seen people that bore a remarkable resemblance to people I know. Rob, Juan—and now you. Or, rather, someone who looks very much like you."

"You've also been knocked in the head a few times," Rob said from behind me.

"It wouldn't explain how I know the Giblumite's name. And by the way, what the bloody hell is a Giblumite?"

There were two or three heartbeats where I thought that I'd be run through there and then, in a stone corridor somewhere beneath the earth in complete darkness. Then I heard the sword go back in its sheath—loudly and firmly.

" 'Giblum' means square stone," Rodney said. "A 'Giblumite' is a stone-squarer—a skilled stonemason. I am a craftsman, one of the Children of Solomon. My society built the great Cathedral of Chartres, the House of the Lord. There is no structure in all of Christendom more important."

He sounded angry—and impossibly self-important.

"Well done," I said. I heard Rob sigh and could almost hear Rodney scowl in the pitch-darkness.

"It was built to echo the music that would be written within it—the music only one could hear. He who could hear the music would be the one to take the great treasure to its final resting-place, safe from King's men and infidels and evildoers. Apparently you are that one."

"Wait," I said. "Are you saying that the Cathedral of Chartres was built—a century ago—so that someone would write music for it? And that because I can hear that music I get to take the Ark away?"

That was when I truly felt threatened, because Rodney—the Giblumite—grabbed me by the front of my robe and slammed me against the opposite wall of the corridor.

"Who told you that?" he shouted at me, his face close to mine. "How do you know what is concealed here?"

To my shame, the first thing that crossed my mind was: *Does everyone in this bloody century eat onions for dinner?*

Rob was right at my side—I could feel him pulling the stone-mason away. All of this was in complete darkness—I couldn't see faces, or indeed anything else. If a weapon had been in anyone's hands at that moment, I'm certain that someone would've been killed in that corridor.

"How do you know?" the Giblumite repeated.

"He knows because—" Rob began, but I interrupted him.

"I know because *la Vierge sous-Tierre* told me," I said, and left it at that.

The man uttered an oath under his breath. I felt Rob step back from him to stand right next to me at arm's reach.

"Let's all get out of this corridor," Rob suggested. "I've no taste for any more walking in the dark."

The Giblumite didn't answer, but I heard the key-ring again—first rattling in his hand and then a key in the lock of the door in front of us. He clearly had a key he could tell by feel.

The door swung inward, and for the first time in several soft-boiled eggs, light struck our eyes.

—•—

There was a popular movie a few years back that involved a hidden treasure that had been buried for a few centuries beneath a church in New York. When the characters emerged from some sort of dirty cave their eyes were assailed with heaps of gold and shiny bits of all sorts—Fort Knox meets the Smithsonian meets Saks Fifth Avenue.

I would like to say that the sight that met us when we stepped through that doorway resembled that scene. It would have been a just reward in my mind for ten minutes or so in cloying darkness with a Templar guide of unknown powers and a complete stranger who seemed more than willing to kill me because of what he thought I knew.

The truth was more prosaic. We emerged onto a balcony—a fixed scaffolding, really, anchored to the stone of a large cavern by stone pegs a handspan wide. It ran the length of the cavern, which was about the length of a football pitch. The cavern itself was some sort of workroom; it had plinths and sawhorses, pieces of stone and various sorts of joinery to hold it in place, tools and piles of junk everywhere.

And oh yes, lest I forget, a half-dozen apron-wearing workmen with drawn bows aimed directly where we stood.

"Roddy old man," I said as quietly as I could, "perhaps you should tell your lads to put the bows away."

To my annoyance, he took several seconds before making a palms-up gesture to the workmen below. "Peace, Brothers," he said. "These are the Templars that contacted me."

They in turn took several seconds before lowering their weapons. When they'd done so, we walked along the scaffolding to a ladder and then descended, Rodney first, myself in the middle and Rob last to the workroom floor. There were nearly a dozen men in that cavern workroom, including the six that had been ready to practise archery on us a few minutes earlier. They didn't look at all friendly.

One of them, a burly, bearded fellow who looked like he'd been carved from stone himself, placed himself directly in our path.

"We're none too fond of having these two here," he said. He looked ready to spit.

Rob stepped to stand beside Rodney. "Any particular reason, friend?" He asked it as if he knew what the answer was going to be.

"Your day is almost done, Templar."

The burly stonemason placed his hands on his hips. He was twenty or twenty-five centimetres taller than Rob—who was no slouch.

"Not quite done yet, I think."

"It might as well be. You've lost it all: all of Outremer. But instead of redeeming the Sepulchre, what do you do? Sit fat and content on your riches. Your pride and your greed will soon be paid back and more."

I saw hatred in the man's eyes: not mere resentment—for I knew from our experiences thus far that Templars were known for their arrogance—but actual, visceral hate.

This had a chance of turning into something like a hideous American telly programme—the sensationalist kind, with lots of social misfits and shouting—except that there were no stage-hands to break up the fight.

My quarterstaff was loose in my right hand; I had a fair idea where the big man would move and how I could counter him if he chose violence. The problem was that there were many more of them than there were of us—even if Rodney could be considered part of 'us'.

"You're right," Rob said levelly. "When Grand Master De Gaudin left Saint Jean d'Acre, I was aboard one of those ships. I knew that my foot would never be set in the Holy Land again, and the same is true for every other member of our Order—servant, sergeant or knight.

"But I'm not here to argue that point with you, friend, and neither is my companion. We've asked for your help, and your brother"—he gestured to Rodney—"has agreed. Are you prepared to challenge that offer?"

The man wasn't ready for that concession or that question.

He was still angry—hatefully, perhaps violently angry—but didn't appear ready to go against Rodney.

It was a brilliant piece of crowd control, worthy of any stage performer or politician I'd ever seen. The entire dynamic of the room changed.

"Many of your Order never even placed their foot in the Holy Land," the stonemason said at last. "Many who walked there never returned. But Tripoli and Acre and Krak des Chevaliers are just names now, lost forever." He looked around him. "I do not fault *your* bravery, Templar, merely the determination of your Order to do as it has promised to do."

He stood aside, but his glance followed us as we passed through the group of workers to cross the room. I looked over my shoulder to see him standing there with his arms crossed, the others surrounding him like some sort of tableau from a bad TV historical drama.

—•—

"You should not have had to face that," Rodney said. We were walking along a wide, well-lit corridor; half of the corridor had a smooth-worn track that was used for carts—there was a complex rope pulley system used to pull them along.

"It doesn't trouble me," Rob answered.

"But it does," Rodney said. "If you were in Outremer at the end of the Kingdom of Jerusalem, then he is not angry with you. Still, that he dislikes the Order of the Temple is something that disturbs you, Brother."

"Why does he hate the Templars?" I asked. "What have they done?"

"More because of what they have *not* done," Rodney answered. "He feels that the Order has betrayed its obligation to protect the *routes templières* and to redeem the Sepulchre . . . and it seems clear that the King of France feels that way as well."

"Do they speak often?" I asked.

"What does that mean?"

"Nothing. I meant nothing."

"You give offence easily, Initiate," Rodney said, scowling. "Are you suggesting that—" He paused, not wanting to speak the other stonemason's name. "That he is in communication with the King's men?"

"No, I didn't mean that at all. Does the King even know of your—guild?"

Rodney looked at Rob. "He does. Your peril is ours as well."

We walked on in silence a few dozen more paces.

"Where are we going?" I asked, finally, feeling as if both of my companions knew something I didn't. I had begun to feel something: the hair on my arms and on the back of my neck was standing on end.

"Deeper within the Hill," Rodney said. "These caves have been here since long before the cathedral above was built. Their walls are the sinews of the earth—and the telluric force is strong."

" 'Telluric'?" It sounded like science fiction, and dated stuff at that.

"Earth-path," Rob said.

"Heard of it."

Rodney's eyebrow went up. I recognised the facial expression: it usually had to do with an industry job that wasn't going to make much money.

We began to hear the sound of water ahead of us. Not long after, something came into view: a slow-moving underground river running in a shallow channel; there was a wooden bridge with stone pilings built over it. The pulley cart track ended at a manually-operated winch for hauling stone pieces up through a hole in the ceiling a half-dozen feet over our head. The cart itself was drawn up near the winch; it was empty.

"We're beneath the church's ambulatory," Rodney said. "This water flows in a semicircle beneath the church; the arc of the ambulatory corresponds to this river."

"And the centre of the circle—" Rob began.

"Is the place where the old transepts intersect with the choir," Rodney answered. "It is the focus of power within the cathedral—and where the priest stands."

"Water and earth meet," Rob added.

"This warren of caves is fairly extensive," I said. "Are there tunnels that lead out of Chartres?"

"Of course," Rodney answered. "But only a few have that information."

"Including us."

"Yes. And excluding the King's men."

"Unless someone tells them."

Rodney stopped walking, a few paces short of the bridge. He turned to face me. "And does that comment mean 'nothing' as well, Templar? Or are you truly making an accusation this time?"

I took a deep breath. "I know that you said that our peril is yours. But any of your friends back there could save their own skin by turning us over to de Bec, or to Nogaret. Do they hate our Order enough to do so?"

"What makes you think they might?"

"I have no reason to believe or disbelieve *anything.* I just know that some of them—including the big lad that confronted us—hate the Order of the Temple. If it came down to saving his skin or being hanged with us, I'm willing to accept the idea that he'd save his skin."

"He sees what he wants to see—but he also feels that the Order no longer believes that the Holy Land is important to you Templars. Based on the writing of your own Grand Master, I'd tend to agree with him."

I looked from Rodney to Rob. Fortunately, my guide came to the rescue.

"The Grand Master wrote a letter last year," Rob said. "He argued that an army of twelve to fifteen thousand knights would be enough to return to Palestine in force and drive the Saracens back into the desert."

"Fifteen thousand—" I thought about the idea. A knight was not just one man in shining armour: he was one well-armed fighting man with three horses, a squire, a page or two, a few servants . . . that was more like an army of 100,000. "That's absurd. There aren't enough troops in all of Christendom. If there were, Granada would fly a Christian banner."

"That's right. And most of the kings aren't even willing to contribute to such an army. Grand Master DeMolay knew that no one would agree—he just wanted to have his plan in plain sight so it could be dismissed, thus absolving him of all responsibility."

"You're very cynical," I said. "Is there any chance that he's right about the number of troops needed to take back the Holy Land?"

"Right?" Rodney smiled, tight-lipped. "I expect he *is* right. Maybe Bonomel was right as well—'Neither cross nor law helps nor guides me against the evil Turks, God curse them! Rather God wishes to help them destroy us.' "

I didn't answer. Bonomel wasn't a name I knew. But Rob evidently did, and he looked angrily at our guide.

"If that's what you believe, then you have no need of helping us," he said quietly.

"Bonomel was one of yours."

"No one spoke those lines as we left the Holy Land behind. No one in the Order believes that today."

Rodney didn't answer, but led us across the bridge and the river. Whoever this Bonomel was—and Rodney said he was a Templar—had pissed on the leg of the Order.

I felt a chill run down my back as we crossed the water. Rob said, "Are you all right, lad?"

"I'm fine."

I wasn't: there was something between my Templar friend and the stonemason—something they both understood and was out of my ken. In the meanwhile, we were some hundreds of feet deep in the earth with folk that hated us between our present position and the only exit I knew from this place.

Even aside from the semidarkness and the closed-in feeling, the nearness of the water-path gave me the creeps. It was very nearly too much for one day: the dream, the music, the interrogation; the initiation with Gran, the walk through the darkness, and now this: walking through underground caves over underground rivers, heading for the secret hiding-place of a thing of legend . . . and a few hundred feet above us, king's men who wanted a secret I didn't quite possess.

"Quiet," Rodney said. We had reached another narrow passage. He took flint and steel from a shelf and used it to light a torch that he took from a cresset on the wall. With it held in front of him, he led us through the passage and into a smaller chamber; just at the edge of range of the light I could see another door.

Rodney walked forward, his torch held high. I could see the floor we were crossing was laid out like a huge checkerboard, square black and white stones as far as I could see in the torchlight. Rob's face was one of rapt attention—the symbolism was meaningful to him. It meant nothing to me, though I wished that it did.

We reached a bronze door just over the height of a tall man. It was decorated with bas-reliefs showing the building of a great structure: hewing stone, transporting it to a building site, fitting and finishing. To the left and right were tall ornamental pillars with a Hebrew letter on each. The door looked solid, as if it weighed several tons.

Our guide closed his eyes; his lips moved in silent prayer. Then he placed his right hand on the door and pushed gently inward; there was no sound of machinery—in fact, there was no sound at all. The heavy door simply swung inward. Glancing backward at me he walked through the doorway, the two of us following.

Within the chamber it was dark but for the light of the torch. Unlike in the outer one, where light seemed to carry its proper distance, the darkness here seemed cloying, close and heavy like a weight on our shoulders. I didn't want to get more than a pace or two from Rodney—I'd had enough of being alone in dark crypts for one lifetime by then.

"The Lord said that he would dwell in the deep darkness," Rodney said quietly. "The priests of the Temple placed the Ark within the *sanctum sanctorum* so that the Lord could come to rest beneath the wings of the cherubim."

He gestured, and I could see something resting on a small block of stone: a box perhaps four feet wide and three feet high, gleaming gold in the darkness. The top had two carved statues of human figures, faceless but with wings extended and almost touching at their points. Each corner of the box supports had a gold ring secured to it.

I was having another Indiana Jones moment, like the one with Gran, but with fewer special effects and more chills down my spine.

He hung the torch in a cresset. "This is the greatest of the treasures found beneath the Temple," he whispered, his voice hesitant as if the darkness were swallowing up the words. "My grandfather constructed this chamber to hold it when the cathedral above was built. I have never seen it with my own eyes."

For reasons I can't explain, I reached my hand forward—but Rob grabbed my hand before it could touch the surface of the Ark.

"You must not touch the *kepporeth,*" Rodney said. "It would strike you dead."

"Kepporeth?"

"The cover. The Mercy Seat," Rodney added. Rob let go of my hand, shaking his head slightly.

"How are we going to carry it?"

"The same way it was carried in here."

After a moment when Rodney was probably reassuring himself I wasn't going to do anything else stupid, he bent down in front of the Ark and picked up two long poles made of smooth wood.

"We're going to carry it out of here on those? What if we slip and accidentally touch the side of the—*kepporeth?*"

"This is how the Levites carried the Ark into the Holy of Holies," Rodney said. "We will use them to carry it out of this chamber—but we'll transport it within a larger box that will shield it from detection—and protect us from the danger."

Faraday cage, I thought. I must have said something, because Rodney gave me the same look Rob had gotten used to giving me. "Nothing," I added.

He took each of the poles and carefully threaded them through the rings on either side of the Ark. They extended two or three feet out on either side, with room for us to stand in between and lift the entire affair by means of the poles. Rodney gestured Rob to stand between the poles in the front, and myself in the rear. He picked up the torch from the cresset.

"Gently," he said.

Gently, with the darkness cloaking us, we carried the most precious artifact in Christendom out of the chamber, passing between the pillars and through the bronze doorway. When we had come onto the checkerboard floor once more, Rodney pulled the door shut behind us.

PART II

A SONG IN STONE

Ignoranti, quem portum petat,
nullus suus ventus est.
(If one does not know to which port
he is sailing, no wind is favourable.)
— Lucius Annaeus Seneca,
Epistulae ad Lucilum, 71:3

Lord, now lettest thou thy
servant depart in peace,
according to thy word.
For my eyes have seen thy salvation,
which thou hast prepared
before the face of all people;
a light to lighten the Gentiles
and the glory of thy people Israel.
— The Gospel of St. Luke, 2:29-32

CHAPTER 13

THE ROADS OF CENTRAL FRANCE SCARCELY DESERVED THE NAME. They had been good enough for us to walk on, particularly when the weather was fine; but they were hazardous and far less forgiving for a cart. But with the cargo we carried it was the only choice.

—•—

We carried our precious burden through dimly-lit passages until we reached a hand-operated pulley lift.

"Set it down here," he'd said. "You work the winch, Templar. I'll go up first and make sure it's all clear."

"I don't think so," Rob answered. He squinted at the stonemason in the dim light of a flickering torch.

"You don't trust me."

"What makes you think so?" He smiled slightly. "You take Ian with you."

Rodney scowled. I looked from my friend and guide to the Giblumite, who was clenching his fists.

"All right," he said at last, gesturing to me to climb onto the lift. I didn't know whether he expected me to object. He stepped next to me, and Rob began to work the mechanism.

Slowly we rode up, the wooden platform shuddering as it encountered rough spots on the adjacent rock wall. To my surprise, the lift was fairly quiet; just the sound of the rope passing over some unseen pulley above u, and the occasional bump of wood against stone interrupted the silence.

It took most of a soft-boiled egg for us to make it all the way up. I could see a roof above us and light leaking through shuttered doors on one side of the shaft; there was a chock attached to each rope that halted the lift when it reached the correct height.

"Best have that staff of yours at hand, Initiate," he said quietly. I assumed a fighting stance, not knowing what to expect.

He nodded and turned away, then said, "Do you trust me?"

"What?"

"Do you trust me, Initiate? Any more than you trust the Templar down there?"

"I've known him for—"

"Yes?"

He interrupted me, as if he was aware how little I knew Rob. After a moment of thought, I realised that he probably could reach some reasonable conclusion: this was Rob's twelfth pilgrimage as a guide, and all of them had come through Chartres.

"I trust him with my life. Why do you ask?"

"Because you're being used," he answered. He took a step forward and gently knocked on the wall: three times, then a pause, then once more.

"What does that mean?"

He didn't answer, but someone did from the other side—three times, then once in response.

He knocked once, and so did the other.

"Ready?" he said to me, very quietly.

I didn't answer this time. Whatever I was to be ready for, I was armed and tense—it would have to be good enough.

A portion of the wall opened where there had been no door before, and someone thrust a torch directly through. Rodney stepped back with a curse. A moment later the torch was withdrawn and a rough voice said, "Who comes here?"

"A man of Giblum. Are you trying to get us all killed?"

"Password?"

"Rabboni."

The man in the doorway handed the torch to someone else behind him. I could make out a heavy-set man in the dim light, and through the opening I caught wind of an unholy stink.

"Can't be too careful. Are you alone?"

"No. There are two with me. I vouch for them. One is below working the lift."

"We'll work it from here," the man said. Rodney gestured to me and I stepped through the opening into what looked like a storeroom; the man I'd seen and the man holding the torch stepped aside and we gave each other the visual once-over.

I didn't know what they made of me, but from the smell, and the piles of cured hides, I could tell that these two lads were tanners. An apprentice was already standing at a crank mechanism a few paces away and through the door I could see Rodney descending on the lift.

I wondered what they'd make of the Ark—but it didn't take long for me to find out: six or seven minutes later Rob and Rodney arrived, and between them they carried it through the doorway into the room. During the intervening time I had found a place to lean and watch; they'd had nothing to say to me.

"What do you mean bringing that through here, Giblumite?" the senior tanner said, hands on hips, as they set it down on a clear area of the floor. "Someone's bound to sense it."

"Not if we take it away," Rodney said. "You're going to help me build a crate for it."

"We are."

"Aye, you *are,*" he said. "And you'll be lending me a cart to transport it."

"Where?"

"Do you want to know, craftsman?" Rodney said. "We're taking it to—"

"Peace," he interrupted, holding up both hands, palms upward. "No, I don't want to know. You'll be paying for the cart."

Rodney gave a scowl to Rob, then one to me for good measure, I suppose. "Yes. Of course."

"You risk everything by removing it from its *sanctum.*"

"Our choices are getting fewer by the day," Rodney answered. "You may help us or not as you wish, craftsman. But our time is short."

Time might have been short, but the moment seemed to stretch out forever as stonemason and tanner gazed each other down; it was like bad Shakespeare. Finally the tanner looked away. "We'll help you, and consider our debt paid."

"Done."

"Done." The tanner turned to his companion. "Alain, get the cart ready. In the meanwhile, I'll be imitating our Saviour and doing some carpentry."

—•—

By the time we'd left the tannery, Rob had briefed me on the plan he and Roddy had developed. We would travel to Amiens, a journey of roughly a hundred and fifty miles—likely about ten days if weather favoured us—with the Ark concealed in the crate we built in that storeroom. With no sense of the state of things in our Order, we'd avoid Templar hostelries; we'd set out for Evreux in Normandy, then turn east, cross the Seine and make for Beauvais and eventually Amiens.

It was pitch-dark when we left Chartres, and it came to me as we bumped along the road in the near-darkness that it had all happened in one day.

It led to the most logical outcome. While Rodney drove the cart and Rob kept him company and kept watch, I went to sleep.

And, of course, I dreamt.

—•—

I was in Chartres Cathedral again, standing before the Labyrinth: the arrangement of white stones placed in the centre of the floor a dozen metres beyond the Royal Portal. A soft afternoon light fell through the stained-glass windows to my right, bathing the scene with blue light. There were no vendors, no crowds—I was alone . . . just me, the cathedral, and the music.

It was in that dream that I heard it clearly for the first time: the haunting tune that was every haunting tune I'd ever heard. It was the song that sticks in your head, the music that sets off a memory, a hundred fragments that are nothing alone and everything together.

The healing music of Rosslyn washed over me in that dream, echoing from the cornices and the triforia, rolling from the west end of the nave to the pillars of the choir and back again, echoing in the very stones of the floor and the 'forest' of roof-braces thirty-three metres above my head. It was for this music that the cathedral had been built.

It was why I was here.

"Beautiful, isn't it?" a voice said behind me.

I whirled, quarterstaff in my hand, wary. The music faded almost to inaudibility.

"Your pardon," the voice added.

A man walked into the light. He was a slight, somewhat elderly man with clear, deep eyes. My first impression was of a hunchback—or at least someone whose natural position was slightly inclined, as if accustomed to bowing; but it seemed that he was being drawn upright as he stood in the cathedral.

"Yes," I said. "Yes, it's very beautiful. All of it."

"And it all goes together, yes? The music and the architecture. The tones and the stones." He smiled. "The pale echo, the reflection of the Divine."

Considering what was in the basement, I thought, *I shouldn't be surprised.*

"Monsieur," I said after a moment. "You have me at a disadvantage."

"Ah. Yes. I am Adam, called *le Bossu* by my detractors. Adam of Arras."

"Adam de la Halle."

"Your servant." He did bow then, a gentle, graceful gesture, but the surroundings seemed to pull him upright.

"And this music . . . this is your work."

"I am merely the conduit: the means by which the internal becomes external," he answered. "The music came to me and I brought it together. But my work . . . no, it's the Lord's work. I am the vessel through which the Lord speaks."

Rather like the Ark.

The idea struck me suddenly. The Ark of the Covenant, the curious device that Moses was caused to construct, was the means by which God spoke to the Israelites: the vessel through which the Lord spoke.

"You wrote the music that I can hear."

He came up to stand next to me. "Yes, that's right. I wrote the music and heard it in my mind . . . but only you can hear it as we do now."

He fell silent and looked off into the distance, the afternoon sun passing through stained glass painting his face with soft light.

The music continued in the background, the harmonies joining and parting, rising and falling, like the curved arches in the Lady Chapel at Rosslyn, hundreds of miles and hundreds of years from where I stood in my dream.

You wrote music that you couldn't hear, I said to myself. But it pervaded half the music I'd heard in the fourteenth century . . . so he'd heard some bits, but never the entire song—what I was hearing just now.

"That's right, Ian. I could hear it here"—he touched his heart—"but nowhere else."

The use of my name made me concentrate intently on him, as if he'd just come into focus. "You know my name."

"I've always known your name," Adam replied. "And I always knew you would come."

"From the future."

"Yes. From the future. It shouldn't surprise you to know that no one from this time can presently hear the music."

"Not all of it," I said.

Adam nodded in agreement.

"You know what's going to happen, Ian: the King of France and the Holy Father had become such bitter enemies that His Highness arranged for a brutal attack on His Holiness . . . and as a result, there's a new Pope who doesn't dare show his face in Rome. Your Order is about to be struck on its blind side by that same monarch, and soon there will be not one, but two Popes, dividing the Christian world into two hostile camps. And then will come the greatest scourge of all: a plague so terrible that those who survive will think that it is the end of the world.

"I thank God that I am not around to see it."

I thought about this for a bit then said, "We have our own problems back in the twenty-first century, Adam, things that would make all of this look like a walk along the High Street. What makes you think anyone will hear the music then? What is this all about—and why is it *me?* Rob can't answer, Gerard didn't answer, Gran wouldn't answer. How about you? You wrote this music. You started all of this." Adam began to protest, but I shook my head. "No, don't be denying it: *you started all of this.* Maybe the Children of Solomon knew you'd be coming to tea, but whatever inspired you, you started it. Why me?"

"It's hard to explain."

"Is that so. Try it out. I want to know." I stepped toward him; he stepped back, more than a little fear in his eyes. "I've come this far. I'm this close. I want to know."

Slowly Adam de la Halle, the composer of the elusive music that had become Rosslyn's song in stone, raised his hands to his mouth. *"Amoun,"* he said.

A sudden jolt on the would-be road from Chartres shook me awake. I cursed loudly and repeatedly, and it echoed off into the night.

—•—

We rested the horses not long after the sun rose. Our breath was visible; it caught the morning light, a stark contrast to the mugginess of the day before; there was no sound other than the water on the stones in the creek. It reminded me of that first morning in

Santiago, eating empanadas, feeling at peace for a brief moment and forgetting that I'd been penalty-kicked seven hundred years into the past.

Rob and Rodney walked a short distance from the wagon and held a brief animated conversation. I'm not sure how much of it was about me, but each man glanced in my direction at least a couple of times—enough to make me curious, but not enough to make me want to interrupt them. Finally Rob walked away and came over to where I was adjusting the harness on one of the cart horses. He didn't seem too happy.

"Anything wrong?"

"Nothing. Everything." He turned away, the morning sun giving sharp relief to his features.

"And you say that I baffle *you.*"

"Do you know where we're headed, lad? We're on our way to Amiens with—with that." He slapped the side of the cart. "And with him." He jerked a thumb at Rodney.

"I thought that was what you wanted to do."

"No." He walked away to the back of the cart and hoisted himself onto it. He leaned back against the box containing the Ark of the Covenant—then hesitated, as if he suddenly realised that he was putting his back against something that had rested within the Holy of Holies. Then he shrugged; we'd carried it on wooden poles through caves under Chartres. He let himself relax, adjusting his seat in the back of the cart.

"But—" Now I was confused. I pulled myself up to sit beside him. "But the clues—the poem, the music . . . I assumed that they were all pointing us toward Amiens."

"Yes, certes. The *clues* are, lad. But not the pilgrimage. Not the thing that places me on this road . . . and you too. If any of that still matters."

"Why wouldn't it matter?"

He leaned forward, elbows on knees, chin resting on his fists. Other than when we'd sat in the Templar hostel in Orléans, discussing Nogaret and politics, I'd never seen him so serious, so distracted.

"You came up from Cintra to follow the path to the East, the path to the Light. Father Tomaso—Father Corvão—sent you to Santiago, and the Grand Master sent me to find you. I knew that this would be my last journey along the route; I knew this would be a special trip, that you would be . . . a special pilgrim.

"But it's not about that anymore, is it? It's all about the music no one but you can hear. It's about a hunchback composer. It's—" He placed his hand on the box. "It's about the Ark of the Covenant, lad," he whispered. "I don't even understand this anymore. I'm out of my depth."

"That's a bit disingenuous, isn't it? You've known about the music for some time."

"Perhaps so. I knew that your ability to hear it was important. I'm beginning to see why . . . but now that this—now that the pilgrimage isn't going to the place of the fifth initiation but rather the place of the sixth, I don't know what to do. As for being disingenuous—I'm a humble pilgrim now. Like you, like as not."

"No, you'll not get off that easy. You know much more about this than I do. You've been conducting this business all along—from the time we met—and you must have had a good idea where it was to end."

"I didn't—"

"No, no. Time for truth."

Rob was ready with a quick response but saw the expression on my face.

"Truth, is it."

I took a deep breath. This wasn't going to be easy, but I was tired of '*Amoun*', tired of deception. I needed to understand what he knew—and what it meant for us to be going to the place of the sixth initiation instead of the fifth.

"Yes. Truth."

"When we met in Santiago—" he began, but I put my hands up and he stopped short.

"We didn't meet in Santiago, Rob. We met in Rosslyn Chapel near Edinburgh."

"I've heard you mention it, but I've never heard of the place."

"So you say. Do you remember the morning of St James' Day in Santiago?"

"Of course I do. You'd just hit your head—"

"Yes, yes. I hit my head. But I told you that I didn't feel that I belonged there—not at Santiago, and not in 1307."

"Another one of your mysteries, lad."

"Rob," I said, looking directly at him and holding his gaze, "I was born late in the twentieth century. Two months ago, I passed out in a chapel a few miles south of Edinburgh and woke up in a hostel in Santiago de Compostela. Some of the things I've said . . . some of my confusion . . . are because I've been sent back into the past. This is not my place and it's not my time either."

Rob didn't say anything in response. He closed his eyes; his lips moved almost imperceptibly, perhaps in prayer.

"You don't believe me."

"If I had said that to you, lad, and you were me, would *you* believe *me?*"

"I suppose not."

"And if we'd traveled together for two months, prayed and fought together—and if I were your guide through four initiations—would you believe me if I said something like that to you?"

"Rob, when were you born?"

"Twelve fifty-five."

"If I were born in that year, I couldn't even imagine that someone could have come from the future—except if he was a sorcerer or a demon. If I had told you this in Santiago that first morning, you'd have accused me of being one or the other.

"But now we've prayed and fought and traveled together. I've been through four initiations. Do you think I'm a sorcerer or a demon? Do you?"

"No, lad, I don't. No demon crosses the threshold of a church—and if you were a sorcerer you'd be more clever by half and I'd like as not be dead."

"Doesn't leave you much choice then."

"That's a curious turn of phrase," Rob said. "With the pilgrimage off the tracks, I have more choice than ever before. I can even choose to give this all up."

"That doesn't seem like you," Rodney said, coming around the corner of the cart. "And as for you, Initiate," he added, looking at me, "your story is the most ridiculous thing I have ever heard . . . but it explains much."

Rob was already on his feet, standing between Rodney and me. I couldn't see his face, but from behind I could see that he was in a fighting stance.

"I don't like being eavesdropped on, Giblumite," he said, fists clenching.

"And I don't like being deceived, Templar," Rodney answered, looking from one of us to the other.

"I haven't deceived you."

"No," the stonemason said. "But *he* has." He nodded toward me. "I think he's deceived both of us. Instead of being a simple Scottish mercenary fighting in the *reconquista,* he turns out to be . . . what? A traveler in time?"

"Yes. And no." I got to my feet to stand next to Rob, who glanced briefly at me before turning his attention to Rodney once more. "I *did* fight in Spain—and with Wallace in Scotland against Longshanks. And I *did* come from the twenty-first century as well."

Rodney frowned. "I don't understand."

"Huh. You think it's confusing for you—I've been on this trip for almost two months and still haven't made sense of it myself."

"So there are two of you."

"Something like that."

"Which one of you can hear the music?"

"Both can. But the one from the future is here because he can. The one native to this time . . . I don't know. I didn't even know there was a fourteenth-century Ian Graham until I was stabbed in the gut."

"And you're sure this isn't all a fever dream?" Rodney asked, crossing his arms over his chest.

"No. I'm not the least bit sure. But I only know what I've been told."

"By *la Vierge sous-Terre?*"

"And others." I looked at Rob, who returned the glance, a bit alarmed.

"Tell me the future, Initiate," Rodney said. "Tell me something I don't know."

"All right." It wasn't difficult for me to decide what to say. "In five weeks' time, on Friday, October thirteenth, King Philip is going to betray the Templars—seize their holdings and their property, and have them accused of heresy and blasphemy."

It hung in the early morning air for several seconds. Rob looked stunned by the revelation; Rodney betrayed no emotion at all.

Finally the stonemason replied, "I said, tell me something I don't know."

Rob looked from Rodney to me. "What are you talking about? How do you know—why do you believe this?"

I thought about how to reply. As I touched the Tree of Jesse at Santiago, my first inexplicable experience in this century had occurred: Rob—or someone with Rob's voice—had told me just this. I'm sure I learned it in my Highers originally, but I'd been given the executive briefing then, during the first initiation. . . and it had been bleeding *Amoun* ever since.

"Because—" we both began. Rodney nodded to me. "Because it already happened," I finished. "I know how it goes, how it all comes out."

"How long have you known this? Since you met me?"

"Not exactly," I said. "I knew the Templars were destroyed—but not when or by whom. Didn't have the details until the first initiation . . . when *you* told me."

"When I . . ."

"Yes. You spoke—"

Rob held his hand up to stop me from continuing. "Why don't you go eavesdrop on the horses, Giblumite?"

Rodney frowned and gave Rob a hard stare, letting his hands drop to his sides. Rob never stirred; he stayed ready, a soldier waiting for his opponent to make the first move.

"We'd best be moving along soon," Rodney said, with a *this isn't over* expression on his face; then he turned on his heel and walked back toward the horses at the front of the cart.

Rob waited for him to be several paces away, then said, "You've been trying to tell me about the first initiation since it first happened, lad. Now make it quick."

"You spoke to me, Rob. But I couldn't turn around to face you. You were—too bright." He didn't comment, so I hurried on. "You told me about the coming destruction of the Templars, and that Santiago was the beginning of the journey that would end at Rosslyn—the *camino de las estrellas,* the road of stars."

"I know what it means. Go on."

"That's it. You told me I needed to listen; that the other—you—that *you* didn't know all of what you'd told me—and then he dropped '*Amoun*' on my head. Be discreet, you said. Learn humility, you said."

"He said."

"All right. *He* said, in your voice. Then who was he?"

"Tell me something, lad. In your twenty-first century, do you believe in the Saviour?"

It was such a change of subject that I couldn't answer for a moment—I wasn't sure how his question related to mine.

"You mean me, or anyone?"

"You."

"I was raised a Christian. Presbyterian, actually," I said, then at his baffled expression, added, "In my time there are Christian denominations that don't even recognise the Pope as the head of the Church. It started when people began to translate the Bible from Latin into common language."

"So everyone can read it?"

"Why not?"

He laughed. "Then everyone would want their own Bible.

There aren't enough copyists in all Christendom to do that—not in a hundred years."

I didn't want the conversation to wander off into a discussion of movable type; Rodney would only stay out of earshot for so long, and I could see him glancing at us from time to time.

"I know what I was taught as a child," I said finally. "Some of it I believe and some I don't. I believe in God more strongly than I did when this all started—but I find it difficult to *trust in the Lord* as you do. I envy you your faith, Rob."

"All of that and you didn't really answer the question," he said. "But if you do believe in the Saviour, then perhaps you believe in the Lord's angels."

"Angels?"

"I think an angel spoke to you, lad. It used my voice, but it wasn't me."

The sun had begun to feel warm at last. We couldn't see our breath anymore; the two of us stood there silently for a few more moments, lost in our own thoughts.

"I don't trust him," Rob said very quietly, shielding his mouth with his hand as he scratched his beard. "His brotherhood is in danger as well, but kings build cathedrals—he assumes that his services will continue to be needed, no matter what happens to us."

"Then why are we traveling with him?"

"We're not. We're traveling with the Ark," Rob answered. "And so is he. As long as we have a common goal we're allies. Don't forget that."

"I won't."

"I'm going to have to pray on what you've told me, lad. I don't know what I think about it."

"I don't know what I think about it either."

"Really." He raised an eyebrow. "What choice do *you* have?"

"I don't know. I wish I knew. So—what happens next?"

"We're going to the Jupiter Oracle. We—"

"The 'Jupiter Oracle'," I interrupted. "Wait a minute. You mean that the sphere of the initiation at Amiens is governed by Jupiter?"

"Yes, that's right."

It touched off a memory—of a voice speaking in the darkness: a corridor beneath the puzzle-box of Rosslyn Chapel.

The Saturn Oracle, Rodney's voice had said. *Where we expected to be.*

"Rob, where is the Saturn Oracle?"

"There isn't a Saturn Oracle, lad. The Jupiter Oracle is the last one. Moon, Mercury, Venus, Sun, Mars, Jupiter. Six in all. There isn't a seventh."

"Doesn't that strike you as odd?"

"The cathedral at Amiens is enormous. What could come after that?"

My thoughts strayed to a small, unfinished chapel a few kilometres south of Edinburgh, wrapped in mysterious carvings, proof against the centuries of change and tumult.

The Saturn Oracle.

After all the mystery, all of the concealment, all of what I'd been through since awakening in Santiago on St James' Day, I suddenly realised that if I was able to survive the next few weeks that I would find my way back to Rosslyn . . . in my own time, because there was none in this time.

"Let's go," I said, and walked toward the front of the cart, Rob a half step behind.

CHAPTER 14

We didn't trust Rodney—but we all had to take our turn sleeping. Once we had put some distance between ourselves and Chartres, we confined our travel to daylight hours—Rodney took the role of a tradesman, with Rob and I as his bodyguards. We'd agreed on that first morning that one of us would keep an eye on him all the way to Amiens.

On the third day of our journey, Rob was taking his turn sleeping in daylight; I rode next to our stonemason companion as he guided the cart along the road. He'd been silent on the subject of my revelation since the morning it had happened.

"I assume," he said out of the blue, "that the Templar hasn't told you anything about the initiations."

"We've talked about them quite a bit."

"I mean in advance. Before the fact . . . or do you already know what's to happen, since you're from the future?"

"I—" My first reaction was to answer, *Nobody knows about them in the future,* but I didn't say it. "I have taken the experiences as they've been presented."

We rode on a few hundred more yards, and then Rodney said, "That means exactly nothing."

He didn't look at me; I glanced at him, then looked away at the land sloping downward to the Eure river valley below us.

"I'm not sure what you want me to tell you."

"The Order of the Temple is like a lost sheep," Rodney said at last. "They were founded to guard the passage of pilgrims to the Holy Land—or so they would say: but the *routes templières* are all they have left to guard now. Everything they had in Outremer is lost, and they're lost with it."

"Bonomel."

"Yes. The moaning and wailing of Bonomel says it all, doesn't it? 'He will build a mosque out of the church of St Mary.' Most of the members of Robert's Order"—he jerked a thumb at the wagon bed—"don't even know what to do with themselves these days."

"Except escort pilgrims. And legendary sacred objects."

"Most of them don't even do that. Music or not, Initiate, you must realise that only a very few acolytes of your Order even undertake the pilgrimage. Only those judged worthy are even allowed to begin it."

I thought about that for awhile. I wasn't sure whether he was trying to compliment me or just denigrate the majority of the Order.

"They're very stingy about dispensing enlightenment," he added. "You should consider yourself lucky. Still, it should be obvious even to you that you're being used."

"You said that before, at Chartres. Used for what?"

"Aye, there's a question, isn't there. You have a special ability: a unique one, so far as I can tell."

"The music."

"The music. That's right. No other pilgrim has ever been able to hear it—de la Halle's music, composed in Chartres and intended to heal the world."

The healing music, I thought. "What does that mean?"

"I don't know. I thought perhaps you might—but you're as ignorant as the rest of us. So much for the wisdom of future ages . . . assuming you're really from the future."

"I told you I was."

"As you say."

"Roddy, where's the Saturn Oracle?"

The question caught him by surprise. He looked at me sharply, enough so that his attention to the horses faltered.

"There is no Saturn Oracle, Initiate," he answered at last. He clucked to the team, looking forward again. "It is the place of perfect measure . . . it doesn't exist."

"But it does," I whispered back. "It does, and I know where it is."

He let go of the reins and grabbed the front of my robe, pinning me up against the corner of the wagon seat—but unlike in the dark corridor beneath Chartres I could see it coming.

"You know? You know where it is? Tell me. Tell me *now.*"

"Damn it," I said, pulling from his grasp and twisting to face him. "Is that the only response you have to anything?"

Rob's head poked out of the wagon bed behind us.

"Need help, lad?"

The wagon had come to a halt with no one pulling on the reins. Rodney's fists were clenched; I was tensed and ready to throw him to the ground.

"I told him that I knew where the Saturn Oracle is, and he—" I wanted to say *freaked out,* but as usual the language fell short. "He reacted the way he always reacts."

"Let be, Giblumite," Rob said, climbing up onto the seat between us. He was alert—he didn't look as if he'd just had his sleep interrupted.

"He said—"

"Yes, he did, didn't he. What do you know about the Saturn Oracle, lad?" Rob said, without taking his eyes off Rodney.

"I told him that I knew where it is."

"Where is it?"

"Rosslyn. Rosslyn Chapel. That's the Saturn Oracle—and I heard Roddy say so. The day before I—the day before the Feast of St James, when I was sent back to this time—I toured

Rosslyn and heard him speaking to someone in the crypt."

"You're completely daft," Rodney said. "I've never been to this—Rosselain. Where is it?"

"Scotland."

"Ah." He threw his hands in the air and let them fall onto his thighs with a slap. "Scotland. Of course. It's no wonder I've never been there: who would bother to visit a God-forsaken place like that?"

"If I weren't from the Isles, I might take that as an insult."

"In my time, the Isles are part of Scotland," I added. "And Scotland is part of the United Kingdom. Scotland, England, and Wales—Great Britain."

"Now I *know* you're daft," Rodney said. "England and Scotland—the same kingdom?"

"And the same monarch. For more than four hundred years. But that's not what we're talking about."

"The Saturn Oracle doesn't exist," Rodney insisted. "Not in Scotland or anywhere else."

"Not yet."

"And in the future it does."

"Yes. I heard you say so."

"But I—" he began, then frowned around Rob at me. "You heard me say it."

"Yes."

"Perhaps I will be there . . . in the future. I'm not admitting that I believe you, Initiate, but if it were true . . . then you heard something already that for me is yet to come."

Rob rubbed his forehead. "I don't get it."

"I think I do," I said. My television experience had made me aware of the need for visual aids—I glanced around, looking for something, and hit upon the loose threads on one sleeve of my robe.

I pulled them out, one lighter and one darker, and laid them out on the wagon seat while my two companions watched.

"Look at this," I said, taking the darker one into my lap.

"Think of this as my life so far."

"As a soldier?"

"No," I said. "As a—" *television talking head,* I wanted to say. "As an entertainer. Up until my visit to Rosslyn, my life proceeds normally, growing up in Edinburgh. Then this—thing—happens." I laid out the thread in a straight line, left to right then pressed my finger on the middle—and drew it back so that the end lay far to the left of the other, like a backward 'C' with the bottom line far longer than the top. "So I wind up here, in 1307. Back here"—I pointed to the place farthest to the right—"I hear Roddy's voice saying that he's reached the Saturn Oracle."

I took up the lighter thread, placing the left end to the left of the end marking my place in 1307, and stretched it past to where it touched my place in Rosslyn. "Think of this one as Roddy's life. He starts in—whatever year he was born, passes through 1307, and somehow finds his way to Rosslyn in the twenty-first century, where he says he's in the Saturn Oracle—and I hear him. So it's already happened for me, but it hasn't happened *yet* for him."

"Your past is in his future," Rob said.

"Essentially, yes."

"But your past is in the future."

"Yes."

"And your future is . . ."

I looked around me at the scenery, the bumpy road, the wagon; I smelled the smells of horse and leather and wood and unwashed human; I listened to the silence.

"As remarkable as I have found the fourteenth century to be, I pray that my future is in the future."

No one had anything to say to that. I lifted my finger; a little bit of breeze caught the two threads and blew them away and out of sight.

—•—

We had not wanted to use Templar hostelries between Chartres and Amiens; Rodney—and by that time Rob as well—believed that word might reach those who were searching for us. Instead we found places to camp near the road, usually near one of the many little shrines. Rob would usually take a few moments to pray, hoping for a blessing, or perhaps only guidance on whether our course was the right one.

What I knew of Normandy was largely from the twentieth century—the D-Day invasion and so forth. Like most tourists I'd been in Paris when I'd taken French holidays, but not far outside it. But Rodney seemed to know the road well. When I asked him about it, he said that the paths between the locations of the great cathedrals—especially the Gothic ones—were lore of the Children of Solomon: something every journeyman learned. Further, both the roads and the workmen that traveled on them were protected by our own Order; like the pilgrims' paths to the Holy Land, they referred to them as *routes templières*.

—•—

A week along the road, we had stopped to rest the horses at a scenic overlook; the leaves on the trees were just beginning to turn, framing a postcard view of two small towns nestled in the bend of a river below. Beyond I could see steep white cliffs and, upriver a bit, a huge fortress.

I'd stepped away to do some necessary business. When I returned Rob and Rodney appeared to have just finished discussing something.

"Anything wrong?" I asked.

"The Giblumite wondered whether we could avoid this entire matter by turning you over to the Church as a witch."

"What?"

"You have to concede, lad, that your . . . revelation is hard to accept, on its face. But I told him that whether or not it was true, we needed to proceed as planned."

"I'm glad you came to my defence."

"The music," Rob answered. "You can hear it, and the Giblumite knows that. In any case, he has decided that we'd best avoid Rouen," Rob said. "We might be recognised."

"I haven't broken any hearts in Rouen." I shrugged. "At least I don't remember having done."

"De Bec has realised that we're not coming to Paris," Rodney said. "He—and his master—must be looking for us."

"France is a big country."

"They have their ways," the stonemason said, his brow furrowing. "De Bec is a sorcerer; he'll look for our course in the earth-path."

"He thinks we should cross the Seine," Rob said. "Here."

"That's the Seine down below?" I asked.

"Yes."

"Why does it matter where we cross?"

"They'll be searching the water-path as well, Initiate," Rodney said. "This is one of the narrowest places on the entire river. What's more, it's best we confuse matters as much as we can."

"How does crossing here confuse de Bec?"

"The most difficult divination is at a crossroads," Rodney said, frowning. He sounded annoyed, as if he were explaining the obvious. "Also, the church of Saint-Sauveur in Petit-Andély is a place where the air-path comes close to ground level. De Bec may sense us when we cross the river, but he should have trouble following us after that."

"You're saying . . . that he's watching the river? The whole river?"

"Within the Great Tower in the *Palais du Louvre* there is a map—a model, showing all of the lands of France," Rodney said. "It has the towns and cities, the great castles, the great churches—and all of the rivers, marked as accurately as possible. It was constructed on the orders of Monsieur de Nogaret. Even Archbishop Duèze—the Cahorsin—consented to it, though he half accused us of using black arts."

I didn't know that name; from the way that he spat it out, I assumed that he was another villain.

"This is how they dowse for us?" Rob asked. "They use this great model?"

"That's right."

"And how do you know about this?"

"Simple," Rodney said. "We constructed it."

"The map."

"The *Louvre,*" Rodney replied. "The Children of Father Soubise—and then the Children of Solomon—originally built the Louvre for Philip Augustus, Great Tower and all, map and all."

He folded his arms, a pose I'd seen before. *Knock the chip right off my shoulder,* he seemed to say.

Rob didn't reply; he looked as if he'd taken another blow to the side of his head that he hadn't expected.

"If they can use that map to track us," I said quietly, breaking the silence, "then why haven't they just zoned in on the Ark and found us already?"

"Hic amitur archa cederis," Rodney said. "We work through the Ark. It is because we have it with us, Initiate," he added, pointing to the cart. "The *keroubim* keep it from bending the earth-path as we pass."

Keroubim, I thought. *Cherubim?* I didn't understand what he meant, but that was nothing new. "But when we cross the Seine . . ."

"We'll show up on the God-cursed map," Rob finished my sentence and my thought. "They're waiting for us to cross the river."

—•—

We followed the road into Andély le Vieux, a town that looked like it had been there since Roman times. It sat in a bend in the river, water on three sides—a perfect place for a village of weavers and fishermen. There was a wide wooden bridge with stone footings extending across to the other shore, by way of a low, rocky island two thirds of the way across.

According to Rodney, when we took our little cart onto that bridge we'd be visible to de Bec, a few dozen miles upriver. My gut feeling was that we should get that behind us as soon as possible: cross the damn bridge, beard the lion—just move on toward Amiens with the box. But both of my companions disagreed.

"It won't do," Rob said, leading one of the horses to a trough in the courtyard. He looked up at the sky, where clouds had begun to crowd over the river. "It's seemly that we offer a prayer at the shrine."

"Rob, there are shrines every twenty paces. We can't stop at them all."

"We haven't stopped at them all, lad. But we are stopping at this one."

The horse had begun to drink thirstily; Rob walked away from me to unhitch the other one. I followed along.

"What's so special about this one?"

"This is one of the places where pilgrims stop. Not at this time of the year, mind: *peregrinos* headed for Santiago often stop here before heading south. It's late in the season for that."

"They don't close the place for the winter and go south?"

Rob turned from the horse harness and frowned. "This is some future thing, is it?"

I nodded. He shrugged and returned his attention to the horse. "We're going to visit the shrine, lad, and have a sip from the healing fountain. Whether or not it means something to you, I'll ask you to show courtesy."

"I didn't mean . . ."

Rob undid the last of the harness and led the horse past me without a word or a glance.

—•—

He still wasn't talking to me ten minutes later when we walked up the steps and into Andély's Notre-Dame. Like a hundred other churches in France—including the famous one in Paris, the one everyone knows—it was a church especially dedicated to the Virgin. From the outside it was shaped like a cross: a long, long main building extending back from a wide, west-facing portal crowned by two pointed towers, with transepts jutting outward just a bit three-quarters of the way back. Attached and crowded around it were the buildings of Saint-Clotilde monastery.

Another church, I thought—but I hadn't schooled my face to neutrality. Rob scowled at me, as if he had something to say but wasn't about to make the effort to say it.

We bowed our heads and walked slowly up the centre aisle. Afternoon light, now wan and pale with the sun hiding behind clouds, came in through high, decorated windows. It was after Nones; no Mass was being said. In the windows, in statues in a few niches along the walls, and in carvings on the lower piers supporting the choir I saw representations of the church's patroness, Saint Clotilde—a crowned woman with a book in one hand and a little model of the church in the other.

Someone was working through a theme on an organ off to our left. For just a moment I stopped dead in my tracks; Rodney went a few steps farther, but Rob stopped with me.

"What?"

I couldn't help but smile. "That reminds me of 'California Dreamin'," I said. "Seems appropriate."

The melody ran through my mind, but I shook my head and carefully let my face return to the proper level of solemnity. The moment was lost on Rob, of course, and I had nothing really to explain to him about it.

A monk approached just then, and led us to the south transept; there in a side-chapel, with newer construction than the nave itself, was a beautiful gilded statue of the saint—full size, her features lifelike, her expression caught in a transition moment between sorrow and contentment.

There was a hassock before the saint. We crossed ourselves and knelt, bowing our heads in prayer—Rob in the middle with me to his left and Rodney to his right.

After less than a minute Rodney crossed himself once more and pulled himself to his feet; I began to do the same but Rob placed a hand firmly on my arm and looked at me seriously. I considered pulling it away but relented.

"Blessed Saint Clotilde," he said, quietly, folding his hands once more and looking at the saint, "I humbly ask your intercession. Your great humility and holiness is known throughout the world—how you brought the light of our Saviour to this land, how you caused water to become as wine, and how you have always inclined your ear to prayers from those exiled from their native soil.

"I ask . . . not for myself." He looked down at the stones of the floor and took a deep breath. "I ask rather for my young companion, tossed to this place and . . . this time by chance and fate, a stranger to this land and a stranger to himself."

"Rob," I began, but he grasped my arm again, tighter this time.

"We are in desperate trouble," he continued, still looking at the saint and not at me. "Our enemies—the enemies of truth and of light—seek to destroy us. I do not fear for my soul; my place . . . for better or worse was settled long ago. My friend has no such assurance. He has not been given the knowledge he needs, he has not found the wisdom he must possess to carry out the task which burdens him. I was to be his guide, but I have failed.

"Blessed Queen, I don't know what to do."

He squeezed my arm again, then let go and let his hands drop to his sides. I couldn't tell in the light, but he might have had tears in his eyes.

There were a few more distant notes from the organist, but I ignored them.

No, Rob, I thought. *You haven't failed. You're like that bloke in Greek mythology—the one with the rock. Sisyphus. Nogaret is too powerful. De Bec is too powerful.*

And I'm not really much of a hero.

I thought about standing up then, leaving him to pray—but couldn't bring myself to do it. After a moment of consideration, I looked up at the statue.

Saint Clotilde, I thought. *I'm not fully briefed on who you are, what you are, or why you're here. It's a beautiful church; you have the respect of my friend here, which means you have my respect as well.*

I've had so many visions and dreams in this time, it would hardly surprise me if you began to give me some cryptic message about what I'm to do. I'm the star of the show it seems—but to be honest, I added, looking sideways at Rob, *it would be the greatest favour to me if you'd give some solace to my friend.*

He thinks he's failed me, but I'm hard pressed to imagine how.

I don't want guidance. But since I decided to tell him the truth of the matter he has been sorely troubled. But truth conquers all. He told me that.

I don't even know how to properly pray, but if there's anything you can do to help I'd be grateful.

If this had been a costume drama—especially one with particularly impressive special effects—it would have been the moment for the gilded hand of the statue to reach out and gently pat Rob on the head. It wouldn't have surprised me a bit.

Instead, we were merely favoured by a stray bit of sunlight finding its way between the clouds and through the quatrefoil window over the portal at the end of the south transept, warming Templar, displaced Initiate, and gilded saint's statue and casting soft shadows toward the nave. It was there long enough for Rob to glance at me, surprise—or perhaps even hope—on his face. Then the clouds swallowed up the sun once more, leaving us in grey light.

The organist went to work on the Rolling Stones.

We crossed ourselves. I stood, bowing to Saint Clotilde, and turned away. I took a step, then stopped, reaching into my scrip.

"What is it, lad?"

"Just an idea," I said. I searched around among the few coins I was carrying and pulled out what I was looking for: the St Giles medal I had been given at Saint-Eutrope in Saintes.

I turned and walked back to the statue, inclined my head, and then reached out and placed the medal on the corner of the plinth. Rob watched this without remark.

"All right," I said. "I'm ready to go."

—•—

Outside, the afternoon light was gradually retreating in the face of what looked to become quite a storm. Rodney was already attending to the cart and the horses; Rob directed me up a short circular flight of steps to a fountain. We each took a ceramic cup from a hook, dipped it in, and after a moment of bowed heads took a sip of cool, clear water.

"Did you have any luck with the saint?" I said.

"Maybe I did," he answered. He sat at the edge of the fountain, drank deeply from the cup, and then returned it to its hook. "As I knelt there I had an idea; mayhap it was just taking the time to think of it, or possibly the Lady placed it in my thick skull.

"Lad, if you are truly from the future and have come back to be with your other self—then I believe that in order to do what we must, we need *both* of you. The man who fought the Saracen and chose to come to Compostela isn't enough; the man you were—whatever you were, in that unknown future land—isn't enough either. Two must become one."

"My tale is true," I said, and drank my water.

"The Giblumite thinks that this is a Templar plot. But he's afraid, Ian. He knows that this is beyond all of us, and has no more idea than I do what we will find in Amiens."

"Or what will happen when we cross the river."

"Or that. I don't know what will happen either. I can't fight sorcery, lad—if de Bec had found us that night outside of Orléans, I don't know what I would have done. What I *could* have done. Something or someone protected us that night."

"Perhaps luck will favour us again."

"Perhaps Saint Clotilde will favour us now," he answered, standing. "We'd best get ready to cross that river before the heavens open."

—•—

Rodney and Rob took their places on the wagon seat; I settled in the wagon bed next to the crate holding the Ark. As I made myself comfortable, I noticed that one of the laces on my pack had come loose—enough so that some of the contents had spilled out.

I picked up a piece of cloth—the cloak-half from earlier in the journey—but after a moment I stopped, stunned.

It wasn't a cloak-half at all. It was a cloak. The two parts were together, with no ragged edge. As I held it up before me, a bit of metal rolled out of the bundle to land next to my foot. Even with the sky darkening I could tell that it was my St Giles medallion.

"Stop," I said. We'd made our way through Andély and were moving slowly down toward the west end of the bridge across the Seine.

I scrambled on to the wagon seat, the cloak in one hand, the medal in the other. I showed them to Rob, each in turn, while Rodney sat, scowling, perhaps annoyed at the delay.

"Put it on, lad," Rob said. He yielded his seat to me and clambered into the wagon bed. I secured the cloak around my shoulders and fastened the clasp.

"What—" Rodney began to ask.

"Let's cross the bridge," Rob said. "Come on, Giblumite. Before it begins to rain."

Rodney waited a few seconds, as if he realised that something had passed between Rob and myself; then he clucked to the horses and snapped the reins, and we began to move onto the bridge.

It seemed to take forever. Drops of rain began to spatter on us as we moved across. I was sitting on the right side of the wagon seat; somewhere off to my right was Paris, and the Louvre and its map, and presumably de Bec waving his hands at it—or whatever sorcerers were meant to do.

Someone—lots of someones—were looking for us. Lots of someones might well be looking for the Ark as well. It didn't bear thinking what would happen if they found it—or us.

Two become one, I thought, shrugging inside the cloak. *Ian Graham—late of* Ian and Jan—*Gran MacPherson's favourite grandchild. Ian Graham, late of Lamontaigne's Company—who has lost himself and doesn't know how to find the broken pieces.*

Both of us are here now. Bring it on.

We reached the opposite shore just as the skies opened, dousing us with chilling rain.

CHAPTER 15

IT RAINED WHILE THE DAY FADED INTO NIGHT, AND THROUGH THE night as well. We found some shelter in Petit-Andély beneath the arch of a bridge, not far from the massive presence of Château-Galliard—for rain means mud, and we could hardly afford any sort of mishap with cart or horses.

We settled ourselves in the wagon after eating a brief meal. It was waterproof enough, the canvas waxed and without holes; the rain ran steadily down the outside—a storm from nowhere, the worst weather we'd seen since leaving Chartres.

"This has to be de Bec's doing," Rodney said finally. We'd exchanged few words since crossing the bridge; finding a place out of the rain and arranging ourselves for a wet night had taken up our attention.

"Is that something sorcerers can do?" I asked.

"Of course."

"Of course," I repeated. "Then why hasn't he been doing it all along?"

"It takes an effort to do that, Initiate."

"You could call me 'Ian,' Roddy."

"Names have power," he answered. "Truthfully, Initiate, it would please me if you would avoid using mine. Particularly that annoying nickname."

"Every Rodney in Scotland is called Roddy, whether he likes it or not."

"I *don't,*" he said. I heard Rob cover a chuckle by clearing his throat. "Perhaps we should find a nickname for you as well," he added.

It was my turn to smile. "Already happened. My Gran always called me 'Wee Ian'—my father was 'Big Ian', even though I outweighed him by two stone."

"I'll keep that in mind."

"All right. Fine. Well, the Initiate—that's me—wants to know why de Bec hasn't been pounding us with storms all along."

"He doesn't know where we are. Not exactly. He can't just send storms out into the countryside."

"But you think he sent this one."

"It feels so." Rodney was sitting with his knees drawn up; I couldn't see his expression, but he seemed to have his head cocked, as if he were listening to the rain. "It has a sorcerous tang to it. Since we've exposed ourselves to the water-path, I can only assume that de Bec has detected us."

"But the storm started before we crossed the river," I said. "You told me that the—that our cargo—prevented him from following us through the earth-path. How did he know to send this sorcerous storm before he knew where we were?"

That question hung in the air for a few minutes. I couldn't imagine that the stonemason hadn't already thought of that.

"Are you sure this storm is sorcery, Giblumite?" Rob asked, shifting his position slightly.

"No, I'm *not* sure," Rodney said. "I'm not sure of anything. I'm not even sure I know why we're trying to get to Amiens. Do *you?*"

"I thought I did. When we took our cargo from its resting-place it made sense, but I'm not sure now. Ian's been sent here from time to come and knows—*knows*—that His Highness Philippe is to betray the Order in a matter of weeks; why does any of this matter? Is it of any consequence that we even go to the Jupiter Oracle?"

"Isn't what you seek at the Jupiter Oracle, Templar?"

"What I seek . . ." Rob let the answer trail off into nothing. We sat and listened to the rain for a few minutes. The sound was almost hypnotic: steady, heavy, the heavens opened up and letting loose on us poor folks below.

"What do you seek, Templar?" Rodney said at last. "Pray, tell us."

"I think I'd like to know the answer to that myself," I added. "I know what I want more than anything: I want to go home—I want my time and place back. But I don't really know what you want, Rob."

"I want my time and place back as well, lad," Rob said after a moment, during which I suspect he tried to formulate an answer. "But it's gone forever."

"What is it? What was it?"

"The Kingdom of Jerusalem," Rob anwered. "The last Christian kingdom in Outremer."

"I know you were there . . ."

"Almost to the end, lad. I left for Cyprus with Grand Master De Gaudin just before Acre fell."

The rain fell outside for a short time before Rodney asked, "And how did you come to be there in the first place?"

Rob shifted his position again. For just a moment I thought I heard something from within the crate that held the Ark.

"I came into the service of the Order when I was sixteen," Rob began. "I was a *confrère,* a servant in an associate order—a grounds-keeper at Balintradoch, if you can imagine it.

"Not much glory in grounds-keeping, though," he continued. "A few years on, I stowed away on a galley bound for the Middle Sea—and by the time they found me out we were at sea. I was young and strong and quickly learned my way around the ship."

"So they didn't pitch you overboard," Rodney said. Stonemason and Templar both seemed amused by that.

"No."

"And they didn't put you off at Genoa or Venice to find your way back home."

"I wanted to be a man-at-arms, Giblumite. I wanted to fight for the Sepulchre, to shout 'Beauséant', to wear the badge of a Crusader."

"That time is past," Rodney said, his voice tinged with sadness. "Jerusalem was lost at the Horns of Hattin, and the kings of the West had no interest in getting it back. And, I should say, neither did most of your Order."

"We still held land there when I arrived, and for years after. I distinguished myself—I received the mantle of a man-at-arms. I took the vows of a soldier of the Temple and was willing: nay, ready—to die in defence of the Cross."

"Why didn't you?" I asked.

"Why didn't I what?"

"Why didn't you die in the Holy Land, Rob? It sounds as if you wanted to fall in battle."

"If I didn't know you well, lad, I might find that question cause for challenge."

The comment hung heavily in the air.

"That's not what I meant."

"No, I know it isn't. Before God, Ian, I've asked myself the same question. Do you know the story of the fall of Acre? No, I don't expect you do. Saint Jean d'Acre was our last stronghold in Outremer; we were sworn to defend it against Kalaun, the Saracen general. Grand Master de Beaujeu received an offer from Kalaun—if he would pay one Venetian sequin for every person within its walls, the infidels would go away satisfied. The Grand Master proposed the idea to the people of Acre, but they accused him of cowardice.

"He was no coward when he died defending them. And those who remained in the fortress to fight to the last, while the rest of us left for Cyprus, were no cowards either. I sometimes wonder if I should not have been among them rather than one of those who sailed away."

"You're not the only one who lived to fight on," I said. "Do you really think of yourself as a coward? Do you think that you should have died in Outremer?"

"I was still young," Rob said after a moment. "But the Giblumite's brethren—some of them, at least—think of us as cowards. They were ready for violence beneath the Hill of the Strong; didn't they tell us that the Templars' day was done? As for me—God's will be done, I suppose."

It was too dark for me to see, but I would have guessed that Rob was looking at Rodney in the dark, daring him to agree with his professional colleagues. I had seen how much the Order of the Temple was respected—and feared, and despised. And in four weeks it would be betrayed. It couldn't have sat well with Rob, who had served the Order for most of his life.

But he hadn't answered my question.

"Not yet, I would say," Rodney said. "Whatever the Lord has planned for your Order, Templar, there's work yet to do."

—•—

The storm had passed over us by late the following morning. It was still damp, and uncomfortably cold—more so than I would have expected Picardy to be in mid-September. Still, it was better to be moving than staying in one place. After some discussion—at which I was present, but could provide no useful input—Rob and Rodney determined that we should travel onward from Andély to Gisors, where the earth-path—and thus the *route templière*—crossed the water-path once again.

The knowledge that de Bec, or his master Nogaret, or *his* master King Philippe—or maybe all three—were hunched around a relief map in a tower in Paris watching for any sign of us should probably have given me an even greater sense of dread. But as we moved eastward for the next few days, I felt almost relieved.

It's 1307, I reminded myself, *and you're a Templar.* I'd allowed that to be true when Rob, in the first initiation at Santiago, had told me so. It was four weeks away—Friday the thirteenth, the great betrayal.

And yet . . . I felt as if I was whole now, as equal as I'd ever been to the challenge of being chosen for this pilgrimage. I wasn't sure how the two parts of me were supposed to fit together, but it seemed that it was beginning to happen of its own accord.

My mental state at the time, if it could be called that, was remarkable considering the notion that I might be swept up, tortured, burned at the stake for whatever crimes the King of France chose to charge me with. It wasn't that I didn't care: it was as if my resolve had grown to the point that—regardless of the event that I knew was to happen—I was by God going forward, because there was no going back.

—•—

"Why Gisors?" I asked as we came down a gentle hill, the town laid out before us like a 40p postcard. "I assume we have to cross the river, but—"

"It is where the earth-path goes, Initiate," Rodney said. "Haven't you already had that explained to you?"

"In a word, no."

"We are following the earth-path because our cargo helps conceal our passage—"

"I know that, Roddy," I said. He scowled at the name; I smiled for the camera. "I just want to know what the earth-path actually is—is it like the *camino de las estrellas?*"

"That's the air-path, lad," Rob said from inside the wagon. He leaned forward, sticking his head out. "Where'd you hear of that?"

"From you." When he began to protest, I added, "In the first initiation. Remember, I told you."

"Ah."

"An ill-kept secret of our brotherhood," Rodney said, scowling at Rob, "is that there are paths all across the lands of Europe, marking the flows of the earth's energy. This energy—the telluric flow—follows the contours of the earth, concentrating in key places."

"Especially where it crosses other elemental paths," Rob put in.

"That's right," Rodney agreed. "And where the concentration is great, men have always built shrines and temples. The ancients, and the Romans that followed them, established places of worship near underground water flows, at the brows of prominent hills . . . and other places as well. When we build our own places, we make them align to the telluric flow."

"Feng shui," I said to myself, and received the usual blank looks. "Telluric flow," I prompted Rodney. "And it leads through Gisors?"

"There are earth-paths all over France," Rob said. "I'd guess that the way from Andély to Amiens leads through Gisors. But," he continued, pulling himself onto the seat between Rodney and me, "I think I understand Ian's question, Giblumite. Is there any reason for us to pass through Gisors?"

Rodney didn't answer directly, focusing his attention on the horses and wagon.

"Am I due for a mystical revelation, Rob?" I asked.

"This isn't my pilgrimage, lad. But I think we're waiting for an answer."

Rodney pulled the reins, guiding the cart to the shoulder of the road under a small stand of trees.

"You don't trust me, do you, Templar? Do you think I'm leading you into the arms of King Philip's sorcerer?"

"Are you?" I said.

Rodney waited a few seconds too long, I think, before answering, "No."

"Couldn't we leave the earth-path altogether?" I said. "I thought we were following it for some reason—and that the . . . cargo was preventing de Bec from following us. If we don't need to follow it to Gisors, why don't we just go off to Le Havre or something?"

"Le Havre?" Rodney said. "Why would you want to go to Le Havre?"

"Somewhere else, then." I hadn't managed to make myself clear for the thousandth time. "Why are we following the earth-path? Why not just make for Amiens?"

Rob's face suggested that he knew, but was waiting for Rodney to give the answer.

"We're under the protection of my brotherhood, Initiate," Rodney said. "As long as we remain on the *routes templières,* they will be able to help us."

"How?"

"They can *help* us, Initiate," he repeated. "You must accept that as a matter of trust."

"Does Rob trust you on this?"

He waited another few seconds. "Yes. And after we go to Gisors, you will as well."

—•—

Rob had no comment as we came into the town. As with Andély—and innumerable other hills across France where wars were being fought—there was a major fortification on the top of a hill.

Rodney guided the wagon up a steep slope to the fort's outer works, a curtain-wall three or four metres high; above it was a tower that loomed at least five times that. A tunnel through the wall gave access to the inner courtyard, and Rodney didn't hesitate. We plunged into relative darkness and then emerged in a few seconds into bright overcast.

"Is this a good idea?" I asked Rob quietly. He'd remained on the wagon-seat, a wary expression on his face.

"I pray that it is."

Rodney nodded to us and jumped down to the flagstoned ground. Rob followed, taking his staff from beneath his feet; I did the same. We took a few seconds to look around. Rodney was waiting for something—we weren't sure what.

A well-dressed young man emerged from an arched doorway and approached the cart. Rodney stepped forward and offered his hand; the man took it and let the hand slip to Rodney's elbow, grasping it with his other as his own elbow touched his palm. I stepped forward, but Rob held me back.

"I've seen that," I said. "Twice."

"No doubt," Rob said. "But don't interfere."

I'd been given that handshake: first by Juan la Rosa at the second initiation, then by Brother Andre at Saintes. There was some meaning to it that hadn't been explained to me.

The young man seemed satisfied, nodding to Rodney. He beckoned to the two of us, and we followed the other man into the inner apartments.

Stepping into the building, I instantly sensed something: this was the house of a very sick man. It didn't take any sort of expert to pick that up, in this or any other century; there was some composition of smell, sound and light that conveyed it.

Rob leaned close and said, "Now I understand why we're here. You'll show proper respect to the lord."

"He's dying, isn't he?" I answered.

Rob didn't answer, merely nodding, his lips pressed tightly together. "His last journey was too much for him. I believe he was meant to meet us in Amiens, but will never reach it."

"How—" I began, but we'd passed through to an inner door. The young man knocked, and someone opened it.

Before us was a sick-bed. Somewhere among the covers and pillows was a small figure—and I stood stock still, recognizing the dying lord.

This might be my last visit. The Lord gave me strength to get here one more time.

A minute or two before I'd touched the Tree of Jesse at Santiago, the man in this bed had done so. We'd all feared that he wasn't going to make it—but he did: the old man, toothless and coughing, at Santiago de Compostela on Saint James' Day.

"Come closer," the man in the bed whispered, looking directly at me. I stepped close, the others parting to let me approach. There was a little three-legged stool next to the bed, and he gestured for me to take it.

"You know me," I said.

"Yes. You are the initiate who can hear the music."

"Apparently so. You knew that when you saw me in Santiago, I take it."

"I had to make sure." He turned his head aside for a coughing bout, then returned his attention to me. "I wanted to see for myself."

"Who are you, Monsieur?"

"My name is—" He did a bit more coughing. "I am Guillaume, Lord of Gisors."

That ranked him as a person of some importance, of course, but I looked at Rob for some sort of indication what that should mean to me past the obvious.

"I am honoured to meet you," I said in my best Channel 4 voice.

"I have been waiting for you, Ian," he said. Everyone seemed to know my name. "I knew we would meet again. I had hoped—" There was a pause; he looked as if he would succumb to coughing, but it didn't quite come. He took my hand in his: my rough, calloused, not particularly clean hand between his two aged ones.

My hand in God's hands, I thought.

"I had hoped," he finally said, "to see the lamp of your soul revealed at Amiens, at the sixth initiation. But the journey to Santiago was almost too much for me."

"I'm sorry."

"Don't be. We have met—and met again. And now you are here. Everything has a purpose. The eye is the lamp of the body. If your eye is sound, your whole body will be full of light."

"I've been told that."

His right eyebrow went up. "Have you." He gave my hand a little squeeze. "I have something for you, Ian." He looked away and nodded at the younger man—his son, perhaps, or his grandson, who stepped over to a shelf and brought down a leather-bound volume. He presented it to the lord, who let go of my hand to take it.

"What is this?" I asked.

"I am soon to depart this life, Ian," he said. "This is my greatest treasure. There is no land, no precious stone, no work of art so valuable as this book. I give it to you."

He placed the book in my hands with the reverence of a priest. I took it, looking again to Rob and Rodney for some indication of what had just happened.

"Monsieur," Rob said, "is that—"

"Of course," Rodney interrupted, before Rob could give me any useful information. Whatever Rob thought it was, it clearly was.

"Go ahead, young man," the lord said in his fading voice. "Open it."

He smiled slightly, as if he had completed some great burdensome task. Perhaps he had.

Ian and Jan several times had had guests who brought some valuable thing into our studio: a piece of artwork, a delicate item of jewelry, a rare book. We had been fairly well coached at the correct way to show reverence for the thing—so that the studio audience would give the proper 'aaah' when it was examined on close up. I wiped my right hand on my robe—my palm was sweating—and slowly I drew it open. There was no audience to make the right noise, but Rodney and Rob appeared to be holding their breath.

I expected the book to be some sort of illuminated manuscript: the kind of thing you see under glass at a museum, delicate vines intertwining ornate capital letters, beautiful, structured lines of carefully placed characters spelling out words no one but scholars read. Instead, what I saw before me were rows and rows of numbers.

They were arranged in threes and written with little or no ornamentation: Roman numerals, a single number followed by a bullet and then another number in the hundreds:

I • CCCXVII	II • DCXLIX	I • DCCCIII
III • XLII	I • III	I • CXVI
I • CMLV	III • CVIII	II • CCCLXXXI

Hundreds upon hundreds of rows of these numerals, arranged side by side, three columns to the page. I gently turned the first leaf over and the second and third pages held the same. Without proceeding further I could tell that there must be fifty or sixty leaves to the book. If they were all filled there would be hundreds of thousands, perhaps a few million, numbers.

It was a code: a mathematical expression of something—God knew what. Rodney's eyes were filled with astonishment; Rob's, reverence. If a mirror had been held up before my eyes, I'm fairly sure they'd be filled with confusion.

"What is this that I hold in my hands, my lord?" I asked.

"It is that which heals the world," he answered almost too softly for me to hear. His eyes were closed, his hands laid gently on the coverlets of his bed.

"Is this . . . music?"

"It is the key," Guillaume de Gisors said. "The key."

I closed the book and laid it in my lap. The tooled leather of the cover was of ornate design; it was some sort of abstract pattern that didn't make sense.

I looked up at Rodney and Rob, still transfixed by the scene. The young man, the younger scion of the Gisors noble house, was stoic, but his eyes were full of tears waiting to be shed. I looked back down at the book in my lap.

Suddenly a picture leapt up at me from the leatherwork. It was two designs intertwined; my hands were placed on it in just such a way as to allow me to see them separately and then together.

The first was the outline of a chalice: a wide-brimmed but simple cup, flared from a broad stem and standing on a fluted base.

The second was of a fish.

I didn't understand what the information in the book was intended to convey—but the symbolism was too obvious even for a dull-witted, temporally displaced, less-than-devout ex-Presbyterian to miss.

"I am honoured beyond words, my lord," I managed. Glib telly personality that I was, I couldn't think of what else to say.

"By your leave, my lord," Rodney said, inclining his head respectfully, "we will be on our way."

The old man's eyes came open just a crack. Slowly, he raised his hands to his mouth, placing index and middle fingers to each corner, then let them fall to the coverlet.

"Dieu vo garde," he said. God keep you.

CHAPTER 16

WE CONTINUED OUR JOURNEY TO AND THROUGH BEAUVAIS, home to another Gothic church that had collapsed and was being rebuilt. Rob rode on the wagon-seat with Rodney while I sat next to the crate containing the Ark of the Covenant, the Holy Grail in my lap. I had two of the most extraordinary, sought-after artifacts in human history within reach.

There was no way to say that it blew my mind in *langue d'oc;* and there I was, still unsure why I could hear the music, or how this would all end.

As we traveled I looked through the Grail-book. My first impression was that the entire volume was merely filled with these cryptic numbers; but there was a sort of order. The book was divided into twenty-four sections. Each of the first twenty-two was labeled with a larger numeral drawn in gold; the twenty-third and twenty-fourth were more elaborate and instead of the number bore an inscription—Latin ones that were in a different hand and read: IESUS FILII JOSEPHUS . . . Jesus, son of Joseph, and IESUS FILII MARIA . . . Jesus, son of Mary.

But what did the numbers mean? My companions seemed to be waiting for me to tell them. Roman numerals weren't so foreign: every film and telly programme had them in the credits—V for five, X for ten, L for fifty and so on. I couldn't see any pattern, but there were definite limits on the numbers in the lists. Each was a one, two or three followed by a bullet and then a number or, in a few cases, a slash mark that I took to mean zero—there was no Roman numeral for zero, I remembered from Maths Highers, that was an Arabic invention. So the first three rows were:

1 • 317	2 • 669	1 • 803
3 • 42	1 • 3	1 • 116
1 • 955	3 • 108	2 • 381

The highest number I found to the right of the bullet was 999.

Decimals, I realised, as the cart traversed a particularly uncomfortable bump. They're decimal fractions. 999 is .999, 42 is .042. These are numbers between 1 and . . . and, it seemed, something just over 3; at least in the first several pages, the largest fraction I found following a 3 was 141.

It hurt my head to think about it. Jesus, the son of Joseph and Mary and not incidentally the Son of God, had been reduced in some fashion to some millions of numbers between 1 and 3.141. The outer boundary stuck in my mind, tugging at some painful memory from my school days, until it struck me as we camped one night, two days after leaving Beauvais.

—•—

"Pi," I said aloud.

The days were now brisk and the nights downright chilly; a half moon was high in the sky. Rob was repairing a piece of leather from a harness. Rodney was stirring the kindling in our fire.

"Pardon?" the stonemason said.

Rob had been traveling with me for two months and was used to having me say things he didn't understand. He set the harness aside and leaned forward, elbows on knees, chin on his fists. "Say on, lad."

"Pi. The numbers in the Grail-book—none of them are larger than pi. About three and a seventh."

Rob looked helpless, Rodney curious. "And what," Rodney said, not looking at me, "do you suppose that means?"

"I haven't the faintest clue."

"Would you two explain to me what you mean?" Rob asked.

"About what?"

"What do you mean by 'pi'?" he said.

"Pi is the ratio of the circumference of a circle to its diameter," I said.

Rodney's eyes brightened. "Archimedes' constant," he said. "Interesting."

Rob looked mystified, his brows furrowing. I picked up a small stick from the pile of brush that hadn't yet been fed to the fire, and came over to kneel next to where Rob sat. I drew a circle in the dirt and marked the centre with a dot, then drew a line from the centre to the edge of the circle.

"This is the radius of the circle," I said, pointing to the line with my stick. "And this"—I traced the circle itself—"is the circumference. Take any circle, and this bit will always be an exact multiple of *this* bit." I touched circumference and radius in turn. "What Roddy calls Archimedes' constant I was taught to call by the Greek letter 'pi'." Evidently that term was later than the fourteenth century, but I had no way of looking it up.

"Any circle?"

"Any circle. It can be as small as this one, or as big as the moon."

Rob squinted at the sky. "That's not very big."

"The moon is thousands of miles across," I answered immediately, and moments later regretted it; Rob looked more dubious than ever. The moon was about the size of a 20p coin held a handspan from the eyes—it went through phases to be sure, but never got bigger or smaller.

"It doesn't matter how big or small the circle is, Templar," Rodney said, unhitching me from the uncomfortable moment. "The ratio is always the same—a number a bit over 3. The great Archimedes found it by the method of exhaustion."

I didn't remember that particular fact, or any other fact to contradict it—but the mention of a Greek seemed to give it the ring of truth for Rob.

"Why is it 'a bit over 3'?" He asked. "Not 3? It seems overly complicated."

"The Lord works in mysterious ways," Rodney said, clearing his throat and spitting into the dark. I wasn't sure if that was just spitting or some sort of sarcastic punctuation.

"There's no number in the book greater than pi," I said, returning to my own seat. "The smallest number is 1, the largest just less than pi."

"It must have something to do with circles," Rodney ventured. "These are dimensions, then, like the boundaries of an arch or a tower."

"Our Lord and Saviour is not a circle, and He is not a tower," Rob said, a trifle angrily. He looked down at the circle I'd drawn, and scuffed it with his boot. "I'm not sure I like the direction this conversation is going."

"I meant no disrespect—" I began, but that seemed to bother him more. He pulled himself to his feet and turned his back, walking into the dark—not toward the place we'd set aside for a privy but rather the other direction, toward a smaller stand of trees and the bank of a small creek from which we'd drawn water earlier in the evening.

I began to get up and follow him, but Rodney touched my arm and I subsided.

"I don't understand what just happened," I said.

"Let him go, Initiate. As this business continues, he understands less and less. Something offends him, but he cannot bear to simply pluck it out."

—•—

I waited a few minutes and then stood and followed. Rodney frowned but didn't try to stop me this time. I walked to the cluster of trees; there was a slight downslope to the creek where I found Rob kneeling on a dry, flat space, a shadow against the moonlit water.

"Nunc dimittis servum tuum, Domine," he said without turning. *"Secundum verbum tuum in pace: quia viderunt oculi mei. Salutare tuum*

quod parasti, ante faciem omnium populorum: lumen ad revelationem gentium, et gloriam plebis tuae Israel."

I had heard Rob speak and sing many times during this pilgrimage; he had a beautiful singing voice and a pleasant speaking voice that combined a soft Scottish burr with whatever language he was using—Occitan or, in this case, Latin.

Two months ago I wouldn't possibly have placed the prayer, but the Compline office was part of my life now and I knew it very well.

Lord, now lettest thou thy servant depart in peace, according to thy word: For mine eyes have seen thy salvation, which thou hast prepared before the face of all people; a light to lighten the Gentiles, and the glory of thy people Israel.

It was the Canticle of Simeon, the devout Jew who had been promised by the Holy Ghost that he would not die before he saw the Saviour.

"Are you ready to die now, Rob?" I came down the slope and squatted down beside him. "I don't think your work is done."

He turned his head to me. "I've done what I was expected to do. But it was the Giblumite's choice to cross the Seine at Andély, lad. He knew we would come to Gisors for the . . . for the book. He can be your guide now."

"That's not my choice, my friend. You already tried to walk away. What makes you think I want you to?"

"The Giblumite wants me to."

"I don't know what the—what Roddy's agenda truly is."

"You don't know much of anything." In the moonlight I could see a faint smile on his face. "You know that the Order is to be destroyed; you know that we have been waiting for the one who can hear the music. But you've been manipulated, deceived and led by paths you know not. If things had been different, you might well have had a chance to grow closer to God. As it is . . ."

I pulled myself down to sit beside him.

"When I first met you—"

"In the future?"

"Yes. At Rosslyn. When I first met you, you told me the story of Zerubbabel. Wine is strong; the king is stronger; women are stronger still—"

"But truth conquers all. It's from Esdras."

"That's right. And I've spent the last two months trying to figure out just what constitutes truth. When I decided to tell you who and what I really was, I thought—I knew—that it would be hard for you to understand what that would mean. But truth really *does* conquer all.

"So here's some home-grown truth, Rob. I have grown closer to God. I never really knew what I thought of Him, or what He thought of me, or what I was supposed to be doing with my life. I would never have guessed that this was it . . . but I've seen great wonders. Two of them are in our cart, things of legend. Most people in the future don't even think they exist—and yet I've seen them.

"And I've had a chance to meet you, travel and fight and laugh and pray with you. If that doesn't bring me closer to God, I don't know what could."

He looked away and into the creek.

He crossed himself. "If I were the blessed Virgin, lad, I could tell you that my soul doth magnify the Lord, but instead I am a poor and humble seeker. If I've brought you at all closer in your journey, then I've accomplished my task in part."

"You're closer to God than I am—something for me to strive for." I took a small stone and tossed it into the water; the image of the moon shattered, spread out, and slowly re-formed.

"You think so."

"Yes. I think so. And I don't give a damn what Roddy thinks on this subject. We need him, we need his help. But my relationship to God has nothing—*nothing*—to do with the pilgrimage."

"We should pray," Rob said.

I shifted from a sitting to a kneeling position; as the water settled back to calm, Rob and I sent our silent invocations into the night sky, hoping they would reach their destination.

—•—

Rodney had been reserved and grim for most of this journey; the business with the Grail and the Lord of Gisors seemed to trouble him. Rob's spirits, on the other hand, seemed much lighter after the night I had my insights about the Grail-book's numbers; it wasn't quite like our earliest times together, but he seemed more confident that he had a place in our journey.

For my part, I only had one further question about Gisors; Rodney provided the answer as we traveled through the countryside of Picardy.

"Why was something as precious as the book," I asked him at one point, "kept in a place like Gisors?"

"Do you find something wrong with Gisors, Initiate?" he answered, a question to a question.

"Nothing at all. But I would've guessed it to be guarded and hidden like the Ark. It was, I don't know, sitting on a shelf in the lord's bedroom."

"Hm." Rodney scowled, a practised expression. There was something else I was obviously supposed to know. "You have some understanding of the earth-paths," he said. "Gisors was an important node for centuries—not just because the path crossed the Epte at that point, but because of the Elm."

"What Elm?" He'd capitalized it, so I did as well.

"The Elm of Gisors. For centuries kings had met beneath it to discuss peace. It stood in the *Champ Sacre,* the Sacred Field, and was a powerful nexus for the earth-path. It was . . . until King Phillippe cut it down."

"Our King Phillippe?"

"No, the second of that name. It was in 1188, when the tree had grown so great that nine men linking hands could barely encompass its trunk. The English King Henry—Curtmantle—had his army sheltered beneath the tree—and Phillippe announced that he would cut it down to take that shelter away."

An image of fellow Scot David McCallum from *The Lion in Winter* flashed through my mind. "Go on," I said, thinking about the stage-play as Rodney continued to talk of it—narrative history fighting with the theatre drama I'd seen as a schoolboy. Surreal, really.

"Henry placed iron bands around the tree to protect it. Even Queen Eleanor could have told him that such an act would weaken the tree by severing its connection with the earth-path—though I suspect that he was far too proud to listen to advice.

"In any case, Phillippe did cut the tree down, then stormed back to Paris in a huff, claiming that he had not come to the Sacred Field of Gisors to play the role of a woodcutter.

"But what is most important about this tale, Initiate," he said, allowing himself a bit of a smile as I was about to ask him why the hell any of this mattered, "is that the cutting of the Elm—which truly happened—represents far more than a simple act of spite by a king whose royal line seems to possess that trait in abundance.

"By severing the Elm of Gisors, Phillippe was symbolically severing his relationship with Henry, and the French from the English. Both, you see, were descendants of the Merovingian dynasty—and thus both bore the blood of the House of David in their veins."

That caught my attention. "Wait. You're saying—" I tried to gather it all in, the elm, the kings, and the genealogy. "You're saying that the kings of England and France are descendants of *Jesus?*"

"Not necessarily. But there are related bloodlines." Rodney looked up at the cloudy sky, as if he were simply looking for rain and not blasphemously undermining fundamental Church doctrine. "Truly, the Bible says nothing about Jesus' actual descendants. But there are accounts of such: repressed by the early leaders, declared heretical by the Church's hierarchy. And even if the Saviour Himself had no descendants, there are—or were—close relatives who did. And the Gisors Elm symbolically represented them—and when it was cut down the two branches were sundered. All that remained was the book you now possess. After the Elm was destroyed, Lord Guillaume's great-grandfather Jean hid it away, waiting for the right person to come."

"So . . . you're saying that the Grail-book is related somehow to Jesus' family bloodline."

"Sangreal. Holy blood. That's about right, Initiate, and that's what the Children of Solomon—my brother stonemasons—have always believed, as well as those charged with the custody of the book."

"But what does it mean?"

"I think we were hoping you could tell us. The other night you realised that the numbers were in a particular range; does it mean anything to you?"

"Not really."

"And—it's divided into sections, you say."

"Twenty-four. The first twenty-two are numbered; the last two each bear Jesus' name and that of His father and mother. They're all different lengths: some long, some short."

"Does that mean anything to you?"

"No. But it must mean something to someone. The lord said it was the key—not the music, but the key. Does it combine somehow with the music only I can hear?"

"I'd expect so," Rodney answered. "But I don't know how."

I wish Juan were here, I thought. It was the first time I'd thought about our Asturian friend in weeks; I hoped he was safe, though I suspected otherwise.

"I've never heard all of the music together," I said. "But the numbers in the book seem much more complicated than simple music. There's some relationship that we haven't discovered yet."

"Yet," he repeated, as if unsure whether we might ever find it. I had no answer for his doubts, only the realization that time was growing ever shorter for the path we took to be completed.

—•—

We came at last to Amiens on Friday, the twenty-second of September, two weeks after leaving Chartres. I had no idea what to expect; Rob had no more briefed me for this initiation than he had for the four others, except to note that Amiens—the Jupiter Oracle—was the grandest church in all of France, and that it had been repeatedly destroyed by fire.

Does that mean that it's on the fire-path? I had asked, half-joking. But Rob's face was serious when he answered.

Correct in one guess, lad, he said. *That makes it the most dangerous of all.*

As it happened, however, danger arrived first from a not unexpected direction.

—•—

Even at some distance from Amiens, the ground thrummed with the sound of turning wheels. Wind and water: the Somme flowed through the centre of the city, putting its power to work—and the steady breezes blowing across Picardy kept windmills in constant motion day and night.

It was not as pervasive as at Toulouse—but there was a smell in the air and in the water as we approached the dyeing and weaving capital of northern France. Wind and water crushed the plants that became the dyestuff; the looms clacked from dawn to dusk, enriching the Amiénois.

—•—

"This does not look good," Rodney said as we approached the Porte Gayant, where the *faubourg* of Vignes crowded against the city wall. There were a half-dozen men wearing fleur-de-lys tabards present, watching travelers go by, but their attention seemed fixed on us.

We were sitting side-by-side, myself in the middle. I looked at Rob, who shrugged.

"We bluff," Rob said.

"Oh, that'll work." Rodney snorted. "They're waiting for us, Templar."

"Why?"

"We'll ask them," the stonemason said. "As they arrest us, we'll ask them."

"Do you have a better idea, Giblumite?"

He spat off the side of the wagon.

We came up to the gate. The guardsmen took up positions, blocking our forward progress.

"Can I be of service?" Rodney asked.

Two of the guardsmen approached the left side of the wagon. One took hold of the bit on one of the horses, and began stroking its muzzle.

"I said—" Rodney began, but another figure approached from the gate. Rodney didn't recognise him but I did: we'd seen him in an open field north of Orléans.

"Master de Bec," Rob said aloud. The cat was out of the bag: he was waiting for us.

"Well met, Templar," Guilbert de Bec said. "You've led me a merry chase." He stepped to Rodney's side of the cart, giving a gentle wave to the two guardsmen—who didn't look happy to be so airily dismissed.

"Glad you enjoyed it," Rob said. "What do you want?"

"At the moment, only to talk."

"What, out here?"

"No." De Bec squinted at the sky. "Perhaps somewhere more genteel."

"Genteel." Rob chuckled. "What makes you think we want to go anywhere with a . . ." He lowered his voice. "a sorcerer?"

De Bec looked over his shoulder at the two guards nearby, close enough to have heard it even though Rob had said the word softly.

"Thank you for sparing my tender feelings, Brother," he answered. "But they"—a quick jerk of the thumb—"are well informed about my activities."

"All of them?"

"Oh, spare me," de Bec said. "I've been called worse, and by men whose codpiece is heavier than yours, Templar." I saw Rob tense as if he was about to surge from his seat—and then slowly and deliberately relax. "But I have no wish to sling words," de Bec continued, "or anything else out here in the road."

He looked beyond our cart. Two or three others had come up behind us, intending to pass through the gate and into the city.

Rodney didn't answer; he looked pointedly at Rob as if to say, *This one's your call, Templar.*

Rob in turn took a few moments to collect himself, placing his hands palms down on his thighs.

"So," he said at last. "What did you have in mind?"

—•—

We went to a public house called Le Maison des Fleurs hard by the church of Saint Martin on the west side of the city. We turned the wagon off a narrow street and passed under a gated arch into an inner courtyard.

Rodney indicated that he intended to remain with the wagon while we went inside and "supped with the Devil," as he put it. Rob was on edge as de Bec led us within; the place was empty even approaching the dinner hour. This had obviously been planned in advance.

A bottle of some Rhenish wine and the remains of a round of cheese were in the centre of a trestle table. One of de Bec's guardsmen served as cup-bearer, pouring from the bottle into three ceramic cups, and then stepped away, perching on a tall stool to clean his fingernails with the point of a small dagger.

"I don't want to waste your time or mine," de Bec began. "I know why you're here."

He nodded at me, sipping wine from his cup. After we saw him do it, Rob and I drank as well.

"Frankly, I can only compliment you on your skill. You wouldn't bother coming to Amiens if you hadn't gotten your business done in Paris—though I cannot imagine how you passed unnoticed."

Rob didn't miss a beat. "Keep imagining. Go on."

"To complete your pilgrimage, though, you'd have to come here sooner or later. The . . . Jupiter Oracle, isn't that what you call Notre Dame de Amiens? It seemed only logical for me to come here to wait for you."

"To what end? So that we could share a last cup?" Rob put his hands around his cup, the tiny ruby in his ring catching the fading sunlight through the open shutters. "You might as well have arrested us at Porte-Gayant."

"Arrested—" de Bec smiled. "You wrong me, Templar. I don't want to arrest you . . . as long as you're willing to cooperate."

"Cooperate? How?" I said. Rob looked at me sharply. After a few minutes of conversation with the man, I'd found that he was well-spoken and polite; I'm sure he was all of the things Rob said of him and more—but he reminded me a bit of David MacDougal of ITV.

"I want you to share your findings with me."

Rob looked at me, then back at the sorcerer. "Findings? What findings?"

"The manuscript. De la Halle's manuscript."

"What makes you think we have it—or that we'd share it with you even if we did?"

"Oh, you have it," de Bec answered, nodding at me again and sipping his wine. "And you also have your heart's desire—someone who can hear the music. As for your reason for sharing it with me—simple, really: I make a far better friend than an enemy."

"I don't take your meaning," Rob said quietly, but I suspected we both knew what he would say next.

"Let me make it clear in terms that even a Templar sergeant would understand. If you're not inclined to work with me, I will simply turn you over to my master. Monsieur will use far less polite, and far more persuasive, methods."

"Why haven't you just done that?" Rob asked.

"Because then I don't get what I want. The manuscript disappears into Monsieur's hands . . ."

"As opposed to—"

"My uncle Michel's library," de Bec finished his sentence. "You get what you want; I get what I want—"

"And Monsieur?" Rob asked quietly. "What does Monsieur get? I don't think he'll be happy with your betrayal."

"He does not know what this is about," de Bec answered. "To him this is another valuable thing: a treasure for *his* master. No, I think both prince and minister will have plenty to keep them occupied in the next few weeks."

Rob shrugged, as if he didn't know—or care—to what the sorcerer was alluding. We suspected that he meant the attack on the Order, but it wasn't clear how we could already know of that.

"I don't trust you," Rob said finally. "I expect you to betray us at the first convenient opportunity."

"So you don't want to work with me?"

"Didn't say that," Rob said. "I just want to put this in terms that even a tainted black sorcerer can understand." De Bec's face grew angry, but he didn't respond. "Since you've found us—by whatever means—you are in the position to interfere with our task here. Given that, I'm willing to consider 'working' with you.

"Bear this in mind, however." He placed his palms down on the table and looked at them, rather than at de Bec. "We have something you don't—and you can't—have. We have him." He nodded at me; his eyes were full of emotion: anger, anxiety, fear all rolled into a ball. "You can torture; you can kill. You can likely do things that my faith in the Lord prevents me from doing. But you can't *hear the music.* You need our help."

"That is so. I'm surprised it took you until now to come to that obvious conclusion, Templar."

"We do nothing for you before we get our business done," Rob said. "Vespers Saturday until Terce on Sunday, he'll keep vigil at the cathedral. Then we'll talk."

The sorcerer considered this for a moment, wrapping his long fingers around the cup before him. Rob's hands, stretched out on the table, were scarred and callused—a warrior and worker; de Bec's bore a few stains—most likely ink, or something from a laboratory—but didn't appear acquainted with either war or labour.

"Agreed," he said. "I can wait that long."

Rob stood up; I rose to stand next to him.

"We'll be on our way then," he said, and turned to walk toward the door.

"Templar," de Bec said, without standing. We stopped, but didn't turn around.

"However you slipped into and out of Paris, don't expect your luck to serve you a second time. Any sign of betrayal and our partnership ends."

Rob's hands made fists. He looked back over his shoulder at de Bec, sitting at his leisure, his hands still wrapped around the cup.

"Our dealings are no partnership, sorcerer. Don't deceive yourself—and don't flatter yourself either."

They held each other's gaze for several seconds. Finally de Bec looked away.

"Until Sunday," he finally said, and made a dismissive gesture.

CHAPTER 17

In the end, the dispute between Rob and Rodney about where we would lay our heads was decided by Rodney. He was unsure about the trustworthiness of his own brotherhood and its attitude toward the pilgrimage—and toward the removal of the Ark from its hiding-place—but was also dead set against going near the Templar priory. He was sure that the Order of the Temple was rife with spies working for Nogaret or directly for the King.

Instead he found a safe-house for us, located on one of the many canals of Amiens. After passing beneath the city-wall near Pont de Dursame, just below the gate we had used to enter the city, the Somme split into a dozen different tributaries. All of these ultimately rejoined beyond the eastern wall. Collectively, the Amiénois called them the *Chemin de l'Eau*—the Boulevard of Water—and they provided power to dozens of wheels that helped make the city prosper. Our lodgings were in a presently-unoccupied dye warehouse which was smelly but at least dry, and afforded some relief from the constant clack-clack of the wheels turning on the canals. It also had plenty of room for the cart—though we transferred our treasures to an upper level, concealing them among crates and barrels from the place's former business.

Rodney seemed to know everyone and had knowledge of current events and local affairs; he gained acceptance through gestures and quiet words, but sometimes had to resort to showing some sort of document, after which he readily obtained what he needed.

"That's his 'horse'," Rob explained quietly to me as we watched one of these transactions from the upper storey, taking place on the quay on the other side of the little canal.

"Horse?"

"That's what I've heard it called. It's a sort of . . . pass. Marks him as a fellow of the craft. So *that* bloke there"—he pointed to a thin, balding man who was doing most of the talking, looking very much a Laurel to our traveling companion's Hardy—"is a member of the Children of Solomon."

"He's a stonemason? He doesn't look it."

"They're not all stonemasons, lad. He could be a costermonger for all I know. He's a, well, a *confrère* of sorts. A fellow traveler."

"What does he have that Roddy wants?"

Rob leaned forward, squinting, trying to get an answer to just that question. After the two men had talked for a bit longer, Laurel handed Hardy a leather tube; they exchanged a handshake I recognised—one of them grasping the other's elbow as they gripped—and Rodney tucked the tube in a sleeve and made his way along the canal-side, crossing a little wooden bridge and then making his way into our building.

He didn't make any secret of his destination; we all assumed that de Bec knew where we were. Assuming that the sorcerer did feel he needed us, he truly would wait until I'd gone through my vigil. Rob had stood up to him to buy us time.

Rodney came up the stair into the upper storey. He knew we'd been watching the entire exchange.

"What's in the tube, Roddy?" I asked.

"A bit of insurance." He took a seat on a nearby crate and removed the end cap from the tube, then drew out a roll of parchment. Placing the tube next to his boot, he carefully undid the ties that held the roll and opened it across his lap.

It was a map of sorts, with the major gates of Amiens—Barbacanne, Dursame, Gayant, the great Porte Montrescu, and so forth—marked around the edges, and the myriad canals and waterways inked in. A few major buildings were delineated as well, particularly the cathedral and the Hôtel-Dieu. But most of the map was a sort of network of connected blots, each annotated in tiny Latin characters. My first impression was of a London Tube map—or the incredibly complex Paris Métro.

"Please tell me this isn't a map of the sewers, Giblumite."

"Certainly not." Rodney scowled. "This shows all of the underground vaults, and how they connect."

"Vaults?" I said.

"Vaults," Rob said. "I've heard there are hundreds of them," he continued, a smile coming across his face. "It's storage space, dry places for wine-casks and woad-sacks and such."

Rodney didn't answer. He traced a path with his finger, running from a series of marked vaults not far from where we presently sat, and then through tunnels along and beneath the nearby canal to another vault group just within the cathedral close, and farther to yet a third group just within the wall at the southeast corner of the city, near the church of the Prieurs de Saint-Denis.

"I expect we will need an escape route, both for ourselves and for what we carry," Rodney said. "It's possible that de Bec has this map, but he may not expect us to have it."

"He won't betray us right away," Rob said.

"No. Your little pucker-up"—he used an Occitan expression: *bec-a-bec*—the closest I'd ever seen the stonemason come to humour—"bought us two nights and a day, Templar. He'll wait until the sun rises on the Initiate on Sunday before doing whatever he intends."

"But he doesn't know about our cargo," I ventured.

Rodney snorted. "Let us not make any assumptions."

"He may or may not know, lad," Rob said. "It's hard to tell whether we should believe what he said—that he thinks we somehow went through Paris and weren't detected or captured. We assumed that he was looking out for us on the map in the Louvre because we hadn't turned up and walked into a trap.

"On the other hand, he may be lying to see how we react—and may well have felt us cross the Seine at Andély, which means he knows that we followed the earth-path and likely went to Gisors."

"Does he know about the G—" I caught myself before saying *Grail.* "About the lord's treasure?"

Rob looked at Rodney, then back at me. "He might know, he might not. Difficult to say."

"And our . . . original cargo?"

"Aye, well." Rodney rolled up the map of the vaults and tucked it back into its tube. "That's harder to say. It would be a great prize for him.

"He does know," Rodney continued, "that the Order of the Temple excavated 'neath Temple Mount in Jerusalem; he might well know what they found there—treasures and ancient knowledge. If he reasons that he hasn't been able to track us because the—because it is keeping him from doing so, then he'll reach the obvious conclusion."

"He hasn't been able to track us before," I said. I related our previous encounter with Guilbert de Bec, north of Orléans: his unsuccessful attempt to use a lodestone to locate us. "We didn't have it with us then—why didn't it work?"

Rodney shook his head. "Perhaps the Lord protects innocent initiates," he said. "The important thing to remember is that you can't assume that anything that viper tells you is the truth. What he says about his knowledge, his intentions, and his motives are as like to be lies as truth."

"I don't think I needed to be told that," I said.

"*You* sat at table with him. I have no idea what you need to be told, Initiate."

There was another tense silence. I wasn't sure what Rodney wanted from us—but I could readily tell that he was frightened. He had charge of incredible treasures; he had a dangerous man watching him who would clearly covet them. And he knew, as we did, that a reckoning was coming that might cost him his life.

"Nothing happens until Sunday morning," Rob said at last.

"No," Rodney said, getting to his feet. "A great deal happens before then. While you prepare your Initiate for his Templar vigil, I'll be busy." He picked up the tube and tucked it into his sleeve. "You do what you need to do, Templar, and so will I."

—•—

So, in the midst of intrigue and menace, Rob and I prepared for the sixth initiation by paying a visit to Amiens Cathedral.

My Gran had a collection of postcards that her father had sent home from the Western Front, where he'd been one of the victims of Haig's misguided attempt to win the Great War along the Somme in 1916. Among them was a sepia-tinted picture of Amiens Cathedral, a common tourist destination for British soldiers on their way to the front several miles to the east; it was the only time that my great-grandfather ever visited it—he was killed by mortar fire sometime shortly after the packet arrived by post.

The cards were set on stiff board pages protected by glassine; the Amiens one was set on the same page as one showing a ravaged church with a Madonna and Child statue, hanging down past horizontal from the spire, bent but not broken. The two images—ornate Gothic façade, bombed-out ruin with the statue holding on by its toes—had always been favourites, side-by-side in my mind. Peace and war, a beautiful sculpture and a grinning skull.

It was what crossed my mind as we made our way through the streets and across the narrow bridge-canals. But as with so many things on this pilgrimage, what I actually saw didn't correspond with the sepia-toned postcards that I had in my memory.

"The towers are missing," I murmured, as we stood before the west façade, admiring the huge rose window and the triple arches adorned with hundreds of carvings, mostly hidden by early-afternoon shadows.

"Towers?" Rob looked at me curiously for a moment, then thought about it and said, "They'll be added later, I take it."

"Yes." It looked a bit forlorn without them, but the stone was new and fairly clean—there wasn't centuries of coal smoke and such gathered on it.

"Rob," I said as we walked across the *plâce,* "why is this initiation a vigil?"

"Because it's the last one, lad. Or is meant to be."

"But what about—"

"Last one." He stopped walking and looked at me from toes to top. "This is the Jupiter Oracle. From here the only place to go is to the place of perfect measure—the place that doesn't exist. At least not at present."

"Am I going to have some sort of vision here?"

He frowned. "In your time, lad, what would a guide say to a pilgrim? Would he tell him everything that will happen?"

"In my time—" I sighed. "In my time, Rob, there is no pilgrimage. These places aren't . . . they aren't the same. My great-grandfather came here during the Great War, not as a pilgrim or even as a worshipper. He came just to look at the place."

"The 'Great War'?"

"Yeah." I smiled. "The 'War to End All Wars.' He was killed somewhere near here. Six hundred years from now." I only knew that because I'd been to the War Memorial in Edinburgh Castle and looked it up: MACFARLANE, GORDON LEWIS, name and regiment, and the date in 1916 he died, leaving a widow and two young girls . . . and a book of postcards. "But that's another subject. I still want to know what this is going to be about."

"It's to be about—" Rob looked away, anywhere but at my face. "Wisdom. The actualization of the Word, wisdom enthroned. More than that I will not say—except that I have no earthly idea if any of this matters, as we were to go to Paris first."

"So why am I bothering at all?"

"What?"

"Why should we even bother with this vigil, Rob? If you're not sure if it's even valid, why waste time?"

"It's not a waste. You're here, *it's* here—" He waved toward the cathedral. "And if we go ahead with the vigil, we have a day and a half before we must deal with de Bec."

He began to walk again toward the middle of the great three-arched portal, leaving me to follow.

The centre arch of the cathedral entrance consisted of a tall pillar—a *trumeau*—placed between two doorways. Deep in the recess of the fantastically-sculptured archway, the doorways themselves were dark; I couldn't make out what lay behind them. The *trumeau* was fairly easy to see in the grey afternoon light: a full-length statue of a man under some sort of canopy, with another, more impressive statue on the top. Rob had told me about that one on the journey to Amiens: they called it the *Beau Dieu*—and it was an impressive sight: the resurrected Christ, one of His hands raised in blessing and His feet resting on vanquished serpents.

Just as we reached the wide stone stairs, however, a familiar figure stepped into our path.

Rob stopped on the lowest of the stairs and waited, his right hand loose on his walking-stick, as the man approached. We hadn't seen him since Chartres, when both of us came close to killing him in the crypt. We didn't even know his name: he was just a tough in the employ of our sorcerer enemy who now claimed to be our ally.

"If you're looking for trouble," Rob said quietly as he came out from under the ornately-carved central arch, "we'll give you more than you've already had from us."

The other stopped, hooking his thumbs in his belt. "Be at peace, Templar," he said. "I'm not interested in starting anything with you—though I owe you a few sharp kicks for the courtesies you gave me."

"You're lucky to be drawing breath," Rob said. "Now get out of our way."

"But of course," he answered, stepping aside and bowing

elaborately, gesturing for us to pass by with his hand. "I'm eager to see what happens next."

"It doesn't require an audience."

De Bec's man shrugged by way of response.

Rob gave him one more murderous look and then walked up the steps and passed through the portal to the right of the *trumeau*. Our shadow followed a few paces behind.

"We're going to split up," Rob said. "You need to pray, lad, and I believe that he's more likely to stay with you than follow me."

"What are you going to do?" I remembered the incident in the crypt below Chartres—and wasn't thrilled with the idea of having an eye gouged out.

"There's a clue that led us here. I aim to find it."

"So I'm the bait again."

"Aye," he said. "Or perhaps I am. But each of us can take care of himself. Stay in plain sight. Walk the labyrinth," he said, gesturing toward an ornate pattern in the floor of the cathedral, spread out before us—an even more elaborate version of the one we'd seen at Chartres. "He doesn't know what we're looking for."

"Neither do I."

"So much the better," Rob said. "You won't be giving anything away."

With a nod to me and a glance over his shoulder at the soldier, he walked up the nave a bit and then across to a side-chapel. Our shadow knew he couldn't follow Rob and keep his eyes on me, so he decided for the latter choice. As I stood before the pattern in the floor, he took up a position near one of the massive support pillars and crossed his arms, watching what I did.

The cathedral at midafternoon, with Nones past and Vespers a few hours away, was uncrowded: not empty—there were too many canons, acolytes, worshippers, and scribes. But I was the only one standing before the labyrinth.

"Aren't you going to walk it like a good penitent?"

"You know," I said without looking at the man watching me, "I don't even know your name."

"Armand de Got is my name," he said—stated, really, with pride echoing from every syllable. There was a pause, as if he was waiting for me to say something. The name didn't mean anything to me, so I concentrated on the light and dark lines in front of me.

"De Got," he repeated.

"You said that."

"My father's brother is the Holy Father," he added after a moment. "Bertrand de Got. His Holiness Clement."

That caught my attention. I looked at him. "You're the Pope's nephew? The French Pope?"

His face turned angry. "He's not French, you ignorant oaf. He is from Languedoc—he's an Occitan."

"My mistake. Well then, Armand, why don't you mind your own business and let me pray."

"Mind your tongue," he answered, his fists clenched.

"Or else what? You'll do—" I turned and walked toward him, stopping a pace away. "You'll do what you tried to do in the crypt at Chartres? I don't think your master would be very happy with that. We're all friends now, no?"

He didn't reply. I had spoken quietly, but I thought I heard my words echo in the dark spaces of the cathedral above me.

"Don't bet your life on it."

"Looking to scare me, are you. If you're the Pope's nephew, Armand de Got, you're clearly not his favourite one, or you'd be doing something important—you wouldn't be assigned to just watch me pray."

Then I turned my back on him and returned my attention to the labyrinth. I waited, but there was no sound: he neither approached nor stalked away. I resisted the temptation to smile at what must surely be a temporary victory.

The pattern was bigger than the one at Chartres and shaped differently: it was octagonal, extending almost the entire width of the nave, set off at the corners by a checkerboard mosaic. At the centre there was some sort of octagonal design, but I couldn't make it out without crossing the pavement.

I could have just walked across to see, but I thought perhaps this might be part of whatever mystery Amiens held for me—so I took Rob's advice and began to walk it, following the dark lines as they led me slowly around and around. Whenever I found myself facing Armand de Got I made sure to give him a top-notch Channel 4 smile, the sort I always reserved for first-class celebrities on *Ian and Jan*.

There you go, I thought. *Make sure to send my best to your uncle.*

A labyrinth isn't a maze. Such patterns have no dead-ends, no junctions—no false turns, just a single, convoluted path that visits all corners and ends ultimately in the middle. It wasn't a challenge per se—though I suppose it might have been, if I had taken it on my knees as I later saw some penitents do; Rob told me that it was considered to be a substitute for making a pilgrimage to Jerusalem, no safe thing. Even so, by the time I'd been walking for a few minutes, I began to realise that if the path were unravelled it would be the length of a few football pitches laid end-to-end.

So in the fading light of a late September afternoon I followed that path around and about, inward and outward, with a hostile Armand de Got watching me do it. When I came at last to the octagonal stone in the centre, which showed an even-armed cross with an angel hovering just beyond each point and four robed figures in between, I turned to face him, folding my hands in prayer.

Bring it on, I thought, smiling at him again.

I waited for something to happen: a stray bit of sunlight through a window above the triforium, a snatch of the Rosslyn music, some part of a vision . . . but there was nothing.

This would be an excellent time for a dramatic moment, I thought. But no dramatic moment was forthcoming. There was some saint I should pray to, I suppose, but I couldn't think of one at the time.

Armand de Got and I held each other's gaze for at least half a minute: he, the well-dressed and well-trained bravo, I the temporally displaced Templar initiate—until I saw Rob walking toward me from the direction of the western doors. Evidently de Got heard him approaching, for he turned, giving a backward glance to my friend, and stalked past.

"Give you any trouble, lad?" Rob said, jerking his thumb at him, as the man passed through the doorway.

"He's the pope's nephew, did you know that?"

"Believe me, the Holy Father has a lot of nephews. And they all have jobs. He's more of a simoniac than Boniface was."

"He's not the favourite."

"And not even in the top half when it comes to smarts. He's no threat." Rob held up his hand, walking across the labyrinth-pattern to where I stood. "And yes, I know he was willing to do great personal harm to you in Chartres, but he's not the one we must worry about."

"You don't look worried."

Rob smiled, looking away. "I'm worried a-plenty, Ian. But not about the likes of him. It's the sorcerer that concerns me—and what he'll do if the music falls into his hands."

"But only I can hear it. He still needs me, doesn't he?"

"That he does. But he doesn't need you to be able to walk or talk or see."

The comment settled into the quiet of the cathedral nave. I knew what Rob was implying.

"So he's going to watch and wait and see what happens at my vigil."

"That's right. And while they watch you, we'll be watching *them.*"

"We?"

"The Giblumite and myself. And others."

"Which—"

"Best not be asking that, lad. Come, let's walk about and see the relics."

Armand de Got stayed out of sight for the rest of the afternoon. Rob and I had a good tour of the huge cathedral; it seemed even bigger than Chartres, where I'd practically had vertigo looking up at the roof-trees. The pillars that lined the nave, separating it from the side aisles, were as broad at their base as the Gisors Elm had been reputed to be—I'd guess that nine men linking hands could barely stretch around. High above my head, pairs of pillars ended in fluted capitals that supported pointed arches. Galleries overlooked our position—I suspected that we were being watched from there, even as we strolled innocently among the relics and riches of the church.

I let Rob be my guide. In every corner, on pillars and walls, cornices and ceiling-panels and architraves, he pointed out symbols and patterns. Even-armed Templar crosses, alchimetical marks, flutings and decorative curves—all with meaning. On the north side of each great pillar Rob pointed to marks—☽, ☿, ♀, ☉, ♂, ♃—that corresponded to each of the spheres: the Moon, Mercury, Venus, the Sun, Mars and finally Jupiter. There was no mark for Saturn, the last 'fixed star' anyone in this century knew. There was no sense in bringing up anything beyond that, of course.

Finally, we wandered into one of the side-chapels in the ambulatory at the east end of the cathedral. There, sitting in a little alcove in the wall, was a skull. Not just your average horror movie skull, but a gold-adorned, bejewelled thing, its crown gashed just above one temple, laying flat upon a salver or plate mounted in the wall. Its empty eyes had been fitted with dark stones, opals perhaps, giving the entire display an even more sinister appearance.

Rob bowed his head and folded his hands in prayer. I followed suit, wondering what the hell this display was all about. Some saint that had been martyred here in Roman times, I supposed.

I closed my eyes for a moment.

—•—

Initiate, a voice said.

I opened my eyes as suddenly as I had closed them, and found myself in the same chamber, surrounded by flames. There was smoke in the air and monks and others were dashing about, carrying objects—altar cloths, candlesticks, anything they could manage.

Rob was nowhere to be seen, but through the smoke I could make out the skull on its dinner-plate directly opposite, its eyes and the gash in its head glowing a sort of dark blue. No one seemed to take notice of it.

"What—" I began, and caught a lungful of smoke and began to cough.

There is little time, Initiate, I heard in my mind, and knew that the hideous thing was talking to me. *This is Amiens, where the four paths meet.*

I squatted down where the air was better. No one seemed to pay heed to me either. "Why is it burning?"

One path is dominant, the skull said in my head. *Water-path and earth-path cross here—but in this time, the cathedral cannot touch the air-path. Thus the fire-path is dominant.*

"*This* time?"

Nearly a hundred years past, it replied.

"Who are you?"

I am the one who came before. After me came one more powerful, the latchet of whose sandals I was unworthy to stoop down and unloose. Yet I too was man born of woman and doomed to perish—to have my head struck off my shoulders and given as a gift.

"Head? You mean—" Somewhere off to my left I heard a great noise: some vast section of roof or wall collapsing. A rush of heat washed over me; I covered my face with my hands, trying to shield myself from it.

My mind raced. Scripture and I had been indifferent acquaintances, but the last two months had made us much more intimate. Only one beheading came to mind: John the Baptist.

One who came before, I thought.

"You mean," I said, uncovering my face slightly and looking at the skull opposite, "you're John the Baptist. You're John the Baptist's head."

It is so, the skull answered. *When I preached I told those who came to me that they should make a straight path. Yet now in this time of sin, nothing is what it seems.*

"What do you want me to do?"

Use your eyes, Initiate. See truth. No darkness can stand before it.

"What's—" Another wave of heat. "What's happening?" I said, without uncovering my face.

—•—

"I'm not sure, lad." Rob gently pulled my arms from my face and helped me to stand erect once more. He looked in my eyes, and gently touched my forehead. "Is something wrong?"

I looked around. No panic, no fire or smoke; no one rushing past. No waves of heat or great crashing sounds.

"Rob," I said slowly, "has this cathedral ever burned down?"

He looked at me, then back over his shoulder at the skull set onto the wall—the Baptist's skull—and then back.

"Four times," he said. "Never *this* one; but the last great fire most of a hundred years ago destroyed the great church that this one was built to replace." He let his hands fall to his sides. "Why?"

"When did the Baptist"—I pointed at the skull—"take up this address?"

"How did you know—"

"I know."

"A monk brought the relic back from Constantinople after the Crusade," he answered. "Took it right out of a church there and brought it here. Many places claim to have his blessed skull, but this is the real one."

A more skeptical man—for example, the one I'd been before St James' Day—would have asked him how he knew that, but the last few minutes were enough to convince me.

"And it survived the fire."

"Aye, it did, by the blessing of God. And this great house was built to honour it. This is where you'll make your vigil tonight, lad. Here before one of the greatest relics in all of Christ's Kingdom." His eyes shone, his voice was full of emotion.

I looked past him and at the skull. It seemed inert and lifeless; no inner light glowed out of it . . . but moments earlier, surrounded by smoke and fire, it had spoken to me.

See truth, it had told me. *No darkness can stand before it.*

Truth conquers all, I thought. It kept coming back to that.

As we stood in that tableau—Templar, Initiate, and skull—the Vespers bell began to ring.

CHAPTER 18

"THERE'S REALLY NO REASON TO BE AFRAID, LAD," ROB SAID AS he stood up. He looked from me to the skull and back.

Somewhere he'd found a cushion to serve as a hassock: it was placed several paces away from John the Baptist, so that I could kneel there and face the relic. I didn't want to take up that position just yet—I'd be doing so soon enough.

"I'm not afraid of that," I said, pointing to the skull. "I'm afraid of closing my eyes. Every time I do I seem to get some sort of vision."

"That's the purpose of the vigil. It's the purpose of the entire pilgrimage, Ian—particularly for you."

"It's frightening."

"I can stay with you for a time if you'd like."

"I think I would." I took a deep breath and knelt on the cushion. I'd brought the now-seamless cloak with me; I had placed it on the tiled floor before my position, neatly folded.

Rob knelt beside me, his hands folded. He seemed totally at peace: as if this were yet another night in his life—not the last stop of the last pilgrimage he'd ever guide. The thought of the destruction of the Templar Order appeared to be the furthest thing from his mind.

"Rob," I said after some moments of silence.

"Silence is golden, lad."

"Whose vigil is this, yours or mine?"

He sighed, but smiled. "All right. What is it?"

"What's going to happen tomorrow? De Bec thinks we have the manuscript but we don't. We're carrying two relics we think he knows nothing about, but he might. I'm supposed to be possessed of all of this ancient wisdom—but I'm afraid to close my eyes. And as for Roddy . . . I don't know if we can trust him as far as I can throw him." The analogy took a moment for Rob to figure out, but he seemed to understand the general sense of it. "And I have no idea what this vigil is for."

"It's the sixth initiation."

"But I haven't had the fifth initiation."

"Don't remind me."

"But—"

"But, but, but. Tomorrow will take care of itself in God's good time," he said. "The manuscript—if it even exists—is here somewhere. If we can't find it, de Bec can't have it either. We have all that we need in there." He reached over and tapped me lightly on the temple with his knuckles—about the spot where the skull of the Baptist was pierced.

"And which de Bec won't hesitate to torture me to obtain."

Rob shrugged. "He'll have to get past me to do it."

I was reassured by my friend's loyalty, but it didn't make me feel that much safer. We fell silent for another while.

At last Rob stood, placing his hand on my shoulder. "I'll be nearby, lad. No harm will come to you this night—the Lord is with you." He made the sign of the cross and bowed respectfully to the Baptist, then turned and walked away, his footsteps echoing softly as he made his way along the darkened ambulatory.

So, in the quiet of the night, I was left alone with the holy relic set into the alcove. I let my eyes close for a moment—I was willing to let happen whatever was to come, just to have done with it—but there was nothing to see. When I opened them again, the skull was still grinning back at me.

I remained silent for just a few minutes; then whimsy struck. Without even meaning to do so, I found myself imagining the set of *Ian and Jan,* where I'd spent so much time.

"Let's give a warm welcome to our first guest—John the Baptist. Glad you could be with us today. So, Mr 'the Baptist'," I said at last. "May I call you John?" It was my finest interview style; I smiled, turning aside from the alcove to show my best side to the camera . . . "I'm told that this great cathedral was built for you. What do you think of that?"

There was no answer, no immediate vision or revelation.

John the Baptist had baptized Jesus in the River Jordan; he was one of the first, if not the first, to recognise him as the Messiah. The story had been repeated to me by Rob as part of our tour after my brief colloquy with the skull earlier that evening. Wore the hair shirt, ate the wild honey and locusts, taught baptism and repentance; and like most who rebelled against the status quo, Mr the Baptist made some powerful enemies, and one of them caused him to be beheaded.

"But it looks like you've really turned it around now, John," I said. "Thirteen hundred years on and people travel from the four corners of the earth to look at you. If that's actually your skull, that is—and if it matters that it's here in Amiens.

"The Ark I can understand. It's a work of art: a beautiful piece of craftsmanship. And the Grail—whatever it is—is clearly a treasure. But a jeweled skull . . ." I closed my eyes again, waiting for enlightenment to descend, *Sicut ros Hermon qui descendit in montes Sion,* I added to myself: *as the dew of Hermon that descended upon Mount Zion.* I'd heard that psalm a few times in the last few months.

But there was no enlightenment: not about the skull, not about my vigil, nothing.

A chill ran across my shoulders and down to the skirts of my garments. I picked up the St Giles medal and tucked it in my wallet, then took up the cloak and wrapped it around my shoulders.

"I think I'll go for a stroll, John. Care to join me? No? Well, don't worry—I'll be back after a bit."

I stood and bowed to the relic, crossed myself, and walked out of the chapel.

—•—

The nave was not completely dark, nor completely empty. A few of the side chapels had presence-lamps lit, and there were shadowed figures attending them, perhaps at prayer, perhaps to watch me. I walked slowly down the nave; the roof-trees were invisible, only the faintest light from a sliver of waning moon making its way through the high windows far above my head.

Interviewing John the Baptist's skull had been a bit of fun—made me feel like I was home. *No,* I thought, pushing back the memory: *not the little cottage in the shadow of St Giles*—my real home, in the twenty-first century.

"Of all the people on the earth," I said to the darkened cathedral, "why was I chosen for this? Entertainment? My fine profile?" There were no cameras here, no sweeps or ratings, no advert executives deciding that *Alex and Lily* was more likely to sell soaps and sweets than *Ian and Lily*.

"This really stopped being amusing when we were walking across Spain," I added. It sounded more assertive—and more flippant—than I actually felt.

There was nothing here but a dark cathedral, a man out of time, and a mystery that no one wanted to explain. My exuberance, or confidence, or whatever the hell had possessed me to tell off Armand de Got and the sorcerer that waited for dawn to come, seemed to have drained away with the night.

Nothing and no one answered my questions.

—•—

At last I came to the labyrinth. The beginning of the path was on the west side; I didn't walk across the pattern but instead circled around through the north aisle to approach it from there.

I briefly considered the idea of walking the pattern on my knees as I'd seen pilgrims do both here and at Chartres—but if that were a way to do penance, I had more sins than a thousand feet of knee-scrapes would offset; and if that were a way to avoid a pilgrimage, then it would be meaningless since I'd done the route already. Walking it would suffice.

While I stood there considering this, I caught a glimpse of someone walking along the south aisle. About my height and build, the man seemed to stop for a moment to observe me. I turned to face him and took a step closer—and for just a split-second I saw his face.

It was my own, looking back at me, a faint smile playing across my lips. It was the same expression I'd seen at Tours, when I'd received a half-cloak from the same man.

I was so startled by the vision that I didn't say anything. The figure took a step back into the shadows—I heard no sound of footsteps retreating. Snapping out of it, I took two quick strides—but there was no one there.

I felt the chill again. Was this the purpose of the vigil—what I was meant to see this night? My heart was thumping in my chest: shadows flickered in the light of candles that wavered in the breeze.

No harm can come to you, I thought, remembering Rob's words. *The Lord is with you.*

I leaned against the nearby pillar, trying to calm myself.

"I am *really* starting to piss me off," I said to no one in particular. The idea of it made me smile as well—the facial expression I'd just seen. Was that other me looking from the shadows, watching my puzzlement, listening to me profane that holy place? I don't know if I cared at that moment. I'd heard from Rob, from Juan, from Lamont and Lamontaigne, and finally from Gran MacPherson. Now I heard—nothing. For a moment I'd seen me, but no wisdom had come from that.

I wondered how many hours it would be until dawn and whatever the sorcerer de Bec had in store for us—and how terribly frustrating it was to never, ever know what I was to do.

—•—

I walked the pattern, singing "Awake My Soul" quietly to myself, counting the soft-boiled eggs. I was bone tired: too much tension, too many mysteries, not enough sleep . . . I imagined two of me, one on each side of the labyrinth, following the dark lines as they turned and swept in and out of the octagonal arrangement on that floor: never crossing, never meeting, like a continuous braid. One would reach the centre and wait for the other to come—*aragonesa a deux.*

There weren't two of me, though. There was only one. I reached the centre of the labyrinth and stood on the octagonal stone, angels and evangelists peeking out from beneath my sandalled feet. The moon was high by then—I could see it peeking through a window above me, no bigger than a coin, retreating last quarter . . . by next week it would be altogether dark. While we'd walked the pilgrim's path from Finisterre to Flanders, from the edge of the world to its centre, summer had faded into autumn.

I wonder what MacDougal and Rodney and all the rest in my time made of it all, how they carried on after their star had vanished somehow from the baptistry at Rosslyn.

I knelt on the centre stone of the labyrinth. Tears came to my eyes and I let them come. The floor was cold and hard; my hands rough and calloused, my beard itchy, my joints and muscles full of aches. The betrayal of the Order was three weeks away and there was nothing I could do to stop it—and I believed in earnest that I would not escape from this time and finally go home.

I felt in my heart that I had failed.

—•—

When the Matins bell rang, I came back to myself; I must have fallen asleep kneeling on the stone floor. I stood up stiffly and made my way to the south aisle, near where I'd seen my own image; as the celebrants of the night office came into the nave, their voices singing:

> *"Salva me, fac Deus!*
> *Quoniam intraverunt aquae usque ad animam meam . . ."*

Save me, O God, they sang. *For the waters have come up to my neck. I am sunk in deep mire, where there is no foothold; I have come into deep waters, and the flood sweeps over me. I am weary with my crying; my throat is parched. My eyes grow dim with waiting for my God.*

It was a psalm—Rob would doubtless know which one. At every liturgical office, the choir began by singing from the psalter. During the course of a season, the monks would work their way through the sequence. It was not chosen for me, but it still seemed highly appropriate. I felt overcome and adrift; my face was stained with tears, my body stiff from kneeling on the hard stone.

Salva me, fac Deus, I thought, walking slowly up the aisle, back to the chapel. The choir continued to sing the psalm as I found my way through the dimly-lit church.

As I approached the chapel, I caught another glance—a cloaked figure darting out of sight. I was fairly sure that someone had been in there; I flattened myself against the inner wall of the ambulatory and listened intently, but there was no sound.

Too late, I crept slowly along the wall hoping for another glance. But whoever had been in this part of the ambulatory had gotten away, unless it was just my fogged mind playing tricks.

Maybe it was me, I thought, brushing a bit of dirt from the end of my own cloak.

I counted to a hundred and stepped into the chapel, where Rob had paid for a half-dozen beeswax candles to provide soft, buttery light. No one was there—just me and the skull.

"Well," I said softly, returning to my kneeling-pad. "Did you miss me, John?"

—•—

Not long after the second night office grey light began to leak through the high windows, lending light and dark features to the nave. I heard footsteps coming toward the chapel; I'd sat and prayed, conducted a complete interview of Mr 'the Baptist' in my mind, counted eggs and engaged in a witty conversation with my Gran . . . but mostly I'd daydreamed about movies, popular music, rugby and cricket.

In the meanwhile my fourteenth-century self was trying to sort out the possibilities for what was to come tomorrow. A good soldier he was—*I* was—not wanting to be caught unawares. It gave me a few moments of shame, knowing that my modern self's cavalier attitude was in direct conflict with the reverence that my medieval persona felt in a place such as Amiens in the presence of a relic so holy.

I hoped that the vigil wasn't going to be a disappointment for Rob. No one had told me that Jupiter ruled this sphere; no one had given me a new title or a new name. I had also hoped that my prayers and solemn moments out in the nave might have brought some result—but it wasn't to be.

Rob stepped into the chapel. He looked as if he hadn't slept much, but seemed to be at peace.

He turned and bowed to Mr the Baptist, then began to return his attention to me—but stopped, a curious look on his face. He cocked his head, examining the relic, and then took a few steps closer.

He reached out one hand and carefully, softly touched the skull.

"Is something wrong, Rob?"

"I . . . I don't know." He didn't look back at me. "Do you notice anything different about the relic, lad?"

I concentrated on the skull. It looked back at me, perhaps waiting for the next interview question.

"Not that I can tell."

"Not that you could tell," he said. "It's . . . I can't properly say."

"I wasn't here all night—I walked down to the labyrinth."

"I know. You took a wee nap."

"Rob," I said, standing up, "Nothing happened. I . . . no one came and gave me the secret word. I don't know what was supposed to happen—but whatever it was, it passed me by."

Rob stepped back from the relic and bowed. He turned and faced me, placing his hands on my shoulders. "I feared it might happen."

"What do we do now?"

"Now? We go and hear the word of the Lord. In a few hours our sorcerer will come out from under his rock—and we'll tell him nothing."

"So you don't have a plan."

"No. Not as such."

"Good. I like it. No plan."

He dropped his hands to his sides, taking another glance at the skull. "No plan," he agreed, smiling. "But we're not beaten yet, lad. The Lord is with us."

I didn't have an answer for that. Rob and I turned to leave the chapel and, in the half pre-dawn light, I almost collided with someone. The other man lost his balance and I caught him, grasping hold of his right elbow with my left hand; he pulled himself upright and took hold of my right hand in his, stepping forward into the candlelight.

"My God," I said, looking from the handclasp to the man's face, then at Rob for explanation.

"Who is this?" Rob asked. "Do you know him?"

"Yes," I said. I let go, letting my arms fall to my sides. "We are awake—this isn't a vision?"

"No," the man answered. "It is not. I don't know you by name," he added, his Picard accent colouring his speech slightly, "but I know why you're here."

"Why?" I asked.

"Who *is this?*" Rob asked.

"Unless I am much mistaken," I said, taking a deep breath, "this is Adam de la Halle."

CHAPTER 19

"YOU KNOW ME," DE LA HALLE SAID. WE HAD TAKEN A STEP back into the chapel; the poet bowed respectfully to the relic, then returned his attention to me.

"I thought you were dead. You told me—" I began, and he looked at me curiously. Rob sighed; he was used to this.

"Perhaps you should begin again," de la Halle said after a moment.

"You said you know why I'm here," I answered after a moment. "That's the question I've been asking myself every day for the last two months. But before you tell me, I'd like to know why *you're* here."

"Well," de la Halle said, "there's a story to that. I have come here to meet you. And as for being dead: I would prefer that the world think that I was dead. I even wrote a play about it: *Jeu de Pelérin*. Perhaps you know it."

We shook our heads and shrugged. De la Halle looked disappointed.

"Ah, well," he continued after a moment. "No matter. I have come to Amiens because I learned that something remarkable was to happen here, at this time."

"At Lauds?" Rob said.

"In late September of this year," de la Halle said. "At this time in history. It was predicted by use of a remarkable machine."

"A machine?" Rob asked.

"A machine?" I echoed. "You mean, like a—" I wanted to say *computer,* but had long since learned why I couldn't. "A thinking machine?"

"In . . . a manner of speaking. You"—he gestured to me—"are the one who can hear my music: actually *hear* it, not just imagine it. After I composed it in Chartres, I realised that it would be better that my whereabouts remain unknown. So I traveled about: to the great city in the East—Byzantium; to Greece; to Rome; and at last I found myself in Catalonia. There I met an extraordinary man, who showed me a machine that plotted the motions of the fixed stars."

"Who was this man?"

"His name is Raymond Llull."

"Llull." Rob's fists clenched. The name meant nothing to me, but it wasn't having a good effect on him. "An incendiary. A preacher who would give our order over to the King of France, who speaks of Crusade as if he knows aught of it."

"He is no great supporter of the Templars, 'tis true," de la Halle responded mildly. He didn't answer Rob's accusation—but didn't deny it either. "But he is a seeker after truth. Some years ago he went by ship across the Middle Sea, bound for Alexandria, hoping to find some remnant of a book of great wisdom."

Rob and I looked at each other; my face remained impassive, but Rob was unaccustomed to unforgiving cameras. De la Halle seemed to note this and continued. "His ship was caught in a storm and he nearly drowned—but he survived and was pitched up on an island near Crete called Antikythera. There he met up with an artificer who was working to repair some sort of ancient machine; together they were able to rebuild it—and construct a second one. And a third."

He reached into his wallet and drew out a wooden case perhaps two handspans long, one hand wide and a few fingers deep. On the cover of the case was a curious emblem: two characters—A and Ω—and an opened human eye with lines radiating out from it placed in between. He opened it carefully, using a hook-and-eye latch on the side.

Within the case was a wonder.

My immediate association was with my paternal grandfather's pocket-watch. When I was very young, he'd had to bring his watch in to have the internal mechanism adjusted and had taken me along with him; we had walked down past Netherbow on the High Street of Edinburgh, then under an arch and down a set of narrow steps past a tea-shop to a tiny jeweler's shop. There on a baize cloth, an ancient wisp of a man—a cartoon character—had carefully opened the device to reveal the gears and intricate parts within.

I was only a lad, but the complexity of the watch determined me to avoid ever working on anything so exacting. It was probably what pushed my career into broadcasting, to my Gran MacPherson's everlasting dismay.

De la Halle held an extraordinary mechanism in his hands. A large circular silver plate was secured within the case; it was bisected by two strips that met in the middle, where a gear with many tiny teeth was placed to drive other gears, which drove other ones—there must have been more than two dozen in all. Around the edges there were inscriptions—in Greek, I presumed—and outlines that looked like star-patterns. There was a thumb-wheel at the lower edge that caused the entire apparatus to turn, and a series of small pointers on the underside of the mechanism that moved along scales, indicating something—it wasn't clear what.

"I've never seen anything like it," Rob said, astonished.

I didn't want to say that I had—but I certainly hadn't seen anything like it in the fourteenth century. It looked like something from the British Museum.

"There *is* nothing like it," de la Halle said quietly. "And it takes great wisdom to interpret what it shows. But I have learned—and it has shown me that this is the time for matters of great import."

He moved the wheel slowly with his thumb, causing the gears to turn. I noticed that many were labeled with a symbol similiar to the ones I'd seen on the great pillars in the nave; the two largest bore the emblems ☽ and ☉—the moon and sun.

"It's a model of the heavens," Rob said. "And you say that Llull found this device . . . in Greece?" He said it with disdain—as if Greece were inhabited by cavemen.

"It was apparently a device of antiquity," de la Halle said. "The few dozen people on Antikythera claimed that it had been built before the birth of our Lord."

I was from the pocket-watch era: truly, I was from the digital wristwatch era—some distance beyond gears and intricate mechanisms like this item. It looked like a piece of nineteenth-century technology, though I could tell that the part of myself native to this time was very impressed with the little machine. I couldn't claim to be knowledgeable on the history of technology, but even I knew that the ancient Greeks—or the fourteenth century Greeks, for that matter—had never built anything like this. I think I expected de la Halle to reach into his wallet again and pull out a PDA and a mobile.

"Tell me of these matters 'of great import,' " Rob said, suspicion continuing to dwell in his voice.

"It has been a momentous year, Brother Templar," he answered. "Not long after the Baptist's feast-day"—he nodded respectfully at the alcove—"the English lost their king. Fra Liberatus died. And there are vipers everywhere, so many that even the *Beau Dieu,* as they call him here, cannot keep them underfoot." He smiled, as if he were playing to an audience. He was speaking of the statue of the Lord on the *trumeau* at the cathedral's main entry, where He trampled His enemies. Rob didn't seem impressed with his word-play.

" 'Fra Liberatus'?" I asked.

"The leader of the Fraticelli. He was to be received by the Holy Father, but died on his way to Avignon—da Clareno governs the Spirituals now."

Rob nodded, knowingly. More pieces I didn't recognise on an ever-expanding chessboard.

I looked out of the chapel; it was starting to become light. Lauds, the dawn office, would begin soon—and with it would presumably come Guilbert de Bec.

"We have one of those vipers within reach," Rob said. "Guilbert de Bec is here."

"I'm surprised he could pass the threshold," de la Halle answered.

"He hasn't yet," Rob said. "But we're expecting him presently. He's looking for the music."

"My music."

"That's right. He believes that we have it."

"Do you?"

"Only in Ian's thick broo," Rob said, rapping his knuckles gently on my temple. "We . . . believe that it's hidden somewhere in this cathedral."

"Really." De la Halle smiled knowingly. "Why do you think so?"

"Creatori serviunt omnia subjecta," Rob said, *"sub mensura, numero, pondere perfecta."*

De la Halle's smile grew broader. "Well done, Templar. Well done. That's right: it's here, if you know where to look."

"We don't," Rob admitted. "We know it has to do with Walter de Chatîllon—but it's a big cathedral. And we don't know if de Bec might be a step ahead of us."

"I doubt it."

"Do you know him, sir—"

"Adam is my name," de la Halle said. "No other title is necessary—particularly considering that I'm dead."

I was caught up in the moment—was this a vision?—then I realised that he was joking.

"Adam," I continued. "Do you know Guilbert de Bec?"

"Only by reputation. What he is and what he thinks himself to be are two very different things. But you should still be afraid of him: knowledge with power is dangerous, but without power might be even more so."

"By reputation," Rob said. "Meaning . . ."

"The Lord of Gisors."

"Wait," I said. "You've been to Gisors?"

"The young lord directed me to come here. He said that the key had been given to your keeping."

In the distance we could hear the strains of singing: *Laudate deus*—Praise ye the Lord—the beginning of the psalms that gave the dawn service its name: Lauds. During our journey we'd heard the early morning office frequently; it began with the last few psalms, praising God and commanding all creatures great and small to do so as well.

The choir was approaching; the great church was filled with more and more light with the coming of day.

"If the book of music is important to de Bec," Rob said, "then friend Adam would be even more so. We should make ourselves scarce."

"What, and leave me alone?"

"No, lad." He placed a hand on my shoulder. "Not alone." He beckoned to Adam, who nodded; before I could say another word they slipped out of the chapel and away.

I stood speechless for a moment and then glanced at the relic, resting comfortably in its wall-niche. Without anything better to do, I took up my position on the hassock and waited, the sound of the choir growing ever louder.

—•—

De Bec and two of his men, including Armand de Got, found me still kneeling after Lauds ended. Whatever levity had kept me in good company during the night had fled with the light—I was too on edge to further interview John the Baptist or worry about how the rugby matches were going.

I looked up at him, declining to stand. I composed myself with experience borne of numerous interviews with unpleasant people, and gave him a calm, smiling glance.

"Fully enlightened?" he said, looking slightly annoyed.

"One night in a cathedral is scarcely enough for that," I answered. "I was thinking about taking a few more days."

"That's not what we agreed."

Now I stood up. I had ten or fifteen centimetres and two stone on de Bec; his bodyguards were bigger, but I was closer. For a moment my fourteenth-century self had a thought about choking the living hell out of him just to get rid of the proximate problem, but restraint, good sense and civility prevailed. In retrospect, I think that de Bec must have seen that idea cross my mind; he stepped back, almost colliding with the two well-armed men behind him.

"We agreed," I said, "that we would return to our discussions after my vigil. As for me, I haven't heard the word of the Lord nor had anything to eat, and you can wait for those things to happen before we talk further."

I clenched my fists and stood my ground.

"Monsieur," de Got said, "we can—"

De Bec held up his hand to silence his guard. "We can wait. Come along," he said—and to me, "we'll be in the plaza outside the west portal when you've finished."

With a flourish of cloak he turned and departed—a movement that gave me a brief moment of déjà vu, but it didn't resolve into anything I could recognise. His two bully boys followed; de Got cast a hostile glance over his shoulder, which I turned back with a winning prime-time smile.

—•—

Rob was waiting for me outside the cathedral. He handed me a jug of wine and gestured me to a seat on the edge of a fountain while he remained standing, scanning the plaza.

De Bec was watching us from twenty paces; he was in conversation with a well-dressed burgher with an ermine-trimmed cape and a medallion of some sort on his breast.

I took a drink from the wine and handed the jug back. "What happens next?"

"There are two hands of the sorcerer's friends scattered about. I count only two of us, perhaps three if we count Master Adam. And one of de Bec's friends appears to be a provost of His Grace the bishop."

"So what do we do?"

"I have a plan."

"I thought you said you didn't have a plan, Rob," I said. "You have a plan now?"

"*We* have a plan. Adam believes that de Bec can be deceived. He thinks that without enough knowledge to tell the difference, he will accept a reasonably complex ruse."

"This is incredibly dangerous."

"It always was dangerous. And no game. We have come too far to place such great treasures in the hands of—"

De Bec had approached during this comment, and Rob fell silent. He folded his hands in front of him to face the sorcerer and his attendants.

"Templar," de Bec said. "It's time for you to make a choice."

"What do you want?"

"You know what I want," he answered, exchanging a look with Rodney. "Give me the manuscript for the music only he can hear." He pointed at me without a glance in my direction. "Without it, you can take up your post in my lord bishop's prison."

"He has no authority to command me, and neither do you."

"Authority." De Bec sniffed. "My authority," he hissed, "is the order of the Keeper of the Seals of the great and noble lord King of France. If your Grand Master troubles himself to make application to him for your release, then he may do so—though frankly, I can't say as he would even stir himself for two such unimportant figures."

He paused like a showman, glancing over his shoulder toward the provost, who watched the scene from a distance, perhaps waiting for it to sort itself out.

"Cooperation would be much easier," he said at last.

Rob held his gaze for several seconds, then looked aside at me.

"All right," he said. "We'll cooperate."

I felt as if I'd been kicked in the stomach. Even my well-trained television face couldn't keep up with my emotions, and for the second time in less than an hour I felt like killing Guilbert de Bec—or at least wiping the smile that appeared on his face.

"I'm glad you could see reason," de Bec said. "I don't know why everyone says such insulting things about you Templars."

Rob didn't answer. He reached behind him and picked up a bound volume that appeared to be a bit smaller than A4-size; he opened it slightly to indicate that a number of sheets had been added into the back, showing the blocky musical notation I'd seen elsewhere. The front part seemed to be some sort of sketchbook; I saw drawings of machines, animals, buildings, and a number of other things.

"This is de la Halle's work?"

"Yes," Rob said. "It's inserted into a fair copy of Honnecourt's sketchbook. I'm sure you're familiar with it." He held the book out, gripping it tightly and then letting it go when de Bec put his hands on it.

The sorcerer could scarcely contain himself when the book was in his hands. His smile grew even wider; the lips were pulled back over the teeth in a way that made me want even more to beat the crap out of him.

A moment later that feeling was multiplied.

"Take them away," he said to his guards. He turned on his heel and walked across the plaza, leaving us in their custody; they moved to seize us, but Rob offered no resistance—but also didn't let them get too close.

"I thought we had a deal with him," I said finally, as they began to herd us away from the fountain toward a long, low building on the north side of the plaza.

De Got laughed. Rob shrugged. "There's no trusting a sorcerer."

—•—

We were escorted not at all gently to the building where de Got unlocked a door. There was a narrow set of stairs leading down; one of the other guards picked up and lit a torch, then locked the door behind him. We went down with four in front and two behind; I was reasonably certain we could have overwhelmed them and got away, but Rob showed no sign of wanting to do so.

The number of choices that led to this outcome fought for my attention. Had Rob trusted that de Bec would treat us fairly? Had de la Halle betrayed us—or had Rodney? I didn't say a word, but tried to read something in my friend's face. It was perfectly composed and totally opaque.

At the bottom of the stairs we found another locked door. Again, de Got had a key; he placed it in the lock and swung it wide, allowing us to enter a vaulted chamber. I took two steps in and stopped, wide-eyed.

This underground vault was at least fifteen paces wide in each dimension. Above us, the ceiling was constructed of curved beams that met in groups of four, joined by pendant bosses. There were a half-dozen of these groups, and every one of the curved beams was decorated by square projections every few centimetres. The undersides of the bosses were ornately carved into faces.

It was the spitting image of Rosslyn's Lady Chapel.

Someone shoved me from behind, making me nearly sprawl. I looked away from the ceiling at my captor as I regained my feet.

"Move along, you," he snarled.

I took one more glance at the ceiling before letting myself be shoved along through the vaulted room and into another corridor.

—•—

Whatever de Bec had in mind for us, it wasn't based on the immediate infliction of bodily harm. The corridor led to another door; just beyond it was a floor grate. It was unlocked and we were forced to drop a few metres into an oubliette—which at least was mercifully dry. When it was locked again, our guards—and their torch—departed, leaving us alone and in the darkness.

In the quiet I could hear the soft murmur of Rob praying. I didn't want to interrupt, so I occupied myself with pacing out the dimensions of our cell. It was four in one direction, three in another; I could not jump high enough to touch the grate above.

"Lad," Rob said when I'd finished determining the dimensions of our prison.

"What were you thinking of?"

"Calm yourself," he said. "Just settle down. You've had a long night."

"Calm—" I went to the sound of his voice and blundered into him. He placed his hands on my shoulders but I shrugged them off. "Calm? You want me to be *calm?* We're in—a dungeon or something, in the dark, in danger of our lives—and you just gave de Bec the book of Adam's music. He has everything he needs."

"No, he doesn't. And keep your voice low."

"He—" I lowered my voice. "He doesn't? How do you figure that?"

He leaned next to me and whispered in my ear, "I gave him the wrong book."

I didn't move.

"Sub mensura, numero, pondere perfecta," he said. "The true book is concealed there."

The words reminded me that the words of Walter of Chatîllon had drawn us to Amiens in the first place. *Well done, Templar,* Adam had said just an hour or two ago.

"What did you give him?"

"Something else."

"What about—our incarceration? Did you plan for that?"

"It wasn't unexpected. I don't think he'll turn us over to Monsieur, though—we might reveal that he had his own plans."

"He'll just kill us."

"No, he won't." Rob placed his hands on my shoulders again. "The Lord is with us."

"So what do we do?"

"We wait."

—•—

I hadn't slept since Saturday evening, and hadn't had anything to eat since the night before my vigil. Rob had a bit of dried meat in his wallet, and our captor had graciously provided us with a small jug of tepid water (that I was glad I couldn't actually see) in one corner of the cell, so we were able to break our fast. We picked a corner for our necessary functions and settled ourselves in the other corner to wait. At Rob's suggestion I took the opportunity to rest.

My sleep was dreamless, as far as I remember, but I couldn't tell how long it lasted—when I awoke again it was still dark. I heard Rob's voice softly praying; I joined in, my voice rough and harsh—and I heard new energy in Rob's as I did so.

When we finished, he found my hand in the darkness and placed the water-jug in it.

"Drink just a bit, lad. How was your rest?"

I drank a few mouthfuls of water, then carefully replaced the stopper in the bottle. "I've had worse nights. Or is it still daytime?"

"I'm not sure. I think I drifted off myself for a time. I would guess that it's night now."

"They haven't come back for us."

"Not so far."

"Let me ask you a question," I said, settling myself on the floor next to my friend. "How is it you aren't panicking?"

"The Lord is with us, Ian. He will not forsake us."

"We can't just sit here waiting for a miracle to happen. In three weeks—"

"Yes. I know. I'm not waiting for a miracle."

"You're expecting a rescue?"

"Something like that. Adam knows where we've gone, and he—"

"Adam? We just met him yesterday. This morning. We have no cause to trust him. Our lives are depending on a complete stranger."

"Yes."

"Even if he sends for help, Rob, there aren't too many people that can help us. And even if they want to help us, they have to *find* us, for God's sake. We're being left to rot. No one is coming. No one is *coming*—"

I felt Rob's arm around me, holding me tightly. "Shh. That's not true. We are not going to be left to rot, lad. We will be found. We will be."

Almost too softly for me to hear, Rob began to pray. I joined with him—and at some point I again fell into sleep.

—•—

At least twice, a waterskin was tossed down into the oubliette from above. Once we found a couple of hard loaves of bread near where we were sitting on the cell floor; whether they'd been dropped down or someone had entered and placed them there, we didn't know.

We slept; we ate and drank sparingly; we prayed. We gained strength from each other, though I felt horror at the edge of my consciousness that kept being turned back by Rob's gentle voice.

"If I'd been able to learn something from the vigil, we might not be here," I said at one point. "I brought this on us. On you."

"I'll not hear it," Rob answered. "This is the work of an evil man with an evil purpose."

"I've failed you."

"There's not room in this cell for you, and me, and your self-pity, lad. You are still the only one that can hear the music. I can't hear it, the Grand Master can't, de Bec can't, Monsieur de Nogaret can't. You have been sent here . . . sent to this time . . . for a purpose. You'll not die in this place."

"We've been here for days."

"Aye, at least a few. Think of it as a chance to catch up on your rest."

"I don't see how you can be so confident, Rob. I don't see anything to laugh about."

"I remember a fight one night when I was still in Outremer between two full Knights of the Order. One of them, Sir Giorgio, accused the other one—a Milanese named Sir Umberto—of blasphemy because he claimed that Our Lord would have laughed at a jest. It went from words to blows in a trice."

"Was it a good jest?"

"I don't properly remember, but I imagine it was. But that wasn't the point."

"What was the point?"

"That Christ laughed. Sir Giorgio insisted that there was no evidence in Scripture that our Lord ever laughed—he wept, of course, but never engaged in levity."

"That's absurd."

"Haec est dies quam fecit Dominus," Rob said. *"Exultemus et laetemur in ea."* This is the day which the Lord hath made; we will rejoice and be glad in it. "Our Saviour knew of that text, and carried it out. Of course he laughed, whether the evangelists recorded it or not. I think Sir Umberto threw that at Sir Giorgio, which made him even more angry."

"If only we had something to rejoice in now."

"Lad. Sir Giorgio died of the flux. Sir Umberto died at Saint Jean d'Acre by a Saracen blade. They are both with the Lord now; there is nothing left of them on this earth but their bones, if that. Whatever our state, whatever our peril, we are still *here*."

"In a stinking cell."

Rob laughed; the sound echoed off the walls. It went on for several seconds: not hysterical laughter, but the genuine, joyful kind which came from the heart.

"Placebo Domino in regione vivorum," he said at last. *I will please the Lord in the land of the living.*

"All of this and you're joyful? You're laughing and singing the praises of the Lord from a cell?"

"I wouldn't be the first, lad. What's more, it's easy to praise the Lord when all is sunny and bright. I praise Him then as well; why couldn't I do it now?"

—•—

Some time later after we'd slept again, we were awoken by a sound—a sort of tapping sound. It was the first time we'd heard much of anything outside of the cell. Rob grasped my arm in the dark and guided me to the wall where the sound was the loudest.

"What's—"

"Shh."

I tried to be as quiet as possible. As I listened, I could hear the tapping clearly. It wasn't a metronome sound: it was some sort of pattern: a series of taps, a gap, and then more taps, a gap, and more taps.

There was a long pause at one point; it lasted long enough that I wondered to myself if we'd imagined the entire thing . . . then, finally, it began again: two taps . . . a gap, then three taps . . . a gap, then five . . . then seven . . . then eleven, and then all was quiet once more.

"What's the pattern?" I said very softly.

"What did you count?"

"Two, three, five, seven, eleven. What does it mean?"

"It's a signal. Someone's waiting for the next number in the sequence, I think."

"As opposed to just shouting out, 'Where are you?' " I said.

"Here it comes again," Rob answered, not answering my quip. We listened: two . . . three . . . five . . . seven . . . eleven, and then quiet. "Any guesses?" he finally asked.

An idea suddenly popped into my head. I dug at the base of the cell wall and found a small shard of loose stone. I rapped it as hard as I could against the wall; it made a satisfactory sound. Then I rapped it twelve more times, as regularly as I could.

"Thirteen?"

"If I'm right, it's the logical next number. It's the sixth prime."

"Prime?"

"A number that has no divisors other than itself. Whoever's trying to signal us knows his mathematics."

"Mathematics? Then it must be—"

The tapping began again, this time continuing all the way to thirteen. I obligingly responded with seventeen taps.

There were no more taps. For several minutes all was quiet; then the next sound we heard sounded more like scraping than tapping, and it was very loud—as if it was happening directly on the other side of the wall.

Then, for the first time in what was probably a few days, light came into our cell—through a missing stone set amidships on the wall. It was coming from a torch on the other side.

"Who's there?" Rob said, shielding his eyes from the light.

"Why, Templar," Rodney's voice replied. "Don't tell me you're not glad to see me."

CHAPTER 20

"Roddy?" I said. My eyes were shut: even the torchlight was too much for me.

"You're in there as well, Initiate?" I could hear more scraping. "Good. I thought that devil might have separated you, and it took long enough to find *this* cell."

"How did you find us, Giblumite?" Rob asked.

"Aye, well. I have a map, if you'll recall. And the sooner we're gone, the better."

"Did Adam—"

"He's taking the cart to another safe place."

I opened my eyes very carefully; they watered from the light, but I was able to see that there were three blocks missing from the wall of the cell. As I watched, a fourth block was pulled from its place. A gloved hand was reaching to work on the next one.

"Let me help," I said, digging with my piece of rock. Rodney placed a chisel of some sort in front of me; I dropped the rock and began working with the tool.

Within a few minutes we'd worked a dozen blocks out of the wall, enough so we could squeeze our way out of the cell and into another chamber. Even in the dim light of Rodney's torch

I could see that its ceiling was similar to the one we'd passed through on the way to our cell. My expression must have made Rodney suspicious.

"No time for gawking, Initiate," he said. He bent down and lifted a long sack from the floor. "We'd best make our way out of here."

"I'll not argue with that."

Rodney raised the torch so that we could clearly see Rob's face. "How are you faring, Templar?"

"After days in a lightless monk's cell? I'll tell you when we get into the light," Rob answered.

Rodney grunted and handed each of us a swordbelt from the sack. "It's good to see that all that praying hasn't addled you. Here, I found these ploughshares lying about unused and arranged to have them beaten. I assume you find no fault with that."

Neither Rob nor I bothered to respond. The sudden change in our fortunes had caught me enough by surprise that I wasn't sure how to react; Rob, who had been far stronger than I, seemed stunned at first—then he visibly pulled himself together.

"This way," Rodney said, gesturing toward an arch that led to a narrow set of stone steps . . . leading down.

—•—

There was no ball of string to lead us through the labyrinth. What's more, this wasn't even the sort that we'd seen embedded in the floors of cathedrals at Chartres and Amiens: there were clearly many paths through the warren of chambers and corridors. Rodney moved with confidence, choosing each branch and turning with assurance. The architecture of these underground passages was extraordinary: patterns in the stone floors, arrangements in the ceilings, stones projecting from the walls in configurations that seemed just beyond our understanding. It was like Rosslyn, but less complete and far bigger—a prefiguring, a series of artists' models, with the chapel in Scotland the perfection of the art.

Twice we stopped to consult his map; he squinted at the parchment under the irregular, smoky light of the torch, then grunted and rolled it up again. I wondered whether he'd spent any time tramping around down here getting ready for this daring escape.

"Roddy," I said after what I guessed to be about an hour, "what's going on up in the world of the living?"

"The sorcerer is having a bit of trouble with his master plan."

"You mean the one in which he tricks Monsieur and gets the treasure for himself?"

"The very one," the stonemason said. "I've a mind to believe that he might have gotten away with it but for the Templar's ruse."

"How so?"

"Well, you know. Like calls to like. If he truly believed that the Templar had given him what he asked for, or if he was a skilled enough sorcerer to know what he had at a glance, then he'd have long since come asking for the real one and then be well away with his prize—off to his Uncle Michel, or perhaps further out of Monsieur's reach." He gestured us along a causeway that was open on one side, looking out into darkness and two or three levels of galleries below.

"But he isn't?"

"Not by half. He had to check, so he put you off in a safe place and from what I hear he has been struggling along, trying to make sense of the manuscript the Templar gave him."

"Does he know that the manuscript is the wrong one?"

"It has the devil's chord in it, so I should hope he figured it out."

"The devil's chord?" I glanced back at Rob, bringing up the rear of our procession. He shrugged, so I got no explanation.

"He has a bigger problem, though: the Cahorsin is here."

"The Cahorsin?"

"Duèze," Rob said from behind us. "Oh, all the saints be praised."

"The next rogue in the gallery. All right, who's Duèze?" I asked.

He'd been mentioned recently—I couldn't remember when. "Someone else who wants me dead or captive, I suppose?"

"He is just as dangerous as de Bec, lad," Rob said.

"Another sorcerer?"

"Worse. A *lawyer.*"

I had to suppress the urge not to laugh. It was television-serial funny: I was being sought by soldiers and ministers to princes and now sorcerers, but now I had to be afraid of lawyers as well. "What is he going to do? Sue me?"

Rodney stopped and drew out his map for a third time, but before he unrolled it he looked at Rob. "Do you want to teach the Initiate the facts of life, Templar, or shall I?"

"Say on," Rob replied.

"The Children of Solomon have relied upon our word and our reputation, the Order of the Temple on its skill and its honour. Yet any society, any group can be brought low by the stroke of a pen in the hand of a lawyer. When your Grand Master de Molay met with King Phillippe this past Eastertide and did not reach an accord, it was the signal for Duèze and his ilk to begin using their pens. Do you recall, Initiate, that I was not surprised when you told me of the coming betrayal of your Order?"

"I suppose you had to give Rob the 'facts of life' as well," I said. "He seemed fairly shocked at the time."

"He was. But he understands the power of the pen. While Christian princes argued over title and precedence, the infidel crushed the Order's power in Outremer. And now Duèze and his ilk are working hard to prepare the legal justification for the king's actions—wrapping a ribbon of half-truths around a scroll of complete lies. The facts that I had to make clear to the Templar were that truth and justice were in no way the issue in this conflict—it doesn't matter whether Philip or his servants are telling lies or not; the legal argument, a tissue of lies, composed by Jacques Duèze, the Bishop of Fréjus—the Cahorsin—will be used to ruin the Templars. And the bigger lies he tells, the better."

The big lie, I thought. *Where, oh where, have I heard that before?*

"I'm fairly sure that I understand all this. He's here because de Bec is here—is he a sorcerer too?"

"Lord, no," Rob said. He peered down at the map for a moment, then cast glances all around into the darkness. "The Cahorsin lives in mortal fear of being bewitched. He suspects de Bec's motives—"

"Good thing," Rodney interrupted. He tucked the map away.

"—his motives," Rob continued. "But that doesn't make him our friend merely because he distrusts our enemy. If the Giblumite is right, he's our enemy too."

"Two enemies who don't like each other are both in Amiens, looking for us. That's wonderful. We have to get past—"

Rodney put up a hand to silence me.

Rob drew his sword and held it ready, turning again to look into the dark.

"That way," Rodney hissed, gesturing toward the end of the causeway, which ended in a rounded arch surmounted by a keystone carved with a symbol of some sort—one of those I'd seen on a pillar in the cathedral.

I drew my weapon as well. Rodney looked as if he were going to douse the light, then thought better of it; he gestured to us to let him take the lead, but Rob shook his head and walked toward the arch, weapon ready.

"Maybe he wasn't ready in Outremer," Rodney whispered. "But he's ready to die *now.*"

"What the hell does that mean?"

Rob placed his off hand on one side of the arch and gestured with his sword for us to come up behind. Then he placed both hands on the hilt and went forward into the dark. We were on his heels.

A few paces farther we came to an abrupt stop.

"Well, well. All the fish in one net. How quaint."

Opposite us, not quite in weapon reach, stood Guilbert de Bec, flanked by de Got and three other guardsmen in his livery. In his left hand, he held a silver plate to which was attached the skull of Saint John the Baptist.

—•—

The room was well-lit. One of de Bec's guards held a torch; Rodney had his own above our heads. The plate reflected brightly and the gems set into the skull's eye-sockets seemed to gleam with inner light. But even more disturbing, we could see something red smeared on the skull's forehead.

"Sorcerer," Rob spat. "And now you are a blasphemer as well. You dare to desecrate this holy relic."

"Enjoy your last moments on the moral high ground, Templar," de Bec answered. "You have no idea what this 'relic' can do. The Byzantines knew; they learned it from Jewish mystics. And I know as well."

Rob stepped forward, but de Bec held the skull high above him. As it moved through the air it seemed to leave a glowing trail behind; Rob stopped in his tracks, his sword held high above his head, waiting to strike. He was posed like a toy soldier—and appeared frozen in place.

"Yes," de Bec said. Arnaud de Got smirked. "That's right, you half-witted would-be mystic. You have no power against the *caput Sophiae*—particularly when in the hands of a true adept.

"Disarm him," he said to his guards. "Or kill him. What thou wilt."

Two of them began to step forward—

—•—

Use your eyes, Initiate, said a voice.

The scene had frozen, as if someone had pushed the 'pause' button on the playback. Rodney stood beside me, torch in his hands, alarm and perhaps horror on his face. Rob was still in position; the guards were advancing toward where he stood, but had only taken one or two steps. De Bec, his face twisted in almost childish glee, held the skull high.

I looked around me. I could move; everyone else was immobile and, seemingly, oblivious.

See truth, said the voice. *No darkness can stand before it.*

"Truth? That de Bec has taken the relic and is about to do us to death with it? I mean—" I struggled for words, trying to think what this all meant. "I mean, if this is indeed a holy relic, Mr the Baptist's broo, how can he even hold it?"

In this time of sin, nothing is what it seems, the voice said. *No darkness can stand before truth.*

I didn't know how much time I had—it could be the rest of my life, it might only be a few seconds. My sword still at the ready, I stepped toward de Bec to look at the skull. It was glowing all right, just as it had done when I'd seen the fire in Amiens Cathedral before my vigil. There were three symbols drawn on the forehead in what I presumed to be blood, mixed with some sort of dirt. My fourteenth-century self had no idea what they were, but to my twenty-first century persona they looked like Hebrew letters. De Bec had mentioned Jewish mystics; I assumed this was some sort of sorcery.

The first character, the voice said. *Rub it out.*

"Only the first?" I was arguing with a disembodied voice. "Why not the whole thing?"

Only the first.

I had no idea why. I reached up to touch the skull; it was scalding to the touch, as was the plate to which it was attached—it seemed to have already started to burn through the glove on de Bec's hand. I gritted my teeth and swiped the dirt and blood away, burning myself as I did so.

No darkness can stand before truth, the voice said as I completed my task. *But death can sweep it away.*

The fingers and palm on my off hand were blistered from touching the skull, but I still held onto the sword with my other—a useful thing, since as soon as I finished the scene sprung suddenly to life. The guards moved at Rob, who found himself able to move; de Bec became abruptly aware that I stood before him, and gave one surprised glance at the skull and then back at me.

He opened his mouth to say something.

I ran my sword directly through him with all of the force I could manage, my anger and disgust aiding the effort. Whatever words he was about to speak never passed his lips: he was dead in an instant. The plate fell from his hands and clattered to the floor.

The third guard never even moved, his face registering shock and surprise. The other two fighting Rob glanced at the sudden sound—and my apparent disappearance; Rob and Rodney never hesitated—they dispatched them with single blows.

The other guard took to his heels and ran down a flight of steps leading out of the room, the torch he carried bobbing in the darkness. Rob began to follow, but Rodney touched his arm.

"Let him go, Templar. There are more important matters to deal with."

My hands were shaking as I pulled the blade from the dead sorcerer's body. The burns were painful, but I needed both hands to get the damn thing out of his chest. Rob stooped down to help me, his face registering shock and surprise.

"Lad, I don't understand what I just saw."

I didn't answer immediately. My fourteenth-century Ian was attending to the task of cleaning blood and bits from the sword-blade; the modern me was trying my best not to retch.

"He did something to the skull," I said. "He drew something on it in blood . . . and dirt, I think."

"And what did you do? How did you burn your hand?"

"I rubbed one of the symbols out. The first one."

"Why?"

"It told me to."

"Meaning . . ."

"Meaning," I said, standing, still shaking, "the skull of John the bloody Baptist spoke to me again. It told me that nothing could stand before truth and I should wipe off the first character from the skull and it burned my hand and I killed de Bec." It rushed out of me in just that way. I carefully sheathed the sword in its scabbard.

Then I retched. It was an impressive display, considering how little was in my stomach; I managed to make it to the corner away from all of the carnage.

When I finally stopped, Rodney was examining the skull. Rob

had picked up the plate, which seemed to have cooled off while I was tossing my guts.

"Those are Hebrew characters," I said.

Rodney frowned at me; Rob looked surprised.

"How do you know?" Rob asked.

"I've . . . seen them before. I don't know which ones they are."

"This is *mem,*" Rodney said, pointing to the middle character. He then pointed to the right-hand character. "This is *tav.* I'm fairly certain that the word written here is *met,* which means 'death'." He looked at me. "Does that mean anything to you, Initiate?"

" 'No darkness can stand before truth,' the voice told me. 'But death can sweep it away.' "

"Then the character you rubbed out must have been *aleph.*"

"If you say so."

"Aleph, mem, tav makes *emet.* Truth."

"You're pretty well schooled in Hebrew, Giblumite," Rob said. "Where did you learn that?"

"You forget our best source of knowledge, Templar. The Temple of Solomon."

Rob didn't appear to have anything to say in response. "Is it all right with you if we clean off the rest of this desecration?" he asked Rodney. "It doesn't sit well with me for the skull of holy St John to have this filth on it."

"If it's really the skull of St John," Rodney said.

"Of course it is."

"Then what is hanging in the alcove in the cathedral? There was a skull there this morning; pilgrims were visiting it as usual."

"This is the real one," I said. "Another one must have been put in its place. Some other skull, gilded and decorated to look like this one. But it was the real one on the night of my vigil, before . . ."

A cloaked figure darting out of sight.

"It was de Bec," I finished. "It was de Bec I saw. He must have put something in place of the real skull and taken it with him."

Rob uttered a curse under his breath, then said, "Then we'll have to put this back."

"We'll do no such thing," Rodney said. "You"—he pointed at Rob—"and *you* in particular," he added, pointing at me, "are in mortal danger. We will do exactly as planned: meet up with Adam at the outskirts of the city and take the treasures to Paris. The skull of the blessed Baptist will simply have to go with us."

Rob didn't seem too happy with the idea, but nodded.

"I only have one question, then," I said, straightening out my clothes as best I could. "If this is the skull of John the Baptist, whose skull is on display in Amiens Cathedral?"

—•—

There are two kinds of labyrinths. The type we had seen through our travels—the one in the nave at Chartres, the one at Amiens—were single path: there was only one way through. It might require a considerable walk, weaving in and out of the pattern, but there was only one way to proceed. (The minotaur didn't live in that sort, I'd guess—sooner or later he'd be able to walkabout in search of a nosh and find himself outside and that wouldn't do.)

The caverns under Amiens were the other type.

We got away as quickly as we could from the place where we'd encountered the sorcerer and his lads. Rodney changed our route: the direction he'd intended would have retraced de Bec's steps to the surface, and there might be more folks waiting for us along that path. Instead, we followed a longer, more circuitous one that ultimately led us into chambers that were actually being used to store dyestuff, bolts of cloth, barrels of ale, and bales of hay. After passing through a few of these, we found ourselves at the base of a rope ladder. Sheathing our swords we climbed, Rodney first and Rob last, with me in between.

Adam was waiting for us in a horse-barn, cart harnessed and ready to go. It was a filthy day, chilly and damp, but the fresh air—even tainted by the smell of the dye-works and the other foul odours of the city—was wonderful, like a perfumed garden.

After a quick glance around the otherwise empty shelter, Rob bowed his head and offered a whispered prayer. Even given the urgency, neither Rodney nor I moved to interrupt him. I remember speaking a few words of thanks myself.

"The sorcerer was on his way to interrogate you two," Adam said to Rob and me. "He's—"

"Dead," Rodney finished the sentence. We climbed up into the cart; the stonemason took the reins with Adam beside him, while Rob and I made ourselves as comfortable as we could on the wagon bed. My burned hand was bandaged as well as could be managed, but that was likely to take some time to recover.

There were a number of tanned hides in the wagon; we crawled in under them, concealing ourselves as well as we could. Rodney handed us the satchel with the skull-relic and we tucked it in among the other items in our precious little collection.

"Well, *that* will come as interesting news to the Bishop," Adam said. "Dead, eh?"

"The Initiate killed him," Rodney said. "I'm still not sure how. But I think we'd best be well out of Amiens before His Grace decides to start interviewing accomplices. Do you have . . ."

"Yes. It was undisturbed, and it's concealed in the wagon. What do you plan to do?"

"Leave the city."

"Yes, of course. But where do you plan to go?"

"Paris."

"So you'd rather our two Templar friends are tossed into a dungeon on the Île de la Cité than remain in one here in the city of alchemists. Won't Monsieur and his associates be waiting for us at the gate of Saint-Denis?"

"I have a plan."

"Saints bless us," Rob said from our hiding place. "The Giblumite has a plan."

Rodney clucked to the horses. I couldn't see his facial expression but could've guessed at the scowl. "Listen here," he said at last to Rob, "you are in *my* cart, snugged up next to *my* relic, relying on *my* skill and luck to get us out of this God-cursed city undetected. You've not eaten in quite some time, you stink even more than usual, and you'd still be sitting in the dark in that cell if I hadn't come to fetch you. Your plan nearly got you and the Initiate killed. So we'll be following *my* plan and I'll thank you to go along with it. Are we agreed on that?"

"I am your humble servant," Rob said. "But friend Adam has a point."

"Amiens first," he said, "and Paris next. Now be silent, Templar," he added quietly. "We've reached the gate."

From my concealed spot I heard booted feet sloshing in the mud; but to my surprise I heard Adam speak and not Rodney.

"Good day, my friend," he said. I'd been in Amiens for a few days and noticed the Picard intonation, the Amiénois slightly different from his own; the man had it perfectly. "You must forgive my cousin here, mute since birth."

"What are you carrying?"

"Hides. We spent all of a night in Saint-Michel with lame Jean—"

"He's a sour one," the other agreed. "If he worked half as hard as he complained, there would be more sous in his wallet."

"He has a few more of our sous than I wanted to leave him. Look." I heard a slight jingling of coin. "We only have a few extra left. My father and uncle will be pleased with the tanning job, though."

"These are fine coins. So many we see here are clipped."

"They have not passed through so many hands.—Perhaps you would like to keep one or two as souvenirs."

"You are most kind, good sir."

"It is nothing."

"God speed you safe to your home," came the answer. In a few moments the cart was underway again; cobblestones gave way to ruts and the sound of wooden wheels on the occasional board.

A few minutes passed in silence; then I heard Rodney grunt. "Mute since birth," he said, annoyance in his voice.

"Picards and Gascons don't get on well as you know, stonemason. A word past your lips and he'd want to search the cart. He wouldn't stop until he found something."

"Your performance was admirable."

"A lifetime of listening to words. You should be glad I'm along."

"We are," Rob said from his own hiding place. "You are a light in dark places, Adam."

"Your servant."

Rodney grunted again. "I am to endure eight days of this revelry. My cross to bear."

The road noise and the gently falling rain combined to make me drowsy after that. The events of the last few days, and the terror of the past few hours, had exhausted me; ultimately I went to sleep.

For a change, there were no dreams.

CHAPTER 21

WE TRAVELED ALMOST FIVE DAYS AFTER LEAVING AMIENS, DURING which time it did nothing but rain. My hands quickly recovered from their burns though I could still see where I'd handled the skull. I could also still almost feel the fire that had surged through the skull of the Baptist when I touched it.

It was October now and the air had a raw, cold edge to it: the first hint of winter to come. It added to the gloom. Adam was our guide and our voice—he knew every accent and dialect. Roddy was his usual sullen self, and Rob simply wouldn't talk. We followed another *route templière* as we made our way south, passing through a deep forest straight out of an adventure movie—a canopy of trees blocking out the grey sky to either side of the road. It took us a day, an evening and part of another day to make our way through.

During the night we spent there, after we made camp, Rob and I took a dip in a sluggishly flowing stream. It came much to the surprise and concern of our two fellow-travelers that we would be willing to bathe, but the two of us and our clothing emerged smelling, if not completely fresh, at least not quite as offensive. It was a far cry from what my modern self was used to, of course, but it was at least a positive step.

The following morning when I woke, I had the same feeling I'd first felt when we were coming across Aquitaine toward Toulouse: a line passing near where we'd camped, something I couldn't see but rather sense.

"Rob," I said, pulling myself onto the lip of the wagon, "is the earth-path strong here?"

He was attending to one of the rear wheels. "Eh?" he said, coming into view.

"Earth-path."

"This is a *route templière,*" he said. "Of course the earth-path comes through here."

"But there's something else, isn't there?"

Rob pulled himself up on the wagon to sit beside me. "The Order didn't create the paths, lad. It just protects them. They were there long before we were. They are anchored by things much older."

"You told me this near Toulouse. The earth-paths follow the contours of the land, and towns grow up where paths cross. No town here."

"There are things older than towns."

I looked at him, waiting for the explanation. He didn't answer but instead jumped down to the forest floor, indicating that I should follow.

Perhaps no more than a few hundred metres from where we camped, we came into a clearing, sloped slightly downhill. Embedded in the ground were three huge stones spaced a few metres apart: each was shoulder-height, large enough that I probably couldn't encircle them with my arms.

The feeling of earth-path was strong enough to make me light-headed. I leaned on the centre stone and it grew even more powerful: I was driven to my knees. Suddenly I could hear music welling up: a crescendo that drowned out the forest sounds and the dripping rain.

I let my hand drop to my lap and the music receded into the background, but the lightheadedness didn't go away.

"What is this place? Some sort of Stonehenge?"

"These are the Three Little Sisters," he said from what seemed to be some distance away. "They stood here when the oldest tree was only a sapling. The earth-path descends into the bones of the earth here." He approached me and I felt each step—the music echoed them with percussion.

I felt his hand on my shoulder.

"Time for truth, lad," he said. "This is a place of truth. The Giblumite especially fears this place: here even his secretive heart is open to the all-seeing Eye."

I looked up at Rob as if through the wrong end of a spyglass.

"I don't understand."

"You said that you are from the future," he said to me, his face stern. "Do you still profess that belief?"

"Yes."

"You swear it by our Saviour and all his saints?"

"Yes." A few months past I might not have done, but the words held meaning for me now. "I swear it."

"And that the head of the blessed John the Baptist spoke to you and gave you power to defeat the sorcerer."

"Yes. It was just as I told you. Do you want me to swear that too?"

The music rose to almost painful volume. I clapped my hands on my ears but it did no good.

"You *must* tell the truth in this place, lad. If you are lying, there is no power under Heaven that can save you from the Lord's wrath."

"I don't understand . . . why you would doubt me now. After all this." I was bent down almost to the ground, barely able to see.

"Something the sorcerer said. He called the skull of the Baptist the *caput Sophiae.* Do you know aught of that, Ian?"

"I don't know what he was talking about. I don't even know what that means—it's a head," I said, recalling the Latin, but not sure what it meant. "Sophia's head."

"That's right. Sophia was a pagan goddess of wisdom. Now tell me, in your future time—do they have such things? Talking heads that profess wisdom?"

The music faded away; my vision slowly cleared. I looked up at Rob and shrugged his hand from my shoulder; I almost laughed in his face.

Talking heads, I thought. *That's what I was—a talking head that professed wisdom. People used to turn on the telly to hear it.*

And now . . .

"Nothing like what I saw under Amiens," I answered, and it was the truth. "What are you afraid of?"

"I don't know what you mean, lad." He stepped back, alarmed.

"This was a test," I said, standing up. Stray drops of water came loose from leaves above and fell onto my head and shoulders. "A test of truth. You wanted to come this way, to come to this place, to test me—because something about that head scared you."

"Everything about it scared me," he said. "Do you know what the 'Baphomet' is?"

I spread my hands wide. "No."

"There are enemies of our Order who have accused us of—of worshipping a head." There was going to be a different word at that spot in the sentence, but I wasn't sure what it would have been. "If the head of the Baptist was the Baphomet, it could have . . ." He trailed off.

"It could have *what?* Taken control of me?"

Rob didn't answer.

"It isn't enough that I saved all of our lives because I can hear voices coming from gilded skulls. It isn't enough that I've followed the path of light all the way to this point even though I don't really belong here.

"See here, Rob: we've lived in each other's laps for almost three months, faced every sort of danger, and you still thought—what? That I was, I don't know, working the other side of the lane?"

Rob turned away and walked to the southernmost stone. He didn't turn to face me.

"We have ten days left," I said. "Ten days before every Templar in France—and most other places—will be arrested by the King and his servant, and you're playing games with me."

"It's not a game, lad."

"Ten days," I repeated. I walked to where he stood and grabbed his shoulder, spinning him around. "But I'm not going to make it home, am I, Rob? All of this is for nothing. All of the initiations, all of the people and places, is all going to be for nothing." I grabbed him by the shoulders. "I'm heartily sick of this. I don't want to be in this century anymore. I don't want to be on this pilgrimage—I've learned quite enough already.

"I don't need the artifacts. Find a safe place for them—you'll have already done that: the Ark is lost in my day, the head of John the Baptist has been replaced anyway, and the Grail book—I don't even know what it is.

"It's all irrelevant. I'm irrelevant too." I let my hands drop to my sides. "This entire quest is irrelevant." I turned away and walked toward the edge of the clearing.

The music seemed to well up again for a moment, and then faded away. I stretched my shoulders and then sighed. I wasn't sure if I was angry or depressed or some unpleasant combination.

I turned to face him. "What's going to happen in Paris, Rob?"

"I have no idea. I know that we're following Adam's lead to get into the city undetected, but I have fear in my gut about taking these treasures there."

"Do you trust him?" I asked.

"I trust in Almighty God." Rob crossed himself. "I am compelled to trust Master Adam as well. Come, lad," he said at last. "We'd best be going."

—•—

In the clearing Rodney was busy with the harness; Adam was nowhere in sight—likely off attending to that which everyone must do from time to time. I went to the rear of the cart; my head was still buzzing a bit from the feel of the earth-path.

After a few moments I was distracted by Rob and Rodney, who were arguing in loud whispers, continuing this bad costume drama soap we were acting out. Adam came up to where I stood; he had a faint smile on his face.

"This is the point in the drama where the hero turns away from the other players and speaks to the audience," he said.

"The fourth wall."

He appeared puzzled for a moment, then nodded. "The stage has three walls," he said. " 'Fourth wall.' That's a pleasing phrase."

I looked away from him, attending to my pack.

"The Templar took you to the Three Sisters, didn't he?"

"Of course. Another mystery that everyone knows about. Yes, he took me to the bloody rocks and asked me some questions about Amiens."

"Amiens."

"Yes, Amiens," I answered. I looked at him again; he stepped back at my obvious anger. "The second-to-last stop on this absurd adventure. It doesn't matter. The only person I might trust doesn't trust me; our stonemason friend has his own agenda; and you—I don't know what your game is. I don't think any of this matters at all."

"That would be true," Adam said, "except for the music."

"The music doesn't matter either," I said. I wasn't sure whether I believed it or not at that moment, but the idea that I'd been subjected to yet another test of truth was making me angry enough to say it. Whatever game the troubadour was playing didn't interest me at that moment either.

"No," Adam said. "It matters very *much,* friend Ian. It matters more than any of this. The music is the most important thing."

"Can you tell me why?"

"All of the portents point to it. But that's not the answer you were looking for, is it, Ian? Let me do better. The music, when combined with the Grail-book, describes the Divine. It's the pattern that Master Llull was looking for."

"Is he hiding in the woods somewhere nearby, waiting for some revelation?"

The musician glanced around for a moment, as if it were part of the drama—maybe he was imagining what he'd say through the fourth wall.

"No," he said finally, "he's still in Castile, playing with his *combinatoria,* proving the truth of Holy Scripture through his charts." Adam reached into his wallet and drew out a wooden something. At first I thought it was the Antikythera device; but it was simpler, a round, flat wooden disk that had markings—words set in concentric circles in tiny, almost unreadable print. "This is one of them."

He handed it to me. The disk wasn't a single circle: it was four concentric ones, each with a little wooden knob that permitted it to be turned independently of the others. The words were separated by horizontal lines, so that various phrases or groupings could be made depending on their position. Each section of each circle had a single letter beside the word.

"I don't see how this proves the truth of Scripture," I said. "Why would he bother? Doesn't he believe it himself?"

" 'Tis not a lack that brings him to make these devices," Adam replied. "This is an expression of his faith. Each combination represents a phrase from holy writ; no matter how you turn the wheels, you always get one. The letter codes are in great charts—I've seen them: C-G-T-A, C-G-A-T, C-T-G-A, and so on. It's rather like music in a way, all of the combinations."

Something about what he said struck me as familiar, but I couldn't place it. I handed the wooden circle back to Adam, who tucked it away.

"You said he was looking for a book of wisdom when he was on his way to Alexandria," I said. "Did he ever find it?"

"No. The book he sought was the one given you by my lord of Gisors—but he does not know aught of it, nor would he know what to make of it if he did."

"And you can make something of it, I suppose."

"I know that each note in the music goes with a line in the book somehow."

"But the book has hundreds of thousands—millions of lines," I said. "Is the song that many notes?"

"No. But the music can be repeated from the beginning when you reach the end."

"What do the numbers mean?"

"I cannot say."

I shrugged. "Whenever the two—" I tried to say stand-up comedians; it came out "*jongleurs* are done with their argument, we can continue to Paris and get this quest over with."

"Paris, yes," Adam said. "But first Senlis."

"Senlis?" I knew that our road reached there; Rodney had spoken of it. "What's in Senlis?"

"Bees."

—•—

We came to Senlis as the sky was darkening toward evening. It was like a beautifully-built stage set: huge angular walls three or four times a man's height encircling a cramped little town with a dozen church spires peeking up over them. It was a perfect backdrop for a costume drama; the little town, fortified and turreted, lying on the banks of a slow-moving river.

We entered through the Porte Saint-Rieul—the northern gate of the city—with the church of the same name on our left. The walls were three or four paces thick; I wondered to myself, looking out from the back of our wagon, what they were intended to protect.

Our destination turned out to be on the south side of the town. We traveled through narrow lanes around a small inner oval, the oldest part of Senlis from its days as a Roman town; over a bridge over a sludgy ditch that Rob called *le Fosse;* and at last to a small hostel adjoining the Carmelite priory.

"Come," Adam said, as we dismounted from the cart. Rodney snorted; Rob's eyebrows went up, but he stepped down from the cart to stand beside the minstrel.

"I've a weakness for honey-cakes," Rob said. "Lead on, Master Adam."

"Honey-cakes," Rodney grunted. "I'll stay with the cart."

Adam led us under an archway into a garden. As soon as we emerged, I heard a sound and smelled an odour that brought back memories of summer. And then something else pulled me up short, also reminding me of summer: a familiar face once again, dressed in unfamiliar clothing.

"Brother David," Adam began, "may I present—"

"Mac," I said.

The monk who was approaching us was of average height and build, dressed in the brown robes of a Carmelite friar; his hands were folded in front of him, his face serene in a way that—in my memory—David MacDougal's face had never been. He stopped short, one eyebrow raised like Mr Spock on the old sci-fi programme.

"Brother Ian," he said. "Welcome back."

Rob and I exchanged glances. Adam looked pleased, like an interested theatre-goer with a fine plot unfolding before him.

"I—" I began. "I mean, I've never—"

"That is not a name I use now," he said. "Here they usually just call me *l'Écossais.*" Brother David smiled slightly, as if this meeting confirmed something in his mind. His voice went from curiosity to assurance. "But in York they indeed called me 'Mac' for 'MacDougal,' as I told you when you were here at Michaelmas."

Thoughts chased each other through my head. *Michaelmas,* I thought. *September 29—but I was in a lightless prison under Amiens on Michaelmas.*

"I wasn't here at Michaelmas, Brother."

"Oh?" David smiled quizzically. "Aye, you most certainly were. You assured me that when you returned you would profess to have no memory of it."

"I told you that."

"You did."

"Brother David, on Michaelmas day I was—" Rob was looking directly at me; he let one eyebrow lift, as if he was waiting to see what I was going to say. "I was far from here. I could not be in two places at once."

Could I? I wondered. I was completely bewildered. *But there was Rob and Mac and Rodney . . . but they're in two times, not two places.*

It was all too complicated.

"God upon His Throne makes crooked paths straight, Brother," Brother David continued. "Please be welcome again to our humble priory." He shared an additional smile with Adam.

"I'm not sure which crooked path brought me here."

"I have considered your proposal," Brother David said, "regarding Master Adam's plan to ask for our help in conveying you to Paris."

This time Adam seemed taken aback. *Must be a mystery he hasn't seen,* I thought. *Go talk to the fourth wall now, troubadour.*

I didn't say anything at all.

"Perhaps we should discuss this plan," Rob said. "Since everyone is so well informed."

"In due time," David answered. He gestured us along a flagstoned path that led through an arbor and into gardens beyond.

As we walked the buzzing sound and the sweet smell became more apparent. In a wide, open barn, protected from the drizzle, we could see other Carmelite monks, wearing thick gloves and floppy hats covered with veils, moving through a haze of smoke trailing from kettles. They walked between wide tables that held cone-shaped wicker boxes. Bees moved languidly among the working brothers, who were withdrawing honeycombs from the boxes and setting them aside.

"Heaven flows with milk and honey," Brother David said. "Those are the skeps, which hold the hives. The brothers are a bit troubled; the honey harvest has been scant thus far—a poor omen."

"No honey-cakes?" Rob said, mock-serious. "I had my heart set on them."

"I think we can oblige you. We have honey stored by for just such an occasion."

—•—

Brother David was as good as his word. After the Vespers service we gathered in the refectory and enjoyed an excellent simple meal—including coarse honey-cakes—with the Carmelite brothers. Even Rodney pronounced himself satisfied.

David, meanwhile, deflected all questions: what we wanted, why we were there, how I came to visit Senlis on Michaelmas even though I was trapped in an oubliette in the dark at the time.

While we sat quietly the rain fell outside. From the windows of the refectory we could see other brothers moving from skep to skep through the smoke, drawing out the honeycombs and setting them aside as the bees buzzed languidly around them.

"Tell me more about your order," I said after we dined.

"Didn't you learn about it on Michaelmas?" Rob asked. "When you were last here?"

"Pray refresh my memory."

Brother David folded his hands on the table in front of him and scanned our little group. In another time and place the mannerisms were familiar: a boardroom at the BBC when I was in my twenties, before *Ian and Jan*, before Mac moved on to greater authority at ITV.

But the serene face made sure to remind me that this was another man, another echo.

"Our order was founded on Mount Carmel a century ago," David said. "We sought to imitate the blessed prophet Elijah, living a life of simple prayer in silence. We do not all observe that vow—it's difficult to deal with the world in a place like Senlis without speech—but otherwise we hold to Father Albert's original rule."

"Did you choose to leave the Holy Land?" I asked.

"It was not our *choice,*" David answered, looking at Rob, who bowed his head, looking at the empty bowl before him. "The Saracens forced us away, just as other orders were made to depart. We took our message to Italy and France, Germany and England."

"God's bees," Rob said without looking up.

"Just so. We dwell in separate cells, gathering the divine honey of spiritual consolation. We believe . . . that we are always in the Divine Presence."

"Under the gaze of the All-Seeing Eye," I said, and David nodded.

"An apt description. God is everywhere, Father, Son and Holy Spirit."

And not just under some bloody ancient rock, I thought. I kept my face passive, but Rob glanced up at me and looked quickly away, seeing anger in my eyes.

David seemed to sense the tension among us. He cleared his throat. "Perhaps you would like to walk through the grounds."

"In the rain," Rodney muttered; but Adam cleared his own throat. Rodney and Adam stood up, as did Rob, and walked toward the door. I made to follow, but David placed a hand on my sleeve.

"If I may have a word, Brother?"

"Certes," I said. The other three went out the door and along the cloister hallway. David gathered the wooden bowls that had held our meal, and with my help we took them toward a sideboard where other brothers were clearing.

He gestured for me to walk with him into the chapter house, empty at this hour of the day. He took a seat on a stone bench; I sat opposite.

"You were as good as your word," he said. "You said that you would recognise me, but not recall our conversation."

"I've never been to Senlis in my life, Brother David. I don't know what the . . . I don't know what this is all about. But on Michaelmas I was in Amiens with Brother Robert."

"You came here on Michaelmas, Ian, and told me that you would return with three friends a few days later—today. I know that Master Adam has brought your group here to Senlis to ask for our help; you told me yourself. He has not detailed the extent of his request as yet, but will do so tonight after Vespers."

"What else do you know?"

"I know of your mission, and what you have in your cart."

"You know about—"

"Yes. You told me."

"I did."

"You did. And since you first visited me I have dreamt of things that I can scarcely understand . . . I have dreamt of myself, or someone who looks just like me. I was not dressed in my habit"—he took a fold of one sleeve between finger and thumb, then let it fall—"and I was a person of authority, the head of a theatre troupe, I think. You were a member of this troupe. I . . . was very unpleasant."

"You dreamt of being—"

I stood up and walked away from him. Mac—David MacDougal, the Carmelite friar—had begun to dream of the ITV producer? Of being the arrogant wanker I'd last seen stalking about in Rosslyn Chapel? There was another link to the future?

"You seem distraught, Brother," David said softly.

"What else did I tell you?" I said at last, clenching my fists. I didn't turn around.

"You said that you had reconciled your two disparate parts. You said that you were at peace."

"You must be mistaking me for someone else."

"In a way, I suppose so. You're not the man you were—or possibly will be. You seem . . . a transitional figure. A man facing two directions: past and future."

Billboard philosophy, I thought; there were no words for it in *langue d'oc. What you see on afternoon television.* "I'm so happy to provide such an example.

"In Master Adam's *goliardes* he has stock figures, did you know? The honourable knight, the virtuous woman, the cunning knave, the wise fool. He graciously speaks through the fourth wall to tell the audience how things are going.

"What am I supposed to be? Did I tell you—when I was here on Michaelmas, which is impossible—that I'd just killed a man in anger? Forgive me, Father. I have sinned, and most egregiously, but it doesn't matter as I'm soon to be arrested along with all of the Templars in France from the lowest to the highest. So glad to be of service."

David waited patiently, my anger washing over him and passing gradually away.

"You have nothing to say," I said at last, turning to face him. "Nothing at all."

"Of your sin, you were shriven. You have already confessed it—"

"At Michaelmas."

"Just so.—Are you angry at me, Ian?"

I paused to think about his question. I didn't know this Carmelite monk; I scarcely knew the man he so closely resembled. Somehow someone who closely resembled me had come to him a few days ago and spilled all of the secrets of our pilgrimage.

I didn't like being in the dark, though you'd think I'd have become accustomed to it by now.

"No," I said. I walked over and sat beside him again. "No, Brother David. I'm just tired."

"No, you are most definitely angry. But I'm pleased to hear that it's not directed against me."

I put my head in my hands. "What happens now, Brother David?"

"When your companions return from the courtyard, Master Adam will detail the plan to convey you all into Paris. After listening patiently, I will bring it to the Father Abbot, who will agree to help you."

"Just like that."

"Ian," David said after a few moments, "we have already had four days to decide."

—•—

In the end, it was just that easy.

The Carmelite enclosure was hard by the southern gate of Senlis, where the sluggish river Nonette flowed by. Master Adam and the Carmelite abbot were old acquaintances, but even so the minstrel was surprised at the abbot's willingness to lend us a river-boat and Carmelite habits.

I assumed that I—or whoever the hell it was that had come to Senlis at Michaelmas—had done a good job of convincing him.

While one of the night offices was being sung, the four of us and Brother David loaded our precious cargoes onto a wide, flat boat suitable for navigating the sluggish stream. A thin crescent of waxing moon peeked through thin clouds, giving us enough light to see but still leaving us largely concealed to anyone's prying eyes.

"We'll make the journey in a few days at most, lad," Rob said to me as we lashed down the wooden crate containing the Ark. "With de Bec dead and the Cahorsin either still in Amiens or on his way to Paris, there might be no one watching the water-paths. In any case, that"—he gently patted the crate—"might conceal us."

" 'Might'."

He looked at me, his face only dimly visible in the moonlight. "We're trusting in Master Adam, who knows people in the Paris constabulary. And we've got faith that the Lord has delivered us this far."

"Will there be any more little 'tests' on the river, Rob?"

"No. No more tests, lad. I . . . had to be sure."

"And are you sure?"

"No." He lifted his pack from the wooden dock and placed it carefully into the boat, turning away from me. "No, I'm not. It was wrong of me to subject you to the Three Sisters, Ian, and I beg your forgiveness."

It wasn't the answer I'd expected—it was almost too direct, too honest.

"Rob, I . . ."

"No time for this," he said, standing up and walking back along the dock. "There are still things to be done before we leave."

He left me standing there wondering what to say.

—•—

From Senlis, the Nonette—a narrow, sluggish river—flowed north-west to the Oise. Somewhat wider, and considerably more swift, the Oise flowed into the Seine at Château-Conflans, where the Archbishop of Paris took his holidays (as David was quick to point out to me as the boat took us out into the channel).

We rowed gently, the current taking us downriver through the darkness. From time to time we heard a distant church-bell or animal noises—birds being flushed from their perches as our boat disturbed the water—but it was largely quiet. Rodney sat near the front, with Adam just behind; Rob and I took turns rowing, and Brother David manned the tiller, steering us toward and then away from the banks of the river according to some pattern only he could recall. Just as we were about to push off, as I was thanking him for his help, he had told me that the abbot had given him leave to travel with us to Paris.

"Someone will need to return the boat," he said, with a gentle smile.

We reached the confluence with the Oise just as dawn was breaking. The two rivers met at Chantilly; *Ian and Jan* had done a location there to cover the horse-races, and there had been the wedding of that footballer at the fairy-tale château . . . but there was no huge château looming near the river—it was just a river town, full of dirt and smell—very fourteenth-century.

The Oise was wider and swifter; we were able to leave most of the work to David. The rain had mostly passed, giving us a cool, grey day; Rob and I dozed and left the oars in the rowlocks, enjoying the rest we hadn't gotten during the previous night. Our boat was not alone on the river; there were many travelers on the Oise between Chantilly and Pontoise where it joined the Seine, and Adam kept up a running commentary with Rodney and David, spinning elaborate tales from the smallest of observations. I think if I had not been so tired or so worried I might have enjoyed this remarkable performance far more.

Rob appeared to ignore it all; he found a comfortable position half-sitting, half-reclining with his back to the crate, placed his floppy pilgrim's hat over his face, and went to sleep as if there was nothing at all that required his attention.

—•—

We passed into the wider and busier Seine late in the afternoon. Rob and I took to the oars: where the smaller rivers had carried us along with them, we were now moving against the swift main current to go upstream to Paris. David took turns with us, but neither Adam nor Rodney seemed inclined toward it.

"I would only upset your rhythm, Brother," Adam said to me as I worked away with my back to him, sweating heavily despite the damp air and chill breeze. "I was not born to row."

"It's not my chosen profession either." I let off for a moment and looked over my shoulder. "But—rhythm? I would think that would be second nature to someone like you."

"Ah!" he said, smiling. He reached into his travel pack and produced a fiddle and a short bow. "There *is* something I can do for you."

Rob grunted without turning. My place was astern of him; he continued to row, and I turned back around and took it up again.

"Be careful, Carmelite," Rodney said. "He's going to play the Devil's Office with that thing."

"Really!" David smiled. "Say on, stonemason. I'm eager."

"Didn't Saint Jerome say that to pay a minstrel was tantamount to sacrificing to demons?" Rodney continued. "He called them *turpis,* scandalous. They played just for the sound of the music, not for some higher calling."

"Content cum instrumentis," David said. He leaned back, grasping his knee with his folded hands. "But King David drew a demon out with the playing of his harp. I think this criticism of minstrels is a bit hysterical."

"Thank you," Adam said. I could almost hear his smile. "Now, if I may, Master Rodney—"

"Too bad you don't have a *tabour* in there too, or I could accompany you."

Adam didn't answer, but gave a little experimental pluck to the strings of his fiddle, and then began to play an intricate tune. He tapped his foot as he played; and slowly, almost indiscernably, did exactly what he said he'd do: match the pace and rhythm of his music to the regular strokes of the oars as they dipped and pulled through the dark water of the river.

A few minutes later David took my place, giving me a chance to rest; Adam continued to play. I pulled St Martin's cloak from my pack and wrapped it around me; a few moments after that, the lilt of the music and the steady sound of rowing put me directly to sleep.

—•—

The trouvère was an Englishman. He knew jests and songs in many languages; that made him entertaining to many of Lamontaigne's company, whose common language was the patois of the battlefield.

With the company in camp waiting for *el Justo* to decide where to send us next, there was plenty of opportunity for him to make his coin as he moved from one group of tents to the next. He slipped easily from English to Gaelic to *langue d'oc* to *langue d'oeil* to one or another variety of Italian; we had all learned the words for "look out" and "friend" and "your mother too, bloke" in most of them, but that was as far as it usually went—but this fellow could not only sing but joke with each of the groups, drawing their applause, their laughter and their silver.

By nightfall he had gathered a fair crowd around him and had reverted to his native language. He had put away his flute and his *musele,* choosing a small *viele* instead.

"Let me sing to you of a pair of birds," he began when there was quiet. "The owl and the nightingale. The owl—"

"Birds?" someone shouted. "Sing about women!"

"Peace," the troubadour said, placing the *viele* in his lap and raising his hands. "There is much in their tale about the fair sex." All around, people hooted encouragement; he'd made many friends during the day.

After a few moments Lamontaigne's men settled down again and the troubadour began to sing.

The tale of the two birds began slowly. The nightingale, a sweet-voiced bird, sang to men and women and encouraged them to love; the owl, dour and dirty, recited the Hours. Repeatedly almost coming to blows, the two engaged in a long debate about what they should sing, why love was good (or bad), whether this life should be one of joy or sorrow . . . when the minstrel took the nightingale's part he smiled and exchanged winks and smirks with the audience, and when he sang as the owl he was discordant, frowning, warning us that we would be companions to devils in the next life.

He held us. His talent and skill as an entertainer and the boredom of the camp combined to make a rapt audience of a hundred hardened mercenaries on a warm late-spring evening; the battlefield seemed far away. When he had finished—hundreds of long couplets, astonishing really, all from memory—he stood and bowed deeply. Coins rained into the floppy hat that passed through those who had sat and listened. He accepted the plaudits, slaps on the bank and handclasps as he passed through, at last collecting his hat and making the night's earnings disappear into his wallet.

When the moon had dropped lower in the sky I was sitting before the last of the cookfire, my tentmates already abed. The minstrel passed close and stopped; for reasons I couldn't explain, I nodded to him, gesturing to a place nearby. A stoup of wine lay next to me, and I raised it; he took his mug from its belt-hook and accepted half a cup, sipping it with satisfaction.

"You sang very well," I said. "You're far from home, Englishman."

"And you, Scot." He smiled. "But I'm not the Hammer and you're not the Bruce, so we can be at peace. You enjoyed my tale, then?"

"I didn't think I would do. Two birds arguing about the Kingdom of Heaven? You might not have found us so willing to listen."

"My choice," he said, sipping the wine. "But I was not here to sing to everyone."

I didn't answer.

"I am here to sing to you, Ian Graham."

My hand was on the hilt of my weapon in a moment; the minstrel didn't move or change his expression.

"You'd best explain yourself."

"Something is about to happen, Ian," he continued, in the same quiet voice. "Your life is about to change."

"Is it now."

"There are two parts of you," he said. "Part of you is the owl: fierce, heedless of others' opinions, cruel when needful—not easily turned, a realist, who knows that violence and death will come. Yet part is the nightingale as well—seeking joy where you can, leaving the past to the past because the future is so uncertain.

"Nothing is forever, Ian. Not Lamontaigne's company, not the *reconquista,* not King Edward the Hammer, not the Bruce; not England or Scotland, nor you nor me nor anyone."

"Didn't the nightingale accuse the owl of being a bringer of news no one wanted to hear?" I said, not letting go of my weapon. "How do you—how do you know who I am?"

"Ah, so you *were* listening."

"Answer my question. Are you a devil or warlock, then?"

"The nightingale accuses the owl of that as well."

I allowed my blade to come a handspan out of its sheath.

"Peace, Scotsman. I mean you no harm."

"I don't need riddles."

"You will need to know what to do when the world changes, Ian. Will you continue as the owl, or choose the path of the nightingale? You'll need someone to guide you."

"And who might that be? You?"

"Heavens, no. I would recommend the worthy Abbot Tomaso at Cintra in Portugal." The minstrel smiled a bit more broadly. "They call him *el Corvão*—the crow." He touched the side of his nose. "On account of . . . well, it'll be obvious."

"What will he do for me?"

"If you're lucky," he answered, "he will place you on the path of light."

"Who shall I tell him sent me, on the unlikely chance that I find my way there?"

"Who?" He drank off the last of his wine, then took a fold of his sleeve to wipe the last drops away before hooking it to his belt. "Tell Father Corvão that you were sent to him by Adam."

—•—

"Adam."

I woke with a start. The dream hung there in my mind for a few startling moments: the minstrel, his song, and Lamontaigne's encampment as familiar as anything I'd known—but then it drifted away, leaving me unsure what I'd just dreamt. In moments it was gone, a wisp of fog curling away on the dark river.

The day had faded into dusk; Adam was stowing his fiddle away and settling back onto his seat. Only David was rowing now, slowly and gently: before the bow of our boat I could see a cluster of buildings on either side of the river. We were steering toward a dock to starboard, at the base of a tall, narrow tower. On the opposite side of the river a larger, more imposing tower loomed near the bank; torches were alight on the parapet, and I could just barely make out the Valois banner in the approaching darkness.

"The Louvre," Rodney whispered, pointing. "The Royal Tower." And to Adam: "Your plan had better be a good one, minstrel."

"Have faith, stonemason," Adam said. As we came hard by the quay, Adam stepped off onto the stone piling. He touched a guardsman on the arm and said something to him, out of range of our hearing.

The guard seemed annoyed at first, then as Adam said something else to him, his face turned to surprise.

"What do you think he told him?" I asked Rob.

"I wouldn't venture to say, lad," Rob said, sitting more upright, straightening the folded sleeves of his Carmelite robe.

David chuckled. "At last, the virtues of serving in a house with vows of silence. You don't read lips then, Brother Robert."

"And you do."

"Yes," David answered. "The constable was shocked when Master Adam told him who he was."

"Why should that shock him?"

"Because everyone thinks he's dead," Rob interjected. "Our minstrel friend went so far as to write a play about his own passing. He's worked very hard to convince all about that he died twenty years ago. For a simple guardsman to know him, I'd guess he cut quite a figure here in the king's city."

"That's his plan?" Rodney said. He'd been watching from the prow during the entire exchange, feigning indifference but clearly trying to hear the words that were said. "That's it? Why on earth would we want to play on his celebrity?"

"Do you have a better idea?"

"You know I don't—" He almost said *Templar*, but finished the sentence with an offhand gesture.

"Then we'd best be patient, stonemason. If Master Adam's celebrity admits us to Paris, even under the watchful eyes of . . ." he gestured toward the dark tower of the Louvre above us—"Monsieur and his master, then so be it."

"God's will."

"Be done," Rob added, crossing himself. David and I copied the gesture.

Adam had finished his conversation and was returning to the boat. He seemed serene as he stepped from the piling onto our little vessel. We gathered around to hear what he had to say.

"I have sent word to my old friend Johannes de Grocheio, the Master of Arts at the Sorbonne. He will vouch for me—and, of course, for my companions."

"Without telling the entire city that we are here," Rodney rumbled back at him.

"They will know that *I* am here," Adam said, smiling, placing his hand on his chest. "De Grocheio and I were very close years ago; he will be glad to have me back in the theatrical circles. With such a brightly-lit lantern, dim candles should go unnoticed."

"I assume you mean that in a figurative sense."

"Certes, stonemason," Adam said. For a moment he glanced at me as if to say, *There you are beyond the fourth wall; hope you're enjoying this.*

"So what do we do now, Master Adam?" Rob asked.

"We wait for the messenger to return."

So as the dark descended on Paris, we waited in the small boat that had brought us here from Senlis. The Louvre tower, some few dozen paces away from the river, loomed above; the fires lit on its top gave it a very Mount Doom aspect, as if someone within was scanning about for us . . . as perhaps they might be doing, using that map Rodney had described.

Finally the messenger returned. When Adam stepped up to meet him, he gestured beyond the minstrel to two of us still in the boat: Rob and myself. It gave me a sick feeling in my stomach, made only worse by Adam's next words.

"It seems we're expected," he said. "I am to go to de Grocheio's house, which is hard by the river, and take the two of you with me."

"Just them," Rodney said.

"Aye, that's right. You can make the boat fast upstream a bit near the Quai Saint-Germain, and we'll return for you as soon as this is sorted out."

"I don't find that particularly appealing," Rodney answered.

Rob stood and made his way from the boat onto the piling. "You should do as you think best, Giblumite," he said without turning around. "Come along, lad, we'd best see this on to its conclusion."

I hesitated for a moment; in the dim light of torches lit along the dock, I could see Rodney's anger and David's relative serenity. I really had no idea how else to proceed, so I followed Rob off the boat and onto stone, a bit shaky after our time on the river. We didn't look back as we followed the guardsman and the torchbearer into the narrow, dark alley that led away from the quay.

—•—

My knowledge of Paris in the twenty-first century could not possibly help me. Somewhat west of where we were would have been the Champs de Mars and the Eiffel Tower, but there was no sign of them in this time of course. This might be somewhere near the Quai d'Orsay: with the Louvre across the river, and Notre Dame on its great boat-shaped island somewhere off ahead, we had turned onto the left bank, what would someday become the university district.

"Who is expecting us, Master Adam?" Rob asked as we walked through the darkness, our hands near our swords as if we were expecting to be mugged.

"The messenger brought back word merely that we were to come—we three. It was not phrased as a request."

"Why us?" I ventured.

"They must know you're here as well," Adam replied. "I don't know what that means regarding your—burdens. I'm sorry, I can't act in this play—I haven't learned my lines as yet."

"We'll just improvise," I said.

"Yes," Adam said. "I suppose we will."

He was quite accurate: we had only walked a few hundred paces and made only one or two turns before we came upon a good stone house set apart from others on its row; it had a stout door with a heavy knocker consisting of two figures—from the look of them, an angel and a devil locked in combat. Adam reached to lift it but the door opened first—someone had been waiting for us.

With little ceremony we were ushered into a sitting room where two figures stood. One was a greying, balding, well-dressed man who might have been athletic once but clearly enjoyed a good buffet; the other was a tall, stern, bearded figure with eyes that seemed piercing even in the dim light given off by the candles set in sconces around the room.

Rob was clearly stunned—the color drained from his face.

"Ian," he said at last. "I—I have the honour to present Monsieur Jacques de Molay, the Grand Master of the Order of the Temple."

CHAPTER 22

However it might look on the tube, very little reaches the screen that hasn't been scripted. On *Ian and Jan*, we would frequently have "visitors" who hadn't been announced; it was a way to keep viewers from switching channels if they didn't like a segment. The production folks used to call them "drive-bys". Jan and I worked hard to act surprised—and pleased—when a "drive-by" walked on to share a portion of our afternoon visit. The studio audience was prompted to applaud wildly as well.

It was the first thing that came to my mind when I came face to face with de Molay that night.

A special guest on our show today, I thought. The studio audience applauded wildly.

"Well met, Grand Master," I said, assuming my best telly persona. "I've heard a great deal about you, sir."

"And I you," de Molay said. "Your travels have been much on my mind."

Is that so, I thought. "We were unable to come earlier. But . . . forgive me, Grand Master, I don't know why you're here tonight."

Adam cleared his throat. "You knew we were coming."

"I did," de Molay said. "The presence of these Brothers was noted in Amiens, and I had the approaches to Paris watched. As for you, Master Adam, your appearance was more of a surprise."

Rumours of his death were greatly exaggerated, I thought. Adam didn't answer; he seemed to be looking out through the fourth wall, probably thinking much the same thing.

"It is my pleasure to entertain you, Grand Master."

"This is no game, minstrel. I hope you realise—"

"Johno," Adam interrupted, smoothly turning his attention from the Templar commander to his fellow artist with the skill of a stand-up comedian shrugging off a heckler. "How fare the performing arts here in Paris?"

The Grand Master was speechless; so was Rob, who looked shocked—apparently he'd never seen anyone interrupt de Molay before.

"Things were better when we were young—and you were alive." He gestured to benches set beside a long table made of dark wood. Adam took a seat and reached for a wine-bottle set next to a collection of small silver goblets. de Grocheio took a seat at the head of the table. Rob and I remained standing, ignored; after a few moments of glowering de Molay sat as well, arranging himself so he could rise and draw his weapon easily.

"Well, yes, I imagine so."

"Nowadays," de Grocheio said, "any sweet-talking rustic can come into town and rub his bow against his *viele;* if he's an enterprising lad his pockets will soon be full of *sous.*"

Adam poured himself a goblet of wine, then did the same for de Grocheio. He glanced at the Templar Grand Master, who waved his hand. We were still invisible, which didn't seem to bother Rob a bit.

"I thought only guild-members were allowed," Adam said.

"What's written down in the statute-book has very little to do with the price of onions in the marketplace. So." He drank deeply from his wine-cup. "Tell me, Adam—what brings you down the Seine after twenty years?"

"A rowboat."

"Answer the question," de Molay rumbled. "Or I'll have your ears."

"That's what every performer wants, Grand Master," Adam said. "But I beg you to remember that I am not one of your *confrères* and have never placed my hands between yours to pledge vows."

"I still hold some authority here."

"We hear that evil days are coming," Adam said, glancing at me. "But speaking of *confrères,* my lord, perhaps we should invite the brothers to join us at table."

He gestured to places as if he were master of the house; de Grocheio watched with amusement while de Molay seemed to glower even more angrily. Adam ignored both, but poured wine into two more goblets and pushed them in front of us.

Rob briefly murmured a prayer and then took a sip from his cup. I did the same. It was better than anything I had had so far—priories and pilgrims' hostels weren't exactly front-page adverts for *Wine Spectator.*

"We would like to know, Adam," de Grocheio said. "Should I be avoiding you—or booking a performance?"

"Neither, I hope. I came to you, Johno, because I want to help these folk. You see . . . Brother Ian here can hear the music."

"The music? You mean—"

"Just so. And that means that our dining companion here who so ardently wants to make a trophy of me needs to convey them—and what they carry—to a safe place."

"What do they carry?"

"You would not believe it if I told you."

"And it would be unsafe to speak of it, I trust," de Molay said. "Tell me, Brothers," he continued, looking down the table at us. "Does . . . Monsieur know that you are here in Paris?"

"I do not think so, Grand Master," Rob answered. "He sent his hound de Bec to Amiens after us, but it seems that the sorcerer had plans of his own. He believed—or said he believed—that we had already been to Paris to visit the Mars Oracle and came afterwards to Amiens to complete Brother Ian's pilgrimage."

"But you had not," de Molay said, just as the Master of Arts mouthed the words *Mars Oracle?*

Well thank you, Jesus, and all the saints, I thought. *I finally meet someone who knows less than I do.*

"No. We left Chartres and crossed the Seine at Andély. We went from there to Gisors."

"Gisors?" de Molay said. "We heard that Lord Guillaume had died."

"Not before we visited him, my lord. But by the time we reached Amiens, de Bec was waiting for us. We eluded him—"

"How?"

"We killed him," I interrupted. "*I* killed him, to be specific. Beneath Amiens. In the labyrinth."

"With a ball of pitch," Adam said. "Or something like."

"Something like," I said. "And now we're here, sir, to finish—whatever it is that we're doing."

"The Jupiter Oracle," de Molay said to Rob. "Did anything happen there?"

De Grocheio held up his hands. "Is this the best place and time to discuss—sorcerers and oracles and—other matters?"

"Likely not," Adam said. "But we must of necessity discuss them. Do you have a better venue?" He looked owlishly at his old friend and took another sip of wine, smiling for an unseen audience.

An hour later, with the moon up and darkness fully cloaking the city where its rays did not dart, we made our boat fast at the small landing beside the great fortress of the Paris Temple. The imposing structure, a huge pile of masonry decorated with narrow gates and tall towers, had a great stone pier with a small gated door set a few paces back from the river's edge. Through this door we carried the crate containing the Ark—David and Rob maneuvering it slowly and quietly up a narrow flight of stairs to a guardroom. They seemed to have decided that I was to be kept at a distance—I entered before the Ark did, and wasn't allowed to touch the crate or the two men carrying it.

As I stepped across the threshold I stopped for a moment: something had changed—the almost-invisible water-path that I had felt very strongly from the Seine had disappeared, like a candle being snuffed out.

Once the precious cargo was safely placed on the upper floor, Rob took me aside.

"Tell me, lad," he said quietly. "Do you feel the earth-path here?"

I paused a moment and closed my eyes. "No, not a bit."

"And the water-path from the river just below?"

"No."

"The Temple walls block all of the paths. That's why you weren't to carry the Ark. Someone might have felt it."

I opened my eyes. "I thought that the only one capable of 'feeling it' is feeding the worms under Amiens."

"He's not the only one. Monsieur has a certain talent in that direction. And as for His Majesty . . ." he let the sentence drop.

"The King is a—"

"He is possessed of great skill and wisdom," Rob said, cutting me off. "I don't properly know what he can or cannot do."

"Neat sidestep," I said. "You haven't said a thing, but you've implied much."

"That's what comes of traveling with a minstrel, a Giblumite and a—visitor from beyond the horizon. Come on, lad. We'd best go and see what the Grand Master has to say."

—•—

It would have felt safe: the first really protected place we'd found in weeks for the Ark, the Grail and the head of the Baptist . . . except that I reminded myself that this entire fortress was to be betrayed to King Philip less than a week hence.

It came as news to the Grand Master.

All of us, Rob and I, Adam, Rodney and Brother David as well had convened in a private chapel near de Molay's apartments. He was sitting in a polished wooden chair near a banked fire; it was cold and draughty in the room. His face was barely visible in the gloom, but his eyes were bright with anger and the fervency of a lifetime devoted to the cause of his Order. It was more than a little scary.

"You have done well to gather all of these relics, Brother," he said to Rob. There was no trace of warmth in his voice; it was as if he were stating the obvious. "They will be safe here."

"I wish I could agree, Grand Master," Rob said.

"What do you mean?"

"This Temple," Rob said. He rested his chin on his hands, showing how weary the last few days had made him. De Molay looked disapproving, but Rob appeared not to care anymore. "This Temple is no safe place, my Lord. In a matter of days it will be betrayed."

"Betrayed? To whom?"

"To his Majesty the King of France."

The Templar Grand Master snorted. "Nonsense. The King has done me a great honour—he has invited me to join in the funeral procession for Princess Catherine, not a week from now."

"What day would that be, sir?" I asked.

De Molay frowned at me, looking annoyed at my interruption. "Thursday," he said. "The twelfth."

"The next day all of the Templars in France will be arrested and put in chains," I said. "The King of France will betray the Order. October the thirteenth. Friday the thirteenth. It will ever after be considered a day of ill luck."

"How do you know this, Initiate?" de Molay growled. His hand strayed near his sword. "Are you planning to be part of that betrayal?"

This time it was Rodney who snorted. He had found a comfortable place in a dimly lit part of the room.

"That it were that simple, Grand Master," he said. "Wait until Brother Ian tells you *how* he comes to know."

De Molay's gaze fixed me in place. My throat was dry; I felt him taking my measure without saying a word.

"Go on, lad," Rob said quietly. "You'd best tell him."

Truth conquers all, I thought.

"I know this to be true, sir, because for me . . . it has already happened, centuries before I was born. You—your Order, and all that is going to happen to it—is history to me."

The Grand Master's hands continued to rest on his thighs, his sword hand not far from his scabbard.

"This is as good as black sorcery," he said. "What are you suggesting?"

"I can hear the music," I answered. "I first heard it in a Scottish chapel that won't even be built for another century. It was more than five hundred years old when I was born. Grand Master, let me be as honest with you as I can be: I am from the future. This is not my time."

"And you know of this betrayal."

"I . . . yes. I know it is to happen, and that King Philip will be the instigator. And for you, and for the Templar Order, it will not end well."

"I place my faith in the Holy Father," de Molay replied. "I answer to no one but him. He will not permit anything of the sort to happen."

"When you see him," Rodney said, "ask him about the devil's bargain he made in the Forest of Angèly."

De Molay stood up, his chair falling back. In three strides he was standing before the stonemason.

"That," he said, "is a foul lie. I will have your apology, or I will have your head."

No one spoke for several moments. Rodney had physically threatened me several times during our trip, but I hadn't seen anyone do the same to him. Rob and I kept our seats; de Grocheio and Adam, who hadn't spoken since we'd convened in this room, appeared frozen by the confrontation.

Rodney didn't answer at once. Slowly, his hands in sight, he rose from his place to stand before de Molay.

"Grand Master," he said at last, "you count de Got as your master, your protector, and your friend. You are mistaken. He is none of those things. He is no right heir to the keys of Saint Peter; neither were his two predecessors. There hasn't been a lawful Holy Father since poor Pietro de Morrone starved to death at the hands of the lawyer Gaetani. *This* pretender to the Holy See does not even dare set foot in Rome, but remains instead in Avignon.

"He is not prepared to protect you. He is a creature of this French king, body and soul—even if he did *not* make a secret treaty with him at Saint Jean d'Angèly two years ago as rumours say, he owes his tiara and his papal throne to King Philip.

"And as for being your friend . . . he has no friends. And though it gives me no joy to say it, my lord, *neither do you.*"

He slowly sat down again, but looked up at de Molay in the gloom. "Now, Grand Master, since I am not prepared to offer any sort of apology, you can go ahead and take my head. For all of the damned good it will do you."

The Templar Grand Master made no move to decapitate the stonemason, but remained standing before him, his back to us.

"Brother Robert," he said after a long pause, "do you believe the tale of this Initiate?" He remained facing Rodney, who appeared completely at ease, as if he were waiting to be served a mug of ale.

"Yes, Grand Master," Rob said. "I believe him. I believe that Ian hears the music and that the Mars Oracle will grant him the powers of the fifth initiation."

"What happened at the Jupiter Oracle?" de Molay said.

"Nothing."

I interviewed John the Baptist's skull, I thought. "Nothing, Grand Master," I agreed.

De Molay turned around to face us. His fierce expression had settled into sadness—and, perhaps, fatigue.

"We'd best get ready," he said at last.

—•—

Dawn came and with it mass at Lauds. Our first instinct was to lay low, but Rob wanted to see Paris. Adam pointed out that even if Nogaret or the King's officers decided we were worth plucking off the streets, they'd think twice in view of the plans to move against the Order in a matter of days. It wouldn't do to tip their hand and show their hostility.

Nonetheless, though it seemed that Grand Master de Molay would have wanted it otherwise, we chose to go out incognito in our Carmelite habits with Brother David as our escort. As soon as the Grand Master gave his leave, the three of us made our way through the portal on the west side of the Templar enclosure and into the city of Paris. Adam and de Grocheio had their own business, as did Rodney; we parted company there and went our separate ways.

In the present day, anyone exposed to any kind of mass media gets dosed with an impression of France's great city long before he has any chance to visit. I'd been there a number of times—during school holidays, on vacations, and as a working member of the entertainment industry. *Ian and Jan* had done locations from bistros on the Place de la Concorde and the café on the Eiffel Tower, as well as an interesting walk through left bank restaurants looking for 'best bargains'. . . that was the Paris my modern self remembered. Chic, trendy, self-assured: a city full of contradictions, future and past mixed together. Many Brits hated Paris and the smug Parisians, but I'd always loved it.

To fourteenth-century Ian, it was nothing like anything he'd ever seen. Far more crowded than Edinburgh, more tightly packed than any of the cities of Aragon or Castile—muddy, loud, its narrow, twisting streets full of the same breed that would walk through it seven hundred years later, not hesitating for a moment to shout at or push past a trio of hooded Carmelite friars.

It was festival time: the Festival of Saint-Denis—and the streets were even more busy than usual. Brother David was most at ease, pointing out things as we passed: the hundred spires of the various churches; the shops of the ink-sellers, paper-makers, cloth-vendors, goldsmiths, leatherworkers . . . pedlars of vegetables and eggs, trinkets and relics . . . beggars and blind men, mendicant friars and scribes on their errands for noblemen and scholars and merchants, constables of the Prevost of Merchants armed with truncheons walking slowly through the streets, yielding only to a lord's carriage or a procession of monks and otherwise given more leeway than most pedestrians received.

Rob was quiet. As we moved through the crowded streets he kept the same grim, determined expression on his face. He clenched his hands into fists as we walked and then seemed to forcibly relax them.

"You seem troubled, Brother," David said to Rob as we came out of the covered stalls of the Halles market at Les Champeaux. It was drizzling; a raw, cold breeze met us as we walked along the *planches*—the planking covering the marshy area near the Grand Pont.

"Troubled," Rob answered. He stepped under an awning, out of the way of a slow-moving cart piled with something foul-smelling. We joined him. "You might say that. It's troubling walking through this city knowing that in a matter of a few days . . . something is to happen."

"These aren't your accusers," David said, gesturing.

"There we differ, Brother," Rob said. "Of course they are. Any of them could be an informant, an accuser, a betrayer. And we're clearly being followed."

"By whom?" I asked.

"I'm not sure. But they're not very good. But even if we avoid them, there are more than enough folk that hate our Order—that would be glad to join a mob to watch it happen."

"You don't think there would be an outcry?"

"I would be surprised."

"That's a rather depressing view," David said. "I—"

Before he could complete the statement, he was interrupted by shouting in the broader street along the quay. "Give way, give way!"

The crowd was moving—or being driven—out of the path of a covered carriage, making its way westward. The shouters—tough-looking men with royal fleur-de-lys tabards—were being heeded: no one seemed interested in a fight.

"Caroche," Rob said. "Fancy."

The caroche—four-wheeled, with a perfectly-matched pair of white horses drawing it—was ornate, gilded on its frame and pillars, bearing the royal emblem on its doors. As it approached I could see one of the passengers: a younger woman, sitting sedate and quiet among the hubbub. As if there was no one else on the street, she turned her head slightly, and we locked eyes.

"Oh, my God," I said, taking a step forward. "Liz."

"Brother?" David asked, placing a hand on my sleeve. "What is it?"

The woman in the carriage looked directly at me, her face relaxing into a smirk. It was my ex—or a spitting image of her. And from the look on her face, she knew me.

"All right," I said. "That's enough." I began to push forward toward the carriage; I shrugged off David's hand.

"Brother—" I heard behind me, but I didn't care. If Liz was here—and knew me—it seemed to bring everything back: the time and place I belonged, the future that I'd come from . . .

"Liz!" I shouted. "I want to talk to you."

She never looked away, but I saw her mouth form a few words: *poor fool,* she said. *You poor fool.*

"Liz, why—" I began to answer, but I suddenly felt myself being grabbed from behind, and something hard and blunt striking against the side of my head. I was tossed hard into a nearby wall; the hood of my robe slipped down as I landed on my arse, good and hard.

"And stay away," the tabard-wearing bravo said to me, wiping his hands on his trews and turning his back.

By the time I was able to gain my feet again, the carriage was well past. The crowd had moved in to fill the gap; there was no way to reach it. David reached me a few moments later. Rob was nowhere to be seen.

"Is something wrong, Ian?"

I straightened myself out the best I could, pulling the hood back over my head. "That was . . . that was my—" I wanted to say 'ex-wife', but there wasn't any easy way to say it. "We were married."

"That looks to be one of the Queen's ladies-in-waiting," David said. "She's your *wife?*"

"She was. In another place and time. And now she's here. And she knew me."

"I don't understand," Brother David said, looking puzzled.

"Here's something that's easier to understand," Rob said. He had come up on my other side: and he wasn't alone. He was holding a boy by the scruff of the neck—someone else familiar. "Here's who was following us."

The boy made no effort to escape, but tried to shrug off Rob's hold.

"Let go of me, Brother," he said. "I need to speak with you."

"Thierry, isn't it?" I said. It was the young lad from Orléans—the brother of Juan la Rosa's dead comrade-in-arms. "What are you doing here?"

"I was looking for you. For both of you."

Rob hadn't let go yet. "Certes. And why would that be?" he asked, shaking him a bit.

"I need your help. I want revenge against the sorcerer de Bec."

Rob looked from Thierry to me and back. "For what?"

"The best reason of all," the boy answered. "He killed someone close to me—and to you. He murdered Brother Juan."

—•—

A secluded corner of a loud wine-shop in the lee of Saint-Germain-les-Près was the most privacy we could manage. Thierry had grown even in the few months since we'd last seen him at *La Maison de la Coquille* in Orléans. Death and necessity make a boy into a man.

"You came to Paris to find us," Rob said when we all had cups in hand. "How did you know we'd be here?"

"I didn't come to Paris at first to find *you,* Brother," Thierry said. "I wanted to press my case with the Grand Master of your Order. I thought that since Juan had been an Initiate, the Order might take an interest against his murderer."

"You didn't get in the door," I said.

Thierry frowned. "No. But this morning, as I was in Les Halles getting something for Ysabeau—"

"She's here as well?"

"Yes, Brother." He looked at me, pride and fear mixing in his face. "I would not leave her alone—she is with child."

Rob gave me a look that I'd not seen since Orléans, when he had said *All women are trouble, lad.* I rubbed the bump on my head from my encounter by the river.

"You were in Les Halles," Rob prompted.

"And I saw you. I thought perhaps you would be interested in helping me. You were Juan's friends."

"You said that de Bec killed him," Rob said. "How do you know that?"

"We saw him do it. The sorcerer came to our house late at night, not long after you left the city; Juan bade us hide in the loft—he thought that we might be in danger. Instead—" Thierry paused, taking a drink of the wine. "De Bec and his men looked as if they had ridden far. They had no interest in us: they wanted to know where you had gone. He refused to tell them anything. So they—so he—"

In the pale torchlight within the wine-shop Thierry's face was ashen. I didn't suppose that he had never seen death before, but this was probably his first brush with violent death. It was a fairly new experience for me as well.

"They killed him," Rob said. David placed his hand on Thierry's hands.

"They took his head," Thierry said. "They killed him and took his head. I don't know what possible use de Bec would have for such a thing and I don't want to know." He gripped his cup tightly. "But I want to do the same to him."

" 'Revenge is mine,' " Rob quoted, and when Thierry moved to protest held up his hand. "You need not worry about that. De Bec is dead. He tried to kill us in Amiens, but the Lord favoured us instead."

"And . . ."

"And," Rob said, "if my guess is correct, Juan's head occupies a position of honour."

I thought for a moment, trying to follow what Rob was saying. Then it struck me all at once.

Is something wrong, Rob?

I . . . I don't know. Do you notice anything different about the relic, lad?

Something was different all right. At the moment Rob had said that to me, de Bec had already taken the Baptist's skull away. The *caput sophiae* had been replaced by another skull, gilded and decorated and mounted on a plate. I felt like laughing hysterically: Juan la Rosa's skull was now a relic in a chapel at Amiens Cathedral.

At least he'll enjoy hearing the choir, I thought.

"His death is avenged," Rob added finally. I can't imagine what expression was on my face at that moment. "Now. What would you have of us, young man?"

"I don't know. I . . . for the last few months I've only had one goal—to plead my case before your Order." He shook his head. "I suppose I'll have to find work to support my sister and her child. Paris is a big city; someone will need a servant."

"My Order, perhaps," David said. "I will need to return to Senlis—you can accompany me there."

"I don't want charity, Brother," Thierry said.

"And I'm not offering it." David smiled. "Tell me, my son—do you like honey-cakes?"

—•—

Our accomodations were on an upper floor of the conventual building. They were spartan—two wooden pallets, straw bedding, thin blankets; a small fire-place; a prie-dieu in the corner, its hassock well worn from thousands of knees.

As the sun reached the horizon, no more than a bright smear in the grey sky, we could hear Guillaume, Notre-Dame's bell, ring out the Vespers office.

On the morning of the sixth day hence, the Templar Order was due to be crushed by the King of France—and there I stood, dressed in a clean white Templar habit, listening to the sound of a great bell. Rob stood beside me; he, too, had been given a white habit to wear, though as a *serjeant* he was only entitled to the more modest brown one.

Apparently for this evening, at least, those restrictions were waived. After Matins, a small group of us—Rob, myself, and four Knights including the Grand Master himself—would leave the

Temple and journey across to Notre-Dame to enter the cathedral and perform the initiation at the Mars Oracle. In the meanwhile, I was left with my guide and friend to pray and meditate. I felt like doing neither.

"I don't suppose you'll tell me what is going to happen," I said, looking out across the Paris skyline. It looked strangely barren without the Eiffel Tower: Notre-Dame dominated the nearby vista, with the spires of other churches also prominent.

"I don't know what might happen to you, lad," Rob said. "But I can't imagine it matters whether I tell you the form of the ceremony. This is the Mars Oracle: the bridge between the spiritual and temporal worlds. Here the warrior is made to hold the light of the whole world—and visualize the 'word in the air'."

"Whatever that means."

"I'm telling you what I know."

"Can you explain it to me?"

"No. The Mars Oracle will make it clear, or not. You will receive the initiation or not. The music—"

"It all comes back to that, doesn't it? I'm supposed to know what to do. I didn't know what to do in Amiens, and nothing happened there."

"It might not have been your fault, lad."

"And if—this—succeeds, will we go back to Amiens and do the Jupiter Oracle again?"

Rob didn't answer.

"I saw my wife today. My former wife." Rob frowned as I said that. "In my time, husband and wife can choose to part from each other. She *knew me,* Rob. She knew it was me—even though the Ian from *this* time couldn't have hoped to meet a queen's lady-in-waiting. One more mystery.

"I don't see how any of this matters. Next Friday the king is going to beat down the doors of this place and haul us all off to a dungeon. The best we can do is take the relics off somewhere and hide them so that *he* doesn't find them."

"You don't want to perform the initiation?"

"I—I don't know what I want. I want to go home. I don't want to die. After all this"—I held the sleeve of my tunic between two fingers; it was a beautiful garment, a museum piece—"I'm not a Templar. Not really. I never asked for this quest, this pilgrimage."

"This is old ground, lad. You can only go forward. Look at all we've gone through to get you here: what do you want to do—disappear into the crowd? This initiation may be your only way home."

"How do you mean?"

"They say . . . that the fifth initiation gives insight into all times and all places. No one has ever understood what that meant. But no one could ever hear the music before. You told me once that your guide at this Scottish chapel told you that the music would heal the world—now you have the Grail-book, the manuscript of Master Adam's music, and the ability to hear it. If you could return those things to your own time . . . it gives meaning to all that we have experienced."

"You think this initiation will let me travel in time?" I grabbed him by the shoulders. "You think that it will send me home?"

"This is the path of light, lad," he said. He placed his left hand on my right elbow, then drew my right hand down to grasp his own. "I have asked you many times to trust in the Lord. I'm asking you to do so again."

The light had begun to fail outside. Guillaume had stopped chiming; maybe the hunchback was taking a tea break.

I didn't know whether it was true or not, but in that moment I began to believe that I would go home again.

CHAPTER 23

WITH FULL NIGHT UPON US, ROB AND I WERE ROWED ACROSS from the Temple landing to the Île de la Cité. A wind had picked up, carrying with it a hint of rain. At the pier at the base of the Rue Cloître Notre-Dame—which ran past the cathedral to the southern end of the island—the rope-ladders, unanchored at their bottom ends, twisted into spirals; it drew my attention as we came alongside. Rob caught hold of one and held it by one leg, turning and turning it around until it was straightened out.

I looked up into the darkness and saw Rodney, Adam and David at the top of the ladder, waiting for us to climb up. Clearly this was to be more than just a Templar affair.

The sound of the other ladders distracted me. Each was made up of short lengths of stout rope, anchored at regular intervals—and each twisted around, a barred spiral . . .

"Are you coming, lad?"

"DNA," I said. "They look like DNA."

"We need to get inside," Rob said, looking at the sky. "Storm coming."

Up he went, with me following. *This is the day the Lord hath made,* I thought. *Let us rejoice in it.*

—•—

We entered the cathedral from the north door, alongside the passageway between the chapter house and the main building. Within, a mass was being performed: a tall, gaunt priest in an off-white robe was administering the Sacrament to a small group of communicants, while other groups milled about, ignoring the activities near the high altar.

"That seems disrespectful," I whispered to Rob.

"Get used to it," he said. "Our Lady's church is in use at almost every hour of the day and night. Clergy come from all over France to preach, to say Mass, to pray. It's the mystique of the place."

"Our . . ." I turned to look over my shoulder at our companions. "The plans for the evening—how are they affected by that?"

"Not a whit. We'll not be using the sanctuary—we're going down below."

"Into the crypts?" I shuddered slightly, remembering Orléans and the darkness.

"Below that. We're going to take a trip back in time, Ian. Before this great Lady was built, this was a holy place—where water- and earth-paths meet."

We were walking toward the west portal as we spoke; near the middle opening I could see Grand Master de Molay, with three other splendidly-attired Templars, waiting for us. *Not making a secret of our festivities either,* I thought. It was almost as if this was the last roll of the dice—Monsieur might be waiting on the cathedral steps, but we were going to do what we came to do.

As we reached them, I thought to speak—but Rob placed a hand on my sleeve and I kept silent.

"Come," de Molay said.

We went in silent procession along a side-aisle and then descended into the crypt. Less crowded than the church above, there were still a fair number of the faithful present—in prayer or contemplation. Without a word, the Grand Master led us through to the far end of the crypt-chambers, where four Templars stood guard.

"See that we remain undisturbed," he said, and gestured. A great iron door was opened and we passed through; one of those who had accompanied de Molay took a proffered torch in his hand and we went through the door and onto a narrow stone stairway that spiralled down. After Brother Adam passed through, the door was firmly shut and we heard a bolt being drawn.

Somewhere below I could hear running water.

"This section is older than the church itself," Rob said quietly to me. "The choir is located directly above this place. You should be able to feel the earth-path here."

I nodded. It was strong enough to make me a bit faint, as if the incense and the closeness of other bodies and the heat from the torch wasn't already doing so. If Rob hadn't been beside me I think I might have tumbled down that stairway; just the same, I reached a hand out to steady myself and felt dampness from the rough-hewn wall.

"How much farther?"

"It turns seven times in all," Rob said. "That's three so far."

De Molay moved forward at a steady pace, and we kept up. I tried to count the steps to maintain my concentration but quickly lost count—I had all I could do to manage to count the turnings.

At last we passed under an arch decorated with bas-reliefs, the only one of which I could pick out featuring a robed, headless saint holding his haloed head in his hand and a cricket-bat in the other. No one else seemed to give it a second look.

The Templars moved around the edges of the large room we had entered, lighting torches in sconces. It was twenty or thirty paces across, a large mosaic floor encircled by a flagstone walkway; I noticed that the brothers hadn't stepped on the mosaic at all. The ceiling was held up by six huge columns, each bearing a carved symbol of the sort we'd seen at Amiens: one for each of the six Oracles.

As my eyes became adjusted, I took a good look at the floor. It was a labyrinth, something like the ones I'd seen at Chartres and

Amiens—but it was composed of white tiles crossed by two different sets of coloured ones. The paths intersected at several places, while dodging out of the way of each other elsewhere. The final destination of each was a great rose pattern in the centre. On two sides of the mosaic there was a stepdown from the brick walkway; each was the starting-point of a labyrinth path.

"My Brother," de Molay said, "you have been brought to this place where water-path and earth-path meet to receive the wisdom of the Mars Oracle. Your guide and companion, Brother Robert, attests that you are true and trusty, a worthy and faithful servant of the Light.

"Are you prepared for your journey?"

"No, Grand Master," I said. "I am no more prepared than I have been at any time during my quest."

I thought that honesty was in order: but it clearly wasn't the answer he was looking for. He frowned, but even in the dim light I saw the faintest smile on Adam's face; he winked at me.

In my mind, I imagined polite laughter from the audience. "I'm ready to begin."

The Grand Master nodded at Rob, who guided me by the elbow along the walkway to one side—the west end, I thought, though I wasn't sure.

"What do I do?" I whispered to him.

"Trust," he answered. "And hope."

"What's going to happen next?"

"Eleven times, nothing has happened, lad," he answered. "But this time—I don't know. Maybe nothing."

He let go of my elbow. "Go with God."

During the course of my journeys, my spiritual experiences had always been solitary ones. At Santiago I heard the voice behind me and I was alone; Juan la Rosa had spoken to me in a vision at la Dalbade in Toulouse, Abbot Tomaso at Tours, Gerard Lamont at Orléans, my Gran at Chartres—and I'd had my dream of the skull of John the Baptist at Amiens. Each time I had been alone—there was always the possibility that it had been a dream.

That October night I was far below the Cathedral of Notre Dame, in the centre of Paris in the centre of France, with Templars and others on hand. Whatever was to happen, I would have witnesses.

I placed my foot upon the first step of the labyrinth-pattern, and heard a sharp intake of breath from Rob, still standing beside me. I looked back at him and then across the mosaic; a quarter-turn around the room—near the north wall, if I was standing near the west—there was another Ian Graham, his foot also on the pattern.

"Hello, Ian," he said.

"Fancy meeting me here."

"Did you expect someone else?"

"Did I expect—" I almost laughed out loud. "Is that what this all comes to? Two of us—two of me—"

"You should follow the labyrinth, Ian," my double said to me.

I walked forward along the path as he suggested. As I walked, he did the same. When we reached one of the places where one labyrinth path dodged around the other, the other Ian stopped.

The torches seemed to flicker and dim. The northeast corner of the room glowed brightly; I covered my face with my hands. We all did. From the brightness I heard the voice that was so much like Rob's.

"The first initiation, Ian," the voice said. "When you placed your hand in God's hands, I told you of the *camino de las estrellas*, the path of light, and instructed you to be discreet. The earth-path intersects the water-path there at Finisterre, the end of the world."

"And then you disappeared," I said, my eyes still covered. "You disappeared and never came back."

"Have a care," my other self said.

"It was the first of a long series of half-explanations," I said. "*Amoun.* Very well: from the time I put my hand on the Tree of Jesse in Santiago, I've played the part of a good pilgrim—praying like I've not been taught, looking for clues like Sherlock bloody Holmes."

The voice didn't respond, but I heard Rob—the real Rob—say "Sherlock who?" behind me.

" 'If therefore thine eye be single, thy whole body shall be full of light,' " the voice said. "You followed the path, Ian. Reluctantly, but you followed."

"Fulfilling the fears of paraskevidekatriaphobics everywhere," I said.

"As you said."

My opposite number stepped forward on the path then, and the light faded. As I took my hands away from my face, I looked around the room; de Molay and the other Templars, as well as my other companions were astonished.

"I begin to understand," Rob said quietly. "He spoke to you at Santiago. In my voice."

"More or less," I said. I took a deep breath and walked forward, almost as if I was being pulled along the labyrinth path. I was now in the southwest corner of the mosaic; my other self had reached the northeast, where the bright light had been.

Just as suddenly as the light had appeared, Juan la Rosa was suddenly standing on the centre rose.

"Hello, Ian," he said to me, then turned to the other and repeated himself.

Rob and the other Templars crossed themselves.

"Juan," I said, "I learned that you'd been killed by that bastard de Bec."

"Don't feel responsible," he said. He looked off in the distance, cocking his head as if he heard something. "I made a choice; you respected it. Better me than you."

"I can't accept that."

"You must, Ian, you must. Your pilgrimage was more important than my life—and the sorcerer didn't get what he wanted, did he?"

"No."

"Then it was for the best."

"I—"

"Shh," he said, holding up his hand. "You wanted to know what was happening," he said quietly. "Listen."

From somewhere, we heard the faint strains of music. Perhaps it was from above—singing in the choir that was far above us; or it could have been someone on or alongside the river that couldn't be far below.

It was a portion of the great music that I'd heard in Rosslyn and every other place along this journey. And now, in this ancient cavern below Notre-Dame, everyone else could hear it too.

"What's happening?"

"Abaris was here, Ian. And Hermes as well. But it was always visible to the all-seeing Eye. Just as the Moon governed the first initiation, so Mercury governed the second." Juan crossed his arms over his breast. "It was the place where your soul was first measured, Ian—at la Dalbade. The symbol of the second initiation is the caduceus: the staff of Hermes. To you it has a different meaning." He uncrossed his arms and held a caduceus in silver that he'd produced from somewhere; it caught the torches' flickering light. "The braided stair—the helix."

"DNA," I said.

"Yes. Lost over the centuries—it was mistranslated as the *Sant Graal*, the holy cup. But it is the *Sangre Real:* the royal blood. The blood of the King of Kings—and its secret was caught in this music"—he raised the caduceus so that it flashed in the light of the torches—"and encoded in the stones of Rosslyn Chapel."

I suddenly had a thought, my mind flicking back to the rope-ladders, twisting at the end of the dock. The twisted helix: the code of life.

What I remembered of my Highers included the knowledge of the twenty-three chromosomes . . . and I was reminded of the Grail-book. Twenty-two numbered sections, then one labeled IESUS FILII JOSEPHUS . . . Jesus, son of Joseph, and IESUS FILII MARIA . . . Jesus, son of Mary.

"The Grail book. It's a map. A genetic map."

"The *Sangre Real,"* Juan agreed. "Unlocked by the music of Master Adam."

"It didn't have to mean your death," my other self said, before I could bring myself to say it. I felt a great weight come onto my chest, a burden I couldn't dismiss.

"I'm afraid it did, friend Ian. It always did. But now I can hear the music."

He leaned his head back, smiling broadly. He spread his arms out, hands now empty . . . and vanished as if he had never been.

I spun around, looking at the other faces, looking for some sign or indication. Finally I turned to face my other self.

"He's gone."

"He's dead," the other Ian said. "And he was right: he made a choice, and we respected it."

"But—"

"Everyone dies."

I looked down at my hands, still scarred from the burning skull I had grasped beneath Amiens; scratched and calloused from three months in the fourteenth century—and a lifetime as a soldier in Scotland and in Spain. I felt as uncomfortable in this place, in this body, as I had been since St James' Day, a lifetime ago.

"Which one of us is real?" I asked him. "Me—the one from the future—or you, who actually belongs here?"

"We both are. The music created us."

"How do you know?"

He didn't answer but instead walked forward. The paths of the labyrinths brought us both forward, almost to the rose pattern—but as they tend to do, turned us away again, until we reached another place in the room.

"Orléans is where Lamontaigne told us that, do you remember?" the other Ian said, hands on hips. " 'Most people are echoes, no more . . . the background music of other people's lives.' Pithy."

"Good material for a self-help book. If I were still entertaining I could tell the audience to take it with them on beach holiday."

"He told us to serve mankind," my counterpart replied. "And to find the music and bring it—to *me.*"

The music had continued to echo through the chamber. Rob looked stunned; David and Rodney were watching with rapt interest. Adam's eyes were full of tears: he knew it, every note and chord. He'd written it—and somehow created me. Us.

"Happy birthday," I said.

"You asked how this made you a warrior. Do you understand now?"

"No."

He looked at me, one eyebrow raised Mr Spock-like, and smiled. I'd used that face at any number of guests at the *Ian and Jan* coffee-table over the years.

"Neither do I."

"Why are there so many echoes of things I know?" I pointed to Brother David. "Why is *he* here? Why is *Liz* here?"

"They were always here. You act as if this is a play acted out for your benefit."

"Well? Isn't it? The background echoes . . . are you telling me that they're not the echoes of *my* life?"

"No," the other Ian said. "It's what you—the Ian from the future—have always believed. But this is bigger than you."

He walked forward again. I felt compelled to follow suit, as the music began to rise into the section that sounded most like Poulenc. The paths skirted the edge of the mosaic, bringing me alongside de Molay, who stood in the centre of the walkway on the eastern side. I paused for a moment, bowing slightly to the Grand Master as I passed. He looked, if not serene, at least confident—secure in his faith that this would all turn out.

My opposite number stopped at another place where the two labyrinths almost intersected. The music had changed—now it was the distant sound of a portative organ, voices even more distant circling around the tune as if it were some sort of elaborate dance.

"Now you know where the music was written," the other Ian said to me. "And you know who wrote it—and why. But not how."

"The composer's here. He's standing right over there—I could ask him. What amazes me isn't his talent: it's that every note had to be exactly right. No improvisation—the Grail-book required that the music fit the definition, or the whole thing wouldn't work. And he didn't even have the book to work with. Or did he?"

"I don't know," the other Ian said. "When Master Adam was in Chartres, the Grail-book was only a few days' ride away. The real question is whether he knew how the music in his head and the numbers in the book would go together to produce . . ."

"Jesus' DNA," I finished the sentence. I took a deep breath and looked around the room at the others, watching this performance, wondering what they'd make of it: and I noticed that none of them were moving. Even the torches' flicker had slowed to be almost completely still.

"What's happening?"

"I don't know," the other Ian said. "I . . . we seem to be alone. Together."

"Why?"

"I don't know. Maybe there's something they're not meant to see."

Without waiting for him to decide, I stepped forward on the labyrinth-path. Once again it drew us toward the centre of the mosaic, so that we approached the rose pattern from opposite sides: I was walking northeastward, he southwestward, until we were scarcely a pace apart.

"What happens next?" he asked me.

"I was hoping you could tell me that. This is your century."

"But not my quest."

"Meaning what?"

"The broken pieces of my life. The Scotland I left behind, my time as a soldier in the *reconquista*—all that I've seen and heard, all that I know that I should never have learned, except for you. My other self, my self of the future.

"What's beyond that door in Gran MacPherson's apartment, Ian?" It seemed strange to hear my name spoken to me in my own voice. "What were the noises beyond that window?"

"Edinburgh," I said. My heart was heavy, my voice thick. "Home."

"Not for me."

I'm not sure just what moved me to do so, but I reached my hand out, my arm stretching out from the narrow path of the labyrinth. I felt a prickly sensation stretching from my wrist to my shoulder. Almost in unison, the other Ian did the same. It was like the painting in the Sistine Chapel, except I'm not sure who was supposed to be God and who was Man.

Then our fingers touched, and the entire room disappeared.

—•—

I was standing before the low stone wall again. The raven winked back at me from a tree a few paces away, its eye catching the unknown light. Somewhere far off I could still hear the music, a waterfall of sound.

I looked up and saw the *camino* crossing the sky.

"Here? I'm back here—after all this? What's happening?"

"This is the spiritual transformation of suffering, Ian," Rob's voice said. But it wasn't really Rob: it was whoever—whatever—had appropriated Rob's voice at the first initiation.

"Tell me what that means."

"You were to have received this initiation before you went to the Jupiter Oracle, but circumstances intervened. You have almost lost hope, Ian."

"Sue me."

The first time I'd been at the stone wall, I'd been unable to turn around; but there'd been only my twenty-first century self at the time, without the strength of a fourteenth-century soldier. But now the memories of my two lives had stopped being separate: they had become a mixture. I was both of those Ians now, and they seemed to be getting along.

I whirled in place and saw Rob—or a figure looking very much like him, except bathed in light—an angelic apparition. Part of me wanted very much to look away and drop to my knees before him.

"You're not Rob."

"No," the figure said. "No, I'm not. Would you rather I appeared as your Gran?"

"No. I'd rather that you showed yourself as you really are. If that means I get the smiting I deserve, then so be it. I'm tired of the deception. I'm tired of being pushed about like a chess-piece. I'm—" I put my hand on my head, feeling like I had a five-pint hangover. "I'm just tired."

The figure smiled. As I watched his features transformed: he became shorter and older, his beard grew thicker and whiter, and his back became slightly bent. He held a walking-stick in his hand, and as he moved toward me I could see that he was lame. The glow around him had shrunk to a faint luminescence.

"Who are you?"

"My name is Giles," he said. "There's a church built in my name in your home city. Rather complimentary likeness, if I do say so."

"Saint Giles." I reached into my wallet and drew out the medallion I'd been given at Saintes; it *was* complimentary—he sat beatifically, a sheep nuzzling up against one hand while he gazed off toward brighter worlds. I put the disk away.

"It's been you all along, I suppose."

"Yes."

"Brilliant," I managed, not sure what else to say.

"From the beginning," he said, "you haven't accepted the purpose of this journey and your role in it. But without you there is no journey: there is no purpose."

"And the others? Background music, isn't that right? Like stage-hands on a telly programme. The folks at the end of the credits that no one ever knows about. Couldn't do the show without them. Rob, Rodney, Adam, even de Molay I suppose—if they're lucky they get into the history-books, if not they just disappear."

"Each served a purpose. Even Juan—"

"Oh, yes, *Juan*. At least he gets to play his part as comic relief. Hanging up in place of the true head of John the Baptist. That's rich. I'll be sure to praise the Creator for His efforts there."

"It should mean more to you than that."

"It does. I just . . . don't know what it means, really. After all of this I really just want to go home and be done with it."

He had limped over to where I stood. He took me by the elbow, a firm grasp—an old man's hand. "I can understand that. I hope that it will be possible for you to do so. This is the fifth initiation, Ian. Mars governs this sphere. There is but one God, and all paths lead to Him—but the path of stars leads to a new Heaven."

He paused. I looked at him, expecting him to vanish in a burst of light, or for me to land back in the chamber beneath Notre-Dame; but nothing happened.

"That's it?"

"No. That's not 'it'. This is also the sixth initiation. Jupiter governs this sphere. You are the Eagle now, capable of hearing the unspoken Word in the material as well as the spiritual realm, and walking the path of the stars." He gestured; the music began to sound as if it was being played on my Gran's old phonograph.

I waited for the same special effects to take place.

"That's it."

"Not quite." He walked me to a yew-tree and picked up something lying at its base: a bundle of dark-blue cloth. "Someone needs this."

He unfolded the bundle to reveal half a cloak, parted in the middle, and handed it to me.

"You're joking. I'm to go back and—"

Giles smiled up at me; I had two hands' height on him and probably outweighed him by two stone—all that fasting, I supposed.

"Yes."

I took the bundle—

—•—

Before me, his back turned, a man was standing and contemplating the beautiful rose window above. I draped the cloth over my arm and cleared my throat; then I managed, "Peace be with you."

The man turned. For a moment I couldn't move or say anything: it was me—or, rather, it was a past version of me; I looked uncomfortable, out of place, suspicious.

"And also with you," I—he—said. "I'm sorry, I didn't hear you approach."

"I didn't want to interrupt your contemplations, Brother," I answered. "You seemed . . . rapt."

"Distracted. There's a lot to see."

"It's what's left of an old sanctuary in our new church . . . you're right, of course. It's easy to be distracted. I believe you dropped this," I said, handing the cloth to him, just as had happened two months ago.

"I don't think so—"

"No, I'm sure," I said.

"As you say." He took the bundle from me.

"I'm sure you will find it useful," I said, knowing that it would be the case.

"I suppose." He turned away—he was going to ask something about the window—

—•—

But I abruptly found myself standing next to Giles again, his hand on my arm. I was empty-handed.

"Nice trick."

"You did it, not I. I merely showed you where you should go."

"And gave me the goods."

"True." Giles smiled, just like the medallion; I supposed I was standing in for the next available sheep. "Where will you go next? Oh, yes . . . Amiens."

It was dark all of a sudden. We were walking along the aisle of a great church; the music had come down to the faintest tune in the background.

Giles squeezed my arm and pointed, then stepped back into the deep shadows. I turned to look where he had indicated: and again I saw myself, standing on the Amiens labyrinth. My other self happened to look directly where I now stood: he looked startled, angry perhaps, and took a step toward me—

—•—

But I was near the yew-tree again, the stone wall nearby.

"You know," I said, shrugging off his hand, "You are *really* starting to piss me off."

Giles scratched his beard. "You still need to go to Senlis and obtain the abbot's permission to take Brother David and a boat to Paris."

"My mysterious visit on Michaelmas, when Rob and I—some version of me—was in that stinking cell underneath Amiens."

"Just so."

"What if I don't? What if I don't want to play this silly game anymore?"

"What did the Baptist tell you, Ian? *See truth. No darkness can stand before it.*"

"All I see is that I'm being manipulated. Again. Still."

"If that is so," Giles said, "then you must accept that it has already happened. And that to do otherwise would cost you your life."

—•—

Life, I heard, echoing in my ears.

I was somewhere else now: on horseback, on a hard-packed dirt road, at night again. I was in armour—*and a fine suit it is,* my fourteenth-century self noted. The earth-path was underneath me as I rode; there were five others, similarly kitted out, all riding together. As I watched, the leader—better dressed than any of the others—raised one gauntleted hand to call a halt.

We were in the middle of somewhere, but nowhere I recognised. Three of the others, including the leader, dismounted; one drew out flint and tinder and lit a torch, while another pulled a scroll-tube from a saddlebag and opened out a map.

"I'm sure they must have come this way, my Lord," he said to the leader.

"Could they have come this far?" the lord asked. He drew off his tall sugarloaf helmet and hung it from the saddlebow. In the light of the torch I recognised him at once.

The last time I'd seen that face, it had been full of fury and glee—and the man who wore it had been holding a blood-smeared gilded skull above his head.

De Bec gave the briefest glance at me; I'd not taken off my helm, and decided on the spot that I wasn't going to. The sorcerer looked away, swept his hand in a circle, and then tapped the map spread out on a saddle.

"They could be anywhere. They could even be hiding nearby."

"Cowards," one of the others said, raising his helmet visor. It was de Got, the Pope's nephew, whose acquaintance I made at Chartres.

But that hadn't happened yet—not if this were the road from Orléans. I was crouching in the underbrush not ten paces away, and Rob was up in a tree, watching this all happen.

The lord whirled at the voice. "Mind your tongue, varlet," he said angrily. "They are *Templars.* Whatever crimes their order has committed, His Holiness—and our Master—has not condemned them yet."

"Surely a matter of time, my Lord," de Got answered, his voice sardonic. "But I beg your pardon if I have offended."

De Bec looked back at the map. After a moment he started to pace; for just a moment he looked over at where I would be hiding, but then turned back to the man holding the map in place.

"Lodestone," he said, without looking back.

The other man rolled up the map and tucked it under his arm. He reached into a saddlebag and drew out a small pouch of dark cloth, placing it into the lord's outstretched hand, then laid the map back out across the saddle.

De Bec removed his mail gauntlets, handing them to me without a glance. He undid the lacing on the pouch and drew out an ovoid stone the size of his thumb, suspended on a metal chain. The lodestone was night-dark; I could hear a far-away hum that changed pitch and volume as it spun around, now aligned with the earth-path, now crossing it.

Cupping the stone in one hand and holding the chain with the other, he carefully moved his hand over the map and then let go of the stone—which began to spin free and then swing slowly back and forth.

"What—" de Got began, but the man who held down the map hissed and the Pope's nephew fell silent.

No darkness can stand before truth, I thought. *The truth is . . .*

I didn't know how to end that sentence. I knew what de Bec was trying to do, because Rob told me—was just about to tell me, really: that the sorcerer was looking for a disturbance in the earth-path, one that we would have made as we walked from Orléans to Chartres. He hadn't found anything that night.

The truth is, I thought, *that there's nothing here. There's nothing to find, you murdering bastard,* I repeated, gripping the reins of my horse tightly with my free hand.

The stone, which had been swinging up and down, began to steady. I closed my eyes to concentrate harder, not sure what I was doing—or, indeed, if I was doing anything.

I heard de Bec cursing and opened my eyes. He had scooped up the stone—the hum cut off abruptly—and dropped it into the pouch. Without even looking at me he took the gauntlets and drew them on, then accepted his coif and helm. One of the others was grounding the torch in the dirt nearby.

Without a word, the six of us turned and began to ride back toward Orléans.

—•—

"Wait," I said. The yew-tree was in front of me again; the momentum seemed to push me forward, making me stumble. Giles reached a hand out to steady me. "Wait. They're riding back toward Orléans—where they'll find Juan and kill him."

I grasped Giles by the shoulders. "Send me there. Send me to Orléans—I'll stop them from killing him. I can save his life. He was never meant to die so that we could escape."

"No," Giles said.

"Yes." I shook him. "You have to. I can't stop the whole damn Friday the thirteenth thing, but I can save Juan's life. I—he could hear the music, right here, right now. Send me back!"

Giles reached up and, with a gentle patience, removed my

hands from his shoulders. I might have resisted—his hands were aged, thin, and none too strong, but I didn't feel that I was able.

"No," he repeated. "If that were possible, Ian, I would do it. But what happened has already happened, and it colours everything that comes after. Juan la Rosa is dead—but Ysabeau carries his child. Someday that family will leave France and come to Scotland, seeking freedom of worship. Many generations later . . ."

"Sean Ross."

"Just so. If Juan were to live, the outcome would be different."

I turned away from the saint; my heart was heavy, my fists clenched. I wanted to cry, or hit something, but wasn't sure which.

"It's all still a mystery," I said. "There are so many things you haven't explained. Like my ex-wife. Tell me, Giles," I said, turning to face him. "Why did I see Liz? Why is she in Paris here in 1307?"

"Polyphonic duplication."

"What?"

"The emergence of polyphonic music created her," Giles answered. "I told you that as Gérard Lamontaigne. Don't you remember?"

"I remember the crack about most people being no more than background music. Is *that* all she is?"

He didn't directly answer; instead he gave me his gentle, saintly smile. "She is here and she is in your present as well, as you will see.

"You must go to Senlis on Michaelmas day. And then return to Notre-Dame." He placed a hand on my back. "This is the sixth initiation, Ian. Jupiter governs this sphere. The path of light leads to the centre of true knowledge.

"You can go home again, Ian. At last you can go home."

—•—

I stepped off the mosaic alone. The torches flickered at their normal rate; I looked from face to face. As I stood there, tears streaming down my face, I was also speaking with Brother Adam at Senlis; I was touching the Tree of Jesse at Santiago; I was receiving a helping hand from Juan la Rosa, following Gerard Lamont through the darkness, hearing the words of Walter of Chatîllon to Poulenc's music at Chartres, taking tea with Gran MacPherson, bearing up the Ark of the Covenant, praying with Rob in the darkness of the oubliette, shouting to Liz in Paris, driving my sword through de Bec's chest—

I was in all of those places, doing all of those things, and yet here as well. It no longer mattered the order in which I did them.

Rob was first to reach me, and he placed his hands on my shoulders, his face bright, his eyes full of light.

"You did it, lad," he said.

"I can go home."

"What you have brought," de Molay said, approaching me from the other side, "you must take with you. The relics must be conveyed to their true resting place. A guide will direct you there."

"Where?"

"The Saturn Oracle," he said. "You must take them to the Saturn Oracle."

—•—

A boat was waiting. Rodney and Adam bore the crate containing the Ark down to it, along with a small reliquary for the skull and a wooden box for the Grail-book and Master Adam's manuscript. William MacLeod was waiting there.

Rob stood next to the Grand Master on the dock. I'd assumed that Rob was going to be the guide: it made sense—he had done so during the entire journey, from the time I awoke at Santiago.

"Protect the priceless things, lad," he said. "And take care of yourself."

"Rob, if you stay here, you'll be arrested with the rest of the Order. You know what's coming."

"I was spared at St Jean d'Acre," he said. "I left the Holy Land alive. I'll not abandon my station again."

"But—"

"The decision is made," he interrupted. "I have no fear. I have seen miracles, and I've heard the music of divine measure. My faith is unshaken."

I had no answer for that. Truthfully, I hadn't had any doubt of Rob's faith; it had carried us through the entire journey, even in that dark cell under Amiens.

De Molay's hand was raised in blessing as Brother William and I rowed the heavily laden boat out into the Seine, heading upstream and away from the Île de la Cité.

CHAPTER 24

UPSTREAM FROM THE TEMPLE IN PARIS, A BRANCH OF THE SEINE makes its way off to the east, snaking its way beneath bridges and buildings. Well before the fourteenth century the sprawling city had covered it over, making it into an underground river; it wasn't all that pleasant, a place where runoff pipes drew waste water from the buildings above, where the muted sounds of the city echoed weirdly around our boat.

"Where does this lead?" I asked after we'd been underground for several minutes.

"To the Saturn Oracle," Brother William answered.

"That's in Scotland."

"This may take us a while, then."

"You're a very funny man, Brother. Don't think I've forgotten your little joke, shutting me up in the crypt under Saint-Croix."

He didn't answer, merely kept rowing, stroke after stroke, bringing us further and further into the darkness, while the candle in the little lantern in the bow burned down. Finally it burned out entirely, leaving us in complete darkness.

I let the oars slacken in the rowlocks. "I hope you have a plan now, Brother William."

There was no answer for that either. I leaned forward to tap him on the knee—but in the dark couldn't find anyone else in the boat. I was alone in the dark.

"Giles," I said, loudly enough that I hoped he heard me, "I could use your help again."

There was no answer; the echoes told me I was in a small cavern of some sort. A few seconds later the boat, drifting without anyone to row it, bumped up against a pier.

Nearby, someone switched on a small torch. I recognised the face immediately: Rodney Weiss—not dressed as the stonemason who had been my traveling companion, but in a nice Brooks Brothers suit.

"Glad to see you, Ian," he whispered, grabbing the bow rope and making it fast around a metal post driven into the stone of the pier.

"Roddy?"

"In the flesh, old boy." He helped me out of the boat; I took the reliquary and the box out and set them down. With one of us on each side, we were able to lift the crate containing the Ark of the Covenant onto the pier as well.

"It worked," he said. "I'm sure of it. It's all here."

"Yes—but where is 'here'? It could be anywhere—Orléans, Chartres—"

"The Saturn Oracle," he said. "Where we expected to be."

The conversation was familiar; I was trying to place it when I heard a voice.

"Rodney? Roddy, what are you doing there?"

It was my voice. Rodney cursed and snapped off the torch.

"What now?" I whispered to him.

"Sir. Sir, that area is off-limits to visitors." It was William MacLeod's voice. *I'm out there,* I thought. *This is the first day I was at Rosslyn.*

Rosslyn, I thought. *I'm home.*

"I heard something. I heard . . . I'm sorry," my voice said. It seemed reedy and higher-pitched. "I thought I heard something."

"I'd be surprised. Those are the crypts . . ." the voices receded off in the distance.

"We're under Rosslyn Chapel," I whispered to Rodney.

"Yes, we are. Look, Ian, I'm sorry, but—"

"About what?"

"This."

In the dark I never saw it coming: a sharp thump to my head. I felt myself falling—I thought I was headed for the water, but long before I landed I lost consciousness.

—•—

I was lying in an exceptionally comfortable bed, and there was the smell of antiseptic in the air. I opened one eye, and my attention was immediately drawn by a small flat-screen television mounted on a flexible arm just above the foot of my bed. There was a plastic bracelet on my left hand; I could feel a pinch on the top of my right—an IV needle, running from a bottle of some sort of clear liquid.

I hadn't tried to draw attention to myself, but a nurse noticed that I was awake; she took my left hand in hers and looked at her watch, counting my pulse. She seemed familiar—and it came to me at once: I'd seen her in my dream, just after my first visit to Rosslyn.

Rosslyn.

I was home.

"I—" My mouth was dry as dust, but I continued anyway. "I beg your pardon, miss, but what day is today?"

"Shh," she said. After fifteen seconds or so had elapsed, she put my hand down, and placed a small plastic cup below my chin, tucking a straw into my mouth. I drank several gulps of cool water.

"Thank you," I managed.

"It's Thursday, sir," she said.

"Yes, but what day—"

"It's the twenty-seventh of July, Mr Graham," she said. "How are you feeling?"

Like I've been dragged all over fourteenth-century Europe, I thought. But I took a deep breath and flexed my hands and feet. "I feel fine," I said.

"Good." She patted my hand. "No lasting aftereffects. A few of the people up at the chapel got it worse than you. I would say you're very fortunate, Mr Graham."

"Got what worse than me?"

"Gas. Apparently someone on your camera crew accidentally tapped a gas main. There was a fire—don't you remember?"

"I'm afraid I don't."

"Perhaps that's for the best, sir," she said. "Are you ready for visitors? There's a gentleman who has been asking after you since you were brought in."

"My agent?"

"Mr Weiss has left a number of telephone messages," she said, smiling. She pointed to a side table; several notes were tucked under an impressively gaudy floral arrangement that had Roddy written all over it. "This is a man from the Trust, I believe."

"Is he here now?"

"He's in the hallway. Shall I have him come in?"

"By all means."

"Only a few minutes, sir," she said, making her way out. As she left the room, Rob came in. He was clean-shaven, dressed in slacks and a polo shirt bearing the National Trust logo, and wearing glasses.

I didn't say anything, but managed to prop myself up on my elbows, getting myself into a better sitting position.

"How are you feeling?"

"Question of the day. I'm tip top. Where am I?"

"Royal Infirmary," Rob said. "ITV managed a nice private room for you."

"Nice of them. What happened?"

Rob smiled. "Don't you remember?"

"Refresh my memory."

He came alongside the bed and placed a hand on my arm. "I took you along the path of light, lad. Don't you remember that?"

I must have started away from him. My mind was trying to knit things together: the quest, the relics . . .

"I don't know what you're talking about. I've been having some strange dreams—"

"No dream." He drew the covers back; I was in nothing but a pair of boxers and that most revealing of hospital clothes, the johnny. Before I could snatch his hand away, he drew the johnny up and pointed to my chest.

Clear as day, there was a red scar three inches across: the place where the bandit had stabbed me. I felt something squirm down there, but I'm sure it was my imagination.

He let go; I pulled my clothing together and the blanket up to cover it.

"The nurse told me that it was the twenty-seventh of July."

"So it is. Wouldn't do to have you come back before you'd gone, now would it?"

"But it was October. I spent three months—nearly three months—"

"Time is very flexible," Rob said. He sat on the edge of the bed. "It could have been an hour later for all that it mattered. But . . . some arrangements had to be made."

"For the relics."

"Yes, for the relics. And for you as well. Clean you up." He wrinkled his nose and smiled.

"Rob, the nurse is probably right outside this room."

"Don't worry, lad. She's with us."

" 'Us'?"

"Later. Just be assured that everything is safe."

"Rob, how did you get here?"

"The same way you did, Ian. The music brought me here. I have you to thank for that."

"But—you had it in your mind to remain with the Grand Master. You were fitted out for the martyrdom suit."

"Aye, that I was," he said. "But the Grand Master had other plans for me. There were more treasures in Paris than those in your charge." His eyes twinkled. "And when my work was done, I came forward."

"Were you in another hospital bed?"

"Time is *flexible,* lad," he said. "No, not at all. Rodney and I came forward to a point a dozen years ago."

"So you are—"

"Older. So is Rodney. When ITV decided to do the special programme about Rosslyn, we knew it was time."

"And you knew I'd succeed. You knew—the whole time we were walking through France, dodging Monsieur, fighting de Bec." I looked away from him. "No wonder you were so confident in that bloody oubliette—you knew we'd come through."

"No, not at all. Remember, *this* time—your time, where you'd come from—was in my *future.* The Rob you met in Santiago de Compostela was the genuine article, the real Mackay. I didn't come here until after the pilgrimage was done—I just returned to a place in your past. You were at university."

"I could have been hit by a transit bus, or fallen into the river—you waited all that time for this to play out?"

"We did."

"And Roddy as well."

"Lad. Men have waited two thousand years for the Son of God to return and bring the Kingdom of Heaven. A dozen years is nothing: a step on the path of light." He stood up, straightening the hem on his trousers. "Your effort, Ian, may be the greatest task in the history of civilization. With the book and the music of Master Adam, we have the key to the mystery of Rosslyn Chapel. We have what we have been waiting for."

"If only we could read it."

He smiled. "Get some rest, Ian. We can read it all right."

—•—

The high-tech office was in a nicely-renovated space at the west end of Cowgatehead that overlooked the Grassmarket. On the ground floor there was a science-fiction bookstore; the story of my last few months was probably too wild to even sell there—but if only the proprietor knew what was going on a few floors above.

When I saw Sean Ross sitting at the desk I couldn't breathe properly for a moment. He was sitting in front of a flat screen monitor that showed the cube arrangement in one window and some sort of 3D model in another. Spread out to his left was a stack of A1-sized sheets, copies of pages from the Grail-book.

"Afternoon, Sean," Rob said as we entered the room.

He smiled and turned to face us. "Mr Madson, Mr Graham. Hope everyone's feeling well."

"Tip top," I said. I looked from the sheets to the young programmer. "Rob, does he—"

"I know where these come from," Sean said, pointing to the sheets. "I saw the book myself when they scanned it. I'm . . . it's amazing. Simply amazing."

"You know what it means?"

"I have a good theory." He leaned back in his chair and picked up a coffee-cup with the Irn-Bru logo. "Please have a seat, gentlemen." He gestured to two office chairs, side by side, placed in front of a crowded bookshelf.

"From what Mr. Madson has told me, this is supposed to be a genome map—a description of someone's DNA. A very important someone. The key to the map is the Rosslyn music; with the original manuscript, I was able to make a good diagramme of the Rosslyn stones. There are several hundred times as many lines in the book as notes in the song—it's an exact multiple, in fact: the last time through corresponds with the last line in the book.

"If the book is supposed to describe the structure of the twenty-two numbered genes as well as the X and Y, the numbers have to somehow represent amino acid chains in some way. I tried several different approaches, but I think I've hit upon the solution." He turned his chair to face the monitor, setting his cup down alongside.

He enlarged the window with the 3D model, making it fill the screen. It was a complex pattern, interleaving dark and light patches in a regular order. On the window's title bar were the numbers 1.317, 2.669, 1.803.

"This is what's called a Chladni pattern. I did some research online as well as down at the University; more than two hundred years ago, a fellow named Ernest Chladni did a demonstration at the French Academy of Science showing the relationship between the vibration of a violin bow and the interference patterns of sand on top of an anchored metal plate. It varies, you see, depending on the frequency of the violin movement—the pitch of the note—and the size of the plate. What twigged me to Chladni is the idea that all of these patterns are periodic past a certain point."

"Periodic—"

"They look the same. If the plate is bigger than a certain size, the pattern simply repeats."

"What size?"

"A little over eight centimetres, for notes in the audible range. A tad over three inches."

"Pi," I said.

"That's right. That put me onto Mr Chladni. If you take a plate so wide and so tall, sprinkle sand on it, and rub a violin bow on the side, you get the same pattern *every time*. It's a way of translating a note into a two-dimensional pattern—specify the frequency of the note, and the height and width of the plate and you get a predictable result."

"What does the third number mean, then?" I asked, following the logic.

"Mr Madson and Mr Weiss told me that this book"—he tapped the A1 sheets—"is hundreds of years old. If that's true, then my conclusion doesn't make any sense—there's no way for the author to have this information."

"I don't follow."

"Ernest Chladni was a nineteenth-century scientist—a natural philosopher. He used a violin bow and a metal plate; he drew the patterns by hand. But a modern scientist reproducing the experiment can use a *virtual* plate, and introduce the harmonic artificially. That means that someone with a decent computer can take the Chladni interference surface from two dimensions to three. And with *three* dimensions, what you get is this." He tapped the screen. "This is what you get from the first note in the music, with the dimensions corresponding to the first line in the book. It's a three-dimensional Chladni interference pattern." He pressed a key on the keyboard; the pattern changed. "This is the second." He pressed the key again. "And the third. And so on.

"Now if you chain them all together—say, all of the first section of the book, with the notes of the music running through it as many times as necessary—what you wind up with is *this.*" He opened opened up another window and clicked some control with the pointer. The 3D model began to redraw: a long, sinuous pattern in three dimensions from left to right, an intricate geometric dance.

"It'll take some decoding, but what I think you have there is a genetic map of the first chromosome."

Rob crossed himself; I began to do the same, had a brief thought about my Gran, shrugged, and followed suit. *You're in it fairly deep as it is,* I told myself.

Sean Ross didn't turn around; he was completely engrossed in the delicate spirals of the genetic map he'd created. Beyond the windows, down in the Grassmarket, life went on as usual.

—•—

Two days after that Rodney and I found ourselves on the way to Studio One in Glasgow, ITV's headquarters up north. David MacDougal had sent a car for us; it gave us a chance to catch up in style as we hurtled down the M8.

"Everything resolves itself nicely, doesn't it?" I asked, sipping from a bottle of tonic water. "I do the pilgrimage, find the goods, bring them back, and suffer nothing more than a scar on the belly and a bump on the head."

"You could look at it that way, old boy," Rodney said.

"I never got the answer to the most important question."

"Eh? What's that?"

"Why me? Why was I chosen to do this?"

Rodney laughed. He looked out the window at the highway, then back at me.

"You weren't chosen. You could hear the music."

"How did you know that?"

"I can't give away all of our secrets."

"Ah, yes. The mysterious 'us'. Who are 'we', anyway?"

"Surely you've guessed. 'We' are the Order of the Temple, Ian. We are what survived the trial and execution. Some of the Order reached Portugal, some reached Scotland; some became Teutonic Knights. Some just rode your coat-tails and reached the modern era the easy way."

"The sixth initiation."

"We hear the music now," Rodney said. "And you made it possible. And what you've brought back makes . . . other things possible as well."

"Such as?"

"Healing the world. Think about the world we live in, Ian. Nihilistic, self-destructive: a world with no soul. And do you know what destroyed the world's soul? Not some conquering army, not jazz music, not even some terrible philosophy—it was a tiny little flea on a tiny little mouse. The Black Plague wiped out the Saviour's bloodline, and the world was diminished."

"So—what are you going to do? Clone Jesus Christ?"

"It's a possibility."

"You can't be serious."

"Of course I'm not serious. We've scarcely managed to clone a sheep, for pity's sake. No, most likely the Order is going to take a close look at the genome map, once it's decoded, and compare it to the data on file to see what sets it apart."

"What set the Son of God apart was that He was the Son of God, Rodney. I don't think that's in the genome."

"Oh?" He raised one eyebrow. "You know that for certain, do you?"

"I'm no expert—"

"No. Neither am I. It's going to take a long time to decode the information we have, and maybe we'll understand it better by the time that's done. But—at least there's a chance of learning something. Maybe there's a way to do what the *Sangre Real* is really supposed to do—to heal the world.

"Isn't that something worth doing?"

—•—

At Studio One, David MacDougal performed the sort of *volte-face* that is endemic to the entertainment industry. He was obsequious, complimentary, courteous to a fault. Of course we could cancel the Rosslyn programme, or delay it if I wanted: of course we'd do a full season. Of course there'd be a pay rise. ITV might even want to try out an afternoon talk programme . . . they'd been wanting to do that for a year or two, and with someone with the name recognition of an Ian Graham available, well . . .

By the time we were in the car headed back for Edinburgh, I felt as if I'd been basted like a roast for the oven. Rodney was practically rubbing his hands with glee.

"Roddy," I said, leaning back in the seat cushions. "About Mac."

"He rolled over, then sat up and begged, didn't he? Very risk-averse, these ITV blokes."

"I'm sure the threat of a lawsuit over the little incident at Rosslyn didn't hurt a bit. An incident I still don't remember, by the way."

"That's because you weren't there. But what about Mac?"

"I—" *I was off getting my beard trimmed and my body deloused,* I thought to myself. "You and Rob came forward, and Sean is Juan la Rosa's lineal descendent. I've seen no sign of Adam—but what about Mac? Is he the Carmelite brother in a better suit? They're nothing like each other."

"I'm nothing like the man I was when I met you in Chartres."

"Point taken. Planning to answer my question?"

"They're not the same man, no. The Carmelite brother and the ITV executive are the result of polyphonic duplication. Not exactly coincidence, but it might as well be. You probably saw or met others who reminded you of people from the present day."

Polyphonic duplication, I thought. "You mean like my ex."

Rodney had been riding along with his eyes closed, like an epicure after a satisfying meal. One eye opened and glanced at me under a furrowed brow. "You saw Liz?"

"In the flesh. And she saw me, and knew me."

"Are you sure?"

Poor fool, she had said. *You poor fool.* "Yes, I'm sure."

"That's interesting."

"Is that the best you can manage?"

"At the moment," he answered, "yes. Now let me rest; I'm thinking about how to make you more money."

—•—

I paid a visit to Gran's grave in Rosebank Cemetery, something I had not done since her funeral. She was buried in a well-shaded place, surrounded by shipowners and businessmen, and sharing a spot with her husband who had gone years before her and whom I had not known as well.

The grave was well-maintained; years ago Edinburgh Council had forced the purchase of a number of other more historical graveyards that had been poorly kept up, but the Rosebank groundskeepers seemed to have greater respect for the less-famous dead. The headstone was plain, bearing only their names and dates of death, though there was a border on the top made of linked *croix-pateés* that I'd not noticed on my single visit.

I placed a simple bunch of sunflowers on the grave. "Hello, Gran," I said. "It's Wee Ian. Come to pay my respects. I've come home."

I didn't expect an answer, and fortunately I wasn't surprised. A slight breeze whispered through the nearby trees; I stuck my hands in my pockets and sighed.

"I went through the strait gate, you know. I did what I was supposed to do—I even knitted up the loose ends of the story, those that I could manage. Who knows—I might even be able to do more, now that it's shown to be possible.

"I just wanted you to know . . . no. This doesn't make any sense." I turned to walk away, suddenly uncomfortable with the whole bad idea of visiting Rosebank, of seeing the gravestone that was no more than a calling-card for my Gran's life—and almost walked into an older man coming in the other direction.

"I'm—terribly sorry," I said, stopping short. The man was dressed a bit out of fashion: well-trimmed beard, three-piece suit, cane in hand, like a character from a film. He walked with a slight limp; he tipped his hat to me.

"Hello, Ian."

"Giles," I said. "I didn't know you frequented Rosebank Cemetery."

"I don't. I came looking for you."

"I suppose I should feel honoured."

He gestured to a bench under a large, spreading elm in sight of the grave. We walked over and sat down, side by side; he leaned slightly on his cane.

"I'm not sure what I'm supposed to do now," I said. "I've had this bloody great life experience, and only a handful of people know about it—if I told anyone else they'd clap me in the Royal Asylum."

"Do you want to go out and shout it to the world, then?"

"In a way I do. I lost two days of my life to an accident that—for all I know—was staged by Roddy and Rob, but in fact I spent almost three months in the fourteenth century: the music took me there, and the music took me back, and most of the evidence is buried under Rosslyn Chapel just like the conspiracy nutters have always said it was. And yet here I am—still Ian Graham, still the talking head as ever."

"The *caput Sophiae* of ITV." Giles laughed. "I'm sure your Gran would find that analogy amusing."

"I wouldn't be surprised to find that you knew her better than I did."

"Don't be surprised, then. She heard a little bit of the music: mostly Poulenc. Then it skipped a generation and came out in you. The Lord works in mysterious ways; still does, mind."

"The Lord, and the Order of the Temple."

"The Lord *through* the Order of the Temple. Believe what you wish about your friends, Ian—they followed their hearts and their faith all along. They hoped and prayed that it would all turn out as expected."

"And what if it hadn't done?"

Giles leaned his cane against his chest and spread his arms wide, then brought his hands together with a clap. "Poof!" he said. "The world is changed. Maybe the world *is* changed, and no one knows it. But as for you, young man, you were sent, like Saint James: *Misil me Dominus.* 'The Lord sent me.' And He watched over you and brought you home."

"And now . . ."

"And now you live your life, Ian." Giles got himself to his feet. "You do what you have done, having done a great service for the world. If it heals the world, well and good. If not—"

"Poof."

"Just so." He smiled wistfully, and walked slowly away, whistling something that came from Rosslyn's music.

I sat on the bench for awhile longer, watching the breeze worry away at my bunch of sunflowers. I breathed the air and looked at the sky. Then I stood and walked out of Rosebank Cemetery, intent on living my life.